Interstellar Marine Strike Force

Saviors of Earth

Derek Stone

authorHOUSE®

AuthorHouse™
1663 Liberty Drive
Bloomington, IN 47403
www.authorhouse.com
Phone: 833-262-8899

Published by AuthorHouse 12/06/2023

ISBN: 979-8-8230-1880-7 (sc)
ISBN: 979-8-8230-1879-1 (e)

Library of Congress Control Number: 2023923445

Print information available on the last page.

Monday, July 9, 2131
Dark side of the moon

Corporal Sean Ryan sat down in the briefing room near the central holographic table aboard the Destroyer ECS Robert F. Stryker. Several of the Interstellar Strike Force Marines sat watching holographic images of Chicago. A giant stag beetle-esque monster hovering over the city was the most noticeable thing in the image.

He had been watching the blue tinted radiation patterns that made up beam space surrounding the image. The ship's awareness showed the crew a sight of swirling radioactive gasses and particles that were lethal to them. He found the void between realities a beautiful sight.

The trip home for him had come after spending two years in unending combat. The war had already claimed his father and brother. He could feel their eyes gazing down on him, repeating one word: *failure.* He closed his eyes, trying to rest, knowing it would probably be a long time before he was able to rest again.

A bitter cold pervading his body woke Sean; he must have dozed off after all. Had his suit malfunctioned? Derek stood before his brother, his helmet visor shattered, his armor, instead of the standard green, was scorched black. The ghost reached its arm forward, pointing. "Why did you let this happen? How could you let this happen?"

Sean looked at his gloved hands, then back at the screen. Despite wanting to wake up, Sean instead tried to touch his brother. He reached for the hand. "I followed you into battle. I did this for you! We didn't need blood to be brothers."

Sean's nightmarish war had followed him home. Science had remade his body to be better, and faster, than any human. However, despite his enhanced speed, he was too slow to touch his brother. "You're right, I failed you all!" he said, hanging his head.

His grayish-green eyes were far too world-weary for a twenty-year-old man. Brown hair grew from his head, but something made him feel like it was gray. When he looked up a second time, his next ghostly visitor was his mother. "I'm so sorry I didn't keep my promises! I couldn't save Derek and I didn't keep you all safe," he cried, embracing her.

Sean felt her crack like glass in his arms and let go. In an instant, he remembered the last five years. He remembered the evening news tides of silver machines. How no one had cared. Now Sammy burned before him, screaming as atomic flames ravaged her body.

As the fires subsided and she turned to a pile of ash, he fell to his knees, grabbing at the pile. He scooped the ash up tightly but struggled to stop them from scattering to the winds. He'd failed again. "No, God. Let her be alive," he pleaded.

Mitch shook Sean violently. "Wake up, man. Major Robb will slice you up like ham if he catches you asleep in the briefing room."

Sean looked straight into Mitch's blue-gray eyes. He reminded him of his brother, if he were white and more vocal. An opposite of his brother, yet eerily similar. Sean reached out. "Thank you. Seems only another Newboot will look out for a man," Sean said catching his breath.

"You don't look like you enjoyed your nap. Maybe you should visit medical and get a PTSD treatment. You can't fear the needle and be in the Marines."

"I'd rather not, Mitch. The last one left me feeling fuzzy," Sean said as he and Mitch went to join the rest of their team.

"These assholes could bomb every city into rubble from orbit, yet they would rather take the cities with ground troops. I know that Guardian drones have a brain the size of an orange, but this makes me wonder how the Serkin came up with space travel," Mitch joked, taking the seat on Sean's right.

Gabe, frustrated with the needless small talk, let Mitch know his feelings. "Some philosopher once said hell is other people, but really, hell is just being with you, Mitch."

Sgt. Eric Blake sat down. "Stop fucking with the children, Corporal Short Stuff. That's my job. Well, so much for the ticker-tape parade and welcome home. Eva, is the city of Lviv under attack?" He ran his hand over his long-since healed facial scars.

"Negative. Lviv is currently under martial law, likely waiting to process refugees. The commander is focusing his plans on Chicago. That is where Serkin patrols are the most prevalent," Eva answered Sgt. Blake in the calm monotone common to service AI.

"Hey, Eva, how big is that ship over Chicago?" Mitch asked and ran his hand through his overgrown brownish-red hair. It was slightly longer than regulation would normally allow, but finding the time to adhere to regulations was a luxury.

"Observed lengths for the Type 27 class ship are between five hundred meters and four thousand meters. This ship over Lake Michigan is five hundred and forty meters long, one hundred meters wide, and fifty meters tall." The ship's AI answered, showing a large diagram of the ship over Lake Michigan on the holo-table.

Major Robb walked into the briefing room. His muscle mass alone silenced his underlings. His scarred-up jaw hardly moved as he spoke. "Alright, listen. The safety of our home world has been compromised. Our nearest fleet battle groups are at best eighteen hours away. In the meantime, we have over a dozen cities under attack and calling for support. Chicago, so far, is the only battle that can go either way with our small force." Major Robb spoke soberly as he placed his helmet on the holo-table, crossing his arms over his armor-plated chest.

"Currently, civilians, police, and military forces are pinned down throughout the center of Chicago," the ship's bodiless AI, Eva, added. "All communication is currently overwhelmed with emergency calls. One ship is not worth the effort for their fleet. Mathematical probability is near fifty/fifty for mission success."

"Expect Guardian drone swarms in the streets," Major Robbed added, "and Specter gunships providing close air support. Until we take out the anti-aircraft defenses, our birds won't be able to clear the skies. As such you will have two officers in the field at all times to avoid severing command, and control. Since, Captain Mobati is no longer with us I will be working with Lt. Carver."

The Warrior class destroyer normally kept its Interstellar Marine Strike Force detachment at a full platoon of a hundred men. Major Robb as now down to half that number and had no support drones for his men. None the less he was at least proud of them for not belly aching.

"Military Intelligence has stated there are over one hundred and fifty aircraft on standby to provide air support. Once the skies are clear, civilians can be airlifted out through the O'Hare Spaceport. Currently, that is impossible due to one 128mm anti-aircraft rail gun and four medium Maser cannons. Any aircraft that is at low altitude up to low Earth orbit can easily be shot down by these guns. Captain Kurkov has decided any interdiction of Serkin activity will force their ships away from standard patrols. The only method of viable insertion is Interstellar Marine Strike Force standard drop pods. Once you exit the pods, you will be too small for even Serkin targeting systems to attain target lock."

"We will make our way ground side via jump-packs and won't drop directly over Chicago. Upon making it ground side, head south from the drop point to O'Hare Spaceport. Make all efforts to destroy any anti-aircraft defenses encountered. I have forwarded all navigational data to your individual HUDs," Major Robb finished while scratching at the synthetic skin covering his wounds before securing his helmet.

Gabe raised his arm as he stood up, seeing as he was the shortest man in the unit. "Sir, we have very little information on the enemy's objective. Should we at least try to gather intelligence? We made sure to keep the archives on that outpost world safe, so how did they find Earth?"

"If the opportunity presents itself, we need to prioritize evacuation of the civilians and contact with the local military. Frankly, we know our goals: fight first and ask questions later. Winning in Chicago will be the first step to saving Earth. Let's not have the birthplace of humanity end up like Vieira. Drop in twenty minutes, and keep your suits sealed at all times. I don't care if the air is breathable or if you scare civilians. If anyone has a question…" Major Robb scanned the room for a moment. "Alright, dismissed!"

As the Marines piled out, Mitch looked at his helmet before throwing it at Sean to grab the latter's attention. Sean caught it, instantly knowing it was Mitch's way of seeing if he was paying attention.

"Are you serious? Why do you keep drawing on your helmet? It's against regulation! At this rate, you're going to get busted down to Private again," Sean said, pointing to a large shark mouth around the visor area and an eye next to each of the helmet's side-mounted sensors.

"Eh, what's the point in rank or the money? We've never had any time to spend our paychecks. Worse still, I haven't had a beer in two years and eight months! Sweet Jesus, I sound like a recovering alcoholic!" Mitch tried to remember the taste of beer as he put his helmet on.

"Fat load of good alcohol will do you. There's no liquor out there that can beat our enhanced livers and kidneys," Sean added, securing his helmet's cable to his cyber port behind his ear. He hated the fact he didn't have time to shave the hair covering the link.

The suit connected directly to Sean's nervous system, and he could feel and control his suit by thought. He adjusted his jetpack's nozzle system by thinking about turning right in the air. His HUD flickered to life, and as he walked down the ship hallway, he felt lighter with every step as his mind completely interfaced his actions with the suit at a synaptic level.

Major Robb's men formed up and headed to the armory to collect their weapons and supplies. Sean collected his rifle and additional equipment. Filling his spare ammunition pouches, he collected spare batteries for his rifle, and like many others, he collected extra explosive charges.

Mitch walked up to the armory computer sensor, which scanned his combat armor's Identification Friend or Foe system. The arms rack then released his weapon from inventory and Mitch switched to radio communication. "Oh yeah, M68A1 with a 35mm grenade launcher, fifty round magazine of 6.8x40mm slugs able to punch a hole in forty millimeters of steel armor. This should turn these bullet-head-motherfuckers into pulp," Mitch said, sliding a battery pack into the butt of the rifle as he followed Sean and Gabe to the drop bay of the ship.

"Nix the boasting. The bullet-heads never leave a carcass when they die, unlike their tentacle-headed Guardian drones." Gabe checked his rifle safety and took a seat in the first available drop pod.

The drop bay of the Destroyer was along the center line of the ship just before the main hangar where the Naval Infantry dropships and other vehicles were stored. The floor had a secondary airlock below the drop pods to protect the ship's crew from the vacuum of space. A total of ten teardrop-shaped pods waited as the rest of the Marines began filing into the hangar. The lighting change forced everyone entering to blink a few times. The walls of the drop bay had some of the ship's crew members already secured in the fold-down high gravity seats. The crewmembers not seated were loading supplies into smaller scale drop pods.

"Major Robb, your first and second waves of resupply are ready. We will be finished with the third momentarily," a female deckhand shouted while securing a supply crate into a launch tube.

Major Robb nodded his acknowledgment before entering his pod. Once inside, he focused on his own job. "Alright, you know the drill. Five Marines to each pod. Let's go!" His command console showed a clock counting down.

"We are sealing the drop pods now," a deckhand shouted, closing Major Robb's hatch. When the pods were closed, a mechanical arm sprayed sealing gel along each hatch that would melt away in the atmosphere.

"This is pod 1-4, ready and waiting for the drop," Sean said, securing his rifle to his leg before fastening his restraints to his suit. The deck crew gave him the thumbs-up and then closed the pod. With no windows and only a single light that would change from red to green during the drop, the pod was eerily like a coffin. He felt a slight jolt as the pod was lowered into the airlock. He knew no matter how many times this happened, he would never become used to a drop.

"Confirmed, ready to drop. Captain Kurkov of the ECS Stryker.

This is Major Robb. All teams are ready to drop. Give us a target," Major Robb reported as he felt the pod lower into the Destroyer's launch bay.

With the drop pods loaded, the crew secured themselves as yellow warning lights flashed and the airlock doors opened. Once the airlock doors sealed again, the deck lights stopped flashing. Sean and the other men in the unit sat waiting for the rush of adrenaline to pour into their bloodstreams.

On the bridge, Captain Kurkov, having received the information, began his part of the mission of getting the Marines planet side while avoiding the Serkin patrols. "This is Kurkov, finished threading the needle. Let's hope those Serkin ships haven't decided to change their patrols." Captain Kurkov watched the command screen show each level of the ship turn red as all outer, nonessential decks evacuated for depressurization.

"Captain, the last nonessential deck has been evacuated. Depressurization of those decks should take another two minutes," a bridge officer said.

"We don't have time for a full depressurization of the ship's outermost decks. If we want to get our Marines into Chicago and through the gap between the Serkin ships on orbital patrol, they have to go now. The window is closing." Colonel Mason motioned to the timetables on his own monitor.

"Damn, we have no choice but to accept eighty-seven percent evacuation and depressurization of the ship's outermost hulls. All stations switch from alert status to battle stations. Seal off the decks that can't be depressurized. Engineering crews, transfer all additional power to the sub-light engines and maneuvering thrusters." Captain Kurkov double-checked his harnesses.

The ECS Stryker's navigator switched over to the maneuver thruster controls and began the task of changing the ship's axis to point its nose toward Earth. With the ship at the proper angle, it drifted closer to the moon and pressed the four fusion engines to their maximum thrust of 9 Gs.

The gravitational forces produced by the ship's engine gave Captain Kurkov the distinct feeling of having his stomach and other innards being crushed within his body. The only comfort was that the full thrust burst of 9 G-forces was short-lived. "Sir, four minutes until we pass by the enemy patrol ships," the CIC commander shouted while firmly holding onto his console as the G-forces pushed him down into his chair.

The console feed showed they were now in orbit over the Earth. "Alright, kill the main engines and divert the power to the shields. Let's do what we can not to draw more attention to ourselves." Relieved the main engines had powered down, Captain Kurkov breathed normally again.

As the ship's lower section skimmed the Earth's atmosphere, it drifted over North America. The drop bay opened and released the drop pods as it sped away. For the men inside the pods, there was a feeling of having their stomachs pulled out of their throats as the Earth's gravity pulled them down.

Mitch had grown accustomed to the rattling that made him question whether he was going to suffer brain damage. The worst part of the drop was falling through the thermosphere as the ablative heat shield on the pod slowly peeled away. "You would think by now the scientists could figure out a way to make our Scorpion MK3 Armor stop the drop's heat!" Mitch screamed.

"Five minutes until we pass through the stratosphere. Get ready for the flip," Major Robb shouted, watching the countdown on his helmet's HUD.

As soon as the drop pods reached the stratosphere, the air pressure triggered the retrorockets, and the pod slowed and jettisoned the outer layers upward to burn away. The pod then turned over, pointing the Marines to the ground. The rapid change in force jolted the occupants. To further stall, the pod's parachutes deployed. The light came quickly as the drop pod's floor and seats released the occupants. The occupants went from a seated position to a horizontal fall in moments. The visceral jolt triggered the muscle memory in their legs and arms to help direct their descent.

Once Sean was free of the safety harness, the starting gate opened and it was time to fly. For everyone else, it was merely a drop, but for

Sean, it was an escape. He was free of the dreaded feeling of plummeting to his death in the darkness of the pod. The fear of the dark gave way to a slightly blinding light before he began to descend.

"Here comes the fun part!" Mitch readjusted so that he would accelerate quickly away from the falling drop pod. He then used his suit's jump-jets to follow the set trajectory to Chicago.

Eric spread his arms and legs out to slow his descent. "Alright, there are no flak clouds, so be ready to brake when you see the details of the ground!" His mind was screaming the command to his limbs repeatedly as he glided his way down along with every other Marine.

After several minutes of flying, and passing the last layer of clouds, everyone repositioned their bodies so that their feet were pointing at the ground. Once in the right direction, they fired their jump-jets, which acted as brakes, before touching the ground. They were nowhere near where the ship had dropped them when it skimmed the atmosphere.

Major Robb checked his Heads Up Display and was relieved all fifty men had completed the descent safely, even if some of them had missed their mark. After breathing a sigh of relief, Major Robb issued the first order. "Alright people, I want situation reports."

Marlow leaned against a tree, "This is Gunnery Sergeant Marlow to Major Robb. Twenty-five of us have touched down somewhere on the western side of the Mannheim Road. Do you copy? Over," Marlow said, taking out an improved vision module before he placed it on his helmet. "Sir, I can see their guns. It seems they are trained westward. We are securing our position. Over," he continued to report over the unit's secured comlinks.

"This is the worst place possible to hold up. A parking lot of ruined cars is not the best option for cover. The Serkins could advance at any moment and we'd be fighting in a field of explosive metal heaps. I know chemistry. With fuel tanks full of hydrogen, you won't see the flames in daylight and then all the cars go boom," Mathew commented, lying down with his M79 machine gun near a burnt and broken tree.

After dropping in, Major Robb set about gaining the initiative. He looked at his forearm-mounted computer pad and began gathering his forces. "This is Major Robb. Copy that, Gunnery Sergeant Marlow. You landed off course. We will wait for you to rectify the situation. Attention all units. Wait to advance to the main spaceport terminal on the west side of the eight lanes of Coleman drive."

The twenty-five men who landed off course advanced through the lower section of the highway. They moved from car to car to have some semblance of cover in case they were walking into a trap. The soldiers with machine guns took position to cover their comrades as they moved up. The standard Serkin Infantry was formidable, but their Guardian drones were the true threat. Towering over a man, the drones could descend and ascend walls to ambush their targets from ceilings and roofs.

The worst part of the Guardians was their animal-like ferocity. Each Guardian stood three meters tall when fully erect. They each had digitigrade legs and a pair of tentacle-like appendages that could support their weight. It meant they could take up a position anywhere and fire their weapons from different angles, bypassing most cover.

Marlow leaned up against a car and warned his men. "Keep your eyes open, people. These elevated highways are the perfect environment for Guardian drones. Be ready for some fucked up fields of fire."

The men scanned the elevated highway as the group moved up. Sean and Mitch searched the area, keeping their rifles aimed. Nathan wondered if everyone else felt suspicious finding so many cars without the drivers' bodies anywhere.

Sean picked up a teddy bear as he used his cybernetic implants to switch from sonic vision to his standard HUD. "Sir, I scanned the area. There are no land mines, but shouldn't we figure out what happened to the people?"

Sean checked the bear for blood but found none. He and the platoon continued using the car wrecks lining the roads for cover. Using his jump-pack to leap on top of a weathered tractor trailer, he hoped the slight lift in elevation would give his suit's three-hundred-meter alert zone more reach.

A truck driver had left in such a hurry, the cabin door to the truck was still open, but the truck wasn't looted. Sean knew the Serkins' drones likely terrified any would-be looters into fleeing for their lives, but there wasn't a single drone in sight, leaving no clue to what happened. He jumped down from the truck trailer and began looking up and down the road.

"There isn't time to find survivors. We need to get to the spaceport terminal," Sgt. Marlow said.

So far, if the Serkins had Guardians in the area, they weren't within Sean's three-hundred-meter alert zone. Looking down at the bear, he remembered when his father Trevor dodged traffic to rescue his favorite stuffed bear when he was a little boy. Instantly, he imagined the bear being abandoned as the Guardians attacked. He hoped the owners got away.

"Fuck's sake. People don't disappear from a war zone like a tech fad," Nathan said, passing another empty car as he walked westward.

"Who knows, they are likely dead elsewhere. Look at the ground. Do you see severed limbs and splattered blood all over the place? Guardian drones like to play with their kills; so far the place is pretty clean, for a city, that is." Gabe dismissed the concerns, actively trying to forget the human stampedes in the streets of Vieira.

Marlow's half of the platoon moved forward once they were close enough to the main terminal, and he connected its systems' scanners to his own HUD. Marlow sighed, looking at the massive eight-lane highway in front of him. "Okay people, hold up. No scanners. We clear this the old-fashioned way."

The various support structures of the highway would hide the Guardian drones from their combat suits' scanners. A crow landed on top of a wrecked car and began loudly calling to other birds. It was the first noise loud enough to draw everyone's attention. Sean took a closer look at the bird's blood-soaked beak.

"That is the perfect ambush spot for drones. I'm going up." Nathan activated his jump-jets, and when he was high enough, grabbed the ledge of the highway. After making his way over the hurdle, he leveled his Gauss rifle and made sure he was alone before climbing over the guard railing onto the road.

The rest of the unit would cover him if any Guardian drones had concealed themselves on the upper level. They'd only kill one Marine easily. "Alright, no drones. Get up here and cover me."

Sean followed Nathan. He turned to look toward the neo-traditional skyscrapers with their red and brown bricks flanking intricate glass windows. Those buildings were mixed among the more modern glass and steel skyscrapers. He remembered watching the city as his shuttle lifted off years ago in an ominously cool June.

Several of the skyscrapers he remembered were now gone, and smoke from countless fires across the downtown area had darkened the sky. Sean couldn't watch, but he also couldn't tear his gaze away from the scene. The enemy starship drifting over Lake Michigan was hideous. As gunships patrolled the skies over the down-town area, he knew he had failed.

"Shit! Wasn't there a pair of arcologies on the south side? There's barely even any tracer fire from the ground. The Serkins must have taken out our air defenses ground side," Mitch commented as he stood next to Sean, sharing his view.

"The Grand Boulevard Arcology housed about two and a half million permanent residents and could provide hospital care to an additional five-hundred-thousand. Hyde Park Arcology had similar statistics, and it was gone too. They're right there, where those big billowing smoke piles are," Sean said, pointing to the south side.

"They killed at least six million people in their opening shots. And now there are almost no tracers coming from the ground. The Serkins own this city," Gabe remarked as he watched the skies.

"Fucking hell. Let's regroup first and worry about that later." Sean shook his head before returning his attention to the mission.

Nathan looked into each car before crossing the dividing barrier. Something moving between the barriers caught his attention. "Sergeant, we have civilians. They're alive!"

"This is sloppy work for the Serkins," Mathew informed the gunnery sergeant as the pair looked up at the highway overpass.

Marlow was stunned. "Mathew the Mute Miller can speak? How would you know what sloppy work for a Serkin is?"

"I was at Vieira when they invaded. The Guardians always made sure their targets were dead, and it wasn't clean. We have abandoned cars and there are civilians hiding in plain sight," Matthew replied.

For the civilians gazing upon the armored trans-human soldiers, it was an intimidating sight. Quickly, the adults gathered in front of the children, forming a barrier before Nathan's imposing form. With each soldier significantly taller than the average man and covered in armor plating, the closest human feature were the Marines' imposing shapes.

Sean approached the group and held out the bear he had taken earlier. "Did anyone drop this?"

"You saved Doug," a little girl cried in joy. As she rushed over, Sean could see she had curly black hair and bright green eyes. Clutching the bear close, she returned to her parents.

"Major, this is Marlow. We are securing the elevated highway before moving. We have bad news and good news."

"Give me the good news, Marlow," Major Robb replied, the dread in his voice clear as day.

"We have live civilians, but there are too many for us to escort to safety without transport. If we march them out, we'd be an easy target for the Serkins' drones," Marlow said, motioning for his men to make a perimeter around the people.

Sean wanted to take off his helmet and scream out for his mothers. He would have too if he weren't being watched. Using his HUD system, he activated the helmet loud speaker. "Samantha Hale, Lisa Ryan, and Jennifer Ryan. Has anyone here met any woman with one of those names?"

The civilians glanced nervously at each other as their whispering rose. A man in a tattered suit approached Sean. "No one here with those names. They all sound like Sidonian names. If you are looking for the families of soldiers, they already entered the main terminal."

"Thanks anyway, man." Sean turned away from the civilians. He was disappointed with the news as much as he was with his ability to just turn away. The uninhabited world he'd fought on for the last two years of his service didn't prepare him to endure seeing his home town being turned into a full scale war zone. The sight of the child's toy earlier had sent his mind racing.

Marlow waited for the major's reply while keeping his eyes on the city center, watching the Serkins' air support circling like vultures around a rotting carcass. He had twenty-five men around, and at least fifty civilians. "Sir, we are just inviting a blood bath if we keep them here," Marlow said, contacting the major again.

"The Serkins are getting sloppy. Send the civilians north. Intel confirms there is a firebase where they can find shelter. Otherwise, leave them where they are for now. It's your call. Just remember, you are under orders to link up with me. Those civilians are on their own for the time being," Major Robb said.

"Yes, sir, we'll move out momentarily." Marlow turned his attention to Nathan.

Even with a helmet that obscured Nathan, he recognized the gaze of the gunnery sergeant. It always sent chills down his spine. He approached Marlow and jumped over the concrete divider. "So what is happening? We need all the people we can get to take out those anti-aircraft guns, but we also can't leave these people."

"Indeed. That's why you're going to get them to wait it out." Marlow turned his speaker on, addressing the people. "Alright, people, for now you'll have to stay here. It's for your own safety. We'll come back to evacuate you."

"If you don't want to wait, make your way north to a Marine firebase," Gabe added.

Sean knew how nihilistic and compassionless Gabe could be. He grabbed him by the arm and said to him quietly, "If they do go north, they could be ambushed. Waiting here for us to evacuate them later is the better option. Why did you even mention that bullshit?"

Gabe jerked his arm back. "Because waiting for us to win is a tall order. As a gambling man, I wouldn't back that horse."

Nathan scanned the area, making sure no Serkin Guardian drones were lurking around. The road was discomfortingly clear. "Everyone, please remember it is safer to just stay put. Lord knows how many Serkin patrols there are. Anyone of them could ambush you on the road."

Sean remained silent, glad he didn't break down after making contact with the civilians. Earth was nothing like holding the line. The jump point to the Perseus Arm was an unnamed, habitable world. Most commercial ships built after 2090 could easily make a jump of ten thousand light years with no need to spend a week recharging their engines.

Sean had spent his entire time fighting on a world with no civilians. Now his childhood home was little more than an hour's drive from where he stood. He switched off the safety on his rifle.

"Thank you," shouted the girl, waving her bear around.

Marlow ordered his men to regroup and move on toward the rally point. "Haul ass, people, we risk compromising our mission by standing around with our dicks in our hands!"

Sean waved to the girl before climbing over the guard railing and jumping down.

Major Robb waited at the parking deck across the main terminal. His remaining men approached the perimeter. He headed straight down to speak with his sergeant. "Well, it took you long enough. I know it's a war zone, but twenty minutes, Gunnery Sergeant?"

"Sorry, Major, we had a complication. I won't let it happen," Marlow explained.

Major Robb sighed, saving his complaints. "Alpha and Bravo teams, move up and secure the third floor. Once secured, Delta and Echo teams will use the sky bridge to cross into the terminal and provide cover as the rest of us move in from the ground floor," Major Robb ordered his men. "First things first, Davis. I want those security gates to the terminal unlocked in five minutes."

Mitch stepped forward when called and plugged a small crystal drive into a security panel which began accessing the spaceport's security network. "Easy, network overrides are one thing, but selectively controlling a gate and the security feeds at once are not. So is that an actual five minutes or a theoretical five minutes, sir?" Mitch asked as the spaceport's newer security network began to slow him down.

"It's a hard five. You have till Alpha and Bravo secure this deck. I want all teams to report when they are in position," Major Robb replied as he and the remaining men waited for the gates to open.

Mitch managed to catch a security camera's footage of the gate. "Oh, those arrogant pricks! Major Robb? Sir, Serkin security inside is rather relaxed. Hell, their attack drones are in sleep mode to save power. There is only a Guardian on the other side of the gate patrolling the entrance. I'll patch a feed to your HUD," Mitch said as he shared the HUD view.

Major Robb looked over the entrance on his HUD. "Can you open the blast doors just enough for us to send a few smart grenades in without alerting the entire enemy force?"

"Yes, sir, I can open the gates just right. These doors should be rated to protect us from up to five hundred kilograms of TNT," Mitch said, using his suit's interface to start messing with the blast door controls.

Major Robb checked in with his unit. "All teams, this is a command. Report in. Have you reached your assigned positions?"

"This is Charlie lead. We are ready and waiting for this door to open. Sir, how copy?"

"Bravo lead, the fourth floor is secured. We have eyes on two Specter gunships near the suburbs. Looks like they will remain out of our AO for the moment. Over."

"Alright, sir, I'll make the opening look like a power jolt just in case they're monitoring the system. If we can time the doors just right, we can probably chuck a few grenades in and kill the bullet head bastard and his cyber mutts without a fight." Mitch removed a grenade from his kit.

Sean joined the group by pulling two grenades from his kit. Nathan pulled one as well before looking at the ground level entrance to the terminal. Major Robb gave the three men a simple nod, and the trio rushed across the road up to the entrance.

On the opposite side of the entrance to the terminal, a single Serkin soldier in his dark blue armored suit observed the air defense guns as his drones patrolled the area. Shortly after making its way back down to the first-floor street, the Guardian drone quickly turned its attention to the opening and closing gates.

The Serkin soldier followed his drone to the gate to investigate a humming noise as the smart grenades rolled along the ground. Once the smart grenades spotted their targets, they rolled toward them.

The lone Serkin soldier commanding the drones noticed the sliding grenades. Unlike his drone, he turned to flee before the grenades went off. The grenades' humming noises ceased, followed by an explosion. White-hot shrapnel entered the Serkin's body, flaying flesh from bone, before the shock wave of the explosion turned the remains into a fine purplish-blue mist. What remained of the mangled corpse began to dissolve as the Serkin's armor protocols did their best to keep its wearer's anatomical information out of enemy hands.

The doors opened, and the Marines rushed in to find cover. Major Robb looked around. "Do this by the numbers, men. We have a dead Serkin commander. The drones under his command are going to rush to where their commander died. Dig in and make every shot count!"

"Hey, Mac, you may want to roll with Bravo on the second floor. You're the marksman," Sean said, finding and using a small hallway leading toward the restrooms for cover.

"Yeah, kid, I know. Focus on your job and you won't be replaced." Masa took up a position with his marksman rifle on the second floor food court.

As the Marines took cover positions along the first and second floors, the drones swarmed the building. Windows smashed as the drones filed into an attacking wave.

"Delta 1 to command. We've spotted at least two company strength Guardian drones marching on the first floor. Hard contact in forty seconds max!"

Sean and Mitch looked at their squad leader, Manuel. "Alright, here they come. Get ready! You don't need to worry too much now that the master is dead," Manuel said as he took cover behind a kiosk across from Sean.

The Serkin drones began firing as they pushed forward. Sean leveled his Gauss gun and began firing. They took down a few Guardians instantly and damaged several others as they marched over their mechanical comrades.

The fifty Marines fired short, controlled bursts into the enemy formation as they leaned out of cover. A single Guardian drone broke formation. Using its large muscular digitigrade legs, it jumped several meters to the second floor. As it grasped onto the wall, it fired several explosives into the nearest Marine position.

Each of the Guardian's explosives sent a barrage of dense carbon crystalline shards into anyone unfortunate enough to be in the four-meter area. The drone used the tentacles on its back to hang from the ceiling as it began aiming its particle rifle at the Marines. Sean cursed as a barrage of super heated beams cut into the walls, keeping him pinned.

"God damn it, where are the fucking marksmen?" Sean cursed as he exited cover just long enough to open fire into the advancing drones.

Masa focused his rail gun's sights on the drone's head. His resulting shot left the drone hanging dead from the ceiling for a moment before it crashed down onto other drones. "You're welcome."

"Fuck you, that thing nearly broke our line," Sean replied, watching as the ammunition counter on his rifle quickly dwindled from fifty rounds in the magazine to nothing. "Cover me. I need to reload."

"Yeah, fine, but I'm pretty sure we may need to fall back," Mitch replied and grabbed a nearby M79 machine gun. When he grabbed the gun, he saw it had a full magazine. He pulled the severed hand from the grip and prayed. *Hope these two hundred rounds serve me better than the last guy who used this.*

Sean pulled a grenade and threw it down the hallway toward the departure ramps where most of the Guardians were still massing for a charge. The explosion knocked the Guardians back for a moment. "Should we fall back and get our sergeant before they start shooting at us again?" Mitch asked.

"You go first, I'll cover you," Sean stepped out of cover and kneeled down to open fire as Mitch ran behind him toward the next hallway. "Sgt. Ortega? Talk to me. We are coming to get you. Just hold on. Over."

"Fucking hell shit, get this thing out of me," Manuel shouted into his radio. Several carbon shards had cut through his suit's armor and skewered his leg. The pain brought him to his knees. He crawled behind cover, knowing he'd lucked out when he saw the dead Marine across from him with a long, cooled shard sticking out of his neck and missing an arm.

Nathan pushed up to where the two were. He handed Mitch a grenade. "Move up, draw their fire while I beeline for Manuel. After that, hold your position!"

Mitch and Sean moved up to cover Nathan, the nearest corpsman, as he ran to Manuel's location. Nathan slid over at the last minute, like a baseball player would, sliding to home base to avoid the Guardian drone's fire.

Nathan looked at Manuel's leg. "Oh, for Christ's sake, you can take the god damn pain." Nathan noticed that the nanofibers had already compensated for blood loss, and the damage would do little to hinder the power armor's functionality. He sprayed the wounds with antiseptic, then removed each shard and flooded the injuries with medifoam.

"Oh, give me a break, kid. My leg just got turned into a kebab," Manuel complained, picking up Nathan's rifle for defense.

"Shut up. Hundred years back, I'd only be able to drug you up for a nice long time. After that, you'd be lucky to have a below-the-knee amputation with a metal stick for a leg if you got air-lifted out. Instead, all you need now is a new armor plate and some therapy," Nathan responded, getting Manuel off his feet and letting the muscle suit do the rest of the work.

By the time Nathan noticed the looming shadow over him, it was too late to react. Manuel fired his Gauss rifle three times into a Guardian drone that rushed up behind Nathan. The first two 6.8mm slugs hit the Guardian hard enough to punch through its thick overhanging breastplate, and the third came clean out of the back of the creature's snake-like head. The biomechanical drone stumbled backward, screeching, with its legs clanking and leaking viscous pink liquid onto the floor before collapsing.

"Yeah, and you would be just like your little lesson, a piece of history if not for my shooting," Manuel said, scoffing at Nathan's comments.

After a thumb up confirming Nathan and Manuel were good to fall back, Mitch asked, "So Sean, what's your count? I'm almost certain I have ten." He was thankful that his helmet drowned out the sound of the large 11.5mm rounds coming from the M79 machine gun as it chewed into the charging Guardian drones.

"There are at least two hundred of these things standing. Everyone in the platoon killed at least ten!" Sean shouted, aiming for the enemy drone's head. He landed a shot, dropping a Guardian as another fired his pulse cannon. Sean's armor took the damage, but an indented scorch mark was visible. Sean took cover in the nick of time to avoid a second shot that melted the wall. He removed the empty magazine from the stock and slid a fresh one into its place.

Mitch kept firing, but only slowed the Guardians. "These fucking things are insane. We just killed over ten apiece, and they still keep fighting their way forward!" Mitch threw a grenade at the enemy formation as a Guardian drone's pulse cannon left a scorch mark on his chest plate.

The grenade exploded at the feet of several Guardian drones, shredding them and breaking up the group assaulting the hallway where Mitch and Sean had positioned themselves. Several marksmen lined up ranged shots and began cutting down the other Guardians that were using their back-mounted appendages to climb the walls and flee the spaceport terminal.

With their formation taking too many casualties, the Guardian drones fell back. The Marines advanced from cover down the main terminal, and three Stalker class drones appeared to cover the Guardian drones' retreat. Each was just as large as a Guardian with a similar snake-like head, but the neck ended in a large central eye just above their mouth. They moved more like dogs and could crush anything in their vice-like jaws, but could stand up like a man to use their large dewclaw blades as stabbing weapons. Both attacks were more than able to cut through power armor.

The Stalkers rushed headlong at the advancing Marines. A massive beast stood on its hind legs and stabbed clean through the power armor and chest of an unlucky Marine who had gotten too far ahead of his group. The beast shook its arm, dropping the corpse. The animal turned its sizeable metallic claw, covered in blood, to find a new target.

"Hose those fuckers down. Don't let them close the distance!"

shouted a Marine fleeing from the three large beasts as several others focused their fire on the drones.

The Marines focused their fire on the Stalkers. Round after round bounced off each Stalker drone's skin like a rubber ball. Some of the Marines with marksmen rifles managed to incapacitate a few by shooting each of the Stalkers in their central eye, one of the few weaknesses of the monsters. Mitch fired the M79 into the side of one of the blind beasts.

Sean fired his Gauss rifle's under-barrel grenade launcher at a pair of Stalkers. The subsequent explosion blew the drones off their feet, allowing for a few well-placed belly shots.

Dodging a Stalker's attack, Marlow began firing his M68 rifle into the beast's side, forcing it off balance before shooting its lower neck. He then managed to kick another one into the vulnerable position of having its unarmored lower abdomen exposed. Marlow moved to finish the second, but it rushed forward, and clamped down hard on his right arm, trying to tear it off. "Ah shit, get it off!" he shouted as he pulled his sidearm and fired a round into the robotic beast's central eye.

The last Stalker fell dead, and the gunfire ceased. Mitch dropped the M79 he'd borrowed and approached a dead Stalker drone, kicking it in the head. The monster remained silent. With a breath of relief, Mitch shouted, "I fucking hate these things. It's a stampede only…"

Sean was shocked; he had served with Mitchell Davis for the last few years. It was rare Mitch had nothing to say, neither a complaint nor an insult, and did not boast about his skills. Instead, Sean saw Mitch shake ever so slightly. Mitch was usually only silent when a cigarette was in his mouth. Sean quickly drew Mitch's attention to Marlow by pointing to the wounded man across from them. "Yeah, I know the feeling. We better see if we can aid our corpsman."

Marlow sat on the ground next to the dead Stalker. He could now feel a pain he thought he had long forgotten. He'd last felt this kind of pain when he received his augmentation—the grafting of titanium carbide to his bones, the injections drilled in deep past the muscle tissue. "Come on, god damn, you function, damn it! Come on. Please work for me, baby," Marlow cursed and pleaded, trying to make his right-hand function.

"Gabe, help Mitch and Sean get this thing off the gunnery sergeant so I can work," Nathan ordered as they ran a diagnostic on Marlow's suit.

Marlow took his helmet off before looking up at the corpsman. "Well, what's my damage, doc? I can't feel shit past my elbow."

Nathan pried the drone's mouth open as Mitch and Sean pulled the beast away. He could feel no teeth when he felt around the mouth and deduced the cutting edge was the jaw itself. Turning his attention to Marlow's arm, he removed the damaged armor. "Damn it, your arm will have to come off. Well, it's already off. Your muscle suit is the only thing keeping it on." Nathan prepared a painkiller before the amputation.

"Oh, fuck you! When I get a new arm, I am going to, ah…" Marlow passed out as Nathan shot a sedative into his neck.

"I can't perform a proper amputation here, but the muscle suit will form a sterile bandage with the right cuts. Thank god for smart compression wear." Nathan began cutting into the muscle suit with a laser scalpel, and when he pulled the arm off the suit began molding over the wound.

Major Robb watched over the field surgery while the rest of his men gathered the dead, placing their bodies along the wall with the *Welcome Home* signs. He picked up a sign at his feet and brushed off the dirt. A child had made it with large sloppy letters, macaroni noodles, and glitter. While his men went about securing the perimeter and helping the few wounded, he placed the sign against the wall. *Thank you for this sign,* he thought before taking a look at the time. He had about four more hours before the Destroyer would return. Time was running out, and he knew it.

Lt. Carver presented Major Robb with his noteputer as he entered the security office. "PFC Davis found a functional security terminal. Seems the Serkins shut down the security drones before the attack in the spaceport. Our supply pods have landed with heavy weapons at the terminal entrance. A decent defensive perimeter should be up within the next fifteen minutes, sir."

"Alright, listen up. I want Alpha squad to hold the perimeter and get into the security systems. Our window of opportunity is closing fast, and I'd rather not piss away time on scouting." Major Robb began counting his losses on the noteputer.

The Serkin anti-aircraft defenses could be seen on the central tarmac used by shuttles to taxi from the terminals to the mass driver that would shoot them into orbit. Major Robb looked at his objective and then at his dwindling forces. "Delta squad will help out whatever is left of Charlie squad. Our wounded need to be stabilized. Bravo will collect all able bodies from Delta and move on the target."

Sean stood studying the *Welcome Home* sign and the scene beyond as the civilians, who'd hid on the overpass made their way into the terminal and did their best to stay out of the Marines way. He remembered this place well from about three years ago when he'd left with his brother to join the war effort. He walked over to the terminal gate, looking at the landing pads where large drop shuttles with hundreds of tons of cargo landed. It took him back to the day he left for boot camp.

June 3, 2129 Chicago Illinois

Sean looked at his family and girlfriend. The airport was busy, as if it were any normal day in June. The security drones remained hidden in the walls as the mop bots cleaned the floors. Tourists exited their transports. It was all so odd how the people went about their daily lives, focusing on their vacations, ignorant of the war. At the gate for the military shuttle, a soldier fiddled with his watch, clearly displeased he was dealing with a gaggle of civilians who had just signed up.

The shuttle outside was smaller than a Hummingbird transport. Instead of being egg-shaped, it was a blended-wing-styled craft that would need the mass driver to pass through orbit. His brother had already boarded the shuttle that would transport them to basic training. Sean stood on the other end of the security barrier. It separated those with tickets from the people who were dropping off or picking up travelers from their shuttles.

Sean could instantly tell he'd pissed off his sister Larisa and his girlfriend Samantha. The pair were whispering to each other in obvious agreement, which was strange. The two young women were polar opposites who rarely got along. Even their looks disagreed with each other. Sammy had dyed her shoulder-length hair purple with blue highlights and wore green tights with a pink blouse. Larisa kept her hair long, with its natural black color with no highlights, and wore a dress with matching shoes. He knew he was in trouble if they agreed on something.

Both had their arms crossed, but Larisa was the first to speak. "If you're intent on protecting us, maybe you should serve in America's Army, you big, dumb, stupid jerk!"

"Agreed. The National Guard is more useful now than ever. What's happening out there is a Colony problem that the fleet and Colony defenders should handle. Hell, you're good with guns. The small business Yuki and I are starting could use security," Samantha added with her hand on her hips, clearly in no mood to negotiate.

"Larisa, I told you to behave. We aren't splitting up on a sour note. I expected better of you, Sammy. This is no time to be self-righteous," Jennifer scolded both girls before taking command of the group. "Now, Sean, if you ever feel in over your head, it's okay to walk away at a later date. I promise you won't be cut off, and the same goes for Derek."

Sean hugged his mother. "Thanks mom, but this was Dad's fight, and it's mine too. I don't want to wait for the fight to come here. It'll be too late to make a difference then."

"I know you feel that way, Sean. I won't make this an argument. I'll have enough of that heading home." Jennifer looked at the girls, shaking her head in disappointment. "Please look out for your brother. Losing your father has taken a lot out of him. He's frailer than you think, and despite what he says, he does need you." Jennifer had to stand on her toes to kiss her son on his forehead.

"Of course, tell Mother I love her too, and I promise to come back. Things will get better soon, and I'll write letters home before I go to sleep. I promise you'll know everything I do, but for now, this is goodbye." Sean let go and walked backward for a bit until he absolutely had to leave.

Sean blinked back into reality and found himself staring at the Serkin rail gun-destroyed aircraft and burning vehicles. The tarmac was nothing like the LZ. A battle had clearly been fought and lost outside the main terminal before their arrival. He didn't even try to count the burning vehicles and wrecked buildings.

He took a step back from the windows and regained his focus. *Chicago is a big city, plenty of chances for them all to be safely away from the fighting,* he thought, looking over the civilians.

Mitch sat at the computer terminal in the security office, accessing as much of the spaceport as possible. Surprisingly, many of the power and camera systems were still functional. *Thank you, Mr. Tesla, for wireless electricity systems,* Mitch thought.

As Mathew approached, his helmet instantly altered the man's name to ID him by rank and surname. "Sgt. Miller, what can I do for you? The mainframe is booting up. We'll have eyes on the entire spaceport. Right about now." Mitch had cleverly managed to use public Wi-Fi to bounce all live camera feeds to Major Robb's HUD. He hadn't even used a hacking module like he did with the security doors.

Major Robb scrolled through the video footage on his HUD. "Sound off, PFC Davis. I want to know why every camera in four of the hangars is offline. And how the hell did you bounce signals into my HUD?"

Mitch promptly responded. "Sir, the cameras in those hangars are physically damaged. As for the signals, I logged into the Wi-Fi network and can use the system to feed information to the platoon as needed."

Mathew left the security post and approached Major Robb. "Sir, is it necessary for us to locate the missing civilians? Don't we need those anti-aircraft guns down ASAP? We have five dead and five wounded walkers holding our perimeter. I suggest we take the objective now."

"Fair enough, Mute. You have Bravo and Delta to move on the anti-air defenses. Davis, I want the airport security systems' diagnostics. The power is still on, so there may be some security bots left that we can use to augment our forces. Miller, take PFC Davis with you. I have no need for him here." The major promptly pointed Mathew outside.

Mathew paused. "Alright, listen up Bravo and Delta teams, you're with me. Get your gear and the heavy weapons. We're taking out those anti-air guns."

All twenty men gathered and began collecting heavier weapons—single-shot rocket launchers and Omni-rifles. Masa opened up one of the heavy ordnance crates Echo had brought in, selecting the Omni-rifle. "Oh, now this is firepower. A six-shot man-portable particle cannon—35 kilos of armor-piercing glory!"

"There are only five anti-aircraft platforms that don't pack heavy armor. You, on the computers, tell me the status of the security drones,"

Matthew said, moving toward the security terminal where Mitch was working.

Mitch looked away from the terminal. "So you do talk Mute."

"Just give me the information I asked about, you little mouthy shit," Mathew said, then picked up Mitch's Gauss rifle and threw it at him.

Mitch caught the rifle with his left hand. "Well, Mute, we have fifteen security bots ready to go. Only thing is, they only have nonlethal weaponry. If you want them loaded with live ammunition, it will take another hour."

Mute sighed. "Get the bots ready for deployment as they are. We can certainly use the distractions. Just keep them on station until we need them."

The twenty men strode toward the tarmac of the spaceport. It was a nasty scene to behold the dead security and spaceport staff, as they were all maimed and charred. Crows picked at the corpses until scared off by the approaching Marines.

"Christ, I'm glad we got sealed suits. This has to be an awful smell," Sean said as he looked back at a crow perched atop a smoking police car.

From his HUD, Mitch ordered the security bots to mobilize, and all fifteen robots rolled out of their charging pens onto the tarmac. Each security drone was a tracked cargo bot with its hauling capacity replaced by weapons and armor. Each drone featured enough armor to withstand most small arms and fragmentation from small explosives.

"Alright, listen up. Mitch, send the security drones in to draw the attention of the remaining Guardians defending the target. While that happens, heavy weapons teams will flank and take up positions on the high ground. The Omni-rifles have a better shot at punching through the Serkin vehicles' top armor," Mathew briefed the group as they slowly moved forward.

The men and their security bots walked across the bombed-out tarmac with the hangars. Cover was plentiful from the wrecked aircraft and burning remains of drop shuttles scattered everywhere. The Serkins had even destroyed several large egg-shaped cargo shuttles at their launch pads. Hangars for conventional aircraft were on fire, but the battle seemed to have left more structures intact than outright destroyed.

The Marines saw several of the purpose-built landing spaces for heavy-lift cargo spacecraft. The water used to cool the spacecraft's outer shell after landing was spraying in every direction, and the spaceport's mass driver was leveled beyond repair.

Mathew scanned the area with his suit's radar system before returning to advancing with his rifle raised toward a potential target. "Stay focused on what matters, people. The Hummingbird dropships still have five good landing pads."

Masa looked over the destruction as he moved forward. "God, this is bad. I wonder how many cities are getting hit this hard."

"The ones recognized on the ship's holo-table were Moscow, St. Petersburg, Bussan, and Osaka. It looks like they hit Houston with several airstrikes before moving onto Chicago. Do you have family in any of those cities?" Sean asked Masa as he checked the next corner for the group.

"My mother lives in Tokyo, but I have family in the Osaka region," Masa said.

A few bodies lined the wall of the hangars, clearly having been executed not long after the area was destroyed in airstrikes. The flames from the fire on the tarmac were now behind the Marines who had successfully flanked the anti-aircraft guns. Mathew gave Mitch a nod.

"Alright, I am sending the bots to attack, Sergeant," Mitch said, issuing the attack orders to his drones.

The security bots deftly circled the Serkin's anti-aircraft defensive positions. They began firing their weapons as they charged the Guardians. The Serkin drones quickly left their position to dispatch the attacking security bots. Despite outnumbering the Guardians, the security bots' rubber bullets and tear gas meant little compared to the Guardian's neutron beams that sliced the first five attacking drones in half, causing them to explode shortly after being hit.

The following Guardian smashed a security drone with its fist, and a security bot adjusted its turret and fired rubber bullets at point-blank range with no effect. The Guardian drone then used its particle rifle to shoot the drone several times, obliterating it.

The last security bot was lifted off the ground by another Guardian drone that proceeded to rip its turret off before flipping the drone over and shooting up the vehicle's underside. Once the Guardian confirmed its kill, it promptly went back to standing guard.

While the last security bots were being destroyed, Masa and Eric jumped up to the roof of a nearby aircraft hangar to gain elevation. Masa nearly slipped as a section of roof gave out under his foot. "Fucking hell, watch your step. The high ground may be unstable," Eric said.

"No kidding. I'm not sure how solid the ground will be when we start shooting. Hey, Mute, we're lined up with the Maser cannon and see the four Type 23 air defense batteries. The Serkins parked them in a standard star formation," Eric said as his team had managed to reach firing position.

Mathew was pissed his distraction was short-lived. "Well, there went our distraction. Alright, demo teams move in once the Guardians are down. Everyone with an Omni-rifle, target a vehicle. Everybody else, take out the drones on one.

"Aim for the back of the Guardians' necks. That's where their armor is the weakest," Masa told Eric while leveling the sight of the heavy rail gun at the first Guardian.

"Fuck you. I know where to shoot, Mac. After all, I'm the reason these things run," Eric replied.

"Three, two, and one," Mathew said, and the Marines killed the Guardians protecting the anti-air defenses. He jumped down from cover and lowered his gaze, standing just above where Hangar Road turned into a staff parking lot. Looking out toward Interstate 90, he used his HUD to zoom in on the horizon and saw a pair of Specter gunships patrolling the heavily populated suburbs. "We've got two Specter gunships north of our position. I want these guns destroyed in less than fifteen minutes!"

The Omni-rifle-equipped Marines targeted the vehicles surrounding the rail gun. The particle rifles fired, each releasing a Helix shape of electric light around the stream of particles. The beams of particles hit the Serkin anti-aircraft vehicles' armor first. They were cut, and it caused several electrical short circuits, inhibiting their ability to hover.

The vehicles crashed to the ground before they exploded as the beams cut into their fuel tanks.

The demolition teams moved in quickly. Planting one demolition charge on each of the four short-range Masers, they loaded the rail guns' power sources with C4 charges to destroy the Serkin's long-range rail gun. With that gone, the dropships could descend from orbit safely.

"Ten minutes before those gunships show up to avenge their buddies," Sean predicted as he stood guard over the men planting the demolition charges.

Mitch looked around and saw the anti-aircraft defenses had adequate fortifications. *If we bring vital information to our forward positions, why wouldn't the Serkins bring their vital information to their positions too?* Mitch contemplated. He looked for anything of value left behind.

Sean watched at Mitch as he rummaged about over-turned tables. "Dude, you are playing with their trash?"

"Shut up, man. This isn't trash; this is a mobile computer terminal, intact and undamaged. We can probably discover all sorts of things once I understand the keyboard and user interface." Mitch ensured the computer wasn't booby-trapped before securing it. "This could be a game changer—we have nothing on these fuckers other than there being a few different color-coded ranks for their drone commanders. I hope we can figure out how to use it."

Sean sighed, grabbed Mitch's demolition charges, and slapped one onto the vehicle's turret ring above the hull. "The weakest section on any vehicle has to be right here. At least one of us knows how to follow orders," Sean said, helping Mitch collect the computer before leaving.

"What the hell are you two doing?" Mathew demanded from Mitch and Sean.

"Collecting an enemy computer for information, sir." Mitch presented the computer to the sergeant, hurrying back toward the main terminal.

Mathew cocked his head and reluctantly conceded. "Good work. Alright, people, we pull back to the terminal and protect our new prize. The air force will take care of those gunships."

Major Robb watched from the main terminal as four explosions surrounding the large rail gun were followed by several more minor explosions at the base of the rail gun. After that, the rail gun's turret wobbled and fell over. "Well, we met the timetable. Carver, get the locals on the horn. Tell them to launch their air strike and alert ECS Stryker they can begin the drop."

"Sir, it looks like what remains of the Serkin forces are pulling out and heading to the city," Carver reported, watching the CCTV footage of several Guardian drones all running toward the city.

"This is Sgt. Miller to Major Robb. We have destroyed the rail gun and surface-to-air Masers. Stop. We have bugged out of the enemy AO and are returning to your position now with an enemy computer terminal. Over."

"This is Major Robb. We copy you loud and clear. Local air assets are inbound, and the Serkin forces seem to be falling back to the city. We saw many of their Guardians head east into the city and the air assets are five minutes out. Over."

By the time Miller's team made it back to the main terminal, the air assets had arrived—several large fighters accompanied by drones lead the attack. Over three dozen fighter bombers sped east, destroying any small-scale Serkin aircraft. The human air forces stayed in close formation as they came within the vicinity of the Serkin warship hovering over Lake Michigan.

"All call signs; this is Badger, lead of the Illinois Air National Guard. All air assets follow me in and keep the enemy aircraft off the bombers. Maintain formation and only shoot down small scale aircraft that are in your way. Do your best to keep as many missiles as possible for that ugly ass bug over the lake. Over," the lead pilot said as he flew over the burning alien anti-aircraft guns.

As the fighters attacked, several Serkin aircraft started mobilizing but were quickly overwhelmed by the human suicide drones. The human fighters stayed in close formation as they came within the vicinity of the Serkin warship hovering over Lake Michigan.

The aircraft finally reached the downtown city center, shooting down the occasional Specter gunship that had the unfortunate fate of being in the path of the air strike. The B21 bomber drones' flight paths followed that of the fighters, releasing a swarm of suicide drones before they all banked right flying away, letting the suicide drones swarm the Serkin ship.

As the salvos of missiles and suicide drones made contact with the shields of the Type 27 Cruiser, the missiles exploded one by one, each with a shimmer of blue light that could be seen as the missiles hit the ship's shields. The second and third salvos broke through the shields, peppered the Cruiser's hull, and managed to destroy a small section of the ship's forward, beetle-like pincers structure. The sudden human attack had an immediate effect and the Serkin ship began to flee.

"Well, I don't recognize any of those birds. Are they new?" Mathew watched the planes above his head.

"I take it you aren't from Earth, Mute? America is one of the many nations on Earth to maintain a standing military separate from the Earth Colonial Federation's Armed Forces," Mitch answered the sergeant's question.

"The Federation has more than two hundred colonies, Earthborn," Mute said, moving back to the terminal.

"Run, you cowards. Tokyo and the whole Earth are next!" Masa shouted, watching the Serkin ship flee to the southwest, leaving a massive trail of smoke as it flew away.

"Now that is a beautiful sight. Pity, I got no camera for that," Eric replied, watching the event unfold. Looking around at the ruined spaceport, he finally felt a sense of satisfaction.

Gabe was unimpressed. "They aren't scared of us, they are just playing us. Don't get too confident."

With the thrill of winning cut short, the group returned to the terminal. While Bravo and Delta teams were busy destroying the Serkin air defenses, the rest of the strike teams had set up a small defensive position around a make-shift command post and field hospital. The civilians that were found hiding on the overpass began helping tend to the wounded.

The five dead had survival blankets serving as shrouds, and the wounded were lined up in various stages of treatment across the hall from the dead. Nathan was all but alone in treating the few wounded aside from the civilian helpers. He took notes on each person's condition. "Major Robb, the wounded are all stabilized. Though I don't think we'll see them on their feet again for a while," Nathan said, checking the IV pad connected to the arm of a wounded Marine.

"Alright, return to perimeter defense with Alpha team. For now, we will leave the wounded here. We will have medical teams for them soon enough once the heavy dropships land," Major Robb said, watching Bravo and Delta teams return from across the tarmac.

"Look, an HD-1M Hummingbird. I guess the Stryker let them go early in case the Serkins shot it down." Sean pointed up through the skylight. After entering the terminal, he removed his helmet and went to an open seat on a bench to get some rest with a few other Marines.

As the group returned to the terminal, they saw the survivors' children. "God damn, I envy the civilians. What I would give for a meal and nap," Gabe complained. After watching the children eating for a while, he turned his view to that of the descending dropships.

"It's cool. I'll grab some MREs. It's not like guard duty is going to be hard now." Masa made his way toward the command post the Marines had set up near the first security station, along with Major Robb's command center. The site had MREs, but also ammunition thanks to an earlier supply drop. He noticed a child taking one of the spaghetti MREs. Masa stepped in to correct the child. "Hey, you don't want to eat that one, kid. It's very salty. Take the BBQ pork instead."

Masa reached out his hand offering the boy an MRE with his armored hand.

"Lance Corporal Chikafuji," Major Robb addressed Masa as he spotted him giving food to a kid.

"Shit fuck," Masa cursed under his breath before turning to address the Major. "Is there something you need, sir?"

"Chikafuji, I want you to get some of the men off their asses. Once you have a fire team, move back to the parking deck where we entered. Set up overwatch and await further orders. Don't engage any targets unless you have to."

"Yes, sir," Masa replied, relieved his plan to steal food had gone unnoticed.

"Also, gather enough ammunition for your fire team to make a scouting operation into the city," Major Rob added, looking away from the noteputer.

"Yes, sir," Masa said, leaving to gather his fire team, who was at the make-shift armory. "Eric and Sean, you're up too. Let's go. We got a job to do. Grab some ammo and get a few explosive traps."

The group went over to the supply set-up. "Well, so much for teaching the kids which MREs taste like shit, huh, Mac," Sean said, loading replacement slugs into his magazines.

"The Major wants a team on overwatch at the parking deck across from the main entrance," Masa replied.

"Anyone else once ever think magazines would be thrown away en mass like garbage? I kind of wish the laser rifle program hadn't been canceled. All we'd need to do then is carry batteries about," Mitch complained as he slid a fresh battery into his Gauss rifle.

"No, I was trained on how to use guns by a veteran of the Federation Communist Union War when I lived in Texas. As for the laser rifle— that program cost too much, and every time you fired the damn thing, you glowed like a forest fire after a few shots on an infrared scan. Using the laser rifle gave away your position to anything with modern sighting systems. Gauss rifles can fire a million rounds and barely register on a thermal imaging scan," Masa said to Mitch, taking a newly loaded magazine.

"Most of the guns I used were single-shot weapons. They were typically used for off-the-grid situations in the wilderness," Eric replied dismissively.

"Shut up, load up and let's move out," Masa said. Everyone quickly finished grabbing what they needed, then collected their helmets and headed out to the parking deck. Masa then looked to Mitch, "Davis stay here, and guard the civilians."

Mitch complied with Mac's order and nodded a fair well to Sean as the men moved out. Mitch hardly mined maybe he could do something nice for the civilians. He looked at them, all a sorry bunch. He looked at the kids, and had to do something for them.

ECS Robert F. Stryker
Low Earth orbit over Chicago

The bridge of the Stryker was a beehive of activity. "Captain Kurkov, the ship has reached geosynchronous orbit. We can convert operation systems for atmospheric support," the ship navigator said. She was finishing her tasks in readying the ship for converting its artificial gravity and engines to function as fire support platform safely in the Earth's uppermost atmosphere.

Captain Kurkov stood up from his seat and approached the ground control table at the back of the ship's bridge. "Very good, but we will stay in orbit, helmsmen. It will be easier to retreat and come back if we stay in space. Tell me, Colonel Mason, do you have a plan to take this city back?"

With the city maps on the holo-table in front of him, Colonel Mason stood studying them and the number of soldiers the Destroyer had on hand. "I have begun dispatching several heavy-lift dropships to O'Hare Spaceport. That is where we will set up our FOB. From there, the ground troops can evacuate civilians and push into the Chicago area." He paused, looked away from the table, and pinched the bridge of his nose. "As of now, the Air National Guard here is largely in charge of the skies. If we can get some of our SPAAGs on the ground, we can help the fly boys focus on providing fire support."

"I know that look, George. What is on your mind?" Captain Kurkov questioned his long-time friend.

"At this rate, we can easily win here in Chicago, and that's without most of our drones. These attacks on the Serkins' part are not their normal modus operandi. They are all over the planet, and one ship randomly fled Chicago. Washington DC hasn't been so much as touched. The same goes for the Glasgow capital of the Commonwealth. Things don't add up. They went for the head of state on every planet in the Perseus Arm." Colonel Mason sighed. "I'll stay focused on the mission at hand as always, sir. I suggest we think about this attack as more than one of their usual strikes."

"The Americans probably won't send more forces to Chicago. They fear the Serkins are feigning attack to draw in forces for a full-scale assault elsewhere." Captain Kurkov rubbed his chin, looking over the holo-table.

"What is the real goal here? We are committed to Chicago, but we need to contact NORAD or find a way to access any available government communication systems. I am running an entire operation on the long-range scans and radio transmissions," Colonel Mason said.

"I understand, George. Focus your efforts on retaking this city for the moment. I'll do what I can about the greater situation and see if we can identify where that enemy ship went," Captain Kurkov said. He put his hand on Colonel Mason's shoulder before returning to the main bridge.

"Sir, our LIDAR, and radar have shown the orbital patrols we had to dodge earlier are forty minutes overdue. I think they may have broken off their patrol," the tracking officer said.

Captain Kurkov took his seat and asked, "Where did they head off to? Are you certain our Laser imaging, Detection, and Range system is working?"

"So far, we cannot tell where they are since we lack communication with the planet's command centers like NORAD or the Russian Aerospace Command. With so many satellites destroyed, we are mostly blind, sir. We have our systems, but we need to make contact with local forces directly to get into their networks without hacking," the officer replied.

"So we can't find out where the Serkin ships are going unless we abandon our operation. Very well, we will stay where we are. I will not take the bait for a possible trap, and I want to send out a beam space communication. Let's see about rallying our space forces outside the system," Captain Kurkov said, watching as the third and fourth dropships left the ship.

"Of course, sir. Sending out communications network now," said the radio officer.

Forward Operation Base, O'Hare Spaceport
Earth

When Mitch returned, he looked at some of the kids and noticed one of the terminals still had a functioning flat screen in the central waiting area for passengers. He pitied the kids and decided to search the internet with his HUD. He knew the major was too busy to pay attention, so he did a quick back hack and found some entertainment files online.

It took him very little effort to find something online to distract the kids. He chose cartoons films, not digital. No the kids deserved something with more effort- hand drawn animation. *Bingo.* He thought as he found a copy of *Lady and Tramp.*

Mitch loved old cinema but often found the old attempts at Cyberpunk rather fanciful, if not downright absurd. TV Shows where the internet and computers could create an artificial world of information. One where the hackers would swim through data like an ocean but when technology advanced far enough they find out the opposite is true. There it all was in front of his eyes but there would be no swimming through seas of data. Perhaps if it was like swimming in the sea people wouldn't rely on the AI tech so much. Hacking computers would certainly be less mundane than sitting at a noteputer display.

March 2, 2115 New York City

Mitch silently watched his uncle at his computer station where the screen had numbers and some images placed beside each other. The only sound he could hear besides his uncle's breathing was him tapping away on the computer's keyboard. The speed with which he entered the data was impressive. He approached his uncle; he had to know what this was. "Wacha ya doing, Uncle Allen?" Mitch asked.

Uncle Allen turned to the boy, motioning for the four-year-old to come and sit on his lap. "Come here and I'll show you."

Mitch hurried over and once he was settled in his uncle's lap, Allen began explaining things. "Your aunt and I aren't exactly as wealthy as we appear, but her friends are as wealthy as they are foolish. So we siphon a few sovereigns from their accounts—they don't think too much about their money. In all, I take a bit of it here and there. Right now, this is me erasing the proof I ever took anything." Allen firmly clamped down on his nephew's neck. "You keep this secret and I'll teach you many more. Consider this your first step into manhood; all men keep secrets and all men provide."

Mitch nodded in agreement with his uncle's statement. Having his uncle's undivided attention like this was all he ever wanted. No more would he be left wondering when his nanny would be replaced from his aunt's envy; now he had the attention of the only person she would not replace out of spite. "Anything you want, Uncle, I will do."

Mitch returned to the present as soon as the download and upload of the movie was completed, and he locked the film into a loop. Turning the emergency broadcast off, he switched the flat screen to play the movie. He was no longer needed and decided to rest as he didn't know when next he would get a chance to rest again, if at all. He found a spare seat in the booth with other marines.

Mitch tried making his small space comfortable enough to rest without disturbing anyone else. It was a futile effort, though, as airport seating wasn't meant for soldiers wearing advanced power armor. For a time he just watched the film with the civilians, an odd sight that even he admitted.

Major Robb watched as the large egg-shaped dropships unloaded their cargo. The operation was going well, and he finally had some breathing room. He wanted to relax. However, having fought the Serkins long enough, he knew this was just the calm before the storm.

"We'll have enough forces to attack when the last two dropships unload," Lt. Carver said, scrolling through the logistical reports.

"Better send out a scout team to find a clear path into the downtown area for our heavy vehicles. Have an Ibex made ready for the scout team," Major Robb said to Carver.

Carver sent an order to the dropships as they began touching down to secure a vehicle. "Forward observation team, this is Lieutenant Carver. You are to report to the tarmac when relieved by Sergeant Cooper. Major Robb has a mission for you. Over."

"Yes, sir." Masa secured his helmet and sealed his power armor. His HUD and data bank system came up again. When he collected his firearm, the suit's computer calculated the number of rounds when Masa tilted the weapon's axis to determine the additional mass based on the firearm's weight when empty. "You heard the boss man we're moving out."

Eric's HUD read thirty-six rounds in the lower right-hand corner of his HUD in bold, green letters. Similar readings showed suit's status to Friend and Foe Identification as Sgt. Cooper's fire team approached. "Alright, just in time to enjoy the view!" Eric shouted pointing up at the sky.

Four egg-shaped Hummingbird heavy lift dropships, each firing off their four massive rocket engines brought the ships' rapid pace to a slow controlled descent as their landing gear deployed. Eric walked the spaceport terminal, confident it would not be long now before it was crawling with standard Naval Infantry forces from the Robert F. Stryker. With their support elements, proper medical support and command equipment, they could set up an appropriate base.

Eric saw Gunnery Sergeant Marlow being readied to be moved for treatment. "Watch it, you little twerps," Marlow shouted at the soldiers, only to be silenced by the pain of his arm being moved. "I swear to god, you idiots better cut this thing off properly and put on a decent replacement!"

"Good old Sergeant Marlow is still full of piss and vinegar," Sean commented as the medical teams took the injured man away.

The group passed through the airport terminal they'd secured. It took only ten minutes for the terminal to be crawling with standard Infantry Forces from the Robert F. Stryker. Their general support, medical support, and command equipment had begun to establish an appropriate makeshift base. The group exited the terminal and continued towards the tarmac.

"I'm glad not to be his corpsman," Masa added as the dropship crews began the process of unloading their cargo.

Iron Horse, the 3rd Combined Arms Company based on the ECS Stryker, began to assemble as they exited the dropships. They carried with them several armored vehicles, close-support aircraft, and Infantry. The company's single platoon of twelve M10 Harrison tanks began rolling off the dropships and assembled with the other vehicles.

The tank crews started their pre-combat preparations, as their fusion reactors drove them forward. Each tank differed little in design from the tank models going as far back as the Cold War. The Harrison tank used an old tried-and-true design layout—the driver sat in the hull with the gunner and the commander in the turret. The main gun was a 140mm Light Gas Combustion Cannon sitting in the center of the turret with a smaller coaxial weapon next to the main gun. The M10 tank's fusion engine at the back was similar to past designs running on fossil fuels.

"Alright, everyone stand back. We are rolling out," the tank commander standing on the turret shouted. Even though the fusion reactor could run silently, its start-up phase to full power, was a boastful roar. It was followed by an expulsion of excess heat that blurred the air like the heat waves coming off a fire.

Everyone in the immediate area collected whatever they were working on and quickly fled as the area filled with steam clouds. Even Eric, Mitch, Sean, and Masa with their secured helmets and held up their hands to keep the heat away.

The tanks spun their turrets in unison like synchronized swimmers to have the main guns facing forward. The platoon commander's tank was first to lumber forward; its tracks clanking as the rubber pads prevented the tank from chewing up the concrete like it would rough natural terrain.

"How much longer do you think humanity will need tanks?" Mitch asked Masa as they looked at the tanks.

"I give it at least five hundred years. Believe it or not, we are more costly than much of the equipment being unloaded. Humans can't wear these suits for more than eight hours without, extremely invasive enhancements. Hell, a few years back, the colonial provinces brought up our price tag before Parliament, and they nearly passed the motion to cancel our entire branch. Thankfully, it only killed the laser rifle program," Masa said, pausing to watch the Main Battle Tanks rolled by.

"Yeah, but I can do a running jump and drop a demolition charge down the crew hatch and jump-jet off to the next tank," Mitch replied, catching up with Sean and Eric, who were standing still in front of a hangar.

"Well, the damned bureaucrats are always trying to pinch pennies just before elections. Your little stunning display of awesomeness isn't going to sway an asshole looking for reelection," Masa said as a scene began to unfold at a nearby hangar.

Across the way, a small crowd of Naval Infantry gathered outside the door of a closed hangar. A soldier slid the door open to the right and a group went in. A moment later they came out, none of them looking well. Eric paused, as did Sean, and with their helmets on, it was tough reading their body language for an outsider. Despite this, everyone seemed to know what was on the other side of the hangar door.

Darkness consumed Sean as his nightmare returned, hands filled with his mother's ashes as he knew what they'd found. The missing bodies from earlier had been found. He clenched his fists in anger. "What the hell is going on at that hangar?"

"You know what it is, and you don't need me to say it," Eric replied, watching the horror unfold as hundreds of executed people lay piled on top of each other, like sacks of trash.

Sean fought back his tears. He was medically and psychologically conditioned against combat-related PTSD, but had never fought a war on a populated planet. He could taste his tears as they ran down his face. "My family lives here? God damn it! Just tell me it's not what I think it is, damn it. I need to hear someone say it's not that. Anything is better than that!"

Eric's helmet hid the scowl on his face. "No. You want the comfort of someone saying it's okay. Nothing is okay. And nowhere is safe. You should know that by now, kid," Eric replied. He couldn't see if Sean was crying, but he didn't care. Eric walked away. Life ended and sometimes it ended in a mass grave.

"You alright, man? Oh shit," Masa said, looking at the hangar.

"Let's go. We can only avenge the civilians now and save those still alive," Sean said, jerking away.

Mitch approached Sean. "Hey, man, this awful city heat is always the worst."

Sean looked around; he fought to keep his mind off the pile of corpses in the hangar. *Were Sammy and Larisa in there?* He shook his head. "The cars these days release water from their tailpipes, but city heat is always grimy."

Masa made his way to Eric. "Listen, I can take your shit, but can you try not crushing these kids? It's bad for the team."

"Fuck's sake. They need to screen these recruits better. Kid is weak to break down like this. So what if his mother is dead? The system is letting anyone who passes a few physical tests in while we had to work for our seat at the table," Eric replied, cursing the system.

Masa was furious. "We need more Marines and I suggest you

remember how easy being a hard-ass is when it isn't your hometown! We're NCOs; it's our job to make these kids better."

"Fine, I'll build them up, but I won't hold their damn hands," Eric replied before hurrying to the staging area.

"Well, it's about god damn time you got here! It's not like a city is under attack," Lt. Carver complained as the two men arrived behind schedule.

Behind Carver was a convoy of three M35 Leopard-protected mobility vehicles, four M9 Lee IFVs, and four M11 Ibex general-purpose vehicles lined up. Several soldiers were grouping and creating their units. The dropship crews finally had most of the front-line combat units unloaded and began the processes of leaving for orbit.

"Sir, sorry, sir, we had some issues," Masa replied. "It won't happen again."

"It better not. I want you to load that tachyon uplink into that Ibex. Now, if you do not mind, I will try to get some heavy armor," Carver said, returning to his work.

"I wonder what's going to happen to Marlow, now that he lost his arm," Mitch said, changing subjects as he helped Masa carry the transmitter to the vehicle's cargo section.

"That crazy bastard will probably go for a prosthetic and be back in the fight a few hours later. I swear, there are just guys that will never be good outside the military, and he is their mold," Masa replied, setting his rifle to safe mode.

As Masa's group loaded up their vehicle and prepared to move out, the VTOL aircraft were the last to unload from the dropships before they returned to orbit. Once the area around the dropships was cleared and the crews of the dropships boarded, they lifted off back into orbit to bring down the next wave of troops.

Lt. Carver sat watching the dropship trails climbing up into the sky in his M35 Leopard. He wanted the tanks and tried to argue for them. "Sir, twenty minutes more and we will have twelve tanks. I doubt the local forces and civilians will be any worse off within those twenty minutes."

"Negative," Major Robb replied. "The longer we wait, the fewer people there will be to save. You have two full squads of Mechanized Infantry. Get this done, or I'll get someone who can!"

Carver slammed his fist into the vehicle before he addressed his men. "Alright, people, load up! We are heading downtown to secure Ryan Aerospace Park on West Addison Street; our phase line is Alpha. Check your fire, the AO is heavy with civilians," Carver shouted before he put his helmet back on.

"Who is the acting commander in the scout team, sir?" Sean asked.

"Sgt. Blake, you're the best shot. You get to keep your eyes on the team and streets as you scout ahead of the convoy," Lt. Carver said, tossing Eric a pack of ammunition. "Try to be a leader, will you?"

"Yes, sir!" Eric replied. He hated Carver, but he was smart enough to never show.

Mitch climbed into the rear and manned the Ibex's remote turreted autocannon. He toggled the joystick to check the control system. Sitting in the passenger seat next to Mitch, Sean had no desire to see his hometown's destruction head-on. After starting up the Ibex and making sure all systems were a go, Masa drove with Eric in the front passenger seat.

"Alright, Corporal Ryan." Eric held back his insults for the moment. "We are scouting the city for a viable path in the downtown area. I want you to feed Mac directions the GPS misses."

"Yes, sir. I'll tell you route changes as needed," Sean replied.

Mitch recognized the name and assumed a connection. "So Ryan, as in Ryan Aerospace Enterprises? We got a rich kid escaping luxury?"

"No. That would be my uncle's side of the family," Sean answered.

"That's all well and good, but we are driving into the heart of a city crawling with Guardian drones," Masa said. "Do me a favor, Ryan, get pissed. Use that anger to make these alien bastards pay."

"Yes, getting payback is your best option now," Eric added, deciding to act like the team leader he was supposed to be. "Use your anger. Channel it for the fight."

"This is Convoy Punisher. Call sign is Punisher 01 to the scout team. Our first destination is the intersection of I-90 and West Addison. Do you copy?" Lt. Carver asked. "We will set up a Forward Operating

Base at the Ryan Aerospace Park. From there, our current FOB at the spaceport will be our main base. Scout team, your call sign is Greyhound. Can you confirm? Over."

"Confirmed, Punisher 01. Our call sign is Greyhound. Over and out," Eric replied as Masa sped east away from the Spaceport. "Listen, kid, Sean, we need you to block out the ghosts haunting you."

"You got it. If my family is a ghost, then I'll live for revenge," Sean said, stomaching his concerns about if his family was dead in the hangar or alive in the city. As the Ibex sped eastward, he felt renewed. It was morbid to think his loved ones were a burden, but compartmentalizing was freeing. He closed his eyes, thinking, *I am a failure, but I will avenge you all.*

The group drove straight toward the heart of Chicago as its sky filled with tracer fire from anti-aircraft guns belonging to both Serkins and humans. Both sides were trying to gain the edge needed to claim the city. Several explosions on the ground continued to erupt, as if the streets of downtown were erupting like a volcano.

The US Air force was fighting to control the skies above, forcing Masa to watch for falling aircraft and possible roadblocks. "Shit, there may not be a fucking highway when we get there," Masa shouted as a Serkin Specter gunship crashed into an apartment building.

The collapsing building rained down debris onto the vehicle and flooded the area with dust clouds. Masa managed to brake and turn hard left to avoid the larger building sections. The smaller debris peppered the Ibex's armored shell. The occupants could almost imagine it as heavy rain. Masa returned to the main road. He scraped the Ibex along the sides of the wrecked cars.

"Mac drive right, we'll be fine if we stay on the main road!" Eric braced against the dashboard as Masa jerked the vehicle hard to avoid more debris and abandoned cars.

"Great, there's a whole city of this shit, and we're just a lone fire team. How the hell can we avenge these people if we get killed by collapsing buildings?" Mitch moaned, holding onto his seat while watching the carnage in the streets.

"Bitching and moaning about it won't help me drive through a war zone!" Masa shouted as he pushed the Ibex past a car wreck.

"We know you're Asian. Nothing will help you drive better!" Eric shouted, causing a round of laughter from everyone in the Ibex before he turned the vehicle radio to a military frequency.

"Fuck you, round-eye," Masa shot back, causing more laughter.

Sean took a deep breath as the Ibex crossed over the Des Plaines River. With the Serkin ship no longer dominating the sky, the tracer fire seemingly increased. He felt no better than when he'd touched down. He did, however, find himself with a purpose.

1000 hours
ECS Robert F. Stryker

Captain Kurkov sat watching the security feed as the alien computer system was transferred into the ship's meager research bay to be analyzed. He took a coffee packet out of the nearby wall and began drinking out of the straw. He was about to return to the bridge when the door to the CIC opened.

The Stryker's communications officer entered. "Sir, we have NORAD on the line, finally. We are talking to General Zachary Stone. He has a report for our ground troops. Also, the ship's AI should have a full report on the captured enemy hardware within the hour."

"Wonderful, patch him through to my console." Captain Kurkov returned to his seat.

"Hello, Captain. I'm going to cut to the chase. Some of our surviving satellites are back online, and it's how we tracked your troops. Did you get the information I sent you? It's the last bit of data we could gather," Stone spoke through the radio.

Captain Kurkov pressed a few buttons and brought the man's face up. "My second in command is going over it now. Were you able to track the two Serkin ships we dodged? We could use a heads up on when that patrol is coming back."

"The ships you mentioned have broken off from their patrol route. Both adjusted their headings drastically an hour ago," Stone replied from his war room. "The ships descended into the atmosphere and linked up with the ship from Chicago. We have no idea why they did that, but they came to a stop in the desert. Although we do have other concerns ground side."

One of the CIC officers walked up to Captain Kurkov and handed him a datapad. "Commander, it seems that ODIN has taken notice of our new cargo and is aware of our movements. They also managed to get a few images from a recon drone before it was destroyed."

Captain Kurkov sighed. "General Stone, I will transfer you to speak with my second in command for the time being. I will be with you both shortly," Captain Kurkov said and headed to the private communications room at the back of the command center.

Colonel Mason looked over the NORAD reports. The Serkins weren't continuing their planet-side offensive operations. Compared to their previous assaults focused on steamrolling over any foe, they now merely held the ground they took in the opening attacks. The most informative information was what was happening in the desert.

"Hello, it seems the Serkins have more ships in the desert," Captain Kurkov said, observing the formation of ships. A major tech gap that had impressed him was how the Serkin ships could easily hover in the atmosphere without using thrust.

Mason looked through the reports on the noteputer and then pulled up the area on the battle map to get a better view of the recon photos. "Eva, combine the map with the drone footage and make sure General Stone sees this as well."

Eva responded quickly. "Of course, Colonel, I am combining all data now and sharing it with NORAD."

"There shouldn't be a small flotilla of fifteen ships preparing to defend against a full-scale offensive; what is out there? I know my fiction, General Stone. How many more areas are there besides Area 51?" Colonel Mason demanded, looking at several larger Serkin warships hovering over the desert. He then noticed the movement on the ground. "They are looking for something, but what could be out there?"

General Stone took a cigarette out and lit it as Mason watched. "I believe the Office of Defense and Intelligence called them Overlords. There are ten—five of them stand guard, while the rest dig. We calculate that their plasma weapons at full blast can cut through ten meters of earth every minute. Whatever they are looking for, it's deep underground.

Mason wished for a cigarette and sighed. "At that rate, the weapons will have to cool down for at least an hour. It's why Overlords are rarely seen outside defensive positions. I suggest we keep an eye on it, but we must defeat their fleet first."

"Very well," General Stone said. "I will begin feeding you information as it comes along, but my priorities are reaching the Secretary of Defense and the Joint Chiefs. Is DC safe, or will I need to transfer command?"

"The Serkins have not launched any attacks on Washington DC, but we couldn't reach anyone. We've sent down several tachyon communicators. They should break through all jamming and bypass damaged infrastructure."

"Colonel, do what you can to handle the jamming," General Stone said, taking a deep breath, calming himself, frustrated that he was unable to operate on the same page. "I can give you American assets as support. With the nation's nuclear arsenal, we could help you deal major damage to their fleet."

"Very well General Stone. I am sure I don't need to remind you that other Earth nations have nuclear weapons too. I would hold off until we can start speaking to those powers. Please give me a moment?" Mason placed General Stone on hold. "Of course, they held something back. Typical Earthers, we are supposed to be one nation, and he's worried about his section of the planet," Mason said, disgusted with the situation.

"NORAD could have started a nuclear war with their neighbors if they did use them," Eva informed Mason. "So yes, they held those in reserve, and we would be down one more asset, Colonel. There are more factors than nationalism."

The room for private communications was almost the size of a linen closet and attached to the bridge and command section of the destroyer. It saved time with private communications, but it wasn't the point of this room. When ODIN wished to speak to an officer, they only spoke to that officer and that officer alone. Captain Kurkov stood in front of a small wall-mounted display screen with its few visible sensors protruding slightly. "Captain Nikita Kurkov, SF98-557-132-148-866, born on the Colony world New Saint Petersburg, I am commander of the ECS Robert F. Striker."

The room came to life and a man in a solid black suit appeared. The man was unremarkable, but had a menacing look about him. "Ah, Captain Kurkov. This is Agent Miller of the Office of Defense and Intelligence," the ODIN agent said. "I regret we have to meet under such circumstances."

Captain Kurkov avoided the ODIN agent's attempt at pleasantry. "I am not familiar with ODIN ever having operated under pleasant circumstances. One of my ground forces found a working enemy computer. Also, the earth still has nuclear weapons on standby."

"Very true. I am here to help analyze that computer. Specifically, the wavelength it communicates on and its functions. We have had issues understanding their communications systems, and I'm glad to see something good come of this mess."

"I am lucky to have jumped onto the moon's dark side as I did. This ship may have the latest technology humanity can develop with the Yaren benefactors' help, but jumping in front of a Type 27 Cruiser is a death sentence. I will need other fleets," Captain Kurkov said. "Would you like to come aboard and take the computer?"

"To the point as always. Yes, your ship alone wouldn't be a match for those ships. As for your request for additional fleet support from the 5th Fleet in the Sirius System, they have currently activated to defend the sector. At best, the 7th Fleet at Tau Ceti is preparing to jump to Sol within the next two hours. 8th Fleet at Epsilon Erindai will be here in about five hours. As such, all fleets will be rallying near Mars," Miller said, looking over a report, almost ignoring Kurkov. "Now, I want you to transfer the computer to my ship within the hour. I have a dedicated team and AI programs designed to translate their languages, operating systems, and the like. We may be able to track their communications the way they do ours."

Captain Kurkov couldn't hide his disgust. "Well, what am I supposed to do until then? I'm one ship trying to piece together a counter-attack."

"I am currently on observation. Though if Earth has nuclear

weapons, we could use the neutron radiation and EMPs against the Serkins just before our fleets arrive. The reinforcements will attack a weakened target. I must go now," Miller said, sending a transmission containing vital paperwork and security clearance to Kurkov.

"Very well. I have received your security clearance and request. We will put your ship to use if we can," Kurkov said, ending the conversation. Once finished, he kicked the wall. "Stupid smug intelligence asshole, they can get here in hours to pull rank on me, but can't do the same to the fleet admirals when the capital world is being invaded!"

Colonel Mason looked away from the command table where Captain Kurkov was fixing his uniform. "I take it that went well?"

"We will transfer the captured systems to the ODIN vessel. I can't believe the nerve of some people. That agent can pull rank on me, yet comes alone in a stealth ship for a computer."

"ODIN is probably just focused on the bigger picture. At least, that's how I see it. Also, the Air National Guard is giving the Serkins a real fight in Chicago. And Major Robb has reported they are contacting local forces in Chicago," Colonel Mason said, noticing his irritated CO.

"Well, we have a stealth ship at our command, for what that's worth. The Serkin patrol should be coming around anytime now," Kurkov said, looking at his watch as he entered the bridge.

"Sir, Serkin patrol is still a no-show. This makes it hour four for us," the Radar officer said.

"Sir, our troops have communicated with the local troops in the Chicago battle space. They are requesting fire support," the communications officer said.

"Alright, then prepare this ship for an orbital fire support mission. Bring our turrets online and alert ground troops that our rail guns and turreted Charged Particle Cannons are on standby." Kurkov took his seat as the bridge staff repositioned the ship.

The destroyer used its Reaction Control System to align its starboard side over the city. The Gauss cannons and turreted particle cannons along the ventral and dorsal sides of the destroyer were lined up with Chicago, waiting for a target.

July 9th, 2131, 1240 hours
Chicago

A pair of Serkin gunships made a strafing run on the 290 Interstate Bridges, destroying a large section with their rail guns and missiles. Mitch fired a few rounds at one of the gunships as it flew away from the area. Masa slammed on the Ibex's brakes, bringing the vehicle to a skidding halt. The falling debris from the bridge caused a massive splash that washed several abandoned cars backward.

"Fucking hell, this is just fucking great!" Masa hit the dashboard as hard as he could. Many in the group climbed out of the vehicle for a better view of the area.

"It looks like the next bridge got hit too," Mitch shouted as his helmet began cleaning the face plate of the water. He watched as the enemy gunship was hit with a missile and went down the river.

"Suck it, you drone bastard!" Sean shouted as the gunship went spinning into the ground.

Eric looked at Sean and asked, "Alright, Sean, you want payback? Where's the nearest bridge that can hold a fifty-five ton tank?"

"We can use West Roosevelt Road just south of here. The Army had to have secured it if that gunship going down is any proof," Sean said, pointing south.

Masa turned the wheel of the Ibex and spun the vehicle around, using the accelerator to release his frustration. The traffic in the city had been light enough that he no longer had to play bumper cars, and the vehicle's four-wheel steering made turning around a quicker task. He soon let loose and drove south.

"Alright, head south on South Canal Street—that's likely where the anti-aircraft fire came from, and hopefully, it's still going. From there, we can use the bridge to get the tanks downtown," Sean said, grabbing onto his seat.

"Convoy Punisher, this is Greyhound. Head southeast to West Roosevelt Bridge. Our tanks can cross the bridge there. Army airborne has defensive positions. The bridge can handle the weight," Eric said as the Ibex swerved through the turn from South Canal Street toward the bridge.

The US Army had managed to deploy three Self-Propelled Anti-Aircraft Guns with two on the east side of the bridge. The other was stationed in the riverside parking lot of the Roosevelt Shopping Plaza. It had a large field of fire and was surrounded by whatever the soldiers could find to fortify the position and provide cover.

A Serkin gunship attempted to circle the SPAAG's position and made a strafing run from the south side of West 18th street, trying to hit the vehicle in its blind spot. The attack missed, and the gunship pulled back, using the building as cover.

The second SPAAG on the west side of the Chicago River held a position at a train yard. It locked onto the gunship as it made its second attempt to take down the northern positioned SPAAG. A short burst from the SPAAG's twin 30mm cannons hit the gunship on its left flank. The gunship began spinning as it fell from the sky, crashing somewhere in the Pin Tom Memorial Park.

The third SPAAG held its position in the crossroad center where West Roosevelt Road met with South Canal Street. It had the largest field of fire in the crowded city and was the most exposed. The only physical defenses were a few expandable barricades surrounding it. Masa pressed the brakes of the Ibex as they came across this vehicle first.

Masa brought the Ibex to a dead stop. Eric, with Sean and Mitch, climbed out of the vehicle, stepping over destroyed Guardians. The position had been attacked from the ground, and several Guardian drones, at least a dozen, had failed to take their target out. The SPAAG had several particle burns across its hull and turret. The group used their helmet scanners to attempt to figure out what happened.

Several dead bodies had the telltale, deep cauterized incisions that the drones' particle rifles left on soft body armor and flesh. The battle ground was covered in shell casings from small arms and the SPAAG's 30mm cannon casings. However, the bodies were more spread out, with several severed limbs lying about.

Eric stepped in a puddle of pink goo that had leaked from the drones. "Alright, be careful where you step. Let's not have this thing shoot us, so keep your weapons down."

Mitch stepped on the remains of a Guardian drone before kicking its head like a soccer ball. He switched on his suit speaker and asked, "Anyone still alive over here?"

"Doubtful. This place was their last stand. This M-20 Badger SPAAG can be left alone at a position as an automatic defense. I remember that from an air show Mother took me to," Eric said, using his HUD to gain a detailed view of what happened. "101st Airborne Forces of Chicago, come in. This is Strike Force Marine scout team Greyhound. Please respond. Over."

Masa took a second scan of the bodies in the area. Each dead soldier had several sections of their soft body armor cut straight down to the flesh. Some soldiers lost a limb or two when the particle beam found their target. Masa noticed blood splatter—the Guardian drone must have used the bayonet on its rifle to sever the soldier's limb as the flesh lacked any burn marks.

Mitch approached the fortification around the vehicle head-on, looking into the periscopes for the vehicle driver and commander.

"Anyone home in there?" Mitch asked, waving his hand in front of the vehicles.

The commander's hatch on the M20 Badger SPAAG slowly opened. "Holy shit, so it is you super suit guys! Praise the lord. I knew it was you when I saw the blips!"

Eric pressed the side of his helmet to cease the mute function as the man climbed down. "We're scouting ahead to find a bridge that can hold our tanks so they can cross into the downtown area. Also, what do you mean, you saw us coming?" Eric questioned the commander.

"We tracked some small anomalies on the radar screen toward

O'Hare, nothing we could lock onto or ID. I thought it was scrap from orbit. Thank you, Jesus, for sending us the trans-human soldiers." The commander took out a cigarette. It took a minute before he calmed down. "We have, well, we had a dozen guys guarding this post, but even with our 30mm guns, they didn't last long against these squid heads! I was praying to god to get some help."

Eric figured the man was Southern Bible belt. It seemed odd to hear a black man with a twangy accent. "Can you tell me what the hell happened and how long you've been here?"

"Well, if you must know, Colonel Sledgehammer Sheppard has a command center at Millennium Grant Coastal Park. We got deployment orders last night. We went from busting drug cartels in Juarez to being resupplied at Fort Worth. First boots were on the ground in Chicago at 0300 hours, and we managed to be ready for the attack when that ship showed up. We moved south as that ship took up a position over the lake. Then these things ran at us in waves," the vehicle commander said, spitting in the direction of a Guardian drone.

"Why can't you speak to command?" Eric asked.

"These damn things managed to do two things when they finally hit us. We lost our guards, and they killed our radio to command. My vehicles can speak to each other, and with limited ammo, we've kept our fire limited to protecting the bridge." The vehicle commander pointed to the damaged vehicle's severed radio antenna. "We can use a resupply, if you don't mind."

"If you got here at 0300, then when exactly did the Serkin ship get here and launch the attack?" Sean asked as the commander looked up at the vehicle's communications cluster.

"Scuttlebutt said the ship hit Houston and took down several aircraft on the way here. It arrived at 0830. We were on the streets shortly before 0800, but most civilians on the north side probably never noticed us until the fighting started. That was our last report, and I can't promise you anything other than what I say I saw is correct, alright. At 0930, it dropped off a ton of those damn squid-head fucks at the spaceport and downtown area. All hell broke loose after that," the commander said, taking a deep breath of the cigarette.

"If it went over the city to the lake, did it attack your command post?" Sean asked, not sure of the man's story.

"It passed over the Loop, not where our base is at the Millennium Grant Park. The ship passed over North River and Streeterville. Shortly after that, we made several pushes out from our staging area, but god only knows what went down. My guys pulled back after losing too many of our forces and decided to hold out here so people could get to the evacuation birds. With the various heights of buildings, the blind spots make our job of defending the bridge from air attacks easier."

"Hey, we got Lt. Carver on the radio. Winchester platoon is going to get here first. Their ETA is ten minutes," Masa said, coming over to the barrier where Eric and the vehicle commander were talking.

"Lt. Carver, this is Greyhound. We have a SPAAG team stationed on the bridge. They lost contact with their commander. They will need ammunition and a radio repair," Eric said, calling Lt. Carver.

"Copy that Greyhound. I just spoke with Colonel Mason. We can begin calling in orbital strikes against the enemy. Just make sure you have their Specter gunships somewhere that won't cause heavy civilian casualties," Lt. Caver said. His words ignited a small glimmer of hope within Sean.

"Wait, did he say not to cause heavy civilian casualties? We have people still alive out there?" Sean asked, puzzled.

"Yes, the Robert F. Stryker's thermal scans indicated that civilians are all over the downtown area. They are holed up in various places," Masa replied to Sean's question.

The vehicle commander inhaled his cigarette and let the smoke out through his nose. "Well, if you guys get me some supplies and a radio repair, we'll keep this position secured. Good old Sledgehammer is probably still holding the line." With a final puff, he put the cigarette out and began climbing back into his vehicle.

Greyhound held their position with the Ibex parked next to the rear of the SPAAG, offering it more protection. The Guardian drones' various attacks had chewed through the small makeshift barricades. All the scout team could do for ten agonizing minutes was wait. The ground attacks to take the SPAAG out had been unsuccessful, but losing them was still possible if another wave of Guardians attacked en mass.

Eric took his rifle and peered down the scope toward the park along the riverside, looking for the gunship crash site. The smoke billowing made the area easy to find, but the trees were blocking his view. He then scanned some of the buildings looking for Guardian drones; the weapons they carried had limited range, but their two tentacle manipulators meant they could go just about anywhere.

"Nothing along the northern or southern side of the river. It looks like they are sticking to downtown," Mitch said, looking across the river through the Ibex's turret zoom function. He then swung the turret as far left as it could go and scanned the nearby apartments. "Holy shit, I got a live human in those apartments."

"Wait; can you give me any details? We should try to get them out of there," Sean said, trying to hide his relief that if there were still people alive downtown, his family might also still be alive.

Convoy Punisher arrived first with Lt. Carver's M9 Lee Command Vehicle. A few Drone Trucks carrying supplies were with the convoy, and they, along with the other vehicles, began unloading their troops and supplies. After disembarking their vehicles, a few soldiers started collecting the dead. The rest of the Strike Force Marines who were able to fight came out of their M35s.

"Nathan, Gabe, it's about time you got here. Where is everyone else?" Eric asked, jumping over the barricade.

"Yeah, well, we had some slow drivers holding up traffic," Nathan said, nodding toward the first tank as it began rolling forward.

Two M9s made their way across the bridge first. The troops climbed out of the back and began securing the bridge before letting the tanks cross. The tanks of Winchester platoon split in two, lining both sides of the road. Getting out of his tank, the platoon commander went to Lt. Carver's command vehicle.

Greyhound team began rallying around the Leopards. The majority of the troops looked nervous, but no one slacked off. The squads and platoons formed up with heavy weapons as the light vehicles started crossing the bridge to set up defenses on the opposite side.

"Major Robb is holding most of our guys back for when the VTOLs are ready to fly. They will be delivered to hot spots as needed. Rumor has it the Joint Chiefs are planning to nuke the city," Nathan said, watching the various commanders talk with Lt. Carver.

Sean overheard that and reacted instantly. "Wait, what? Then what are we standing about for? We need to fucking move out now!"

"Calm down, the Serkins are mostly in the downtown area, and we're going to lead the purge," Nathan said, trying to calm Sean. The first M10 Harrison tank began crossing the bridge. "I told you we had VTOLs ready to deploy Strike Force Marines to hot spots. Well, we're going to make those hot spots."

"Looks like the tanks are going over the bridge one by one," Masa said, knowing full well that most bridges couldn't hold an entire squad of Main Battle Tanks on the best days.

The first of the M10s rolled across steadily while its commander sat on top, giving orders to the driver. The first tank made it over without incident and parked near the ruined police station.

"Alright, Lt. Carver, it's almost impossible to perform a pincer maneuver from the ground, so I'm keeping our airborne assets back. I hate doing this, but you must reach the evacuation site first. With the Joint Chiefs trying to nuke the city, Captain Kurkov and Colonel Mason want the local forces out of the local communication system," Major Robb said.

Lt. Carver looked on as a few soldiers crossed. He looked over at Blake and the other Marines talking. "Well, the good news is we can cross the river and head straight to the south side of the 101st Airborne's command post," he said, turning to his command screen.

"The fewer troops you send to the local CP, the better the chance we can find a large concentration of their troops in the Washington area. Head north and hit them before they march on Millennium Grant Park," Major Robb said, watching the next dropships unload their VTOL compliments.

Lt. Carver shouted at the men. "Sgt. Miller, take those Marines and get your asses to Millennium Grant Park ASAP. Captain Kurkov wants Colonel Sheppard to have a line without the Joint Chiefs eavesdropping.

Take that M35 with you as support. You will find the command post on the park's southern side."

"Let's roll out, damn it." Sean rushed back to Ibex.

"We'll follow in the M35 as we head east. Sean, take the Ibex and get us to Millennium Grant Park. You know this place the best," Mathew said, heading back to his vehicle.

Everyone climbed into a vehicle, only this time, Sean climbed into the vehicle's driver seat. He began messing with the radio system, opening the main channel to pick up any open communications and drawing Eric's attention. "What the hell are you doing, Ryan?"

"Opening all channels the vehicle commander said to. We have guys pinned down all over the city. If they are still kicking, we'll pick up their calls," Sean said, slipping the vehicle into drive.

The pair of vehicles promptly sped east on West Belmont as the last tank crossed the bridge. "So, you said civilians are hiding in these buildings, right?" Mitch asked.

"And there is the big silver tentacle-headed reason why, Davis," Masa shouted just as the Ibex's windshield was hit with a particle weapon's fire from a Guardian drone.

The Guardians began opening fire and trying to close the distance between the two vehicles. Mitch took control of the turret and fired a short burst of 30mm rounds at the Guardian drones. The first drone was thrown backward as a 30mm round hit its chest dead center.

Another round hit the next drone in the shoulder, and it severed its arm. One round beheaded a pair of drones as the vehicle fired into their targets. The drone next to it got hit in the legs, falling to the ground as the cannon fire hit the road and caused a cloud of dust to form.

One drone jumped out of the group and used its back-mounted tentacles to climb up a building to get a better line of fire on the vehicles. The particle rifle hit the Ibex's rear hatch, searing the carbon fiber as it dug into the heat-treated armor. It repeated the same shot on the following Leopard, but the shot glanced off the thicker carbon fiber composite armor.

The first chance Sean had, he turned right onto South Franklin to break the enemy's line of fire on the convoy. Nathan followed the Ibex and shouted into the radio, "Forget these drones and keep driving. We'll be out of their particle weapons' range in a few moments. They also won't do much damage, so save your ammo for something bigger."

The Leopard's gunner used the 30mm cannon and large-caliber machine gun to force the Guardian drones into giving up their attack on the two-vehicle convoy. Sean turned the vehicle left on West Quincy Street and returned the convoy to the right path.

Eric sat in the front passenger seat, groaning. "Damn it, kid, slow down. You are pushing the Ibex's smart suspension to the fucking limit!"

"I remember when you bitched about my driving, but this city boy isn't doing any better," Masa proclaimed in a proud tone.

"Shove it, Mac. You trashed our paint job on a dozen parked cars," Eric responded, flipping Masa the bird.

"This is convoy Echo 3 to anyone on this channel. Come in. I have wounded and civilians too! Damn it, we're low on ammo! Come in. Over. You got to get to the Tantrum nightclub, or you'll be counting corpses," a desperate voice shouted on the radio.

Another radio call came in. "Fucking hell, this is sniper team Delta 2-4. Is anyone out there? We are at the Trump Loop Tower on Michigan and East Balbo. We can see the evac site. I need fire support. The train tracks are crawling with these fucking monsters. Is anyone listening to me?"

"Shit, we've been breached! This is defense line Alpha at the Lurie Garden. Drop every fucking piece of ordinance you have on the red smoke. Now, damn it! We got drones inside the line! Bravo and Charlie lines prepare for an assault. It's on y—" the shouting was cut off and the sounds of shooting stopped.

"This is the Robert F. Striker. We have positions for fire support. We see red smoke. Danger close is inbound," replied a crewman from the orbiting Destroyer.

Everyone in the vehicles looked up as high as the smoke from the burning buildings would allow. "Shit, that was a low-powered strike," Mathew said as he watched the air sizzle and felt the strikes hit the Earth.

"Not likely, Sergeant. Lurie Garden is further north on East Munroe, and we aren't actually on a straight path to the south side of Millennium Grant Park. We'll have to get to East Roosevelt Road if the CP is on the southern side," Sean said, slamming his foot on the brakes as the city streets became crowded.

Countless masses from the south and west side of Chicago flooded the streets. Many of those with cars had abandoned them and began walking. The digital displays that remained functional ran public messages in bright red letters, repeating the same message over and over again,

CHICAGO CITY EVACUATION IN PROGRESS. ALL PERSONS MAY ONLY BRING ONE ITEM OF BAGGAGE. NO WEAPONS WILL BE ALLOWED AT PROTECTION CAMPS. PLEASE HAVE ANY IDENTIFICATION READY FOR DISPLAY. OBEY ALL ORDERS BY MILITARY AND LAW ENFORCEMENT OFFICIALS. MARTIAL LAW IS IN EFFECT.

Several Infantry patrols rushed forward against the teaming masses as the civilians fled for their lives. They'd seen the hordes of Serkin Guardian drones coming down on their defenders like a metal tidal wave.

Shit, these people are going to be slaughtered when those Guardians break through, Nathan thought as the two vehicles slowed enough to give the people time to get out of the way.

"Hey, Sergeant, will we be defending these people after delivering the radio?" Gabe asked Nathan as they drove toward the park.

"If we have to, we will. Now shut up and keep your eyes on the road. I won't have you running people over on my watch," Nathan said, knowing that Gabe saw civilians as battlefield clutter to be avoided.

Gabe had no response and kept following the Ibex leading the small convoy as it approached the evacuation site's front gate. A few armored cars had IFVs set up in defensive positions, hiding as much of their hulls behind barriers and sandbags as they could.

The masses of civilians all hurried into the base, too frightened to look backward as the Serkins closed in on the evacuation sites. Thus far, the situation hadn't broken into absolute chaos, as a frightened mob poured into the park looking for protection.

The convoy followed the makeshift road. It had been created by a combination of walkways with the ground destroyed by bearing the mass of combat vehicles leading to the lake's coast. The view was pathetic, both on the ground and in the sky. Troops along the road kept order as best they could while the fleeing civilians watched. The sky above was filled with birds fleeing to the south for safety—scavenging for food from the panicked humans was less important than staying alive.

Gabe and the others noticed the fleeing animals. "Looks like the birds aren't interested in waiting for the carrion," Nathan said with a sigh, realizing how bad things were in the downtown area.

"Well, we can hold up in a sewer or something so long as we aren't at the center of the nuclear blast," Gabe replied over the squad channel.

"Fuck you. We have too many people here. We're taking the city back!" Sean replied in a pissed-off tone.

Gabe rolled his eyes and replied, "Look, kid, I have faced off against them just like this. But not once could we do anything except evacuate the civilians and drop a nuclear bomb. You may as well say fuck reality."

"Both of you shut up. I don't need your banter adding to my bad fucking day," Nathan reprimanded his men. As the vehicles reached the command post, several more orbital strikes came.

A few of the Airborne's light tanks rolled passed the two Marine vehicles, stopping shortly to fire their 120mm cannons before pushing forward. A few Infantrymen followed the tanks while the convoy continued to the command post. Mortar crews had set up near the command post and were actively firing as civilians flooded onto the nearby transport planes.

When the group followed the walking path to the Hutchinson field, the convoy turned south and circled a small bunker. It had a satellite uplink antenna standing on top of it. Sean parked the Ibex near the command post and got out as a sniper climbed on top of the CP and began lining up shots. Much of Hutchinson Field was little more than a military base. The ground was torn to shreds by tank tracks, explosions, or dug-in positions to defend the evacuation site. The four-lane road of

South Lake Drive was crowded with people desperately trying to remain calm, hoping to make their way to the Landing Zone or port where the military loaded people onto available ships in the harbor.

"This area is a few Guardian drones away from a fatal stampede," Sean commented. Everything he knew as a boy was a war zone, and a light tank was burning in the spot where he first kissed Sammy. Now he got to watch as a Serkin gunship came in for strafing run.

Just as Sean thought the gunship would come in and add to the carnage, an Airborne soldier with a MANPAD launcher fired into the side of the gunship. The Serkin attack aircraft's right turbo fan exploded, destroying the wing. The craft instantly rolled as the remaining turbofan in the left wing provided enough thrust to flip the vessel before it slammed into Lake Michigan.

"Fuck you, alien bastards!" some wounded Airborne soldiers who could see the attack shouted while others cheered.

"DPCIM requested fire on grid seven, three, four, five, six, one, direction three hundred and fifty meters northeast of my position. Direction one, eight, zero, zero, right six hundred, drop four hundred. Targets advancing on drone infantry," the mortar commander shouted to the rest of the crew.

"This is our last cluster munitions, sir. We only got high explosive and incendiary rounds left," replied one of the crewmen.

"Defense line Bravo, we are out of fragmentation rounds. Over," the mortar commander said. "Note, we have incendiary and high explosive rounds remaining. We will continue support."

Several soldiers were sitting down on makeshift racks, waiting for treatment at the makeshift medical center. The wounded soldiers already had bio-tex bandages growing into the lacerations and burns to temporarily act as a new skin. Several other soldiers had conventional bandages over their wounds as medical personnel began rationing their supplies. Some soldiers were shell shocked, while others struggled to administer PTSD medication themselves with jet injectors.

Eric walked over to the soldier struggling to inject his medication, steadied his hand and helped inject the medicine into the man's arm. The soldier stopped shaking; his eyes dilated slightly before returning to normal. "Thanks, man," the soldier replied in a disturbingly dreary mechanical voice as Eric then proceeded to help the following few soldiers.

Nathan promptly removed the tachyon transmitter array from the vehicle. "Alright, people, keep the motors running and be ready to move out. I'll deliver the radio, and then we'll see about helping out here," Nathan said, toggling his helmet speaker with a blink of his right eye.

The command post was a large, partially underground structure. It was made of instant concrete fortifications, with makeshift armor plating from destroyed vehicles. The base of the outer walls and roof were further protected with smaller sandbags. The antenna and radio beacons were sticking up and out like random needles on a pincushion as a pair of snipers managed to find a way to use it as an elevated shooting position.

"Sir, they are continuing to press forward. Fire support seems to be having little effect in halting these damn drones. Bravo line is requesting reinforcements," one of Sheppard's officers said, looking away from his terminal.

"Keep the fire support up and reposition two of our Badger IFVs from the front of our base to the north for support. And where's my damn air support? The second wave of VTOLs can take off without escort," Colonel Sheppard shouted as he noticed the Strike Force Marines approaching with a new radio.

"The air force says their birds are refueled and rearmed. Their inbound ETA is fifteen minutes," one officer responded.

"Our Self-Propelled Anti-Aircraft Guns are reporting they are out of missiles. There is also a hostile aircraft on approach," another officer said.

"Tell the crews to refocus their efforts on keeping the gunships at bay with guns. Shoot controlled bursts of fire until we can get them reloaded," Colonel Sheppard said, doing his best to remain calm.

"We have a new command-and-control system for you, Colonel Sheppard. It will give you access to beam space communication and secure communications to the R. F. Stryker," Nathan said after entering the command post.

Several of the soldiers in the command post looked away from their own work to catch a glimpse of a fully armored Strike Force Marine holding a computer system that was well over twenty kilograms in one hand as if it were a pint of milk.

"Put it over there. Are you the ranking NCO for that little convoy?" Colonel Sheppard asked as a Serkin missile landed close enough to the command post to have him stumbling forward a few feet.

"If you want to give my unit and me orders, sir, I won't argue in favor of ECSF taking command," Nathan said calmly, throwing the proverbial rule book out of the window.

"If you can retake defensive line Alpha and secure Bravo line, there should be some leftover defensive drones with small 30mm cannons. They can help you hold the lines," Colonel Sheppard said.

"We'll retake the lines, Colonel. Just tell me what we need to do to secure those lines," Nathan said.

"Retake Alpha line here," Colonel Sheppard said, pointing to the East Jackson parking deck on a battered plastic map of the park. "This is Alpha line. Bravo line is here at the Buckingham Fountain, or whatever is left of it. Many of the old roads cutting through the old park are now walkways. The wireless security cameras are mostly functional, so we can give you a heads up if these bastards try to flank you. Their numbers seem to be high enough that the aliens' flanking maneuvers are pointless."

"Confirmed, Colonel Sheppard," Nathan said. Blinking his right eye, he signaled his HUD that he wanted to switch over to suit communication lines to his fellow Marines. "Alright team, we are retaking these defensive lines. Blake, get your ass elevated and aid the Airborne's marksmen. The rest of you push forward and support our vehicles."

"Good luck. Marine trans-human super soldier or not, everyone in this city needs it," Colonel Sheppard said as Nathan left.

Nathan tapped his helmet's speaker on. "Likewise, sir, and there is our air support." Everyone in the CP watched as two strike fighters came in low. They fired off a load of rockets at everything just south of Butler Field before banking right hard to avoid the downtown skyscrapers.

"My god, they bombed out Petrillo Music center. I had my first date there," Sean uttered in shock, forgetting about the squad's closed communications system.

"Well, they didn't bring down a building, thank god. Just imagine having to use our sonic imaging. Sure its high-end radar feeds a crystal clear image of objects to you, but your best hope time delays come from a radar pulse don't cost you your life. Those old buildings use all forms of materials that could mess with thermal imaging," Gabe said, watching the ground explode.

"Alright, assholes. Stop standing around with your dicks in your hands. We are moving up to retake defensive positions Alpha and Bravo. We move with our vehicles," Nathan said, taking his rifle off his back.

Both vehicles moved through gaps in the defensive wall, with their Marines following close behind. Eric threw a drone into the air to quickly scan the area, slightly improving the amount of information on the area for his comrades.

Eric managed to get a quick view of the lines and used his suit's computer to send the information to the other men in his unit. The lines had fallen apart under the constant waves of Guardian drones slowly encircling several units of the Airborne troops and their vehicles. "Sir, they are swarming on and surrounding Outpost 224. I'll send the nearest group to you now," Eric replied as soon as he touched down.

The US Airborne troops had very little in the way of true protection against the Guardian drones in close-quarters combat. The beasts' powerful mechanical arms and back-mounted tentacles could throw and smash the Infantry.

One Airborne soldier tired, falling back as he fired a series of short, controlled bursts into the center mass of the drone. The standard 6.5mm ammunition used by normal Infantry would do very little to the many layers of armor on the Guardian drone.

Once the drone closed the distance, its foe raised its rifle above its head and swung down the hammer. The Airborne soldier had little time to dodge such a swift strike. The blade on the Guardian drone's rifle sliced through the human's body armor, cutting deep into the man's flesh. The drone then used its tentacles to grab another soldier by the neck, throwing him aside like a rag doll.

The nearby soldiers panicked and fell back. The M20 Badger Light Tank turned its sights on the drone and used its 50-caliber machine gun to fire at the monster, knocking it backward. The drone landed on its back, but used its tentacle to catch itself from falling down. The tank fired its machine gun to keep the Guardian drone down. It took a half minute for the machine gun to finish the beast.

The tank's main gun turned and focused on a small cluster of drones and fired its 120mm cannon. The rounds exploded midair, and the concussive force sent enough shrapnel flying through the air to turn the drones to scrap. The Infantry quickly moved up to retake the position.

The second tank maneuvered out from behind the first and moved up, firing its machine gun to give support to the Infantry. As the next group of drones forced the Infantry from one defensive position to the next, the tanks focused its fire to cover the retreating Infantry.

As the situation deteriorated before them, Nathan ordered everyone out of the vehicles to form a defensive line. The vehicle gunners began sighting the battlefield as the occupants climbed out and moved to what little cover they could find.

"Alright, we got the data. Blake, get to a high point and cover us with sniper fire. Everyone else, move up and relieve the Airborne forces as we go," Nathan said, looking down the sights of his Gauss rifle. With Eric's scan of the battlefield, he managed to find the nearest group of soldiers.

The first wave of drones to enter the Strike Force Marine's sights received 30mm cannon rounds. And several were knocked out of the fight faster than the tanks' old heavy machine guns. Several drones simply bypassed all the Infantry and rushed the tanks.

One drone leaped into the air and managed to land on the second tank as it advanced. The drone dropped its rifle and began tearing into the vehicle. It ripped off the commander's machine gun from the copula's Remote Weapon Station. Next, it went for the vehicle's Active Protection System and sensors.

The first tank spun its machine gun and began firing on the

Guardian drone while its escorting Infantry focused their fire. They were keeping the next set of drones from reaching the first tank. Eric drew his sights on the tank and fired his M90 sniper rifle at the neck of the Guardian drone. The 11mm rail gun slug took mere seconds to close the four hundred meter distance. The slug penetrated the drone's neck, causing its destroyed husk to fall backward off the tank, but not before it managed to destroy most of the tank's sensors.

The damaged tank remained and did what it could with its limited sight. The drones kept up their assault and began firing on the Infantry. The particle rifles of the drones connected with one of the leading Infantry men. The beam cut into the man's body armor and slowly went out the left. Once the beam had gotten off its original target, it severed the man's arm.

The wounded man screamed as his arm fell off—but the wound had been cauterized before the severed arm even hit the ground. As one of the soldiers moved to help their wounded comrade, a second shot from another drone's particle rifle vaporized the upper portion of his head.

Eric took a breath and drew sights on the leading drone. He'd fought Guardian drones enough times to know when one would jump. He elevated his sights to just above the drone's head and fired. The 11mm slug hit the drone in the back just as it jumped into the air. Instead of having a controlled descent, it simply crashed onto the ground.

Sean fired several three-round bursts at the Guardian drones. The 6.8mm rounds from his M68A1 Gauss rifle each had the same kinetic impact as a mid-twentieth century 12.7mm machine gun used on many of the first generation main battle tanks. The only downside of such a weapon was the rifle needed its user to wear the Scorpion MK3 power armor to negate the recoil.

"Mitch, can you cover our right flank from the Ibex? I'll help the Infantry and their tanks," Sean asked as Masa and the others set up a small firing line.

"Yeah, go ahead. Even an Ibex won't be able to climb over most of these defensive walls anyway," Mitch replied, using the RWS's zoom function to hit targets further down the range.

"Belay that order. We move to flank the drones since they are focusing on the tanks," Nathan replied, shooting a drone in the head as it approached the light tanks.

The Infantry surrounding the light tanks kept shooting at the Guardian drones a moment longer before noticing the Strike Force Marines. The drones halted their attack on the tanks and refocused their efforts, becoming more tactical. They took cover and began focusing their fire before making another advance.

Several of the drones slowly withdrew while others opened fire. The particle rifle fire hit the side of the Ibex and boiled into the door. Sean returned fire, hitting the first Guardian drone in the head, causing the group to break up and scatter.

The Guardians picked up their rate of fire, falling back, and the particle beam fire became random. Masa ducked just in time to avoid a blast to the chest. The window on the Ibex's door cracked slightly under the heat and kinetic force. Masa picked himself up and returned fire as the Guardian drones ducked behind the cover of the defensive positions they had previously overrun.

As they backed off, Gabe turned his Leopard's turret to fire on the drones. "They're falling back. We can do this, people," Gabe said.

"Shut the fuck up," Manuel said, driving the Leopard forward.

"Ryan, you're on point. Everyone moving up the vehicles will give us covering fire. Pick your targets and limit the risk," Nathan said, motioning everyone to push forward.

Sean used his jump-jets to make a long jump, crossing the distance toward the first defensive lines. Once airborne, he looked down and began firing into the formation of retreating Guardian drones. "How does it feel to be on the receiving end of a fucked-up field of fire, you pieces of shit?" Sean asked, shooting a Guardian drone dead. The clock counting down to the nuclear strike was constantly in his thoughts. Now was not a time for safety.

Masa quickly followed Sean, landing in one of the defensive lines. He raised his rifle and began firing in the direction of the Guardian drones. All the drones filed into defensive lines and focused their fire on the vehicles.

The drones ignored Masa and Sean for the most part as they focused their fire on the Ibex. "Mitch, you need to get out of the Ibex. I unloaded a full magazine on these bastards. They are under sentient control now," Sean said, reloading his rifle.

"Fucking hell, I hate losing these things," Mitch said, firing off the Ibex's smoke launchers and grabbing his gun. He climbed out and ducked for cover as the vehicle's armor failed, resulting in a small explosion.

Mitch used his thermal vision to find his way through the smoke cloud to friendly forces. That's when he saw a Leopard parked, doing nothing. Mitch climbed into the driver's seat of the Leopard. "Alright, let's get back into this fight!"

"You're crazy. This thing is going to be blown up next," the Leopard's gunner said.

"There are countless people back there, and if we run, those drones will break through. I don't think you want that to happen," Mitch said, driving the vehicle forward to the right flank of the second defensive line.

Sean and Masa ducked into a pathway, moving away from the vehicles as a drone began targeting them. Sean returned fire, killing one drone as it tried to provide covering fire for another advancing drone. Sean ducked backward as a particle beam seared into his chest plate. "Shit, I really should have thought that jump through," Sean said, noting the damage to his suit was minimal.

"You and me both, man," Masa said, slamming a new magazine into the stock of his rifle. He raised the rifle and edged his way to the corner. He leaned out of cover and fired in a burst, killing the leading Guardian drone.

"Their commander seems to be taking more direct control," Sean said as he squeezed off a few rounds, only to miss as the drone ducked behind cover.

The drone ducked out of cover again and returned fire as the second set of drones on the left flank marched toward Masa's position. "Mac here, can you guys hurry the fuck up? We could use some fire support," Masa said. Several particle beams seared holes into the barricade wall.

"I'm coming to get you. Just keep shooting," Mitch said, steering around several of the blockades to flank the defensive drones.

The undamaged light tank moved forward at full speed toward the gap in the defensive lines. Using its coaxial machine gun to pin down the drones, it prevented them from using covering fire for the Infantry. The first Airborne Infantry to enter the defensive line fired a grenade at the group of drones, knocking several off their feet.

A few of the surviving drones threw off their dead comrades and returned fire, shooting the leading soldier's arm off at the elbow and setting a portion of his fatigues on fire. The soldier with the missing arm fell over as his own comrades pulled him back while returning fire.

Masa burst out of cover and returned fire, shooting a drone in the neck with a three-round burst. The head unit fell off, spraying pinkish-colored fluids everywhere. Sean left the entrance of the defensive position and threw a grenade at the advancing drones.

"Get a move on, damn it," Sean shouted as he motioned the group forward, and took another hit from a particle rifle. Sean returned fire, shooting a drone dead, only for the drone behind it to hold it up as a shield.

Mitch managed to drive the Leopard along the rear flank of the second defensive line. "Alright, dude, light those SOBs up," Mitch said to Manuel.

Manuel lined up the Leopard's machine gun on the Guardian drones and began firing into them, making short work of those on the ground. The light tank pushed up, climbing over the makeshift fortifications. "Now this is like shooting fish in a barrel," Manuel said, sending a few rounds down range to finish the drones.

The drones in the trench line promptly leaped out and began a full retreat. The Serkin forces began a controlled withdrawal. Just as the tank lined up a killing shot on the retreating drones, a Serkin gunship fired a burst from its rail guns and rockets before being shot down. The resulting hits blew the turret from the tank's hull and scattered any nearby soldiers with the explosion's shock wave.

"They're falling back. Keep pushing forward," Nathan ordered as they hurried to enter the fray.

The remaining drones in the second defensive line also fled in a controlled retreat. Each drone fired a short barrage to keep the humans from sighting in on them as they retreated.

The Airborne Forces had managed to collect themselves and returned fire in a sporadic but effective return volley. Though the fire did not kill any of the drones, the fire provided a distraction for the more heavily armed and armored Strike Force Marines to line up lethal shots.

As the last few drones made their way back to the first defensive line at Lurie Garden, Nathan took one last shot at a Guardian drone. The shot hit the drone right through its long snake-like neck. It stumbled about for a moment before a second round from Eric's M90 linear rifle finished the job.

"You're welcome, sir," Eric said calmly.

"Colonel, this Sgt. Nathan Caird. Second defensive line has been secured. The drones seem to be in full retreat," Nathan reported, climbing over the barricade into the defensive fortification.

"Confirmed, sergeant. We see them pulling back toward East Randolph Street. I will send the last of my IFVs forward to help my Infantry in the area regroup, but I'm not sure how much help we will be in the long run," Colonel Sheppard said.

"Looks like this little fight at least bought those transports the needed to time to flee," Manuel said. He brought the group's attention to a pair of heavy lift VTOL aircraft slowly transitioning from their take off to forward flight.

Masa leaned against the wall and checked his gun's power pack and the magazine before noticing the transports flying eastward to safety. He looked over to Sean, then out over the defensive wall, where he stared out at the ruins of the park district. "Each transport can hold at least five hundred people. I'm sure your family made it out," Masa said, trying to comfort Sean.

"We have six hours and forty-eight minutes to clear this city out. Not that I recognize anything here, even the cloud gate sculpture is gone," Sean said, staring out at a no man's landscape. The paved walkways and broken water lines that once fed the Buckingham Fountain left the ground an unrecognizable muck.

With the lull in the fight, the ability to count the cost in human lives came to the forefront as the bodies and severed limbs of the previous defenders could be seen lying in puddles of sewage and muck that was once a large walkway in a public park. The dead lay against walls, none without a missing limb or large gash caused by a Guardian drone swinging its large scythe-styled bayonet down.

A trio of MH98 Kestrel helicopters came in from the west. Their quick strafing run on the first defensive position passed the Buckingham Fountain and managed to catch the attention of the ground troops. A few of the Airborne forces pointed up as the helicopters came in low and out of the skyscrapers of the greater downtown area.

"Colt 2-1 to ground forces at defensive position at Buckingham Fountain. Keep your heads down, we got this," a MH98 pilot said as the 30mm cannons and unguided rockets decimated the ground-based drones.

The Marines looked on as the Kestrel helicopters, which were neither gunships nor transports, hammered away at the drones. The helicopters themselves combined both roles into one platform for the Earth Colonial Federation. It was as an added cost-cutting measure. Two of the multirole helicopters came in low and took up overwatch to protect the third aircraft as it unloaded troops.

"Good, we have Naval Infantry on backup. This should bolster our numbers," Manuel said, watching from the cover of the Leopard.

The Naval Infantry squads stepped off the helicopter and proceeded to move up into defensive positions. The next helicopter neared the ground but didn't land; instead, the pilot kept the aircraft steady over the ground. More troops quickly jumped out.

"More bodies for the funeral pyre. Alright, this is it, assholes. You want to save your city? Get on your feet, assholes. We are on a mission," Gabe said, rallying the people around him. He pulled Sean off the wall by his shoulder. He then picked Sean's rifle off of the ground and handed it to him.

Sean checked his weapon, "I am ready."

"Major Robb, this is Sgt. Caird requesting an operations update. We have eyes on Colt squadron and are assisting a Naval Infantry platoon, call sign Reaper. Over," Nathan said as his HUD began labeling each friendly unit in sight.

"We see a massive withdrawal of drones. They are heading downtown and we have been chasing them since Convoy Punisher made it to West Chicago Ave. We are currently stuck at a roadblock on North State Street. The city is full of people the drones corralled into buildings. I'm still waiting for a sit-rep from the ECS Stryker. They should be updating us up soon," Major Robb said, taking cover behind the first M10 Harrison tank of the halted convoy. He began firing on the drones.

"Lieutenant Carver to Major Robb. We have touched down east of Northwest Memorial Hospital. Lots of dead and wounded, mostly police units. I saw a lot of civilians on roof tops waving for an extraction. Do I have permission to extract them? Over," Lt. Carver asked over the radio. He was looking at the windows of the skyscrapers, noticing the scores of people looking out.

"Wait one while I make contact with command. Do your best to keep the civilians out of the firing lines for the moment. Over," Major Robb said, leaning out of cover and using the sights on his rifle to look down the road. He ducked back behind the vehicle just as a drone emerged from cover and began firing randomly at the tank.

"This Punisher 1-1, requesting permission to fire main gun on barricaded drones," the tank commander shouted over the radio.

"Confirmed. Fire Canister shot. Set the round for a maximum effective radius of five meter spread," Major Robb replied, waving a group of Naval Infantry to move toward him.

"Sir, if we don't start moving, those drones could very well circle around us with some AT weapons," a Naval Infantry soldier said.

"I know that, Corporal. You get to Sgt. Roe, then take a squad of Marines and flank around with one of our M9 Lees using West Superior Street to hit those fucking drones from their flank," Major Robb said, sending the man back to one of the vehicles.

A Naval Infantry soldier got shot in the back as he tried returning to the other vehicles. Major Robb leaned over slightly out of the cover of the tank and then returned fire. The tank turned its turret slightly to the right and fired the massive 140mm cannon into the barricade.

The round that left the gun tube reached its target, almost instantly showering the barricade in explosive shrapnel.

"Punisher lead. Please tell me that had some effect," Major Robb ordered the vehicle crew to reply.

"Negative, sir, they brought down an old building to block this street. Those cluster munitions won't do much against all that rubble. If you let us max out the damage on the round, we may have a chance at knocking some of those bastards out," the tank commander replied.

"Negative, we have too many civilians in this area for a full powered blast. Punisher 5-8, bring up the flank and hammer that barricade with your 60mm. And hammer it long enough for the flanking maneuver to work," Major Robb said, ordering another vehicle to move forward.

The first available M9 Lee rolled forward and took a position in between the two lead tanks just as a row of drones began jumping over the rubble. The drones' firing was highly accurate and well-coordinated, nothing like before.

"Here they come," the Naval Infantry shouted from the cover of a building.

The drones took return fire in short, controlled bursts. Instead of the blind rush seen at the O'Hare, only one row of drones rushed forward. They fired while another row of the drones began laying down covering firing on the known human positions. The fighting was about to get much more intense, as those watching saw a single robot slash and bash its way through entire Infantry platoons.

Despite the vehicles firing on the advancing assault with their machine guns, the drones continued forward, marching over their own dead. "You wanted to fire those canister rounds on full blast? Well, now you can make sure to aim high," Major Robb said as several of his Infantry were cut down attempting to return fire.

"Confirmed, captain," replied the tank commander as both tanks raised the main guns upward and fired.

The tanks' buckshot rounds exited the barrels and closed the distance quickly, then burst over the heads of the drones. The canisters containing the shrapnel exploded, and the projectiles shredded the drones. The rounds didn't stop at taking out the drones, but also took out the nearby cars and shattered the windows, killing anyone nearby.

As the barrage of particle weapons fire died down, the number of car alarms steadily became more apparent. "Punisher 3-8 and 4-8 come in. Sgt. Roe, are you there? Alright people, form up and prepare to move over that fucking rubble," Major Robb said when no one answered immediately, giving the area a quick scan with his suit's radar system as well as the thermal imaging.

It took a moment for Sgt. Roe's ears to stop ringing. Even though his helmet was guaranteed to protect him against loud sounds, like explosions by the manufacturer, that didn't seem to be the case with tank fire. "This is Roe. We are fine. We managed to get to North Dearborn. Seems the drones left their flank wide open. Next time, sir, can you at least give a heads up when the tanks go boom? My ears are still ringing. Over," Sgt. Roe replied, noticing some damage on the first M9 Lee.

"Just secure the forward area. I don't want any surprises when my vehicles roll over this rubble," Major Robb replied, motioning his forces to move up.

"Sir, maybe you should take a detour and avoid the ruins all together?" Sgt. Roe responded.

"ECS Stryker, this is Major Robb. Can I get a sit-rep on troop movements? Over," Major Robb radioed the Destroyer. It was holding orbit over the city as several of the Infantry and their Strike Force Marine support moved forward over the rubble. The tanks waited as several Infantry slowly climbed over the rubble. Once the first groups of the soldiers made their way to the top of the rubble, they began the process of waving the military vehicles forward.

Colonel Mason stood hunched over the holographic display of the city as the ship's sensors scanned the city. "Seems the Serkins are focusing their forces on the Streeterville area just across the bridge near the Loop evacuation site. That part is the most populated section of the city. If the reports from earlier are right, the bastards have corralled as many people as possible in that area."

"Alright, that's it people, haul ass. Our next stop is Streeterville!

We don't stop until every last drone in this city is scrap. Find a vehicle, take a seat, or ride on a fucking roof. Our clock is ticking," Major Robb ordered.

The troops not in vehicles promptly rushed to whatever open spot they could find. Several of the more heavily armed Marines simply chose to grab onto the side of a tank. Others rode atop the vehicles as the more conventional troops took seats in the M9 Lee IFVs and APCs.

The M10 Harrison tanks ceased all caution and promptly sped over the rubble. The first tank raised its gun and spun its tracks as fast as it could. Once over the first part of the roadblock, the driver locked the tracks and slid down the rubble. The second tank followed quickly behind, turning its tracks to help reduce the steepness of the pile before it moved forward. The tank then halted after it too slid down the pile of rubble. Major Robb opened the small access door to the rear hatch of the last M9 Lee and climbed in as the convoy finally cleared the debris.

"There will be no stops till we are at the west end of Streeterville," Major Robb said to the driver, and the driver relayed the order over the radio. He wondered what fresh hell awaited him in the city's bustling heart. Millions upon millions of soulless Guardian drones had descended on a plethora of defenseless people.

830 hours
Streeterville, Chicago,

Samantha arrived at the boutique where she served as her friend's model for much of her clothing advertisements. She'd hoped to be an hour early until traffic along Lake Shore Drive was closed and the entire population forced to use alternate streets. For a moment, she pondered if a self-driving car had decided to drive on the wrong side of the street for fun. She knew better, though, as the last company that sold murderous robot cars had gone under before she was born.

The summer morning was at least a comfortable twenty-one degrees centigrade; much of the bright neon lights from the weekend's vibrant night life were finally turned off. City life was a conflicting life for her. She could run to work with ease, or take her motorcycle around town. Then again, the only place she could see grass was in the richest neighborhoods. And shooting the occasional robber who wandered the night was hardly as fun as the movies made it seem.

"Yuki, are you here yet? I guess you were right. I should have just stayed in our apartment, but my mom wanted me to stay the night since we had too much to drink." Sammy entered from the front door. Once she was in, she locked the ancient deadbolt with her key and kept the store's sign flipped to 'Closed'. "Is the dress ready? The shuttle is going to be here at 9 a.m."

Not seeing Yuki toward the front of the store was unexpected. Yuki was always on watch for any number of tourists always looking to get theirs shopping in early. It was something that always made Yuki start swearing up a storm in Japanese. The aesthetics were retro, similar to the mid-twentieth century. It lacked all the holographic ads that used facial recognition to place customers into the ads. Yuki always liked to give the shop a slow-paced, comfortable vibe. All topped off by soft music. The store's mannequins sat atop several racks of clothing. Lingerie, fancy dresses, shoes, and accessories lined the left wall and the sales counter toward the right front.

"I'm back here with that dress you asked for," Yuki shouted. "Seriously, your taste is so dated. Such basic colors as black and white. Vibrant dark purple and bright blues are in now," Yuki added with her shoulder length black hair tied into a sloppy ponytail. She was wearing the store's uniform of a form-fitting pantsuit with a low-cut shirt— Yuki's idea to make men more willing to spend money.

"Hey, you said I could easily make any style look good," Sammy replied, arms cross. "Now tell me, is the dress ready?"

"Indeed, you can. But why do you constantly insist on Mormon extremist styles when you have that body?" Yuki returned to her work. Even with a sowing needle in her mouth, her tone was clearly envious of Sammy's larger breasts. "Ugh, never mind. I need to take the final measurements and make the last few adjustments to the dress."

"Okay, I'll get ready," Sammy replied, stripping down to her underwear. "I really want this reunion to be memorable."

Yuki took a quick look at the holographic image of Sammy and Sean in their Sunday best as children. Content she had matched the clothing perfectly, she handed the dress over. "I'll be taking this out of your paycheck since daddy is visiting us and is intent on taking a look at our books."

Sammy slid the dress on. "Oh, will he be visiting our apartment as well? I don't want to be relaxing and have your old man walk in on me," Sammy asked, looking over the dress's frilled bottom. "Hey, why is this thing so short? I said keep the length to my knees!"

"Oh please, you are seeing Sean for the first time in two years and it's just above your knees by a few centimeters. Also, the fabric is thick enough that you won't be able to see through it if it gets wet." Yuki looked up at Sammy and collected stockings and a garter belt as added finishing touches to the dress. This time when she spoke, her tone was very clearly envious. "Sean is alive. You're lucky, so when you welcome him back, get busy. God, you are so lucky."

"I am sorry about Derek. They both left in such a rush," Sammy said, pausing to comfort her friend. "Whatever you need, I'll do my best to help."

"Derek died. I've made peace with that now. The dead can't love you back. Now let's get you dolled up. That ship will be here in three hours and I still need to tighten the top," Yuki replied, her slim, but round face with almond-shaped eyes attempting to hide her pain. "You know, with so many soldiers returning, we are looking at a new chance for financial growth."

Sammy knew full well Yuki was right. Their business would boom in months. "Hey what's with the garter? I've never worn one of those." Sammy noticed several items set out on a nearby chair.

"Oh, those are to help keep the stockings up. I know the story of this outfit. You wore this outfit when you knew Sean really loved you." Yuki paused, quickly outlining her own breasts to emphasize Sammy's breast size. "Although these girls surely sweeten the deal!"

"Hey, I said don't do that," Sammy slapped away Yuki's hands. "And no jokes about threesomes. I know you and Sean like to tease me for a laugh, but that ends now!"

Yuki dodged the slap with ease thanks to years of taking quick feels. "Hah, too slow. Now hurry up and get dressed!"

Sammy situated the garter belt and sat down to pull on her stockings. The top of the dress had a small black bow in the center of her chest and once tied, it left her with a very near skin-tight fit with a low bust line.

Yuki studied her work, methodically running her hand over the dress. "Seriously, you are enjoying this more than you should," Sammy said, as Yuki confirmed the final measurements.

"Alright, nothing is wrong with your dress now step on out of these." Yuki pointed to Sammy's underwear. "I have your 36D breasts supported by a strapless bra in the dress. However, you can't wear those Plain Jane panties, so here is my gift to your soldier boy," Yuki said, promptly fetching a box. "Now finish changing and can you fetch me some coffee? I have been working all morning and you owe me a bit of extra work. I also left you some breakfast in break room"

Sammy nodded and finished dressing. The smell of spiced breakfast pastries from the local bakery run by the Qualurians was all the direction she needed. The cat people had issues tasting sweet things unless a bit of spice didn't hit their tongues. She snuck an extra, for the taste almost reminded her of the barbeque sauce Trevor made with his sons every Fourth of July.

Eating other people's food always took her back to her childhood. As soon as she finished eating the first pastry, she took the box and some coffee out to Yuki, who began compiling her P and L charts. A fake maternity belly sat in a box on the floor. *Was that Yuki's idea? Maternity wear?*

Sammy handed Yuki some coffee. "Here you go, although I'm not sure you should have any. You're starting to remind me of Samson the Squirrel." Sammy mentioned their favorite Saturday morning cartoon show.

Yuki took the coffee in both hands, drinking it slowly, only to realize it was the instant crap that got Sammy through the day. "We should save the good stuff to pamper your Father," Sammy replied to the look on Yuki's face. "What's with the maternity simulator?"

"Ah well, the troops have come home and are hungry for some action. That action will make babies, which means maternity wear. It's why I felt you should have something a bit more provocative. We should get a head start on the baby boom. I will need a pregnant model." Yuki handed Sammy a small chart. "The baby belly will help us get an early edge until you start to show. Now open my present for Sean."

"Azural brand undergarments," Sammy read the tag as she ran her hand over the soft, delicate fabric. Sammy could see they were lacy, low cut bikini panties with a small bow, combining sweet and sexy. "These are from the Qualurians. We sell them for four hundred sovereigns."

"Yeah, well, today is your first reunion in two years, and it's the same for a lot of other women. Now put them on so Sean can take them off. That troop ship arrives in an hour with your man on it! Now remember, we got to cash in on the baby boom! Expand in all ways, always to succeed in business," Yuki lectured Sammy like a college professor who wanted to hear their own voice. "Hurry up, I fully expect to be an aunt in nine months."

Sammy slid out of her normal panties. "Sure thing, boss."

"Why am I the weird one again?" Yuki asked as Sammy began slipping her leg into the new underwear. "You just can't help but get naked and roam about at home in front of friends."

"Oh, come on, we're both women," Sammy replied. "I never thought you would see me as a baby factory."

"Sammy, I'm alone. The man I loved is dead." Yuki sat down, crestfallen at remembering, and drank her morning coffee. "Worse, I'm sterile. I've even started to envy my mother- and sister-in-law's. My brother is on child number two. In time I'm going to be alone counting coins while you'll be counting first steps, first smiles, and eventually… you'll forget that I ever existed."

"Yuki, you're the most talented woman I've ever known. How could I forget you? I taught you to sow. And look where you took us! I stand around, look pretty, and help you around the shop." Sammy made Yuki look at her. "You'll always be welcome in my life. Be the cool aunt when I have kids."

"You promise? I can't promise you a handsome maternity payout, but we can easily turn part of this building into a decent childcare center." Yuki was thrilled and gave her friend a hug. "I promise to never make a threesome joke ever again."

A loud boom sounded and Yuki's coffee cup shook around on the sewing machine table before finally crashing to the floor. Sammy saw Yuki get pissed. "That coffee mug was a gift from my nephew! It's likely a bomb from the friends of that rapist in the Stalin tank top we beat to a pulp a few months back chucking bombs at our shop!"

As car alarms went off, Yuki instantly remembered the communist riots from three years ago. "If those Californians want to start another smash and grab raid, we won't be victims. Sammy, take the rifle and a vest. They want to loot, we'll shoot!" Yuki ranted as she unlocked her weapons safe. "I won't let anyone ruin our business!"

The safe door opened and Yuki collected the guns. Taking her revolver fast reload cylinder out, she slid six rounds into the chambers. She slapped the cylinder into place and walked to the front of the store. Sammy was still hurriedly getting dressed as Yuki marched into combat.

"Calm down, Yuki. It's probably just a car wreck. We are on the corner of North Michigan and East Ohio Street where car accidents are a thing," Sammy shouted, hurrying to calm Yuki. "There's probably no need for you to go running around like an action hero."

Yuki, now armed, stepped out into the front of the store, holding her polished Magnum .32 Hammer revolver that looked excessively large in her little hands. The scene outside was disturbingly unexpected. Several cars on East Ohio Street had crashed into each other and an M20 Badger and several police vehicles were moving west. Several people lined the road, but all stared straight up into the sky.

Yuki promptly slipped her revolver into the back of her pants as she approached the still locked-down store windows. She had expected idiots in black and red masks shaking their fists, but the sight that greeted her was an entirely different kind of hell.

Sammy approached, equally stunned, holding the company shotgun. "Goddess, what the hell is going on here that needs the military?"

"Store, dim illumination," Yuki ordered the lights lowered to keep attention off the store. "I'm not sure, but my dad would be calling me like crazy right now if he knew about a coming attack. I'll secure the place and you try to find out what's going down."

Sammy went to the break room and turned on the TV, hoping to find any kind of news about what was happening. "Damn, it looks like TV is out. I'll try the internet. Guerilla News is probably well ahead of the networks anyhow."

Yuki secured the back door to the alley and made sure the loading bay door was locked too. She then began laying boxes on the floor in a way that anyone rushing the place would be sure to trip over them. "Alright, if this is another Communist riot, we're ready. They won't have an easy time coming through the back."

"Well, there's no signal and I'm not sure the Californians could do this. The best they had was that riot when we were in high school, so this must be something much bigger." Sammy pointed at the TV while the sounds from outside grew more frantic and confusing. They could hear gunshots, but the sounds that came next weren't identifiable. "It's almost like something is blocking the signals, but I have no clue what could do something like that."

Yuki headed back to the front of the store, holding a shotgun while Sammy held the rifle. "That's not gun fire. It's like a crack of lightning, but it's a clear sky," Yuki said, confused. Just then, a large shadow overtook the city. "Oh god, the sun is blotted out."

Several people ran past the shop, ignoring the two women. "My mom's car is parked out back. Maybe we should bug out of here," Sammy suggested. "We can head west out of the city."

Cars came to a sudden stop as though a major crash had occurred. Police began clearing the street, but many more people just stood in the street staring up that the sky in awe. The city outside ceased being absorbed in its Monday morning woes and were instead terrified of impending death.

"Sammy, what's happening? Who do you think is attacking us? There has to be some explanation for that damn shadow," Yuki said, finally breaking the silence after watching more people fleeing east against the tide of several more military vehicles heading west toward the Trump Tower mall. "How did this happen if we're well within the border walls?"

Sammy tapped the watch on her wrist to search for any news about what was happening. With the shadow gone, a signal finally got through. A holographic image appeared, almost as if Sammy were using magic to broadcast the emergency broadcast system's message.

"ATTENTION CITIZENS OF CHICAGO. PLEASE PROCEED CALMLY TO MILLENNIUM GRANT PARK FOR EVACUATION. ONLY ONE ITEM OF LUGGAGE PER PERSON IS ALLOWED. BE READY TO LEAVE WHEN MILITARY FORCES ARRIVE TO EVACUATE YOU. IF YOU ARE IN THE LOOP OR STEETERVILLE AREA, PLEASE WAIT FOR EVACTUATION TRANSPORTATION FROM POLICE OR MILITARY TO ARRIVE."

"I can't find anything on the news, but the military is broadcasting

loud and clear. We need to remain indoors until they can evacuate us."
Sammy showed Yuki the holographic message on her watch, which was
on a loop. "I guess the media lied AGAIN about this war being over."

Before Yuki or Sammy could speak, a man with three children at
his feet and a fourth in his arms appeared at the door, begging. "Please
let us in. My kids can't run anymore! Please, just take the kids!"

Yuki wasted no time opening the front door, allowing the man and
four kids into the store. Sammy took the smallest child from the man
and he ushered the other children in. "Alright kids, I want you all on
your best behavior. That means you don't touch any—" A bright flash
of white energy grazed the back of his head.

For a moment, the man looked Yuki in the eyes, then his eyes
blinked once more before his body fell onto her. The air smelled like
someone had burned a piece of meat. She fell backward as more beams
of white light fired in rapid succession. Yuki rolled the man's body off
and slammed the door shut, locking it in the hopes it would offer some
protection.

Sammy rushed the kids toward the back of the storefront as the
mechanical monster that fired the killing blow stepped into view. Its
flat, featureless face had four red glowing eyes and a pair of tentacles
standing up off its back, writhing as it scanned the streets. It easily stood
at least two meters tall and walked on legs that clanked with every step.

Another pair of similar monsters fell from the sky, landing on their
feet. The trio then began scanning for targets. The group that descended
took aim and fired on targets Yuki couldn't see. Cracking thunderbolts
followed the white beams of light. Yuki had no desire to be a victim and
promptly fled behind the checkout counter.

Sammy left the children for a moment and moved behind the
counter. "It's a Guardian drone. Serkins are attacking. The net has a
few descriptions of these things."

One of the monsters then noticed the two women. It took aim at the
shop, ready to finish the pair off, when a police car rammed into it. The
drone slammed into the hood of the police car, cracking the armored
glass. A pair of policemen stepped out of the car in full body armor.
One used a shotgun to put down the beast on the car's hood. Sammy

didn't stay to watch. She and Yuki slammed the security door down. The two women rushed the children to the furthest part of the store as the sounds of gunfire quickly ceased.

Yuki took her revolver out and cocked the hammer, unloading it. "Okay, where are those hollow points? It's going to be okay, kids. We'll keep you safe," Yuki said, trying to comfort the scared children, desperately trying to hide her own doubts.

Sammy let the kids go and looked back. "Thank the goddess. I don't think those things are following us. The sounds have moved on, Yuki." She then went to look over the children for injuries but found none. "I'm going to make sure the loading bay is clear. We can't wait for rescue."

"I'm going to take a look up front. I saw a Badger IFV or APC thingy drive by. It may be our ticket out of town," Yuki whispered before cautiously looking out of the door from the backroom into the main boutique. She took a single gulp of air and stepped out onto the main floor. Crouching down, she slowly walked as close to the floor as she could.

A few Guardian drones stood outside the shop. One held the body of a police officer by the neck, confirming the officer was dead. It then threw the body like a piece of trash into the window. The force of the throw was so strong the glass broke and the carbon-coated stainless steel bars bent inward.

Another drone stood atop the police car. Somehow, it had crushed the passenger compartment. The sirens were dead, but the lights were flashing. Once she reached a rack of clothing, she quickly crawled over to the dead man. She grabbed his wallet and tried not to be noticed by the drones. Feeling she couldn't leave him uncovered, she grabbed a dress off the racks to give the deceased some privacy.

As she grabbed a dress off the rack to cover the man's dead body, she knocked a mannequin over. It crashed into the glass. "Shit fuck," Yuki cursed, watching as the crash caused a drone to rush over to inspect the sound.

Yuki had no place to hide as she covered the man's body with a dress. She tried taking a shot at the beast but couldn't find a clear line of sight with the security doors down. The drone used its rifle's bayonet to chop and hack a hole into the security gate. With a proper hole made, it pulled a portion of the security gate open and stuck its head into the shop.

Yuki crawled backward on her hands as the drone stared at her and then saw her weapon. The drone fired at the gun, purposely missing as a warning. As Yuki crawled away from the gun, the drone backed away. Content it had sent its message, it squatted down. Its tentacles lowered onto its back, and it walked away from the store window, taking up a guard-like stance atop the wrecked police car.

Yuki stood up and contemplated spitting at the monster, but it would be unladylike. Yuki took a deep breath and walked up to the front door to test the drone. The drone took notice of what she did, but took no action. "Sammy, I'm not sure we should try leaving right now. Can you leave the kids alone for a minute?"

Sammy handed each child a pastry, hoping the food would distract them. "Now I don't want you guys to worry. I'll be right back. Enjoy these pastries, alright." Sammy stepped out into the storefront, only to see a drone staring straight into the store.

Yuki stood calmly watching the drone guarding the street. "So far it seems that as long as we don't get too close to that door and window, it simply stands around waiting."

Sammy walked into the storefront like Yuki asked. "Yuki, what happened to your gun? And what do we do about that man's body?" Sammy then saw the drone looking straight at them. "Shit! What the hell?"

"When I dropped my gun, it backed down. It's like it's trying to keep us in the building." Yuki took a blouse off a hangar to put out a small fire in the store. Sarcastically she said, "I doubt that thing is in the mood to buy his girlfriend something pretty."

"So we don't leave out of the front of the store. Those kids getting to an evacuation center should be our main concern." Sammy's voice turned cold and stern.

Yuki opened the man's wallet, rummaging through for an ID. "He's a city worker, likely a school bus driver." She then turned to his phone's photo gallery and found a family picture. "Okay, this guy was the girls' dad. Where did the boy come from?"

Sammy took a pair of pants off a rack, knowing heels and a skimpy dress weren't ideal fleeing-for-your-life-fashion. "Regardless of where the boy came from, when you opened that door, we took responsibility for them. I hope you have other shoes than heels too."

"I know our civic duty to our fellow Americans and the next generation. I passed my voting requirements test as well, earning my tier two citizenship with full voting rights. Stop dictating to me what we need to fucking do," Yuki replied, slamming her fist on the counter.

"I'm sorry, it's just that I need to something to do. Do we have any usable guns left?" Sammy leaned up against the checkout counter as she put the slacks on.

"No, I'm sorry. I don't want to be helpless now either." Yuki hugged her friend before returning to the safe and taking out her second revolver. "Good news. I have a second revolver in my safe. Not sure if our rifle and shotgun would help with those drones."

"I'll check the alleyway. Maybe we can sneak out the back." Sammy noticed one of the oldest girls looking out the doorway. "Hey sweetie, it's not safe out here. Go back with the others, okay."

"Where's my dad? I want to see him," the girl demanded.

"He's not with us anymore. I covered his body out of respect," Yuki said, her tone matter of fact.

Sammy shot a death glare at her friend as she turned to the girl. "You are the oldest, correct?" Sammy asked, blocking the girl's view of her dad's body. The girl paused, trying to fight Sammy off for a bit. "I know it hurts. I've buried almost everyone I've loved, but right now, we need to work as a team. I need you to help us save some lives."

The girl started to cry and Sammy gave her a hug. After a few minutes had passed, the girl dried her eyes and asked, "What do I do?"

"Well, I can't keep my eyes on the back and Yuki can't keep her eyes up front if we are watching you guys all the time. So we need you to help us keep everybody calm. If we work together, we'll all get out of this," Sammy said as she helped the girl dry her eyes.

The girl clearly wasn't pleased until she realized she had a very important job. "I have to look out for the others? Like I'm in charge?"

"You bet you're in charge. I also want you to keep the children from listening to the radio at the news." Sammy moved the girl along as Yuki brought out their radio.

"The TV is likely out. The satellites would be the first things hit during a planetary invasion. Can you see if that asshole Truth Tommy is broadcasting? That conspiracy nut job probably loves this," Sammy said, watching Yuki plug in the old radio.

"Fine, I'll listen for the fucking nut job and his water filter ads to save the day," Yuki replied.

"This is Truth Tommy Newton here folks, and guess what? It's finally happened. Mars Man is here to crack down on the man! Yeah, you can sue this crazy legless ass on the mike, but by god, that would be a waste of court time. Not that the judges will be around much longer. The word out of Houston is that Federation Tower went down. You got my number, folks. So if you can get a signal, tell me what you're seeing. I'll tell you this much. The 101st airborne has set up shop in the Loop, so if you can make it there, they will evac your ass to safety. Just give me a call and I'll make sure even more of us survive the Mars Man crack down!"

Sammy looked at her phone's lack of an outgoing signal. "Does he know the phones aren't working? I guess when you're crazy, the phone lines always work." Just then, a shower of glass from the buildings above rained down on the street.

"We should remain indoors if it's raining glass and probably just pray." Yuki noticed that the drone had taken little to no damage from the shower of glass.

ECS Robert F. Stryker, CIC,
Four hours thirty-five minutes
until nuclear attack on Chicago

Captain Kurkov stepped out of the private communications room, defeated. "Damn them all. The Joint Chiefs and the president have no intention of giving us more time," he said, his head hung low as he looked over the holo-table.

"Did you show them this retreat? The drones are all gathered in this one place. They have to admit we are gaining ground," Colonel Mason said, watching the drones in the streets cluster together in one area.

Captain Kurkov shook his head. "No, they think the Serkins are baiting us into a trap. Communications officer, I want to speak to our troops directly. We may as well let everyone know what the situation is. If the US is using a 10th generation stealth drone as a delivery system, we won't be able to stop it until it's too late. There's no reason for keeping this news secret."

The ship's communications operator began the task of opening all military channels. With a swipe of her finger and a few commands typed into the station, she nodded her head. "Sir, we're linked into all our soldiers and even the Army Airborne forces. I've transferred the radio comlinks to your vocal command system in the CIC."

The soldiers approached the bridge into the Streeterville section of Chicago alongside the few functional tanks, APCs, and other combat vehicles, and checked to make sure the downed Guardian drones were, in fact, dead. The vehicles slowly began to break from line formation into a convoy.

The Strike Force Marines and their Naval Infantry took positions around the south end of the bridge, waiting for the other forces to catch up. The multipurpose Kestrel helicopters randomly hammered drones with their 30mm cannons. Civilians from several buildings gazed down upon the war taking place in the streets below them.

Eric sat with a supply crate and scanned the buildings across the bridge. "What is it with people and watching this shit unfold in the streets?"

"Their homes and their city are a war zone. They're trapped and can't go anywhere. They may as well watch the end unfold." Masa finished reloading his magazines.

"Well, we've made it this far, don't get yourself killed, Mac. If you die, I'll lose the only person who knows the best way to berate me right back," Eric said, placing his arm out with his hand open.

Masa grabbed Eric's hand and gave him a quick pat on the back. "Same to you, asshole. If you get killed, I won't have any cultureless round eyes to bash on the firing range."

As soon as Masa and Eric had readied themselves for the fight, their HUDs alerted them to a message override. "Hey, is everyone seeing the same message override I am?" Manuel asked.

"Yeah, I am seeing it," Sean replied.

"Attention all soldiers about to converge on the Streeterville city center. This is Captain Kurkov of the ECS Stryker. For the last five years, I've simply held the line at the Spur Gap to defend the colonies in the Orion arm, as there was nothing to be done to save Vieira. Today I admit to failing my objectives, and by default, you. However, today is the day I say, no more holding the line. Today is the day we go on the offensive. If we fail in this offensive, Chicago will be nuked in the next four hours. But the enemy's command center is somewhere in Streeterville... So I ask you now to gather your strength, put your fears aside, and take this city back. Captain Kurkov, over and out."

"This is Colonel Sheppard of the 101st Airborne division. My objective was to evacuate civilians and retreat. I will not stand by aimlessly as colonists and Earth born persons fight for my nation's people. I now order all Airborne forces not focused on the evacuation of civilians to fall in with the Federation's troops. You heard the man. Take this city back," Colonel Sheppard said over the open channel.

Gabe picked up his rifle and slapped his helmet to make sure his cybernetics connection was still functional. He then walked over to the rest of the group, looking straight at Sean. "Well, kid, you heard the man. He wants an offensive, so save your city. As for the rest of you, I'm genuinely inspired to fight." Gabe slid a new magazine and battery into his rifle.

"It's about damn time we got this show on the road," Sean said, hurrying over to a passing IFV. "Hey, you got room for one more?"

"Yeah, on the roof, man," the commander said, sitting out of his hatch. "You look like you'll be fine there."

"Yeah, that's fine by me," Sean said, grabbing a hold of one of the vehicle's handrail to climb onto the roof.

The first group of soldiers climbed over the debris of the East Wacker overpass and took up positions on the south side of the DuSable Bridge. Several Army Airborne troops began a quick check of the bridge for demolition charges on the underside using the walkway. The few IFVs and light tanks scanned the other side of the bridge, looking for targets that the MH98 Kestrels may have missed, while the Naval Infantry began a single file march to the Chicago River walkway.

"Command, this is engineering team Alpha. The bridge is cleared to cross now. I repeat, cleared to cross now," the Naval Infantry said into his chest mounted radio.

Mitch, Masa, and Eric made a quick jump across the river, landed on their feet, and began using their suits' numerous sensors to find any hiding Guardian drones. "Light tanks, move up first. Let's go, damn it," Eric said.

A pair of MH98 Kestrel helicopters now passed by safely over the bridge, patrolling the area since the Serkin gunships were down. "This is Colt 2-1. So far, the drones are moving north to East Ohio Street and have even made barricades along the way. You armored vehicle drivers better be careful climbing out of the ditch on North Michigan. We have engaged their first barricade at Ogden Park Plaza. Over," said the pilot as the gunner scanned the area with the helicopter's cannon.

"Uh, this is Colt 2-3. I have a mass of drones climbing a building on the corner of Burberry and Ontario. The building is full of people. Both thermal and sonic imaging confirms this. Command, I request permission to engage," the pilot of the second helicopter asked. He was watching as Guardian drones climbed up with their back mounted tentacles. They paid neither the terrified occupants who recoiled from their perches, nor the helicopter watching them any mind.

"This is Colonel Mason. Negative on engagement. This city has had enough civilian casualties. Do not engage. I will divert two Strike Force Marine squads to engage," Colonel Mason said, realizing just too late what the drones were actually doing. "Shit. All units pull back. Those drones are going to bring down the building!"

"This is Colt 2-2. The drones have entered the building on countless floors. I need permission to engage," the pilot said, watching the drones swarm up the building. With no response, the pilot cursed. "Fucking hell! Gunner, open fire with the autocannon. Those people inside are dead either way!"

The helicopter attack had little effect; several drones fell to their death, but many more swarmed inside the building's upper floors. They simultaneously exploded, throwing concrete, mortar, and glass at such velocity it shattered the helicopter's armored canopy with ease. The gunner and pilot of Colt 2-2 tried in vain to shield themselves. The debris also flew directly into the helicopter's rotor blades, breaking all three as the helicopter tried to turn. It fell backward, spinning out of control before crashing into the ground.

As the helicopter crashed into the nearby intersection, the building collapsed shortly thereafter. The top floors compressed like a spring and systematically began crushing each floor below. Finally, the entire building fell to the ground floor by floor as the drones that had swarmed inside it by the thousands self-destructed across every floor.

The soldiers, who had advanced with little resistance up to the Tribune Tower, were quickly enveloped in a cloud of more than a century-old pulverized concrete and other building material. The dust choked the soldiers not wearing full facial protection. Many hacked uncontrollably, even after they managed to don some form of facial protection.

"This Badger 1-5 of the 101ˢᵗ Airborne. We have massive levels of debris clogging up our thermal imaging," the IFV commander said as the troops inside exited. "That helicopter crash and several other factors just blinded us. Motion sensors are functioning on my vehicle."

"Confirmed Badger 1-5. We are deploying sonic pulse pylons to boost your visual capabilities," Colonel Mason said, pinching the bridge of his nose in frustration at his blunder. "Electronics officer, please tell me you have some idea where the Serkins are set up?"

"I am narrowing down the possible locations now, but even with large numbers of drones, the Serkins use some non-observable and untraceable communication system to perform command and control," the officer in charge of electronic warfare replied.

The helmsmen of the ECS Stryker adjusted its position over Chicago. As it brought the bow of the ship and its large Tesla Cannon to bear on target, a series of small cylinders fired down toward the city. The atmosphere burned away the outer layer until the air brakes opened, slowing their fall. The final stage of the units then slammed into the ground.

"Sonic vision assistance pylons deployed and responding. We can even use ambient sounds like car alarms to enhance our own acoustic vision. Damn it all to hell! Colonel Mason, the Guardian drones are popping open water lines. Civilians are entering the Area of Operation," the observation officer said.

"Attention all ground forces, check your fire. We have civilians entering the AO," Mason said over an open channel, trying his best to remain and sound calm. The problems mounted, and he soon missed the days of combat on dead colony worlds.

On the ground, several airborne soldiers fell in with the Federation's troops. The M20 Badger Sean had been riding began unloading their troops from the rear door. Most of them had already readied their gas masks while others simply wrapped their faces in a balaclava and stuck to standard HUDs.

"Ah, what a mess. They brought down a building. It's like the dust storms in California," a soldier said as he raised his collar over his nose and mouth.

"Worse still, the area may have civilians running around," replied another. "Fucking hell. I can see something on thermals, but it's shit. And what the hell was that thud?"

"Hold your fire until you can confirm that what you are looking at is a Guardian drone. Fun fact, you will see the Guardian drones on thermals as slightly shorter than their normal height," Sean said, jumping off the vehicle.

"So why the fuck do we call these things Guardian drones?" one soldier asked.

"The only recorded response from the Serkins to our communications stated a Guardian attack was coming. The bastards spoke perfect English, letting us know that their Guardians were coming to purge us after the Fall of Vieira. At least, that's what I was told in boot camp," Sean replied, taking point as he marched deeper into the debris cloud.

The Airborne troops quickly and quietly followed Sean as their vehicle closed the rear hatch before slowly moving forward into the fray. The remaining Kestrel helicopters pulled away from the fight as Mitch drove up to the rear of the Badger IFV. The vehicles and troops all began filtering onto the six-lane road. Debris still clouded their view, and the cacophony of car alarms and sirens echoed through the city streets.

Masa and Eric stepped out of the Leopard as it came to a stop. "This is going to be a gauntlet," Eric said, grabbing a box of ammo out of the Leopard's storage rack.

Masa made sure his newly issued under-barrel shotgun was fully loaded. "Let me guess, you're going to chicken out and head up."

"I'll provide sniping cover, so keep your HUDs and comlinks open," Eric said, using his jump-jets to clear the smoke and ascend a nearby building. Eric's suit began reading a series of alerts that stopped when he finally slammed through the window of the nearest building.

"Eric, it's Mac calling. Are you okay? Over." Masa asked, having lost sight of Eric. "Seriously, if you died falling to your death, I'm going to kill you."

Eric slowly picked himself up from the shattered glass. "I'm fine.

Seems this building's glass wasn't as well made as I thought," Eric said, looking around the people who worked in the tower, all taken aback by the sudden entrance.

"Well, good. It looks like everyone is about ready to move up. Thermals are clearly shit. Too many fires up ahead. Seems the sonic vision is the only option," Masa said, watching several of the vehicles and disembarked troops slowly head into the city center. He flipped the safety on his gun off and kept his finger off the trigger before following them.

"You want on board, or are you walking?" Mitch asked, opening the door of the Leopard.

"Negative, we're all walking. The majority of the troops on this side aren't equipped with sonic vision. We'll take point with them," Masa said, getting Mitch to climb out of the vehicle. "That means you too."

"One more time," Nathan said, climbing out of the Leopard. The rest of the soldiers marched alongside the four Badger IFVs. The vehicles formed a V-formation as they pushed deeper into the heart of the Streeterville area while several helicopters observed overhead, waiting patiently for the drones to attack.

Meanwhile, at Yuki's boutique, they felt the collapse a few streets over instantly. Yuki grabbed her revolver, and with it in hand, opened the door from the backroom. "Sammy, you may want to look at this," Yuki said, using her sleeve to keep from inhaling the dust cloud.

"It's a debris cloud," Sammy said excitedly, leaving the Go Fish card game that had entered its third hour. "With the right amount of make-shift protection, we can use the cover to escape!"

"Put some comfortable shoes if you haven't already. This is our best chance to escape! We'll use some of the scarves and stockings to make a rope so we don't lose track of the children. We'll tie the kids' wrists together in a line and walk south. I'll get some fabric and use it to cover everyone's faces," Yuki said, rushing to her bags of fabric.

Sammy found a spare pair of leggings and quickly cut off the bottom of the legs with a box cutter, handing the pieces to Yuki. "Can you use this?"

"Yes, the active wear material is stretchy and dense enough—far better than the silks. This will make good masks for the kids, but the effectiveness will be limited," Yuki said quickly measuring some fabric to use as ties.

The oldest girl came out and closed the door behind her. "What's going on? Are we going to leave my dad here?"

Yuki approached the girl. "We're about to get everyone to safety. There's a huge dust cloud covering the street. If we can't see, hopefully, those drones won't be able to see us either. It should be enough to cover our escape. It's our best chance to get south to the evacuation site. We're going to make some protective gear for you before leaving. Now I've relied on you a lot in the last few hours to keep the younger kids in line. I will need you even more if we are to escape."

As soon as the masks and rope were ready, Sammy, now wearing her pants under the dress with sneakers, returned. "Alright guys, we're leaving and I have a new game we're going to play. We're going to see how silent we can be as we leave this building. Now, everyone, hold your hands out," Sammy said, and the children slowly presented their arms.

"You can't leave my dad here," the girl cried.

Sammy looked at the backroom where the other kids still waited. "Right now we have to keep the other kids alive, sweetie," Sammy pleaded, getting on the girl's level. "I know this is hard, but we have to go, and that cloud is our best chance to flee."

"Okay, but I'll stay in line after you just in case you can't get us out," the girl said, trying to sound brave and hide her grief.

"That's right. With you and the kids in the middle, Miss Yuki will help you if we're separated for any reason. But I don't want you to worry. We're going to try our best to keep you guys safe and get us all to the evacuation site together and safely," Sammy assured the girl.

With the children all in a line and tied together, Sammy lead them out the backdoor with Yuki following behind. Yuki would make sure the children stayed together and provide what limited protection her Magnum revolver could as they navigated their way south through the dust cloud.

Sammy's eyes watered and burned as smoke joined the debris cloud from the fires raging all around them. Looking up at the sky, she saw nothing. She kept her hand along the wall of the building in the alley to keep a sense of direction until she could make it to North Michigan.

The cars abandoned in the street provided some assistance in following the road to guide them south toward the bridges out of the downtown area. "Alright everybody, you're doing very well. Keep your hands tightly together, and remember to stay quiet," Yuki said. She kept her hand on the boy's shoulder, who was last in the line of children. Though she was unsure if they were any safer with her or without her watching the group's back armed with only a revolver.

Outside in the city streets, the advancing troops faced a new challenge. While the dust had begun to settle away from the collapsed building, the best visibility anyone had was still only from the sonic imaging their HUD provided, or their vehicle mounted thermal imaging. The four leading IFVs had a clear and easy path thanks to the size of North Michigan Avenue. Despite the clear road and vision enhancing systems, the advance north against the Serkin drones was slow. The lack of any returning fire seemed suspicious, almost as if the situation was bait for an ambush.

"Where are we? The GPS reads we passed Tribune Tower and are at the Bank of America, but I can't see shit through this debris cloud. Hey Marines, anything on sonic vision? The GPS is bugging out," a soldier shouted before drawing a bead on countless sources of heat swarming his thermal vision. "Oh, fuck. I have thermals and lots of them coming out of the building."

"Calm the fuck down. Its people leaving the bank," Nathan said, pushing the soldier's gun up and off the fleeing people. The soldier had no response other than to jerk away before catching up with a passing IFV.

The commander's IFV came to a halt last as the formation stopped. Opening the hatch on the turret, the commander began scanning around the vehicle with a short range thermal scanner. He looked around and spotted several of the Marines and waved over the nearest one. "Hey, you. Any idea what the hell these bastards are up to?"

"Stop waving your fucking hand all over the place, moron. These drones know to go for a unit's commander," Mitch said, jumping onto the back of the M20 Badger.

"Holy shit, don't do that. We've just advanced for more than ten minutes and nothing. These things just don't make sense; even the Cartels and Communists on the other side of the wall use tactics better than this," said the commander, rotating her seat around.

"Yeah, they're probably being controlled directly by a Serkin commander. Now get back in your fucking vehicle and keep the line moving," Sean said just as the commander's head was shot off by a particle beam.

The beam cut a centimeter diameter hole through where the vehicle commander's eye used to be and hit Mitch in his knee, boiling into the armor plating. "Fuck it all," Mitch said, fighting the urge to return fire.

"Everyone hold fire, god damn it! Don't fire at random, you idiots," another officer shouted as everyone took aim and began marching forward.

Some soldiers tried chasing after the Guardian drone, only for their senses to return and realize they were safer with the vehicles. Sean rushed to get ahead of the Airborne soldiers as fast as he could without using his jump-jets. He knew full well they could accidentally fire into civilians.

"I have multiple heat signatures, damn it. All of them are on approach," a soldier said in a hushed tone as he took a knee and prepared to fire.

"Don't you fucking fire or I will kill you myself. There are people still alive," Sean barked as he caught up with the first group of soldiers who'd bolted forward.

"I'm not letting one of those fucking drones slice me open like a Christmas ham," Mitch said, pushing a dead body into the vehicle as the armor plate cooled. He did his best not to flinch, but as a drone exploded, bathing the area in heat, Mitch had no control as his hand started shaking. "Oh shit, not now."

"Fucking hell, the drones blew the building to Kingdom Come just to add to our visual woes. Guys, give me a ping on your sonic imaging,"

Eric said, watching from his perch and cursing his failure to snipe the drone.

"Civvies coming out on the right flank," a soldier sighed in relief as a group of people ran by him.

Masa fired a sonic ping with Sean and Mitch to scan the debris-clouded streets. Eric lowered his sniper visor again. He used his own specialized system to run through the data everyone had collected. Being in an elevated position, he was relatively immune to the psychological effect of wondering if the movements were human or Serkin machine.

The scan finally separated the biological masses from all non-biological masses. The data coming through gave him a slightly clearer view of the city streets. "Dear god, guys, the drones aren't moving. They're hiding in the rubble, letting the civilians come out, hoping we'll gun them all down for them," Eric said, lining up a few shots.

On the streets below, Sammy led their group forward. She could hear a helicopter overhead; the roar of the rotor blades cut their way through the air and clear some of the dust cloud, making their way forward a bit easier, even if only a little. "We're almost clear of the debris cloud. Stay quiet and keep your eyes closed," Sammy said as quietly as possible.

Though quiet, a nearby group of drones still heard Sammy and began moving to follow her. Up the street, a small sensor pylon touched down, violently slamming into the street and coming online. It began a full area scan with a sonic pulse.

"I have civilians advancing on your left, heading south. Two adults, three children," Eric said as the data fed into his HUD. He then looked over the area a second time. "Fuck, we have drones following close behind them!"

Eric lined up a shot with his rifle and pulled the trigger; the round slammed into the neck of the first drone. The creature's neck bowed in at an angle, then fell to the ground. The rest of the drones ignored their casualties and made a mad dash to kill the two women and three children.

Sammy made it to the edge of the debris cloud, where things finally cleared and everything south of the DuSable Bridge was visible. Taking her make-shift face mask off, she was finally able to take a deep breath again. She saw the soldiers all had their guns aimed forward—at least they weren't aimed at their group as far as she could see. Gun shots fired nearby, but she couldn't identify where they were. She looked at the children. "Alright, everyone, we're almost to safety. Let's just keep moving."

Several soldiers moved up, passing by Yuki, who paused for a moment. She heard some faint noise, almost like metal hitting metal, as it stomped down on the ground. She raised her revolver, letting go of the boy as the group kept moving.

A white burst of light came out of the debris cloud and then a scream. The body of a soldier was flung out of the debris cloud. Yuki saw a faint set of four red lights piercing the debris cloud. Taking aim, she fired as the Guardian drone appeared; the bullets from her revolver did nothing to damage the drone.

Eric took aim, making sure the line of sight was clear. He knew he had little time to save the woman in the street. A Guardian drone raised its rifle, and in a swift swinging motion, severed Yuki's left arm from her shoulder. She would have screamed, but the pain knocked her unconscious. As the drone went to throw Yuki's body out of its way, the shot from Eric's sniper rifle went through the metal animal's head. "God damn it," Eric cursed. "I was too late."

Nathan rushed forward to aid the woman, who just lost her arm. He bandaged the limb as best he could and shouted at the other woman. "Lady, get your kids into the back of that IFV, right now!"

Sammy rushed the children to the nearest vehicle and began loading them in first. "It'll be alright, I promise. Just stay in the vehicle and you'll be safe," Sammy told the children, hoping she could go back for her friend.

"Don't leave us!" the oldest girl shouted, grabbing Sammy's hand, holding it as tightly as she could.

Sammy broke free from the girl. "I'm just getting my friend some help and then I'll be right back!" she assured the girl.

Any civilians unfortunate enough to be caught between the Guardian drones and the human military forces were the first casualties.

The drones wasted no time, and with cold brutality, killed with every single shot.

"Here they come. Pick a target and hit them with everything we got," an officer shouted.

Nathan rushed over with Yuki in his arms just as the shooting began. A white beam of light struck a Naval Infantry man dead center and knocked him over. Sammy looked away from her friend and at the terrified girl as tears ran down her face. "I won't leave you, I promise," Sammy shouted, holding the children as the sounds of gunfire began drowning out all other noises.

The column of IFVs formed a defensive line in the street center and fired into the first wave of Guardian drones as they advanced. The 30mm and 60mm cannons of the armored vehicles bombarded the first wave of drones as they rushed forward, firing.

Masa looked upward and noticed that the drone rush was a ploy and shouted, "Eyes up, they're climbing the walls!"

The Infantry began firing on the drones that climbed the nearby buildings, only to be met with a return volley of beam fire. Several drones dropped down into close enough range to turn the gun fight into a melee. With their large powerful limbs, they began attacking the majority of the human Infantry.

The Guardian drones shot several Naval Infantry and Airborne soldiers with their particle rifles —they were the fortunate ones—as the few soldiers unfortunate enough to be near the drones had large bayonets cleave into them before their wounded bodies were thrown aside by the tentacles.

Eric changed his targets, focusing in on the drones that dropped into a melee match with the Infantry lines. As a Guardian drone landed on a M20 IFV, he shot it in the back, turning it to scrap metal.

Sean and Mitch went from firing upward to focusing on defending the vehicles and other soldiers. A Guardian drone soon found itself cut off and grabbed a dead soldier, throwing the body into Mitch. "Mother fucker," Mitch shouted as he pushed the dead soldier off and returned fire.

"Mitch, I need you back here. We got civilians and wounded who need protection," Masa shouted as he covered Nathan. "Staff Sergeant, how much longer before you stabilize that girl and you can get back in this fight?" Masa asked before turning around and firing a three-round burst into a Guardian drone as it tried closing the distance.

"I'm coming, damn it. As soon as I get these guys to stop being a gaggle of targets," Mitch said as he moved to aid several Airborne soldiers.

"She's going to need a few more moments. I can stabilize her, but the cut is real deep," Nathan told Masa as he injected the wound with more medifoam. Nathan bandaged the wound but knew he wouldn't have enough. He then noticed the other woman watching over him. "Hey, lady, help me by placing these bandages on your friend's wound."

Sammy took a set of bio-tex bandages from Nathan before saying, "Right, take this. I don't want to break my promise of getting these kids to safety. Can you load her into that vehicle with the kids?"

Nathan sprayed the wound with disinfectant and exposed it for a short time so the bandages could be applied. "Apply pressure on the bandage so it will enter the wound and plug any bleeding." Nathan did a quick medical scan on Yuki. "Great, she's stabilizing. Just keep the pressure on that wound and she should be stable enough to get to some real help."

Nathan placed Yuki in the IFV and sent the vehicle on its way back across the bridge toward the FOB. Mitch raised the power level on his M68 to the maximum setting. Taking aim at the nearest Guardian, he shot it through the neck before it reached melee range with several of the Airborne soldiers. "Find cover and focus your fire on the drones before they get close, damn it!" he shouted through his helmet speaker.

Nathan took a hit in the shoulder from a drone's particle rifle, but it did almost nothing, as the drone was well out of effective range. He returned fire, the burst killing the Guardian.

The two remaining MH98 Kestrels returned and began firing at the drones that had latched onto the buildings. "This is Colt 2-1, we are clear to engage targets on buildings. Keep your heads down, here comes the rain," the pilot said as the helicopter hovered over the human soldier's position in support.

The helicopter's cannon fired several hundred rounds per minute, hosing the Guardian drones hanging from the building walls. The rounds chewed into the concrete and shattered windows, sending fragments of tempered glass and concrete debris crashing onto the ground with the Guardian drones.

Parked and abandoned cars around the buildings had their alarms go off, causing a symphony of obnoxious noises. "God damn, as if this couldn't get any more fucking annoying," Masa said, finishing another Guardian drone that had made it into close range of the IFVs and vehicles.

"Say it's a Monday and I will fucking kill where you stand," Eric said as he shot a fleeing Guardian drone.

From there, the drones had no choice but to find cover and slowly dig the human defenders out of their defensive perimeter. "Keep drawing their fire. The more time they waste with us, the more time we buy for the others to regroup," Mitch said, lining up a kill shot on a drone as it tried making a shot from cover.

"Colt 2-1, we have a large wave of Guardian drones in sight. We will give you what fire support we can, but our bird is low on ammo. Over," the pilot said as his computer showed that even the helicopter's particle cannons were low on energy.

"This is Badger 1-2. We are okay on ammo here. Just need a minute to reload our main guns," the IFV commander said.

"Hey, Sergeant, what is the word on the rest of the assault? I sure hope it's better than this," Sean said as the IFVs slowly rolled forward, only to have the one leading the group be hit by a large white beam of light in the missile launcher, causing the turret to explode.

"Hey, you know how you said to relax? Well, you can. We have this in the bag. Where the hell is all the good shit you were talking about?" Sean mocked the Guardian drones as he watched the MH98 fire a barrage of rockets and gunfire, crushing their attack before breaking off.

"It'll be twenty minutes before that helicopter comes back, and fuck if I know how many drones are beyond Ohio Street. Worse, they took out one of our IFVs," Masa said as the vehicles, Infantry, and Airborne forces accompanied them, moving forward toward East Ohio Street.

Colonel Mason looked over the very slow progress being made by all the forces. He selected a location where one of his officers had held up. "Lt. Carver, report in. I want a sit-rep. Over."

"This is Lt. Carver. We are at the Northwest Memorial Hospital and have set up a perimeter. The drones are committed to taking this place, but seem to be focusing on street level activity," he finished his report, taking cover behind a police car at the emergency room entrance.

A police officer with an assault rifle broke from cover and fired. The rounds hit a drone center mass but caused minor damage. The officer dove behind cover again as the drone fired back. Several particle beams slammed into the building. "Fucking hell, these are 6.5mm Grendel rounds and they did fucking shit?"

"Those civilians braved that smog, and the IFV lost its commander. It's best they use the smog to flee," Eric said as he lined up a shot.

"No shit, lucky bastards. I hope that thing is out of the blast zone when the nuke goes off," Gabe said, firing his grenade launcher into a police cruiser that the Guardian drones were using as cover. He then checked his HUD to see how much time remained. "Fucking hell, we're just about at the three-hour mark. I sure hope command is satisfied." Gabe reloaded his rifle, slamming a new magazine into the stock of the rifle as the beam fire continued to bombard their position.

One hour forty-five minutes till nuclear strike on Chicago.

Colonel Mason looked over the fighting before him. The captain demanding a victory looked more like a waste of life as the fighting bogged down more with each passing minute. His troops, and those belonging to the United States, had only made marginal headway into the city, and supplies of ammunition were running low. Convoy Punisher was bogged down in the residential area on West Superior Street and could no longer move forward without being overwhelmed.

Mason's forces on the southern section of the city were in better shape. Despite all the Marines and US Army Airborne stalling just south of East Ohio Street in the downtown area. The debris cloud had given dozens of civilians the opportunity to flee into the streets. The troops were using air support to cover the fleeing civilians, and as a result, attack operations had ground to an halt. "Has anyone found any communication sources that could be the drones' command?" Mason asked his communications officer. He watched a bead of sweat fall from the officer's forehead, the failure boiling his blood.

"Yes and no, sir," the communications officer answered, running over various transmissions on a computer screen. "The communications have increased overall. Frankly, if not for the city's security communication systems being in such good shape after the initial attack, maintaining this level of overwatch would be impossible. Plus, with that enemy computer in our hands... Well, I never had the ability to watch enemy communications run parallel to our actions on the battlefield."

"What the hell does that mean?" Mason asked, wiping the sweat from his own brow.

"It means that their drones are actively being fed commands during combat and they are requesting information throughout. All while our communications are traveling side-by-side. Oddly, it seems they don't understand public Wi-Fi or just don't care," the communications officer said.

"Then why the hell haven't you found their command post? We are three hours away from losing this ship's entire ground compliment to a ninth generation stealth nuclear missile," Mason shouted at the officer.

"Well, sir, if these people weren't flooding the systems with calls, I'd have had something sooner," the communications officer said. "But I think I finally found their command post. Took forever, but it's the umpteenth time this sight has received troop movements that matched our own. If we can capture..."

"We may be able to shut down all the drones," Colonel Mason said, finishing the officer's thoughts. "It's a big maybe, but it's better than nothing." Looking over the entire battle, he decided to make the call. He focused on the north side where West Superior Street was. Selecting the nearest group of M10 tanks, he issued the order to move forward. "Alright, I am moving the tanks forward to North Noble Street," Colonel Mason said.

Major Robb noticed the command order and immediately countered it, just as the M10 tanks moved forward. "Punisher 1-1. Belay your order. If you try moving through those suburbs, the drones will swarm you. Command, what the hell is going on? If my tanks move forward, the drones will have them surrounded!" Major Robb shouted as he took cover.

"I am sending a tank forward and you will comply. This city is worth more than one goddamn tank," Colonel Mason said, resending the command.

"Major Robb, it's okay, we'll do this. If it means a win, we'll go," the commander of Punisher 1-2 said.

"Punisher 1-2, fire your main gun for full effect on the first two buildings, then roll forward," Major Robb said.

"Punisher 1-2, confirmed. Fire for effect," the tank commander shouted to his gunner.

Changing its main gun's elevation, the tank fired into the first building on the left side of North Kingsbury Street. The apartment building shattered like glass where the tank's main gun hit. Remains from the explosion scattered everywhere before its roof collapsed. The Marines, despite having sealed combat helmets, could still hear and feel the 140mm cannon go off with each shot. The fire from the drones ceased momentarily.

Punisher 1-2's driver pressed the accelerator hard, and the tank lurched forward, digging its track into the concrete. The tank rolled over abandoned and parked cars with comical ease. The turret of the tank then focused on the second building as it approached from the right. Instead of receiving return fire from the drones, the fire fight died down.

The tank's roof mounted machine guns began firing on the buildings as it advanced, trying to provoke a response from the drones. Colonel Mason watched, praying to a god he once forsook to give him the chance now to save a city.

The tension caused by the Guardian drones' inaction finally broke as hundreds flooded the city street, firing into the tank from all sides as they rushed forward. The first barrage of energy beams fired into the tank's armor, but quickly dissipated over the heavy carbon fiber plates. In return, the Marines' machine guns fired into the drones, cutting many down before running out of ammunition.

The Marines and Naval Infantry fired at the drones, trying to give the tank some support before they began jumping on top of the vehicle. The drones ripped the heavy machine guns from the top of the tank while several others used their tentacles to rip open whatever weak spots they could find. A few dozen drones ceased moving, remaining still on the tank, then the small horde fled.

The drones remaining on the tank each self-destructed; individually, none of them would do much damage. As a group, though, they successfully pierced the tank's already weakened armor, causing it to explode.

In orbit, Colonel Mason and many others had seen such suicide attempts by the drones before. "Tell me you found their command center, damn it," Colonel Mason shouted to his communications officer.

"Sir, they got an order to self-destruct from the Neo Langham Tower on the forty-fifth floor, room number 205," the communications officer said.

Mason looked over the battlefield. The only area that the building didn't have a view of was what was blocked by the Trump Towers. Everything happening on Michigan Ave was well outside its view, but he needed to keep his discovery a secret—the Serkins were not as stupid as he had hoped.

Colonel Mason selected the entire force on Michigan Avenue. "Let's play the baiting game, shall we? Communications officer, issue a retreat order to the forces on Michigan Avenue over the public Wi-Fi as I issue different orders just to see if they are listening."

The officer nodded. "I'm sending orders randomly into open channels, sir."

Colonel Mason selected a unit on his map. He clicked on the recently rearmed MH98. "Colt 2-2, I need a pickup of assets off Michigan Avenue. Carry them to the Neo Langham Tower," Colonel Mason said, turning his attention to another section of the battlefield. "Sgt. Caird, I have a bird inbound to your position. Gather your best men in two fire teams and prepare to capture hostile CP."

Nathan fired a three-round burst to drop a drone as Eric shot the next unit behind it. "Colonel Mason?" Nathan asked, stunned he was being contacted by the second in command of the ECS Stryker. "Sir, I will gather my best, sir."

"I am not sure who or what you will find at this CP. There may be computers and drone control operators. This is new ground for us all," Colonel Mason said, pausing to wipe sweat off his forehead. "I want that win Captain Kurkov spoke of, and this is likely our best bet. Take prisoners and shut the drones down. The details of this operation are on you, given your history with the Naval Infantry's Special Forces."

"Confirmed, Colonel. I will get this done," Nathan said.

Sean hunkered against the rear of an IFV as several particle beams connected with the right flank of the vehicle. Jumping out of cover, Sean fired in return. A particle beam connected where his arm connected with his shoulder. "Fuck, that burns," Sean cursed as he returned to cover.

The suit's computer did a diagnostic test and returned a result of eighty-nine percent functionality. Sean tapped his helmet against the side of the IFV, hoping to knock the system out of place and reset it to one hundred percent, but it failed to work.

"Where is that ammo drop? I'm on my last magazine," Mitch said, finishing his third magazine.

"Davis, Ryan, and Chikafuji, on me now. We're leaving on the next bird," Nathan said, noticing they were the only people nearest to him.

Colt 2-2 arrived and fired a volley of rockets and its own mounted particle cannons as the rear door opened. The helicopter pilot came in and hovered behind the firing line of the IFVs. Nathan climbed on and held the hand railing as the others approached. The majority of the other troops had no idea what was going on, but the fact was clear that four of the few Marines they had were leaving the battlefield.

The men boarded, their body language clearly showing their displeasure with the orders. Each of them took a seat in the cargo hold. It had six seats along each wall of the helicopter bay. There were an additional two seats lined up against the bulkhead next to the doorway separating the cockpit from the cargo hold. The seats were meant for Naval Infantry, not Marines clad in power armor, so each soldier awkwardly took two seats.

"There better be a damn good reason for abandoning the front line like this," Sean said, taking a seat.

Nathan banged his fist against the cargo hatch door control, which sent a signal to the pilot to lift off. "Don't get comfortable. This will be a short flight," Nathan said, collecting a few pieces of equipment as the helicopter jerked upward.

"What the hell is this all about? We just left a lot of people to fucking die! Those guys aren't going to hold long against scores of drones," Masa said as the helicopter jerked hard to the right.

"Enemy CP has been located in the Neo Langham Tower on floor forty-five. This helicopter is going to fly us past the building. We'll move and try to shut down the drones. Captain Kurkov wanted a win, and this is probably the only way we can," Nathan said, taking a pack of C4 foam from the helicopter's storage rack, thanking god it was loaded for special operations.

"What if we can't shut off the damn drones from the enemy's CP," Mitch asked the obvious question.

"Simple, we die in a nuclear strike," Sean said as he began wondering what could be done. "What is the clock down to now? An hour?"

"We have ninety-eight minutes till detonation. The nuke's blast radius is unknown, but it will likely be a low-level air burst to maximize damage potential," Masa added, brushing off the caked-on debris that coated his armor.

"If it's one of our new W99 with a four hundred kiloton blast potential warhead, the blast will hit Oak Park."

"Hang on, we are going skim alongside the buildings as we go," the pilot said as the helicopter jerked upward. "We're going to fire a few rounds into the building. We've passed it before. The Serkins should be none the wiser. You will have an opening by the time the light turns green."

"Alright, stack up and be ready to jump," Nathan said.

The helicopter gunner lined up the targeting reticule and fired several particle cannon strikes into the side of the skyscraper. The glass melted away as it was forced backward by the particle beams. Pulling back hard on his controls, the pilot forced the helicopter to climb rapidly.

The pilot adjusted the helicopter's course to skirt alongside the building. "Drop in ten seconds!"

The group stood up and secured their rifles and other gear to their suits' hard points as best they could. The helicopter's rear hatch opened slowly, giving way to the late afternoon sun. It burned brightly off the skyscraper's panels, contrasting the grim reality of an impending nuclear strike.

The light went from red to green. The men jumped from the back of the helicopter and began a short free fall. Each of them fired their jump-jets and used the weight of their bodies to direct their fall into the smoldering hole the helicopter had left.

Despite their efforts, the landing inside the building was anything but coordinated. Mitch landed on his feet, only to be knocked down by Masa. The pair then slammed into Sean, who hit Nathan, and they all fell into a pile of what was once expensive linens now burning with melted shards of glass.

"Get off me, you twits. Seriously, have you guys ever performed combat jumps? Where the hell are you idiots even from?" Nathan complained as he shoved the others off.

"We passed every requirement to meet drop and flight protocols. I also happened to have finished with some of the highest marks in boot camp. As for where I'm from, I'm sadly from that shithole NYC," Mitch snapped back as he detached his rifle from his suit's hard point.

"Earth borne, seriously, I would take you for colonists. I served in the Naval Infantry's Elite Raider unit for eight years. Did you just join up to see if you could pass the IMSF tests? Damn it all, this place is fucked," Nathan said, dismissing his own question as he picked himself up. "We need to figure out the floor number and move from there."

"As if meeting the standards at eighteen is a bad thing. I was just more fit and capable than some fellow Earth-born Naval Infantry," Mitch said, making his way to the hotel room's door and stepping through to the hallway.

"Scan the floor with your sonic vision. I don't want the door opening to a shitload of drones," Nathan replied, ignoring Mitch's comments.

Sean fired a sonic pulse to ensure the floor was clear of enemy forces.

The scan reported little other than a distinct lack of people. Unlike the densely packed one from before, the floor was lifeless. "Nothing on this floor, sir. If there were people in this building, goddess only knows where they went. All that's left are a few corpses," Sean said, wondering where the being he worshiped as a child was in any of this mess.

"Forget about the dead people. We need to find that command center and shut down the drones," Masa said as the group left the room. "Looks like we're on the forty-second floor. This room is 42B13."

Exiting the room, the group found the hallway lights flickering in the carpeted corridor. The luxurious setting had been reduced to a heap of rubble. Highly detailed and exquisite carpets were ruined with debris and bloodstains and were torn. The small end tables with vases of flowers lay in pieces on the floor, shattered in the chaos.

The complex carved wood molding of the walls lay on the floor next to the cracked baseboard and rested on the dead bodies of the hotel's occupants. A few sections of the floor were soaked as the fire suppression system was sporadically showering the area.

The group raised their weapons and moved toward the stairwell cautiously. As they moved forward, they leaned up against the wall before finding their way up. The stairwell was an emergency system, but the door was blown off its hinges.

Nathan paused for a moment as he looked at the door and noticed a few different markings from a weapon. "This looks like ballistic damage with no burns. They may have their stealth-suited hunter class soldiers here. I've only heard of them, so use your sonic vision."

"Of course you can't see them. They're always wearing suits that make them nearly invisible," Mitch commented sarcastically, as he took point entering the stairwell.

"Shut up and consider that a standing order, smartass," Nathan scolded Mitch as the group began climbing the stairs.

Strangely, the Serkins ignored the stairs as the group climbed up to the forty-fifth floor. The door to the forty-fourth floor remained on its hinges but was still damaged by fighting. A bloody handprint was smeared on the door and its handle. Whoever left the bloody prints had found another place to die.

The group made it to the forty-fifth floor, unopposed. The door was on its hinges and oddly clean. Mitch took a position, aiming his gun right where the door would open. Nathan raised his fist, ordering everyone to stop. He did a sonic scan of the floor. "Alright, cut the power to the door before opening it. The Serkins left the emergency alert system on," Nathan said, pointing out the power lines that fed electricity to the alarm.

Masa took his knife out and cut into the wall, careful to be as quiet as possible, making a hole, thanking god all these luxury hotels had dense sound proofed walls. "Which wire should we cut? It's not a bomb, so it can't be the red wire," Masa joked to relieve the stress.

"Just sever the power wires and let's move," Nathan ordered Masa, who cut the power.

Sean used his enhanced strength and that of his armor to pry open the door as Mitch took a knee and slipped his gun's safety off. "Ready to fire," Mitch added.

Sean finally pulled the door open and Masa moved in first, his rifle raised in the ready position. Masa scanned the hallway. He swung to the left side of the hallway once he'd scanned the right and found nothing. With the area clear, Sean followed Masa and then Nathan. The trio moved forward, heading toward the room on the northern side of the building.

The halls were slightly better lit than the stairwell, but it was still dark enough to hide a Hunter-class stealth soldier. With as many statues and life-size ornamentation in the spacious halls, all a steal-suited Serkin had to do was calmly hold still in place and they could blend in right next to a statue of a person.

The four men made their way to the estate room that easily took up a quarter of the floor. "Alright, according to orders, this is the room overlooking the northern side of the city. Mitch, Sean, line up, you enter through the door. Mac and I will breach through two different holes in the wall using the demolition foam," Nathan said, spraying a line of foam the size of a Marine on his section of wall while Masa did the same on the other side of the door.

"We only need one alive. It'll be nice to kill them instead of their drones for a change," Mitch said, waiting to kick the doors off their hinges.

"Wounding shots only, smart mouth. We need them to operate their equipment," Nathan said, standing back from the foam as he placed a small detonator in the center of the foam. He handed another detonator charge to Masa, who quickly placed his own.

With the detonators set in place, the foam began to burn; a small sizzling expanded and went outwards. When the entirety of the foam had been burned, the wall exploded outward. The inner room shuddered at the shock wave of the breaching charges. The occupants were stunned as the room's air turned into a massive dust ball.

Mitch kicked the door open as a few Serkins took to firing into the cloud of pulverized dry wall. Mitch shot two of them as Masa and Nathan emerged from the cloud, climbing over the expensive couch and moving over the coffee table.

Sean took point as he moved toward the dining area. Firing a three-round burst from his Gauss gun, he killed a Serkin soldier and splattered its purplish blood on the wall. It slid to the ground, coming to rest on the floor. Sean turned to his left; that's when he stopped himself from pulling the trigger. "Hold fire. We got a prisoner!" he said, grabbing the Serkin and forcing him face-first into the wall.

Mitch forced the other Serkin to her feet, away from the computer system she was operating. The Serkin raised its arms and just stared into Mitch's helmet. "Shit, this is literally a first, and it actually breathes O2!" Mitch commented on the fact that the Serkins had no helmets on. "Boss man, this is Mitch. We got a Serkin POW here, and it's got a red marking on its left arm's armor plates."

"You have one as a prisoner? I am going to contact the ECS Stryker," Nathan said as he and Masa split up to clear the remainder of the hotel room. The fact it was a floor-sized room with pointless glass walls and lavish embellishments in bedrooms didn't mean searching would take long.

"No sir. Two males and a female for now, sir. She's also not wearing a helmet," Sean said, noticing the Serkin's facial features.

Their helmets fit closely on their heads, which were somewhat pointed, but their facial features were very human. The eyes had a cat- or snake-like slit, but purple, with a large indigo colored background. The males had a square jaw line like humans, but it ended in a sharply pointed chin with a dimple. The male Serkin had elaborate war paint on his face.

Breasts, though, distinguished the other Serkin as female; she had wide hips, and a much more rounded face. The chin, nose, and ears were equally elongated and pointed. Despite the pointed features, the Serkin woman was far from ugly by human standards. The only striking difference was the various shades of blue skin and rather vibrant hair colors.

Sean shook his head as the uncanny valley-effect finally hit him like a ten-ton truck just ran him over. He bound the prisoners while Mitch held them at gunpoint. Sean slammed the butt of his rifle into the male's stomach, and once he was on the ground, used zip wire to secure his hands behind his back.

Shortly after everything stopped, Masa stormed into the dining room, forcing another female into the room. She wore the same sealed, full armored form-fitting body suit that gave away her sex. Masa threw her to the ground, picked her up, and forced her against the wall with the other prisoners. "I caught this one nearby. It wasn't armed like rest, so I didn't kill it."

"Well, the monkeys have finally taken us by surprise; it only took your kind five years of losing and countless souls to do so. I guess you can gloat," the female Serkin said in perfect English from her place sitting against the wall. She got up and kneeled, placing her hands on her head.

The fact the creature spoke English was little shock to anyone. Humans had been spamming all forms of media into the sea of stars. Nathan simply ignored the comment as the prisoners were finally secured. "Colonel Mason. Enemy CP is captured, as are four Serkins. I will feed you into my HUD."

Colonel Mason turned from the table to watch a tactical situational awareness feed from Nathan. The HUD reported Sgt. N. Caird as the soldier he was following. The image was clean and he could see the prisoners almost as if he were there. "Alright, I am sending you access to the ship's AI. You will get prompts on what to do. Over."

Mitch looked over the Serkin's computer system and tried to figure out if the Serkins used home row keys in a Dvorak simplified keyboard standard. "How long will an Autonomous Militarized Intelligence take to decipher this keyboard?"

"Hopefully less than fifty minutes or we all die in a massive fireball."

Mitch read the text on the screen. He'd seen their text before, but something here was clicking in his mind. He reached out and touched the screen. Several scenes came up with lines of text in the Serkin language along with it. "What the hell are you doing, damn it?" Nathan shouted as he was waiting for the ship's AI to translate all the words.

"Hang on. This is definitely the command screen feeding orders to the Guardian drones. I think I can turn them off, or at least make them stop attacking," Mitch replied.

"Confirmed Private M. Davis. You are the frontline cyber warfare expert," Colonel Mason said, interrupting the conversation.

"Sir, that is correct, and I'm not sure this will work. At least the aliens' monsters don't use security measures in their command posts," Mitch replied as the ship's AI began feeding him a completed translation. Mitch noticed the sheer lack of security to lock the computer.

"Just shut the drones down, kid, the clock is ticking," Colonel Mason said, watching as the battle in the streets dragged out into a slugging match with no possible winners.

Mitch scrolled through the text on the screen as the AI fed him translations. The texts were coming in fast, but he still had to figure out the command structure—everything was a combination of keyboard commands and touch screen.

Sean looked on as Masa went over the enemy's weapons. The Guardian drones used beam weapons but the Serkin weapons were much more familiar looking. Masa had begun to unload the weapons.

"Interesting, they have shard throwing firearms. And these strange-looking knives," Masa said, holding up a Serkin combat knife. It was like a miniature machete had been merged with a scythe. Both sides were sharp, but it wasn't made from any metal listed on the periodic table as far as he could figure out. "It's oddly well balanced; I wonder what it's made of? It's too light for steel, or even composite-like titanium carbide," Masa added as he rolled the blade in his hand.

"Are you really admiring their weapons right before we get nuked? I say we make those things truly suffer before we get fried," Sean suggested twirling the Serkin's knife in his hand. He was trying to take his mind off the fact they were now at forty minutes until the nuclear bomb went off.

"Negative, we will abide by the Sentient Rights Act and Skye Convention on treatment of POWs," Nathan said looking at Sean. "If you suggest anything like that again, I will rough you up myself."

"Understood Sergeant, I won't let happen again, sir," Sean replied, resisting the urge to hurt the Serkins.

Mitch sat silently, ignoring the commotion, scrolling through the images of the command feed. Understanding their system came slowly, and he managed to gather all the units in the city. He still struggled with issuing the drones commands on a grand scale, though. He messed with their orders but struggled to find their off switch. "Damn, there are three hundred thousand of these things still active in the city. All this data is at the scale of an encyclopedia on the enemy," Mitch said, pouring through the data.

"Just find the off switch and kill the drones. The information can wait," Mason said, watching Mitch scroll through the computer systems.

"If I don't know how exactly the drones function, I can't turn the fuckers off...sir," Mitch replied, looking for anything that would give him a rundown on Guardian drones. Mitch had no idea where to begin, typing in more commands within the search section of the computer's mainframe.

"Can the AI shut these things down instead of this kid? A better option than him must exist, so someone find it," Colonel Mason shouted at the Electronics Warfare Officer.

"Sir, the AI would need to have a specialized port and firewall system to prevent hostile worms from infecting our systems," replied the EWO. "It would take several hours to develop one on ship."

"Damn it all to hell!" Colonel Mason cursed as he watched Pvt. Davis work as fast as a human could.

30 minutes until nuclear detonation
North side of DuSable Bridge

Gabe fired a three-round burst into a charging Guardian drone. "Damn it, this is what I get for being inspired. Nothing good comes from speeches," Gabe complained as he took cover behind a Badger IFV.

"Shut your god damn mouth. The last thing I hear before being nuked damn well better not be your bitching," Eric said as she sniped a Guardian drone that had climbed on top of an IFV. Eric could see several civilians fleeing south toward the crumbling defensive line.

The drones ignored the civilians, and all began making a break for whatever defensive lines remained in the street. Eric fired into a drone as it neared a man who tried to help a woman who'd tripped and fallen in the street.

Gabe checked the ammunition in his magazine. The feed on the gun read, 36 rounds remaining. Content as he could be with the ammunition he had, he took a deep breath and exited cover. He didn't need to wait long before plenty of targets emerged, and worse, incoming beams of fire. He fired back a three-round burst, dropping a rushing drone. "That takes care of one. Should we try to find the subway for when the nuke hits? We can survive it if we can avoid the blast," Gabe said.

"You got three civilians and a drone bearing down on them to your left flank. I can't cover them and keep the right flank clear of these things. Again, stop your whining," Eric said, reloading his rifle.

The first IFV on Gabe's left fired its coaxial machinegun as a row of drones emerged. They were rushing forward, overcharging their rifles, firing into the vehicles' frontal armor. The successive barrage of beam weapons managed to cut through the vehicles' forward armor of the driver's position.

With small internal explosions going off as the particle beams hit the ammunition inside, hatches flew open and black smoke belched from them. Gabe decided against checking on the vehicle crew. He moved forward and began looking for more targets emerging from the smoke.

"Did you think you'd get to die on Earth in a nuclear fireball? I admit I didn't expect such a thing to happen on old Earth," Eric said as he watched the IFV next to Gabe billow smoke.

"Oh, now you want to talk? What a god damn hypocrite. Here I am on the street, neck deep with these fucking things, and you want to chat? All after your complain about me pointing out the obvious," Gabe said, noticing a couple of people fall over in the street.

Further ahead, a man had stopped to help up a fallen woman. Only Gabe noticed the man had stopped, along with a single Guardian drone, which was looking around for an easy target. The drone noticed two easy targets and moved on them.

Gabe rushed over to help the woman to her feet just as the drone raised its rifle and tried to bring the bayonet down like an axe. Gabe blocking the attack from the oversized blade, it smashed into his jump pack, cutting so deep into the jump-jets the system blared shutdown warnings. It felt as though the warnings were being sent directly into his brain. He nearly fell on the man he was protecting.

Gabe stood firm and swore at his friend. "Damn you, Eric, where is that sniping support, you dick?"

The drone that had pulled the blade out of the back of Gabe's armor backed off, pausing for a few moments, and Gabe turned to face it down. Gabe's suit was feeding his HUD with jump-jet failure messages and alerts of imminent shutdown. He winked his eyes to dismiss the warnings. "Oh, you son of a bitch," Gabe said, turning around to face the drone. He rushed the drone, forcing its weapon well off target as he forced it to the ground.

The pair hit the ground, and the drone used its tentacles to catch its fall. Gabe managed to force its head backwards but lost his own rifle and had to use his side arm. He pointed the gun point blank at the drone's neck and fired until the pistol's magazine ran dry.

Gabe rolled off the drone with enough time to watch a soldier fire a few rounds to put down another drone. His drone was dead, and the drones' line was all but collapsing. He stood up. The couple had stayed in place out of fear, or perhaps they'd given up hope. If the latter was true, he could relate. "Come on. The vehicle will protect you," Gabe said, rushing the couple to the vehicle's troop compartment.

"Protection from what? Didn't those laser beams cut into your armor?" the man asked Gabe as he helped the woman limp to the vehicle.

"The nuclear bomb," Gabe said, opening the small access door on the vehicle's ramp door. Once the couple was in, he slammed the door shut, preventing the couple from responding to the information he just gave them.

Across town at North West Memorial Hospital, Mute wasn't doing any better. Vehicles and other junk barricaded the main entrance to the Emergency room to provide cover. Across the entrance lay the destroyed remains of drones.

"Holy shit. They just keep coming and it never stops," a panicked security guard said.

"Yeah, that's what they usually do when they have numbers like this. Be grateful they aren't coordinating their efforts," Mute replied, looking for another assault. He wondered why the drones had paused. As far as he knew, they didn't need rest or food.

The pause finally came to an end as the drones began advancing, only this time, the drones weaved in and out of cover, firing at random. "Alright, hold fire till they get into the open and save the ammunition," Lt. Carver said, knowing the drones had no intent of breaking their lines.

Mute stood up slightly, taking a quick look, but no drone opened fire in his direction. "Damn, they are wasting our time until we get nuked," Mute said to Carver.

Twenty minutes until nuclear strike.

Mitch sat working on gaining a universal shut down code for the city's Guardian drone infestation. He was desperate. The colonel was screaming in one ear and his squad was stabbing him to death with their eyes. Sure, he couldn't see their faces through their helmet's visors, but when you had a city with millions of people hanging on your fingertips, nothing could hide that demand for salvation.

"This is what I have, sir. You want a drone shutdown, I think I can do that, but it'll only be city wide. Every other city on Earth will be on their own," Mitch said, his words ringing with uncertainty and doubt. "The keyboard recognizes shut down commands. They don't use Dvorak, but I won't need it."

"Do it, kid. I'm not fond of my ship's remaining troop compliment dying and I won't let the first alien POWs be lost to a nuke," Colonel Mason said to Mitch, trying to reassure the Marine of his job.

"Right, well, here we go. All drones selected in the city are now to shut down regardless of status," Mitch said as he keyed in the commands. The alien keyboard wasn't using the home row system he was accustomed to, but the one thing he'd learned from his uncle was to never be comfortable with a keyboard when messing with a hostile computer security program. "Shut down commands sent now. I'm waiting for a response."

In the streets just north of the DuSable Bridge, the chaos was enough that the Guardian drones became confused on which direction the humans were fleeing. Gabe was no better off than his foes and everyone around him. "Hey, do you have any ammunition left?" Eric asked as he stood up.

"Yeah, I have six rounds left," Gabe said, shooting a drone in the head twice. "Make it four. This isn't good, man." Gabe stood watching as another drone spotted him. The drone he'd shot suffered damage but was far from dead.

The drones both took aim at Gabe. He had little desire to fight back; at this point, he was in no mood to see the city nuked by its own national military. He lowered his gun, letting it hit the ground, accepting he was fighting a lost cause. "Well, I'll see you on the other side," Gabe said to no one in particular.

Just as the drones took aim, the pair shut down. Their shoulders hunched forward, arms dropping to their side. The tentacles on their back hanging from walls dropped their rifles, and their heads drooped over before they crashed to the ground. Gabe looked around. He saw the same sight everywhere. The drones had shut down, regardless of their actions.

Drones that were running forward fell over, crashing down on their faces. Lt. Carver and the soldiers he was with at the hospital also witnessed the drones shutting down. As the charging mechanical beasts rushed the hospital's defensive perimeter, they all fell over, crashing into and over each other comically.

"This is Carver. We are looking at a mass drone shut down in the streets," Lt. Carver said, clearly thankful for a sign from god.

Colonel Mason sighed in relief. "Alert NORAD and the joint chiefs. All the drones in Chicago are shut down. They can cancel the nuclear strike." He closed the battle screen and left to meet with Captain Kurkov.

"Yes, sir," the radio operator replied. "Attention NORAD and Joint Chiefs. All drones received shut down commands. Hostile threats in Chicago have been neutralized!"

Major Robb watched, along with the rest of his men, as the drones fell over. "I read you, Lieutenant. We are seeing the same thing too. Over. This couldn't have come any sooner. The clock is at less than twenty minutes right now. Alright, find a dead drone and make sure it stays that way," Major Robb said as his soldiers began the process of ensuring the drones remained shut down.

"I did it. I shut the fucking drones down," Mitch said in shock. He was now sitting at a major information source once belonging to his enemy. "We actually won this round."

"No time to rest. For all we know, their commanders are aware their drones have been shut down," Mason said. "Cut the network feed to their high command and keep that computer safe until ODIN arrives to relieve you."

Mitch breathed a sigh of relief. "Yes, sir!" Mitch ran through the information on the computer using his suit's record function to copy the data onto camera.

"Jesus, we survived the day because of Mitch," Masa said, looking away from the Serkin weapon collection. "Eric will never believe this one!"

"This is one hell of a day. Do you think we can pocket some of this stuff?" Sean asked, looking at the knife. "This looks more like a jewel than a blade."

"Don't even think about it. ODIN will kill anyone to get their hands on these, and that includes us," Nathan said, looking at the sun setting. He admired the beauty of the city below. Though it had been the site of a major battle, the awe of Chicago still shined through.

2030 hours
ECS Stryker Bridge,

"So you got me that win, if only for the moment. At least we can hold our heads high," Captain Kurkov said to his XO. The bridge crew was working at their stations while consuming protein drinks and coffee, paying little mind to the victory on the ground.

"Only for the moment. We're still one ship against an entire Serkin armada," Mason said calmly. He had little to celebrate. His win was wholly unconventional, and the fight was just begining.

"Well, if it's any consolation, I have an idea. As long as I can contact the Russian rocket brigades, we may have a way to even out this match. Take a look at these recon images," Kurkov said, typing in a few commands into his noteputer.

Mason looked over the images. It was a frightful sight. Several hundred, maybe a thousand, Serkin warships were massing over the remains of the European Union. It was the new third world if he remembered correctly. He looked away from the noteputer. "Not to be rude, but what good will Russia, much less one ship, do against that many ships?"

"It's over the Third World. If we fire off every remaining ICBMs operated by the nations of Earth, we can bombard those bastards without ever placing the Stryker in danger," Kurkov said, scrolling to a new page on his noteputer.

"I see. We can avert any risk of destroying our own territory. But without the other nations knowing what's going on, this idea of yours to use the nuclear weapons of Earth against the Serkin fleet won't do much," Mason replied. He had to admit, Kurkov knew what he was doing. "It could trigger a nuclear war on Earth."

"I can certainly convince the Joint Chiefs of the plan," General Zachary Stone added to the conversation. "Since the president and much of the body politic are missing, the chain of command will fall to them. I know some members of the Joint Chiefs of Staff are planning to run for office. I could probably sell them on this as a campaign slogan."

"Well, there is a chance that any missiles that miss their targets will hit the New Commonwealth Capital of Glasgow and not the Third World," Mason said, directing Kurkov's attention to the Scottish Empire on the map.

"Another issue we have is the Serkins' dig site in the Nevada desert," General Stone interrupted. "I don't know what's in the desert, but we should focus on interdiction there first. If necessary, I can send more American forces to fight there first, but your help would be welcome."

"Our Marines' suits can be repaired and ready to go within the hour."

2100 hours
O'Hare Spaceport field base

As many fires across the city continued to rage into the night, the people began arriving at the Spaceport. Some came in by transport truck or if they were lucky could drive their own vehicle as the road was kept lit by military vehicles powering street lamps. Across the

"Attention. If you are not type O negative, PLEASE do not panic. We have enough synthetic blood supplies to supplement needed supplies," a woman with loudspeaker announced as the civilian refugees of the city entered the terminal area which had been set up as the refugee processing center. "If you have medical certification, please speak to posted guards to be assigned work. We are short staffed and need volunteers."

A pair of helicopters came over at low level, passing the terminal and heading toward the four large egg-shaped dropships. Their own search lights scanned the ground at random before they broke off and returned to their assigned patrol route. A large landing zone had been set up and a barbed wire topped fence separated the refugees from a large tent hospital processing wounded soldiers. The occasional police car made for a gate or used its headlights to illuminate the few areas the spaceport could not.

Printed images of missing people plastered several walls, both inside and out. Inside staff printed any images people had, while others did their best to find individuals' loved ones as armed soldiers stood guard to keep order.

A single MH98 Kestrel came in from the east, and its landing gear slowly opened as the aircraft touched down. A small crew approached as the tail hatch opened. Several soldiers, both Naval Infantry and Strike Force Marines, disembarked.

Despite the recent victory, no one was thrilled—the fight had worn many down to the bone. Mute piled out with the rest and looked over at the nearby refugees. He was thankful to be a colonist and thus disconnected from Earth. In the same breathe he missed his home, he missed his pet Udaloo, and above all he missed Cao. He shook his head and forgot his memories.

"How many hours has it been since you slept, man?" a Naval Infantryman asked.

"It's coming up on thirty-eight hours. Please tell me you didn't invite the media? I am in no mood to be labeled a Nazi by a commie loser who can't define woman," another replied as the helicopter powered down and a maintenance crew approached the helicopter.

"Tell me about it. Can't shoot them unless they throw a punch. Sadly, those dicks aren't stupid or brave enough to try punching us," replied the other Naval Infantryman.

"All Strike Force Marines, report to Hangar 3 for suit maintenance and repairs before you head to the dropships. Everyone else, report to your respective commanding officers for debriefing."

Mute took his helmet off and pushed back the suit's hood that helped seal it off from the environment. He found no line going into the hangar, but when he entered, he saw the dead Marines being stripped of their armor by technicians. "Alight people, salvage what armor plating you can, then send it to the trailer for maintenance," a technician with a noteputer said.

Several Marines stood while having their armor suits removed. Thankfully, Mute soon found that the line for the specially built 'recliners' designed for maintaining the complex muscle suits under the armor was not crowded.

"Alright Sgt. Mathew Miller, step onto the repair and disposal pad," a technician operating the robotic removal arm's computer console said. Mute promptly stepped onto the platform that was attached to a large truck trailer and waited for the robot arms to secure and remove the jetpack. The arms took the jetpack and power plant away for further maintenance. Next to come off was the upper body armor, then the legs and arms opened and fell to the ground.

Another tech picked up the armor for his arms and looked it over. The suit's main weight was comprised of a small power cell and the jump-jets: everything else was light yet durable but easily replaced. Mute watched as the technician decided how much of his armor was good enough to reuse. A third technician then began placing the armored plates in a nearby bin on the trailer after he was set free from the armor plating. "Alright, go to the next station and have a full system check on the muscle suit." The technician motioned Mute onward.

Mitch sat in the recliner, waiting impatiently for his muscle suit to come off. "Seriously, will you get me out of this thing already? I have things to do, so come on already, get it off, doc."

"Oh, shut up. And I am not a doctor. This will take a few minutes as you took a lot of hits from the drones' particle weapons, so the system suffered electromagnetic damage. Your suit thinks you suffered wounds and has sealed up to prevent you from bleeding out," replied a frustrated technician.

"Fine, oh hey, what rifle squad of the platoon are you with?" Mitch asked Mute while he waited to be released from his suit. "How did you get those eyes?"

Mute sat down in the recliner and sighed as several needles poked into his muscle suit. Mute, with his cold mechanical eyes, looked over at Mitch. He was sad he lacked the ability to roll his eyes at Mitch in frustration. "Don't you ever shut up?"

"Yeah, no. I did a lot of that when I was a kid. I didn't have much outside contact, and the only friend I had was a Qualurian my aunt bought." The technician finally managed to turn Mitch's muscle suit off. The suit shrank down, loosening away from his body. In a matter of seconds, the muscle suit transformed into a regular sweat suit, and Mitch's body changed from an overly muscular beast to a more human-like form.

"Alright, looks like the suit didn't take any irreversible damage, which is lucky given how many shots you took from those damn drones.

Also, don't get too comfortable. You'll be needed for a briefing soon enough," the technician said, typing in the release command codes to the recliner.

"Yeah, fine, I'll be back. Just point me to the latrines," Mitch said as the recliner disconnected from his deflating suit. He looked over as his inflated muscle mass gave way and he could feel the crisp night air on his skin. "Oh, that feels much better than temperature controlled electronic pulses."

"Well, Sergeant, good news. It looks like your muscle suit is in good shape. Do you have any complaints about movement or reaction time? Maybe some sore muscles? Even with your improved joints and muscles, it's better to report those problems as soon as they start," the technician advised while typing commands on the keyboard.

"No, I'm just fine, but I have other business to attend," Mute said, promptly leaving as the sound of data ports disconnecting from the muscle suit filled his ears. Mute then pulled the cybernetic plug from behind his ear, disconnecting the control from his head. He felt relief even as a slight shock hit his brainstem.

"Very well. It's advisable you not eat any solid foods. Just stick with the synthetic nutrient drinks that won't produce bodily waste or you'll be in that other guy's situation," the technician said as Mute left the hangar.

Mute, once alone enough at the edge of the hangars, sat down and watched the city skyline. He sighed and took a catnap. The skyline reminded him of Vieira City. A few too many skyscrapers, but with the smoke and fire, it was familiar. Familiar to the first days of the war before everything he loved was methodically consumed and consigned to history. He looked out at the night sky, thinking, *I wonder how long this victory will last.*

Sean and Eric looked on at the refugees on the other side of the fence and then back at the city. Lights came on sporadically across the city, contrasting against the summer night sky with an eerie calm. Aircraft belonging to emergency services and the military could be seen coming and going. Lifting rubble, putting down fires, and transporting what needed to be transported. At least that's what they thought was going on. Both were left out of any information from command besides hurry up and wait.

"Well, it's been saved. It's a little worse for wear, but it's not burning in nuclear flames," Gabe said, sipping on a nutrient shake. "Damn, these are terrible. It's sweet while also being bland and chalky."

"Hope we aren't too late for the other cities," Masa said, looking at a large CH85 Kodiak with Free State Marine Corps markings. In the background, it began unloading ambulances with medical personnel and additional supplies.

"We'll be moving out soon. That's the only reason they would be issuing these to us so religiously. God, goddess or whatever only knows how things are going elsewhere or how long this win of ours is going to last," Sean said, looking over to the refugee side of the spaceport. He wanted to ask about a Serkin counterattack, but knew better.

"If it's any comfort, the north side and much of the south side residential areas still have power and water. The downtown area is trashed, but there has to be some new hell coming. Which is where we'll be going soon enough," Gabe explained, speaking evenly as he drank his nutrient shake.

On the refugee side of the fence, Sammy sat with Yuki, waiting for transport to a hospital with any open beds. They, like so many others who had been stabilized, had to sit and wait next to the runway. The heat of the day had now given way to an eerie cool. Even with the tent having some temperature control, she had chills running down her spine and the blanket they gave her did little to make her comfortable.

"We saved those kids. All are back with their surviving parents. Our perseverance and self-reliance saved the next generation. We upheld the virtues of society," Sammy said, wiping sweat from Yuki's forehead. She tried her best to remember the virtues of the Federation Culture. They were taught to all school children, but looking at her unconscious friend with her missing arm was too much.

"Attention all personnel. Marine transports have arrived. Ensure all critical condition patients are in stasis pods and ready them for transport to Harrison Methodist Memorial Hospital. All stabilized persons will be transported to Saint John's Memorial hospital via ground transportation within the next hour. That is all," the voice over the loudspeaker said as a nurse made their way through the ward.

"Miss, I am afraid we will be moving your friend soon. Her ID number is YN-33-2918. If you have her name, and number you can track her down later. Since you aren't immediate family or injured, we won't be moving you to the same hospital," a nurse said as others arrived to move the stabilized forces.

Sammy stood up and secured her friend's blanket to keep her warm. "I'll be with you all the way up until they load you in the ambulance, Yuki."

At the gate between the civilians and the military portion of the base where the stabilized people were being loaded into ambulances Sean had finally finished his awful nutrient shake. He needed to be alone for a bit. He hoped, maybe, just maybe, he would find his family in good condition. The military ambulances were driving toward the gate between the military's staging area. The available soldiers and nurses came forward, pushing several stretchers past the guards who kept watch over who came and went.

Sean watched this as his family was likely somewhere among the injured. He looked over the group, watching them until he noticed a girl with bright blue and purple hair. "Sammy, is that you?" he called out.

"Sean," Sammy shouted, leaving Yuki's side, but the guards kept her from entering the medivac area. "You're alive; thank the goddess, as our parents would say," Sammy added as she walked along the fence, trying to take hold of Sean's hand.

"You look good despite surviving a war zone. I am sorry to have brought this home. Do you know if my mother Jennifer is alive?" Sean asked as he tried his best to hold Sammy's hand through the fence.

Sammy interlocked her fingers with Sean's and leaned her face against his through the fence. "I am not sure. I was supposed to meet with her and your sister here. How much more of this is coming?" Sean asked, the metallic fence cold against the warmth of his face. He almost wanted to thank the goddess for having Sammy being safe and sound. No, this wasn't enough to restore his faith in some eco-friendly religion. There was too much pain for him to have faith.

"I have no idea, Sammy. I just want you to get a hold of my mother. You can stay with my family as long as you need. It will be better than a protection camp," Sean replied, holding Sammy as close as he could with the fence between them.

"I like living by the virtues of our society and cultural beliefs. Virtue number eight of society is self-reliance. I don't need charity from your family," Sammy replied. "You want to provide for me, then marry me."

"Don't be stubborn right now, please, and I'm being reliable. You'll be taken care of outside a protection camp. It's not like you'd be unwelcome," Sean said as Mute and the others watched. For now he'd ignore them.

"I'm sure Larisa wouldn't want me around," Sammy added, pulling away from the fence as a convoy of ambulances drove through the nearby gate.

"Oh, come on, she isn't that much of a terror," Sean shouted over the passing vehicles, raising a token protest for his sister.

"Attention all combat personnel of the US Army and Earth Colonial Armed Forces. Please report to the field medical personnel. Inspection for Combat Effectiveness will begin at 2130 hours. Vehicle commanders, please report to the motor pool at once," said the voice over the loudspeaker.

"Well, I need to get going. I'll see you later. Just stay go be with my family if you can't find yours. You know, if they're alive, they'll likely head to my mom's house just outside of town on the north side," Sean said, slowly letting go of Sammy's hand.

Sammy sighed. "I'll go find your family once I send Yuki off, so long as you don't go playing hero."

"Damn, these kids today are soft. I bet it's the reason we're fighting on Earth. We're all unified under the same banner and culture of the eight virtues, but what good is that if the people are so soft? All our courage, fidelity, perseverance, industriousness, responsibility, strength, honor, duty, and self-reliance, results in this, so we get our asses handed to us. It's weaklings like him and that mouthy fuck that never shuts up who hold us back," Gabe said on a moaned as he watched Sean and Sammy reunite.

"Actually, Gabe, it's kind of sweet to see young love. Always unhindered by responsibilities," Eric said, crushing his empty packet of nutrient shake.

"Plus, humanity collectively, just like you, found someone in the galaxy taller than them." Masa mocked Gabe over the fact he was the shortest man in their unit. "Now if you don't mind, we want to find the motor mouth and a noteputer. I want to see if the little bugger can get past the communication blackout caused by our lack of open-to-the-public communications satellites."

"Oh, please Mac, you have only 40mm on me, you dick," Gabe replied as he followed the others.

"Can you at least not bother us with your nihilist ranting? If that Mitch guy can live up to his hype just one more time, we may have some old crowd-funded comedies or a marathon of Max Alpha films to binge watch," Eric said, uninterested in listening to Gabe's spout of the obvious.

As the group went to find Mitch, they promptly did what they could to avoid looking too long at the misery they had failed to stop. Their orders were to report for Combat Effectiveness Inspection, but the deadline for that was at 2200 hours, so the group had time to kill and intended to relax.

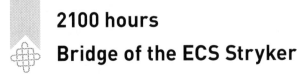

2100 hours
Bridge of the ECS Stryker

"Captain Kurkov, Colonel Mason, our drones are now sending the live feed from Moscow. Local time is 0500 hours and we'll see it in real time," the communications officer said.

"Very good, bring the images up," Kurkov said, looking over his remaining assets and their expanding logistical requests.

The officer typed a few keys and the central terminal displayed the drone footage. Moscow's skyline was filled with tracer fire, and the outskirts of the city had mushroom clouds from the nuclear weapons used to hold off the Serkin's ground force advance from entering the downtown area. The air space saw three large Serkin cruisers slowly moving forward. The Russian were marking Rapiers and outdated attack craft to be used to harass them, but they performed poorly before eventually going down. A lucky few fighter jets managed to ram into the Serkin ship's shields.

The Serkin ships eventually returned fire to unseen ground targets as they began pushing toward the center of the city. The ground exploded. The remaining towers not leveled by the shock wave of the smaller nuclear bombs outside the city collapsed into debris clouds. Several unidentifiable blurs passed the screen just before the video feed went blank.

Mason clenched his fist and shook his head in disappointment. Pinching the bridge of his nose he said, "Well, I don't think Moscow's going to be answering our calls. What's the next likely place their high command officers could be hiding out?"

"Missile command has always kept much of its ground forces mobile on trucks in Siberia. Even going as far back as the first Cold War, they had trucks with twenty wheels that carried ICBMs. Those assets could still have forces hiding out in Siberia. But we can't keep losing recon drones until we have a better grasp on where those mobile launchers are roaming about. Plus, we need to consolidate our win in Chicago," Kurkov said, handing the resupply and losses list to Mason.

"Damn it, I'd say launch all the nukes we have access to, but that would likely backfire, as anyone on the ground could see it as an attack like that coming. What about more cyber warfare? ODIN did pick up that alien computers faster than our MH98s could circle around and pick up the team we sent," Mason complained, reading the list. "Ah, great, Strike Force Marines are down to thirty combat ready men. The Chicago refugees are going to be eating up our medical supplies until the protection camps can receive them."

"If they can get the chance to receive them. The US Joint Chiefs have yet to answer our call for reinforcements. This ship cleared a hole for more forces to land perfectly. The problem is we only cleared the way for ourselves. My request for a win will likely hoist me on my own petard," Kurkov said with a sigh.

Just as Mason was about to respond, the ship's alert system activated. "Emergence signature detected. Scratch that, three, no four emergence signatures detected fifty thousand kilometers behind Luna. Temperature spike is four thousand Kelvin each. Captain, given the distance and heat, they are likely Moscow Class cruisers. I'll confirm it with LIDAR shortly," the LIDAR alert officer said.

"Four ships? The alert from Earth came eighteen hours ago. Our request was ten hours ago. Only Fifth Fleet at Sirius Nader is anywhere near that trip length in beam space. Alpha Centauri, before that, didn't have a fleet with beam space capabilities," Mason said. "I wonder who the commander could be?"

"Hail the four ships. If they have a full Naval Infantry compliment on one ship, we can deploy a full Combined Arms Regiment to supplement the losses in our MEU," Kurkov ordered.

"Hopefully, we won't draw the attention of their fleet just over the horizon." Mason noticed there had been no movement from the enemy fleet in the last eight hours.

30 minutes later
Bridge of the Cruiser ECS, Moscow

The four venerable Moscow battle cruisers finally made their way around the dark side of the moon at a slower speed than normal. The ship's had each added mass in the form of six meter thick composite armor plates from a recent upgrade to a block three standard. The real mass came from upgrading the venerable ships' guns with larger bore rail guns. Admiral Djordje Ilic of Third Fleet stood looking over his bridge crew as the vessel had no view finder to give a view of the space around Earth. He was comfortable with the lower technology vessel. It kept the view of space around Earth on a few computer screens, and Ilic quite happily looked up at bland armored bulkheads.

"Admiral Ilic, we are in range of a single Warrior class vessel. We have LIDAR and IFF confirmation. It is the ECS Robert F. Stryker," the communications officer for the ECS Moscow said.

"Wonderful, seems that we aren't alone," Djordje Ilic said. "We'll need their particle cannons in this fight to punch through the Serkin shield."

The video screen of the ECS Moscow sent a general alert to the Stryker hailing them. Admiral Ilic opened the screen command prompt asking, "Commander of the Stryker, this is Admiral Ilic, have you left us much fight?"

"Yes, Admiral Ilic, there is plenty of fight to go around. You missed Chicago, but the afteraction report should be ready. We're currently figuring out how to deal with the Serkin fleet over Western Europe," Captain Kurkov replied.

Admiral Ilic went over the fleet roster looking over Captain Kurkov's history on his console and selected the overview. Kurkov was another colonist from the area colonized by Eastern Europe, and what the ECSF files had on Kurkov showed him to be resourceful. Ilic closed the file and responded, "You haven't figured out how to turn this around? That is surprising."

"Admiral, we can't contact the Russian missile command to fire their nuclear arsenal at the Serkin fleet. We're in contact with NORAD, but we sure as hell don't want to trigger a nuclear war on the old country," Kurkov replied, looking over the bridge crew.

"I think the colonists the Admiral is berating is us. Tell him we could use someone of his little group's MEUs in Chicago. Also, tell him there is a group of Harvesters digging in the Nevada desert," Mason added, waving the noteputer in his hand at the captain.

"Admiral, we need you to send some troops to Chicago, Illinois. Our own MEU has sustained a great many casualties, plus the civilians need the aid," Kurkov added. Frustration and doubt seeped through every word he spoke. "I am a colonist, too, Mason."

Admiral Ilic watched as the reports from the ECS Stryker began coming in on his commander's console. "Ah yes, that would work. Bombard their fleet while it's over the Third World with Earth's nuclear weapons collection. Shields or no shields, a Serkin fleet won't be able to avoid that kind of damage. It looks like you took the bait, taking back the cities. Although I would definitely avoid attacking that dig site. Their fleet looks poised to attack any force that moves against the dig site."

"Yes, sir, it is why I went to liberate Chicago. Missile Command was relocated to Saint Petersburg some time ago. I say we land some troops there within the hour. It will be the best way to connect with them. We can even supply them with one of our own field communications systems," Kurkov added.

"Very good Captain Kurkov. I will send some spare supplies to Chicago. But I want to focus my forces' efforts on Saint Petersburg until the main fleet arrives." Admiral Ilic issued the orders to begin scrambling his ground forces. "My only concern is that we are stuck with mostly green troops."

"It's better than nothing, Admiral. Although reports on Saint Petersburg are scarce, we'll send a drone to do recon again. We were unable to gather much information on the situation during our first pass. The good news is, the last we checked, no Serkin vessels were in the city's airspace," Captain Kurkov added.

Admiral Ilic looked over the reports that the Stryker's intelligence sent over about the location. He sighed. "Well, seems the Serkins are making an orbital blockade to prevent travel. I will send troop ships in a slingshot maneuver seminal to your performance. They will have an ASF-58 squadron to protect them."

20 minutes later
ECS Moscow, troop section

Attention. Yellow Alert for all Naval Infantry Personnel. Please report to commanding officers immediately.

Victor woke to the buzzing alarm and promptly pulled himself out of his coffin of a bunk. He'd gone to sleep after an annoyingly long shift and almost wondered if he'd simply closed his eyes when the alarms sounded. "*Der'mo*, I should have chosen Siberia, at least there I could have slept," Victor said as he crawled out of the coffin-like bunk.

"Yo, man, you got to speak English. It's the ECF's fixed language," scolded another soldier who woke up.

"Is what- I mean what is your crime that got you forced into the military?" Victor asked the man.

"No, I joined out of high school in New Houston," the man said, tying his boots as the siren blared again.

"Yellow alert has been sounded. Maybe our planet fall will draw their fleet's fire away from the ship in battle," Victor complained. At his sentencing, he was given a choice: Siberia or the military. He didn't want to go to a Siberian prison and perform hard labor for twenty years. However, now it seemed a sentence of ten years of military service with a clean record and a possible chance at earning a tier one citizenship at the end wasn't worth it. Well, that was starting to look like it was too good to be true. He grabbed his boots, realizing that the mundane monotony of military life was about to be replaced with the war of hell. He regretted his choice of punishment as he dressed and reported for duty.

Jason watched as the Naval Infantry men filed into the hangar bay. He had long since been in his powered armor suit. As the ship's highest ranking Strike Force Marine officer, he'd decided to split his forces up and distribute them among the Naval Infantry.

"This will be an air support only operation with a few light vehicles, so I am going to disperse you all among the Naval Infantry platoons to act as support. That means taking point and babysitting," Jason said as he covered his bald head with the standard hood used to seal his power armor.

"Lovely, so we got babysitting duty on the battlefield. Is command too lazy to just give us a drop pod deployment?" another Marine complained.

"Shove it, assholes, and report to your Hornets. I'll send you the mission brief en route to Saint Petersburg," Jason said, dismissing his platoon.

The Naval Infantry, having been armed and equipped, began filing into the dropships, waiting for their commanders to give them their briefings. "First man in, is the last man out, Savinkov," Victor heard the space Texan shout as the group took their seats along the walls of the dropship.

"Feel free to take a particle beam for me. That would be most appreciated," Victor replied. He swallowed his fear of death, forcing the locking mechanism to hold his M65 rifle in place. He then locked the yoke harness restraint down over his chest.

There was enough space for an Ibex or Panther armored vehicle down the center line of the Hornet's cargo hold. Though it didn't look like any vehicles would be loaded. Several of the other Naval Infantry took their seats along the Hornet's wall.

A pair of flight engineers, one in a purple helmet and another with a red, denoting their primary duties involving fuel and ammunition, joined the men. Rolling closely behind the pair was the Pitbull variant of the standard Multi-functional Utility/Logistics and Equipment drone. When the drone stopped, the pair began the process of securing it to the flight deck.

When the articulated wheels were locked in place, one deckhand looked the drone over quickly. "Looks like this might be a long and tough fight. Command wants this drone dropped with the safeties off. Guess it's a hot dropzone. Do you know if this Pitbull is packing enough heat to deal with the issues ahead?" one of the deckhands asked. He removed the safety locks on the drone's turret mounted weapons, seeing as the drones could be dropped while taking fire.

The drone scanned the face of the deckhand with the sensor mounted next to the gun. "Brutus zero one three, online weapon activation confirmed, blue force tracker functional. Combat drop with active hostiles expected."

"That doesn't matter to us right now. We'll cross the hurdles as they come. We need to get these things secured and sent out with the first wave," the other deckhand replied as he began tightening the straps over the drone's rear tires.

"This seems a bit light for a first wave attack. A single Pitbull with only two missiles and its light autocannon?" a Naval Infantryman interjected.

"It's because we're simply probing the area to see if the LZ is viable," Jason said, walking into the dropship. He watched as the flight crews hugged the drone or bulkheads to avoid his fully armored figure. He took a seat near the bulkhead entrance to the cockpit. It would give him the ability to deal with the pilots and the soldiers under his command. He was thankful for the full-face protection his helmet offered, as he could hide his worried face.

Jason had served in the waning days of the FedCom war fighting the Communist Union of Colonies. Now he finally knew how the Union's soldiers must have felt as the end bore down on them. The Serkin war was different. Every time Federation Forces scored a win, the Serkins would change tactics so drastically, their victories were meaningless. Jason knew that now more than ever as on outpost 413 in the Perseus Arm, the Serkins had only been forced off the planet after years of fighting because they were going to attack the Earth instead.

Originally, it was thrilling news, but he should have known better. Vieira was a nightmare he wanted to forget—but now he was about to enter a new nightmare. *Do your job right and you will get out of this,*

Jason. That's all you have to do, he thought. He could only ponder how much longer he could remain in his professional until his last bit of hope faded.

The flight crew, having completed their jobs, began leaving the dropship. The tail ramp started closing, snuffing out the light breaking Jason's train of thought. With the tail ramp secured, the crane lowered the dropship into the airlock. The engines powered up as the airlock sealed and began depressurizing.

Shortly after the cruiser's hangar crews left, the dropship loading ramp closed up. Despite the dropship's larger size, the cargo hold's light dimmed so much before being dropped slowly out of the cruiser; it could be mistaken for a cramped drop pod. Jason had endured worse drops in a four-man pod, but for many of the fresh Naval Infantrymen, it was rough.

Victor felt like he dropped off a cliff when the dropship accelerated away from the ship, which rapidly changed the direction his body was pulled in. Once he was off the cliff, the changes in gravity began, he was abruptly pulled forward, like being shot off the deck of an aircraft carrier's catapult launch system. However, before he could adjust, another intense force of gravity pulled his body down. Victor noticed the IMSF Officer remained calm and asked him, "Is this feeling worse in a drop pod, sir?"

Jason turned his speaker on. "The G-forces in a drop pod simply make it feel as if you are going to puke up your intestines. You'll get used to it. Drops were worse than this back in the Fedcom war. We didn't have any dropships at the time that could perform like airplanes in atmosphere, so the ride down was like a yoyo until you touched down."

Just before Victor could reply, the intercom sounded. "All hands, brace for atmospheric reentry in ten seconds. We'll be in Russian airspace in another two minutes." The cargo light turned red, ordering radio silence as the dropship had entered hostile territory.

"If anyone of you is from Earth, this is your fight. I lost Vieira, my home planet years ago. Millions of people died. Vieira was my home. We lost it in a mere month with no wins, but there was a win in Chicago. We lost back then, but judging from our win in Chicago today, it's clear we can win. There are billions of people who are counting on you to win!" Jason said, trying to motivate both the Naval Infantrymen and himself.

Victor reached for his crucifix, which he had attached to his dog tag chain. He kept praying over and over that his dropship would make it to Saint Petersburg in time. "Make it to Saint Petersburg, save the city, and show the aliens they bit off more than they can chew."

The dropships completed their sling shot maneuver and began the descent through the atmosphere. The craft's large frame was shaped to cut through a planet's atmosphere as quickly as possible, thus limiting the heat stress on the armored skin. Despite this, the interior heated up slightly, though not enough to cause ammunition to cook off and explode, but just enough to make the passengers sweat.

"All troops, Saint Petersburg LZ in fifteen minutes. This is going to be a choppy drop into a hot zone," the pilot said. The black void of space quickly turned into strips of snow white forgiving clouds surrounded by blue sky. The flight computer confirmed a radar lock as the dropship descended/

"Call sign Sylvester to Hornet flight. Maintain course, we'll keep the sky cleared. Over and out," the pilot of the fighter escort said as the four aerospace fighters flew off to engage foes outside the dropship crew's visual range.

The pilots maintained their flight pattern. They closely monitored their instruments as the skyscrapers pierced the clouds over Saint Petersburg. The city had largely been spared any major fighting, or so it seemed at first glance. Upon closer inspection, the aftermath of fighting could be seen on the edges of town, slowly edging its way inward to the city.

"Attention general staff command. We are coming in on a northern vector toward you now," the pilot said. "This is an operation aid to assist you. Over."

"This is Saint Petersburg control. We read you. There is an LZ set up in the pedestrian plaza of the General Staff Headquarters building," the ground controller said just as fire from the ground became visible from the cockpit.

"Confirmed. We see our LZ in Palace Square," the pilot said, descending to street level. The pilot brought the aircraft down and lowered the ramp. "All hands out. Go, go, go!"

The drone unloaded first. As soon as it was clear of the dropship, it began firing its autocannon at hostile targets to protect the Naval Infantry square while the Hornet lifted away. The Plaza LZ had perimeter protection from vehicles in various states of functionality. The Naval Infantry approached a BTR-252 that had clearly been cut in half by a high density plasma charge from a Serkin tank.

Jason scanned the area as the Naval Infantry secured the courtyard. "Spread out and open your fields of fire. Let the drone deal with the heavy armor," Jason shouted as he looked to his right and saw Victor follow the drone forward.

Victor took cover in nearby wreckage as the Serkin HT-22 Hellhound hover tank fired its anti-infantry weapons into the nearby building. The Pitbull drone rolled forward slightly before standing up on its articulated wheels. It fired its missiles into the Serkin tank's flank, dropping like a rock as it exploded.

The Missile command building was partially ruined, and the gate check point was gone, but the Naval Infantry continued forward into the courtyard. Victor stayed behind his Pitbull as it rolled forward through the courtyard and up to the main building. "The enemy armor is history. I am moving into the outermost building." Leaving the drone behind, Victor scanned the area, rifle at the ready.

"Don't get too far ahead of the group! God damn it, stay with the drone," Jason shouted as he and the rest of the men tried securing the LZ before the next Hornet needed to land.

Victor ignored the warning as he climbed the debris into the building. As he searched the building, a Serkin's bullet-like helmet appeared in his eyesight, only for it to disappear again. Blinking, he scanned the hallway. Something was there, though he couldn't see it. Then he saw it. A small bit of blue liquid dropped on the floor.

He raised his rifle and pulled the trigger in the direction of the blood drops on the floor. Suddenly a body fell to the ground—it was clearly female, bleeding bluish blood. The cloaking armor had failed, and the wearer was dead. Victor approached the enemy, but before he could examine the corpse, it dissolved. He had no time to ponder what was happening as an explosion outside cracked the windows, giving him just enough time to duck.

Following Victor into the building, Jason witnessed him kill a Hunter class Serkin. The Serkin's armor had flickered as the bullets damaged its suit's light reflecting stealth technology until it failed, and now the soldier lay dead. If there was one Serkin Hunter, at least two more was nearby, as the Hunters always moved in packs of three. He then knew why the Serkin tanks were not hammering the building harder. Knowing the missile teams were at risk, he used his sonic imaging to find the others.

The Naval Infantry missile teams followed Jason, rushing into firing positions while avoiding being hit by Serkin shards and particle fire. The first team in position aimed for the Type 22 tank. "Fire!" one man shouted as he tapped the head of the man holding the launcher. The man pulled the trigger and sent a rocket into the side of the Serkin tank.

The tank kept moving, and when one missile team tried taking out the tank, they were taken out by a Huntress class soldier. "Keep it up, fire on it till it's dead!" Jason shouted, opening fire on the Serkin Huntress. He was commanding soldiers with little combat experience. They had even less experience dealing with the Serkins' Huntress stealth kill teams. It gave him and the unit an ill feeling they wouldn't win out.

The second missile team fired and sent a missile into the tank, destroying it. The tank sank to the ground with a loud clunking noise. "Focus fire on the drones and push them back!" Jason shouted as the drones broke cover and began advancing erratically. He left the immediate area as soon as the sonic imaging showed him the last Huntress was in the building and likely going to kill the command staff. "You two with the shotgun and SMG, on me now. We're going to save the command staff," Jason said, motioning a pair of soldiers to follow him inside the Command Center.

Victor rushed into building, while outside a wounded Specter gunship spun out of control and crashed into the command building. The floor in front of him exploded. He looked out the window and saw a pair of Russian T-216 tanks moving forward. The first tank fired its 30mm secondary weapon into the Guardian drones that had taken up defensive positions. The second tank moved its turret slightly to the right and elevated its 152mm cannon, firing into the building across the street. He wanted to join the forces fighting in the streets, but focused on the mission.

He looked across the gap in the hallway and tracked the wrecked gunship in the streets below. The building's age could be seen in its scars as the old building materials beneath the modernized façade was exposed to the air. He jumped down to the lower floor, as it was too far to jump to the other side. His first jump was successful. His next was less graceful and he slipped and fell into the basement, missing the second floor when he failed to grab onto something strong enough to support his weight.

Victor managed to focus enough and regain his bearings past the pain coursing through his body. He looked over the rubble and saw a Serkin fire at another soldier. The shards were like knives thrown at speeds no bullet could match. *Shit, that is way too close!* Victor thought as a female soldier fell down dead next to him. He froze when he saw the long blue shard sticking out of her neck.

A Huntress jumped down and Victor rolled out of the way, stumbling. She stabbed into the ground, and he swung his gun in the Huntress's direction, only for it to miss by a good meter. The water pouring down from the pipes mixing with the debris settling made spotting the Huntress easier.

The Huntress swung at Victor. "Fuck, fuck, fuck, and more fuck!" Victor cursed, barely stopping her first slash at his neck with his rifle. He kicked her in the groin and tried to fire his rifle at her, only to realize she'd managed to cut into his short stroke piston, disabling his M65.

The Huntress rushed Victor a second time. Several slashing and stabbing motions flew in his direction, corralling him further down the hallway. "Run, you pathetic thieving ape!" she screamed, chasing him.

Hearing her speaking Federation Standard English shocked Victor. "That you animals have the nerve to speak like victims is disgusting after the millions you've butchered," he said. He swung his busted rifle at the Huntress's head.

The Huntress managed to stab him in the right arm, causing it to go limp. He used what strength he had remaining to punch her in the throat. He knew he was losing blood as he felt lightheaded and could no longer move his hand. With the Huntress on the ground, he grabbed his combat knife and collapsed almost directly on top of his foe.

Before the huntress could respond to his attack, Victor had his knife held firmly at her throat. She tried to resist the killing blow, but Victor swiftly overpowered her, stabbing her in the neck; a few spurts of purplish blood splashed his face.

"Three lives for one. I can die with that," Victor said. Rolling over, panting, and watched the enemy's body dissolve. As he slowly lost consciousness, he noticed a bright light approaching.

Jason showed up just as Victor killed the last of the Hunter class soldiers. He knelt down next to the man and began scanning his wounds. His arm was cut deep enough to sever key tendons and nerves. He took out the medifoam, injecting it into Victor's arm, before slapping a bio-text bandage on to close the wound.

"Sir, for now the assault on the base has halted," a Naval Infantryman reported, and then he saw Victor. The man laid out next a scorch mark where a Serkin had died. "Holy shit, this guy got fucked up," the man said, looking over Victor.

Jason looked up and noticed a roof mounted sentry turret. "They must be manually operated or out of ammunition," Jason said, approaching the large metal door that looked as if an ancient relic had been refitted to modern standards.

"Sir, should we move him to the surface? He is stable but we best get him help fast," a Naval Infantry medic said, looking over Victor's wounded arm.

The sentry turret scanned the room as Jason waved his hands in a fashion similar to a door opening. "Can you hear me? Jason spoke into the turret's camera. We have vital information to give you. I suggest you open up if you want to save your planet," Jason said, looking the turret in its main optic.

The main door slowly moved to the left until it was in the wall. Behind it was another vault-like door that showed its age with tarnished metal. It was made of some form of non-oxidizing metal as it was rust free, despite it clearly using dated piston locks. When it was completely open, two soldiers stood in the gap with armor plating so thick they looked comically fat. As if to remind the Federation soldiers on the other side of the threat, they aimed their weapons and disregarded trigger safety.

"I need to meet with your commanding officer and give him an uplink to my ship's CO. These Naval Infantry are with me and have the equipment to link your CO to the fleet. I also have a wounded man who needs treatment," Jason said. He knew the guards were using old model AK-12s, but he wasn't in the mood to overpower them, not this many years into the war.

"Yes, hurry. Get in and take the wounded through there to the right. Follow the tunnel to the next door," one soldier said, clearing the path for the others to enter.

The group of Naval Infantry followed James, carrying the unconscious Victor down a tunnel. The place had another set of turrets hanging down from the ceiling, and the Naval Infantry clearly winced at the damp mildew scent. There was a small table with a chess set, a few ration wrappers, and a large jug of water on it. The hallway lighting flickered as the doors closed again, leaving the Russian soldiers remaining at their post.

One of the men following James asked, "Have you noticed we're heading toward the Neva?"

"We're well under the river Neva. We haven't been under the building for a while, I guess," James said, estimating the distance they'd already walked. "I guess it would make sense to hide the bunker a bit better than making it just another basement."

The group approached another door, this one no less old but much more advanced. It slid open quickly and the group could see a large command center. The room was ancient but had been revamped several times. Despite the clean environment, it showed its age, as no Russian had ever made an effort to leave a seamless transition between the years.

Those in the room had been silently watching countless screens. Some screens were entirely blank, save for the name and time of location, and the occupants didn't notice the group walk in. A medical officer had managed to arrive. "Place the wounded down. We'll transfer him to medical."

A larger man, not very fit, but certainly not obese, wearing the blue-colored patch with three gold stars of the Russian Air force approached them. "I take it you are here to deliver a communication system?" Colonel General Andrei Zhurav said. "At least I hope you are here to contact me. It's been a few days since anyone here had a decent rest. I hope this visit brings some good news." His uniform was disheveled from more than a day's worth of wear.

"Yes, Admiral Ilic wants to speak with you. Given the advanced nature of this bunker, we figured a direct link would be easy," James said, handing over a data chip.

"Ah, Admiral Ilic. He is a Sidonian of Serbian decent," Colonel General Zhurav said, and plugged the data chip into a computer console. He straightened out his uniform, expecting to greet the Admiral.

The screen provided an image of the Earth Colonial Space Forces' swooping Falcon roundel instead of a visual. "Hello? Is this Western Military command? Is rocket command with you?" Admiral Ilic's voice could be heard coming out of the speakers.

"Yes, this is Colonel General Andrei Zhurav. I have full access to missile command assets. Do you have my American counterpart available? We lost our ability to communicate with NORAD when the attackers took out our satellites." The staff in the command center occasionally looked in Andrei's direction.

"We have spoken with them, and their ICBM systems are ready to launch at the majority of the Serkin Fleet. The enemy fleet is holding its position over the third world of Western Europe, in case any missiles fired miss their targets. If there is a miss, the nuclear bombs would not cause too much damage to any ECF member nations. It will make our actions easier to forgive if we can win this," Admiral Ilic replied. "The rest of the fleet won't be here for another eight hours, but those Serkin ships are going to need to be softened up for this to go our way."

"Very well. I will alert the mobile rocket corps to fire their missiles on targets in orbit," Colonel General Andrei said. He smashed open the case that held the launch codes that would be used to issue commands to the mobile forces in Siberia.

20 minutes later
ECS Robert F. Stryker

"Multiple ICBM launches confirmed across the North American continent and the ocean around the US," the ship's LIDAR operator said. Colonel Mason and Captain Kurkov were watching the event take place on the main console.

"It should do considerable damage. If those nukes are leftovers from the second Cold War, we'll be looking at twelve W98 nuclear warheads in all five hundred land-based ICBMs from the US alone," Kurkov said. Mason, and much of the bridge crew, stood silent as the navigation crew ensured their ship used its RCS thrusters to push it safely out of the ICBM's path.

On the other side of the planet, launches across Siberia took to the sky at the same time. Anyone in the vicinity of the submarines, missile silos, or mobile launchers could see the ICBMs streaking upward into the sky.

Masa went from having his armor plating replaced, to staring up into the night sky as bright lights streaked up to the heavens from the ground. "Hey guys, I think we may have a problem with civilians coming our way."

"Shit, shit, shit. We need to get to the fence where the civilians are likely going to be demanding to know what's happening," Mute exclaimed as he put his helmet back on.

"Shit fuck," Major Robb cursed. Despite being out of the loop, the use of ICBMs from Earth's Cold War era, and the threat of nuclear war, it could not be a good thing to see such weapons launching, especially when babysitting the Chicago survivors. "Anyone in full kit and ready for deployment, assist the Naval Infantry in keeping the civilians on the other side of that fence!"

A small crowd, almost as if told to arrive at the makeshift gate separating the civilian shelters from the military portion of the O'Hare spaceport, all demanded to know what was going on while others simply huddled together in prayer. Earth opinions on nuclear weapon 'hadn't changed much in the last one hundred fifty years. A missile launch on this size and scale only brought bad omens to the already exhausted survivors.

"Someone tell me they remember crowd control tactics from their days in the Naval Infantry? I seriously can't believe we're dealing with this shit," Mitch said before collecting his helmet while looking outside.

"Shut up and get your weapon from the armory," Eric replied before heading off to the gate.

"Any idea what the hell is going on, Mitch? You tend to have all the trivial history knowledge," Sean asked Mitch.

"Well, our government and Russia have both refused to dismantle their nuclear weapons in case any upstart nations start causing conflict," Mitch said as they headed to the armory.

"It was to prevent another cold war like when China built artificial islands on international trade routes. But I'd put my money on them using the weapons on the Serkin fleet in orbit," Sean replied.

"If it works, the taxpayers should be happy to know they won't pay for the ten-year refit of nuclear stockpiles," Mitch said, chuckling.

"Can you blame people for distrusting the military? I mean, for shit's sake, we've avoided any major incidents like rusting aluminum ships with rail guns that melt after three rounds. Face it, rootless globalists' biggest source of funds was faulty military products," Sean replied.

"Yeah, well, I can't stand the fact people made careers on short changing us with the Mk3 Scorpion power armor used in the FedCom War. Worse, our fleet needed one thousand fucking Warrior class destroyers and only got six hundred forty-seven. Now look at us. Our planet is throwing museum pieces at the enemy," Mitch said as the pair entered the mobile armory.

"Any idea if they will work on Serkin shields?" Sean asked one final question.

"Not sure. I mean, every nuke that Russia and America have left will hit in the next ten minutes. That's a lot of firepower. Something will get through. Thanks to penny pinchers, we get to do riot control," Mitch replied, clearly pissed off by the fact he was being deployed against terrified people.

The Serkin fleet holding orbit over Western Europe moved forward as the ICBMs began detonating on the fleet. The shields withstood the first wave of atomic explosions, but as the second and final barrage of nuclear weapons hit, their shield failed, and the ships were torn apart. Hundreds of artificial stars spent off in a matter of seconds, weakened the hulls' ravaged shields. Below on the Earth's surface, the few remaining electrical grids, from France and Germany to New York City, flickered out and died under the massive EMP waves caused by the nuclear blasts.

The Serkin vessels shattered under the heat and shock waves caused by the atomic fires. Several hundred of the ships shattered into pieces as others, still functioning, fled to avoid the barrage. The five ECF warships, however, were prepared to suffer the loss of their long-range sensors as the EMPs and radiation caused their sensors to malfunction. Finally, when the last of the shock waves finally died down, the crews began working on rebooting their needed systems.

"Alight, all hands to red alert. Let's be ready for an assault. There were at least two thousand ships over Europe. Get the drones launched so we can get some eyes on those bastards," Captain Kurkov said as the interface screens used to project a view into space reactivated.

"Confirmed sir, launching recon drones and scrambling drone fighters," the flight control officer replied.

"Defensive weapons and shield are online. Shields protected us from the shockwave, but it looks like the lights are out from the western portion of the Polish-Hungarian Empire to New York City."

"LIDAR alert. We have four Type 35 carrier vessels heading our way in formation. Hold it, they are on a vector heading that will have them passing by us by a margin of a hundred kilometers," said the officer.

"At thirty-five kilometers in length, they are likely the only ships that could survive that bombardment. We should try to take them out," Colonel Mason said as he buckled into his seat.

"Get Ilic on the horn and tell him where to shoot!" Captian Kurkov shouted at the communication officer before turning to the weapons officer. "What about weapons? Can we target them?"

"Targets are moving too fast for our main gun, but the upper and lower hull-mounted particles are ready. The Snow ship-to-ship missiles are ready. All we need are targets," the weapons officer replied, typing in auto targeting commands.

"Get close enough for the turreted particle cannons to gut them. Keep our drones in reserve," Kurkov said, watching as the massive ships moved along.

"The ships are changing their vectors mid-flight," Mason reported, watching the ships' movements on the command console. "Eva, calculate their vector to see if they are heading to Nevada."

Kurkov growled. "Open fire. We'll make sure their ships can't launch another attack on a major city. Safeties off on all munitions. Make sure their damned drone swarms fly into a wall of CIWS fire. After our barrage, bring the main gun to bear on one of the other two ships."

The twin particle cannons on the upper and lower sections of the hull turned. Their barrels raised, and out came streams of super-heated ions speeding at nine tenths the speed of light into the flank of the closest kilometers long vessels. The Serkins' shields buckled for a moment, then failed. The ionized particles collided into the hulls and began to boil the alien metals, finally punching a hole from stem to stern of the Serkin vessel.

A violent decompression near the ship's fusion reactor brought the vessel's engines to a halt. The Serkin ship couldn't return fire before a salvo of Snow missiles peppered the vessel, and the explosions shattered the ship across the ship's hull as it drifted under is momentum. The ship promptly imploded as its alien power source ruptured.

The event repeated with the second ship, but not before it managed to launch a swarm of drone fighters. The Serkin drones exited their mothership, wings extended and engines firing out massive bursts of super-heated plasma. They sped forward on suicidal attack paths against the human ship's defensive fire. The drones began firing their beam weapons into the ECS Stryker's shields. Once the drone fighters expended their ammunition, they crashed into their target.

The Serkin ship fired its main weapon, a bright beam of energy, into the lead Moscow class cruiser, partially gutting the ship in an instant. The stricken vessel was the ECS Glasgow. It had moved in to support the Stryker's operation, only to be shot down. Its engines flared as it began drifting backward from the sheer force caused by the large vessel's main gun. As the three other cruisers retreated, the ESC Glasgow fired several of its missiles as a final act of defiance. Then a second enemy shot fired into the ship's mid-section that traveled toward the ship's engines. The ship's battered hull slowly drifted away as its crew and contents were sucked into the void of space.

The ECS Stryker's drone fighters engaged the Serkin's drones, destroying several groups of them, but were eventually overwhelmed. The next line of defense on the Stryker was the shielding and Close In Weapon Systems. The 30mm and 60mm CIWS systems of the Stryker fired in controlled bursts, destroying as many drones as it could before they could reach the ship's hull. Several drones were destroyed as the ammunition exploded, sending explosive sub munitions into their flight paths.

As six drones slipped through the defensive lines of the Stryker, it turned, using it's RCS to aim its bow mounted Tesla cannon at the last of the two Serkin ships. The drones hit the hull of the vessel, each exploding moments after colliding to maximize damage. The bridge crew could only watch as the external cameras provided them with a view of space before it went offline.

"I want a damage report. Did the Stryker's hull get breached? LIDAR officer, keep track of the ships and get Admiral Ilic on the horn. There is a second ship with its shields down. I want to know that it is out of commission," Captain Kurkov ordered.

"Eva reports no hull breaches. The armor plating held, but the shields are down. It may take thirty minutes to bring them back to full power. The external visual sensor suite took the brunt of the damage," one of the bridge officers replied.

"Send a wide alert message to all personnel in pressurized suits. They are to begin checking for hull breaches in the depressurized sections of the ship," Mason order.

"Admiral Ilic is reporting from the Moscow's battle group. Their sensor sweep confirmed two of the ships made it to the dig site in Nevada. We are to keep observing as the three remaining cruisers regroup at LaGrange point two. It will give us an orbital period equal to that of Earth's," the radio officer said.

Kurkov sat back in his G-force chair and sighed in slight relief. "Deploy a recon drone to keep an eye on that dig site from orbit."

"Sir, we have a message from the admiral," the communications officer said.

"Captain Kurkov, we will be relying on you to maintain and relay communications to the Russians and the Americans. There may be other powers with nuclear arms, but the Serkins are clearly moving to fortify their holding near the Nevada-California border. They sent four of their largest vessels known to mankind. Make sure that area is secure, and we need to know if and when they move," Admiral Ilic said.

"Of course, Admiral. We'll worry about the other nation states soon enough," Kurkov replied reluctantly as the ship's diagnostics began feeding into his command console.

1200 hours
O'Hare Spaceport and refugee camp

The crowd had died down as the nuclear hell fire never came. The skyline looking toward the downtown area was awash as helicopters with searchlights hovered above. Other VTOL aircraft fought the many fires burning brightly in the night sky. Many of the soldiers patrolled the area while hoping against hope nothing would happen.

Eric and Masa sat watching the scene unfold from the top of the airport parking deck. Eric couldn't see past the tinted face plate, but felt something was on his friend's mind. "Mac, you okay?" Eric asked, taking his head away from his rifle's scope.

"Tokyo is not likely going to be on the agenda anytime soon. I hope my mother made it out. I'm regretting a few words," Masa replied, looking away from the scene.

"Stay strong, this fight needs us to make sure those soft-as-shit brats who passed the test to be Strike Force Marines do their job. We can and will win this." Eric hid his doubts under a slightly gruff tone. "God only knows how bad that Davis kid will be now that he shut off the drones."

"You don't have any worries about your family? For all our years of vitriolic friendship you never once mentioned any family," Masa said, turning his attention to Eric.

"I have none beyond you and the corps. Mother and Father are dead; when Mother died, I left home never looking back. She taught me to shoot well enough to impress the Naval Infantry and many years later, here I am," Eric replied, returning to his gaze to the scope of his rifle.

"Thanks. So I heard the drones got shut down all across the tri-county area. ODIN is talking to the motor mouth right now," Masa said, crossing his arms as he returned to waiting.

"I won't miss the little bastard, we have too many kids here," Eric replied.

"We need everyone we can get in this fight. Our entire combined arms regiment suffered thirty-three percent casualties. We still have more fights ahead of us," Masa replied, watching a helicopter fly toward them.

The nearby M96 David SPAAG turret spun forward, locking onto the incoming helicopter before the crew confirmed the helicopter was not a threat and let it pass. The helicopter's bright blue star in a white box on its belly came into clear view of everyone on the upper most parking deck, making it obvious the aircraft was a life-flight helicopter.

The helicopter banked left and headed toward a vacant landing pad in the airstrip area. Sean crouched down to avoid being decapitated by the rotor blades. He rushed over to the pilot's door and opened it. "Can you tell me if Harrison Methodist Hospital is at capacity and if you picked up a woman named Jennifer Ryan or Lisa Ryan?" Sean asked with his helmet's speakers on full blast to be heard over the rotor blades.

"No way could I tell you any of that, man. We've been flying round the clock since you guys cleared the skies. We've had way too many people in this bird to remember two specific women. Now, I need fuel and I got some supplies to trade for it since my airfield got blown to hell," the pilot shouted, pointing to the back of the helicopter.

"Alright thanks, I'll have the helicopter refueled after we unload the supplies," Sean said, shutting the pilot's door.

"No luck finding your family? Didn't you reunite with your girl? I mean shit, take the good fortune you got and be happy," Nathan said, opening the cargo hatch on the helicopter to unload the supplies.

"Yeah, I guess so. What supplies did they give us in exchange for fuel?" Sean asked as he was handed a crate of supplies.

"Looks like biotex bandages and synthetic blood. It'll be good for me in the field, but the people still here could use food that only the Stryker has, and our dropships are grounded. Did you see that flicker in the sky a little while ago? Only Serkin ships have power sources strong enough to be seen from the ground," Nathan answered.

"We killed a couple of Serkin ships, so how are we cut off? That makes no sense," Sean said, carrying a box over to the nearby supply truck.

"Going to orbit is not possible if the ship is in combat. Our Hummingbirds would just be massive targets. As I said, we need to accept our blessings where and when we get them. Like come dawn, every fleet within one hundred light years will be on its way here," Nathan replied, hoping to lift the spirits of his subordinate.

"Home fleet had all Houston class battle cruisers and lost. You think we have anything to hope for?" Sean asked as flight crews began pumping fuel into the civilian helicopter.

"Earth survived a globalist-empowered China. And America survived the Chinese-owned politicians in its own senate before that. Aliens are nothing but one more trial to overcome. We did that all without any help from the colonies. Now we've got the rest of our fleet coming to show the bullet heads what happens when they ruin our world," Nathan replied, his Scottish accent reemerging.

"Thanks, I needed that," Sean said, unloading another box of supplies.

Once the helicopter was unloaded and fueled, it powered up its engine lifted off and left the area just as more aircraft returned to the area. Larger transport planes could be seen flying toward the spaceport coming in from the east. "As I said before, we have more than just the Stryker's troops on our side, Sean," Nathan said, watching the aircraft fly in.

"We have the numbers and the means to win. All we need now is the resolve sir," Sean said, wondering how Mitch was handling his interrogation.

Somewhere at the Spaceport in an unknown hangar, with barely any lighting, Mitch stood alone. He wondered in what part of the O'Hare Spaceport building he was being held since he had forgotten where he was when they grabbed him. Just as he began to remember, a cold voice asked him, "How did you understand the Serkin language on their computer and how did you hack it, Private Davis? We don't have to be this nice to you with the war raging on and all."

"I said it before. The Mk3 Scorpion power armor I wear translated the screen. I've seen their language before on Outpost Planet 432, and per IMSF regulations, I loaded it all into my suit's memory. Their language is simple in alphabetic format from my guess." Mitch tried looking at who was questioning him through the blinding lights beating down on him.

"How did you hack their computer system so well? ODIN usually hires people with that kind of skill set," the voice replied. "You have never seen any formal education in cyber security."

"My uncle. He taught me security systems and how to upload hacking programs via wireless routers. The Serkins' computer was in the middle of command operations. They didn't expect someone to use their systems to access their equipment. I even download their data and turned it over to command. That was, oh god, I don't know the time anymore." Mitch fought to move his arms, but try as hard as he might, he couldn't move them to block the blinding light that shone in his face.

"Very good soldier, your service is worthy of the Flame of Humanity medal. Turn around, walk out of the hangar and back out to the tarmac of the Spaceport. Do not look around trying to find us. It will be better for you that way," the voice said as the lights turned off.

Mitch, having just been released from interrogation with ODIN agents, walked away from the Spaceport building looking for any comrades. While unharmed, speaking to ODIN left him uneasy. Sometimes, citizens of the Federation got a visit from ODIN, even if they did nothing wrong. He looked around, trying to be invisible. No matter where he looked, no massive triangle shaped aircraft lifted off carrying the ODIN operatives away. He knew a hangar was at his back, but it looked bombed out, or at least it had when he first approached it with the ODIN officer that he couldn't describe.

Mitch knew stealth technology had advanced greatly under Right Wing scientists. They greatly valued diversity of thought. Still, Mitch wondered how far it all really went. Could ODIN be zipping around the sky in ships that violated the laws of physics beyond what even

Element 164 was known to break? He just wanted to run away, like a child seeing a horrible monster.

All he could think of were questions. Were the Office of Defense and Intelligence agents masters of the twentieth century UFO? Did they know more about E164 chemistry than the entire human race? Mitch put his helmet on. He hoped to continue blending in as he walked along toward the supply truck, figuring he could fall in with the monotonous task of moving supplies.

"Hey, Mitch, how was your time with ODIN?" Sean asked, noticing Mitch as he put his helmet on. It now lacked the crude shark teeth he'd drawn on it earlier.

"Oh, wonderful, they had a sublime Dutch Apple pie à la mode served by the finest Qualurian waitresses. The even fed it to me while in the nude. You should have been there," Mitch replied sardonically.

"No worse for wear, clearly. You're in time to see some transports fly in and maybe, just maybe, Major Robb won't demote you for disappearing while we worked," Nathan mocked Mitch.

"Actually, if we win this, I'm due for a promotion and the Defender of Humanity's Flame medal," Mitch replied smugly.

"Oh, and where are these ODIN operatives who were giving you the Earth Colonial Federation's accolades? I know E164 can create artificial gravity, but I sure as shit don't see a Red Horse class corvette taking off, so where did ODIN go? Face it, intelligence officers just wanted to ask you a few questions, and they pretended to be ODIN," Nathan replied.

"Yeah, well, they were some damn good actors. I tell you, it was ODIN. I couldn't find their flying triangle, but isn't that the whole point of a stealth ship? It not being a thing you can just easily up and find. I am going to ask this only once, sir. Can I find some shit detail work in the supply depot?" Mitch asked, trying his best not to look shaken.

"Good, you know the most important virtue of the ECF is industriousness, right? Of all eight, none of us would be here without that trait," Nathan said in a fatherly tone of voice.

"Oh, good grief, you don't need to sell me on our culture, dad," Mitch replied, giving Nathan a thumbs up.

"It's always important to remember those things or else you end up a nihilist, Mitch," Nathan replied.

"Yeah, instead of moving supply boxes with our power armor on, we could be scrubbing latrines," Sean added as he handed Mitch a crate.

0800 hours.
Dark side of the moon

Admiral Ilic watched on his LIDAR display as all the ships began arriving. First a few dozen here, then another dozen there. They were all spread out widely across the second Earth-Moon Lagrangian points where the old propellant depots from the race to Mars once drifted.

"This many signatures falling out of beam space with the solar light on us wouldn't be able to hide the immense heat caused by ships exiting beam space. It's only a matter of time before the Serkins' remaining forces mobilize," said the ship's second in command.

"Good, that way we can use nuclear weapons for a second round and not worry about damaging the old-world infrastructure. In fact, split the frigates and destroyers up into four groups of Hunter-Killers. Those wolf packs will assault the enemy's main fleet. They will attack the Serkin flanks, as their ships move to engage our battle cruisers hiding on the dark side of the moon." Ilic scrolled through the information on his command console.

The console between the central command and control officers showed a holograph of the typical Hunter-Killer packs used by the ECSF. Three destroyers flanked by five light frigates in a standing five-point star formation. The larger heavy cruisers and their massive rail guns would hide behind the moon and open fire on any Serkin ships. With their shields down, the Serkins' ships will cross directly into the cruisers' firing lines.

"The Serkins have always gone after the larger group of ships first. The ships holding position on the dark side of the moon will be their first targets. They won't deal with the smaller groups of frigates and destroyers until the main force is gone. At worst, they will soften our smaller ships with their drones. Even if our wolf packs attacked first, they will still focus on our largest ships," the second in command said.

"Our larger ships can't damage their ships when their shields are up. So our only real chance to even the odds is to destroy their shields and force them to turn to engage," Admiral Ilic said, going over the only real advantage the human ships had over the Serkins' tens of kilometers long vessels. He typed in data on the Destroyer and Frigate Tesla cannons into his console. "If our smaller ships use their beam weapons to destroy their shielding first, we stand a fighting chance. Plus, being in this position behind the moon, all our rail gun rounds that miss will aimlessly travel until they hit the sun." Ilic watched the simulation of his plan play out successfully.

"Confirmed, sending information to all available cruisers to rally behind the moon. Also rallying the smaller ships into required flotillas," said the communications officer who had been watching her two superiors.

The navigators aboard the ECS Moscow began the process of repositioning the ship into formation with the other heavy cruisers. And the larger cylindrical vessel powered up its drive engines and pushed it further from the Lagrange point.

The ships maneuvered as ordered. Lighter, three hundred and fifty meter long frigates and five hundred fifty meter long destroyers continued grouping up steadily, waiting in position. The wreckage of home fleet drifted aimlessly. Other ships belonging to the defense flotillas of other colonies and the inner patrol fleet began taking positions between Earth and the moon.

The Serkin ships began moving and the ECS Stryker was there to pick up the movement. "Well, sir, they are moving from orbit over the EU to L2 at full speed. For Serkin ships, it'll be a ninety-minute flight. Our ships can simply make micro distance jumps via beam space. No one has ever seen their ships make pinpoint jumps," Mason said as the alert systems of the bridge began sounding.

"All hands report being ready for violent decompression. I guess it's safe to assume Serkins can travel the long distances in a short period of time, but can't make pinpoint jumps. I'm sure ODIN will want to know this if we can get out of this coming battle alive. All ships in the battle group, fire Tesla cannons first. Snow missiles to follow before repositioning for a second barrage," Captain Kurkov ordered from his seat.

"This is Captain Stein of the ECS Hue. I'm moving the ship into a flanking position with the Stryker, but it looks like we have a full Serkin retreat from the planet and they are coming this way. We'll be able to kill them with our Tesla cannon," Captain Stein radioed in to the Stryker specifically as the ship fell out of beam space incredibly close to the now moving Serkin ships.

"Captain Stein, you need to fall in with flotilla three. Your ship is in the path of incoming enemy vessels, making a beeline for Nevada. You have about fifteen minutes before the first ships will be on you," Captain Kurkov said over an open channel, watching as LIDAR put the ECS Hue into a parallel path with some Serkin ships.

"Fucking hell, send the Hue a message to change their heading. That frigate only has a nose mounted Tesla cannon, a pair of 457mm rail guns, and half our SN-500 Snow missile launchers. The armor is only two meters thick while we have double that. We need to save them. Fire missiles at the Serkin ship," Colonel Mason said only to realize it was too late, as the Serkin vessel running parallel to the Hue began to change heading.

The first Serkin vessel heading toward Nevada began to decelerate and change its course. It slowed and fired a series of burst thrusts, changing its course and placing the ship's main gun directly into the path of the frigate. The missiles hit the Serkin ship's shield and exploded. The missile strike did little damage and the Serkin vessel moved in on its target.

On the Bridge of the ECS Hue, the crew noticed the approaching hostile. "Captain Stein, I am reading a massive heat buildup around the Serkin ship to our eleven o'clock high! Warp engines need another eighteen minutes to spool up. There is neither time for the Tesla cannon to move into position nor time for evasive action," one of the crew members shouted.

"Brace for impact. Emergency response teams and crews prepare for hull breach. Divert all non-essential power to the engines. Fire emergency thrusters. Get as much of the ship out of that thing's way as possible," Captain Stein shouted as the maser fired into his ship. He pressed the emergency release and fired all available Snow missiles.

The ECS Hue fired one hundred missiles from the Vertical Launch System while the hull fired its own RCS. The missiles were turned into the direction of the repositioning Serkin attack carrier. Each missile then fired its engines to full burn as it sped toward its target. The ECS Hue began an emergency evasive maneuver, firing out a massive jet of high-test peroxide, forcing as much of the ship to begin turning.

Despite the Serkins' main weapon being particle in nature, it had the properties of a hydrogen bomb blast concentrated in a beam strong enough to push its target backward after impact, regardless of mass. It traveled at near light speeds and could easily punch through a particle shield.

The Serkin ship maneuvered into a firing position and fired at the Hue, cutting through the starboard hangar and shield generators. Then, the beam then traveled toward the forward section where the main munitions were stored. The ship exploded just as the primary hull began to be cut.

The Serkins' main cannon fired into the Hue's shield for a second. It flickered moments before the front section of the ship containing the ESC Hue's Tesla cannon was severed in a single hit. While not destroyed, the ship was wounded badly, and the bridge bathed in warning lights.

Turning their main Tesla cannon in the direction of the attacking Serkin ship, the Stryker fired their emergency RCS. It pulsed red as it came to life. Firing the weapon, it sent a beam of super dense particles speeding into the Serkin ship. The beam slammed into the bow of the Serkin ship, the blast melting the armor plating away before turning the hull into slag. The ECS Stryker then fired a barrage of Snow missiles into the remaining hull of the ship, finishing it off as the other ships continued to their destination.

"This is ECS Stryker to the ECS Hue. You're welcome. Now, form up with the rest of the flotilla you were assigned to. With your damage, remain at the rear of flotilla one. You'll provide increased point defense," Captain Kurkov ordered as the destroyer continued firing into the Serkin formation.

Admiral Djordje Ilic watched his screen as the Destroyer moved in and saved the Hue on the holograph table. "Hostile ships in outer formation positions have begun their descent onto the target. They will reach the dig site near the California-Nevada border in five minutes. Remaining ships are still on course toward us; ETA seventy-eight minutes. Flotillas, those ships will be in your firing line in ten more minutes."

"Confirmed Admiral. We're in position and waiting. Aside from the ECS Hue, we are at full strength. We're keeping that ship in the rear. We have additional point defense weaponry on station," Kurkov replied, looking at the displayed clock that was hovering over the bridge's view screen.

Stein sighed as his ship was narrowly saved from being sliced in half by a hydrogen weapon. "This is the ECS Hue. Orders received. We'll maintain position and try to reactivate the starboard shielding."

"Hull breaches across all aft starboard side decks. We can't perform any maneuver higher than 2.5 G-forces and the ship's Tesla cannon is offline. We likely don't even have the power to bring the rail guns online," Colonel Ezra said, watching the remaining Serkin vessels begin their descent into Earth's orbit.

"Damn it all, if we only arrived a few minutes earlier, we could have destroyed five of their ships with our Tesla cannon. Flotilla Three will be down one ship," Stein said, thoroughly disappointed in his failed gamble.

Djordje ordered up the Hue's status on a small tactical subset on the holographic table. "Attention ECS Hue. Provide defensive cover formation to the Robert F. Stryker until further notice. Admiral Ilic out." After issuing the Hue orders, he refocused on the enemy's fleet. "Ensign Hanson, how many ships have we killed out of this armada?"

"So far, we have taken out seventy-two percent of their ships with the missile barrage, and thanks to the EMP, only those ten have reactivated their shields. For now, it seems only nine will be making it to Nevada. Unfortunately for us, we're looking at two hundred and seventy remaining Type 270 and Type 35 class ships combat vessels bearing down on us." Hanson scrolled through the LIDAR and drone reconnaissance reports.

"Sir, there looks to be a major increase in ground communications being sent to the Serkin fleet. Our EVA is currently trying to decipher classified communications from their ground troops. It's not likely to happen, though," the intelligence officer said.

"Keep trying and see if ODIN can help. I know they are operating in our AO," Ilic said, watching as his forces began forming into the ordered battle groups. The clock was ticking and his ships could only move into position so fast.

The Serkin ships began entering the first of the human ships' kill zones, and every human ship fired their main cannons early. As the Serkins ships traveled, they passed straight into the path of firing as the beams from the Tesla cannons. After firing, the human ships quickly repositioned in a coordinated group and fired a second volley of their weapons. The humans had developed this tactic over the last five years. It was the most efficient way to cause extreme damage to the massive warships as they traveled from target to target.

Barrage one hit the large Serkin ships, each shot connecting with the largest Serkin vessels humans knew them to have. The Type 270 cruisers came in at a full twenty-seven kilometers long. Highly volatile and dense particles from the Tesla cannons cut deep into the Serkins ships.

Several of the Serkin ships hit with the Tesla cannon kept going, even with the massive damage. The larger Type 270 cruisers were churning along only slowed down slightly. All the Serkin ships that were undamaged by the Human's barrage returned fire, in the form of a maser strikes, and sent out waves of drone fighters at the distant human attackers.

"All ships, fire your secondary weapons. Let your Tesla cannons recharge; we aren't Houston class battle cruisers. Then focus all fire on point defense. The Maser fire will be less likely to target us, and the drones are the real threat," Kurkov said, covertly wiping the sweat from his brow. The only thing to do now was to minimize the damage and hope to take part in a pincer move.

"Maser fire usually won't cut through our four-meter thick hide," Mason commented, hoping to calm the nerves on the bridge.

"The ECS Hue is a sitting duck to those drones; we have to protect them. Even if the Serkins don't turn in our direction, their drones will ravage our ships. They know how to fight us, just like we know how to fight them," Kurkov replied as the ship released its own drones.

The human drones clashed and did their best to stop the vast wave of assaulting enemy forces. Human ships then fired their point defense guns as overwhelmed drones remained in their defensive positions as not to be shot by the mother ships.

Several Serkin drone fighters were intercepted by the CIWS fire of the Human ships formation. The few drones that did break through only managed to damage the outer most section other hulls. The ECS Stryker had a Maser blast hit the recreation deck. The heat boiled away the armored glass and cut through the deck's, leaving it a curled mess of metals as anything not firmly secured to the structure was sucked into space.

Other ships hit suffered minimal damage. A few, like the ECS Iwo Jima, lost its portside supply hangars, with several holes having been boiled into the two-meter thick armor. The super structure was still viable, and had the decks not been depressurized, would have violently depressurized. The majority of ships in the battle group had successfully avoided the Maser fire.

Without the constrained air pressure guiding them, the drones performed flips and rolls that could only be done in the vacuum of space. Serkin drones ignored their human counterparts, doing their best to avoid the human ships' defensive fire. The ones hit by the point defense fire exploded as the fire connected.

"Hostile drones have reached defensive line Bravo. Commanders of the McCarthy and Iwo Jima request drone recall for support from line Delta to Alpha," the communications officer said.

"Negative, the drone fighters will remain where they are. In the next minute and a half, we fire all physical counter measures. The Serkin ships are just out of range. We only need to hold a little longer," Kurkov said as the explosions filled the bridge's view screen.

"Another wave of drone fighters will enter the last kilometer of Alpha zone in sixty seconds," the LIDAR officer shouted.

The few hundred drones remaining sped into the fleet. Some spiraled out of control into the hulls of the human ships. Drones slammed into the hulls of many ships, grouping up on targets, aiming to cause as much damage to the Serkin ships' mission-critical systems. The crew of the ECS Stryker watched as a squadron worth of drones collide with the hull of their ship, damaging the bow particle cannon. After being hit, the turret exploded, shaking the ship.

"Alright, tell the ECS Moscow the ships are outside our range and we lost no ships. All vessels. Respond with damage reports. Any ship with a combat readiness of eighty percent or above, move into the second wave and perform the second wave attack," Captain Kurkov said as his damage reports began appearing.

"Sir, we have an alert from the ECS Moscow. It seems the Serkins are not turning to engage the main force. Their course heading is toward the galactic core; they are leaving the Sol system," the communications officer said. Her voice full of relief as the damage alert sirens still rang.

"Very well. All ships at eighty percent combat operational status, begin supporting the main fleet's harassment operations. They can run, but we have to reduce the number of ships leaving at all costs," Captain Kurkov said, knowing he would need permission to pursue. "Send the request to the admiral."

"Request has already been denied. We are to move our forces to provide orbital fire support over the Nevada desert. Admiral Ilic said he won't split his forces up and run the risk of being locked in an enemy pincer maneuver," the communications officer responded.

"He's right. We can't overextend the limited number of ships we have," Colonel Mason replied.

"Very true. Get into contact with your ground elements and have all other ships ready to drop their brigade combat teams," Captain Kurkov said, unbuckling his restraints.

July 10, 2131, 0130 hours

"Alright, place the added utensils near the bar in such a manner so when the remaining civilians come in, they can eat their food like civilized beings," Nathan said, supervising the group who were tasked with setting up a dining area for the remaining people.

"Attention all troops and support personnel cleared for service. Report to commanding officers at dropship Titan. If your commanding officer is dead, report to reassignment at dropship Belmont by 0200 hours," an announcement rang over the intercom system of the spaceport.

Mitch sighed in disappointment; he'd finally just made his way to the nearest bar to escape the conflagration. He'd hoped to sneak some liquor in while moving supplies. Now he had to leave the building without so much as sneaking a drop. "God damn it, I was so close to that bottle of vodka, then the school bell rings!"

"Shut up, you stupid fuck! First you whined about supply duty, now you whine about combat! You know what? Consider it a standing order to shut the hell up," Gabe shouted at Mitch.

"Alright, you heard the DJ people. Fall in line. All of you are combat effective. Report to the quartermaster and then to dropship Titan for assignment. Move your asses, leave is canceled. Hustle, damn you," Nathan said, smacking his hands together to speed his soldiers along.

The supply trucks and quartermasters at dropship Titan began the process of collecting their equipment and rearming the men. As the soldiers waited in line, many began double checking their gear, then securing their helmets. "Firearms first, ammunition second! Six magazines per soldier," a sergeant shouted as the weapons were passed out. Outfitted, the soldiers who were fully equipped promptly moved on to their commanding officers.

The Strike Force Marines were across the way when handed their rifles. Technicians double checked their armor connection points before issuing them their magazines and releasing their suit's jet packs from their charging ports.

"Alright, report to Major Robb once your outfitting is complete at LZ Bravo and don't waste storage space on food. Bring extra power packs for your M68 rifles. Adjust your suit's temperature control systems for desert combat," Nathan shouted as everyone collected their gear.

"LZ Bravo. That is where all those heavy birds the Army and Air Force gave us are parked," Gabe said. He changed his suit temperature and adjusted the camouflage pattern to a dark yellow broken up by several shades of brown, then secured his helmet. "LZ Bravo is where the CH85 Kodiaks are parked. I hope we won't be sharing a ride with the tanks."

"At least we aren't going to endure the heat of the desert like the Naval Infantry sods," Eric said, collecting a supply belt with sniper rifle magazines.

"This is Major Robb of the Strike Force Marines. Kodiak 6-2 is our ride. Report as soon as you are equipped for combat." Major Robb's voice rang over the unit's comlink.

The group of soldiers hurried into the back of the CH85 where each unit's commanding officer waited. Supplies and vehicles filled the large transport helicopters to the brim. Major Robb stood waiting at the tail ramp of the VTOL's large cargo space as its transverse rotors began cycling. Soldiers piled into the back and took seats along the walls. The CH85 Kodiak could lift just about anything; the interior held a M9 Lee, an Ibex, and countless supply crates.

"This beast normally has space for one hundred and forty soldiers, but we still don't have decent seats," Gabe complained as he stepped over a few crates and sat down. "What the hell are you looking at Ryan?" Gabe asked, looking at Sean.

"You are literally whining that thirty-five of us are now sharing space with combat vehicles. Pity no one issued your short ass the orders to remain silent," Sean said, sitting down across from Gabe.

"Alright ladies, stop the gossip and listen up. We are moving to a staging area in Nevada south of Warm Spring and west of Rachael. The Serkin ships have set up a wide kill zone around the badlands. Our destination is the north side of the Kawich peak. Our estimated arrival time is 0450hours, so get some rest. There is some good news. The bullet heads got their asses handed to them in orbit," Major Robb said before heading into the forward section of the aircraft with the other officers.

"Hey, Sean, you're an American Earther. What the hell is in Nevada that's so special? Isn't Area 51 in the other direction or something?" Mathew asked Sean, who was sitting next to him.

"Not sure Mute, there're a lot of old airbases out there that kind of lost their mystery when we found out about Qualurians. Area 51 is out there, as is the Dugway Proving grounds. I'm not so well read on history regarding aliens," Sean replied as turbulence rocked the helicopter.

"Well, there was a Yaren Memory Core found in Arizona. Maybe they know where more of them are buried. Our technology levels in the 2070s jumped almost a century when we uncovered the first memory core and repaired it. If someone has a fully functioning unit and uses it in the private sector, they could make themselves into the next Nikola Tesla," Masa commented.

"If a Yaren memory core is in the desert and intact, the bullet heads could make an even greater leap forward in technology. As if the Serkins' technology edge now isn't bad enough. One more blow to the might of human ingenuity," Gabe said, leaning back in his seat.

"It means that if we do kick these assholes off this rock, we could end up having the tech to turn the war in our favor," Sean added, hoping to keep morale high. Even after saving Chicago, the fear of a looming defeat still lingered in everyone's minds.

"For the moment, I suggest you rest your minds. If not for the sake of needing it, then do it so I can be spared your speculations," Gabe moaned, the unending talk of hope and changing tides tiring him.

"Oh, forgive me, princess, for having some hope," Sean snapped at Gabe. He wanted to stand up and clock the registered nihilist, but turbulence kept him seated.

"Fat load of good it's done anyone thus far kid. Seriously, grow up and stop pissing away time on something so obviously pointless," Gabe snapped back.

Before the situation could escalate, the officers returned from the forward section. "I hope you ladies enjoyed your fucking gossip. We'll be air dropping in and using Kawich Peak as cover near the dig site, as it's the only place that provides any sort of cover. We'll be dropping in without the Naval Infantry support for several hours, if they arrive at all," Lt. Carver shouted as he walked down the aisle to break up the conversation.

"The lack of support is due to the damage caused by Communist incursions from the Californian border wall having sections being taken down. The environmental mismanagement means a lot of muck high in the atmosphere over California, so don't drink the rainwater. I don't care if you have toxin filters. There's no need for extra risks. Corporal Ryan and Corporal Cortez, come with me," Major Robb said, ordering them into the forward section of the helicopter's hull.

Sean and Gabe stood up and marched into the section of the aircraft that was slightly insulated from the vibration of the two massive transversely mounted rotors. Major Robb took his helmet off. Even in the low level light at this close range, his synthetic skin patches contrasted with his dark brown skin. Raising his right hand, he rolled it, gesturing for the two men to hurry and take off their helmets as he closed the door behind him.

"What have I told you, Cortez, over and over again? Is there some failure in your flight control cybernetics that is affecting your memory?" Major Robb asked, pinching the bridge of his nose.

"Sir, you've told me to keep my nihilist bullshit to myself before, during and after all operations," Gabe responded, placing his helmet under his right arm.

Major Robb was tempted to punch Gabe in the face. "I've had it with your bullshit. Now get out of my sight and speak only when spoken to. Thank whatever pissant philosopher replaced your god I don't beat you," Major Robb said, shaking his fist as Gabe left.

Sean broke the silence. "What about me, sir?"

"Of all the eighteen-year-olds who passed the physical tests and survived the surgeries, I always thought you had the most promise. Your bother Derek, for all his skill and tenacity, lacked the calm professionalism you have, well had, clearly. If that little shit can get to you after a day like this, I think I sent the wrong brother to die at Outpost 89. Get out of my sight, rich kid," Major Robb spat as the flight chief exited the cockpit.

"Oh, Major Robb. The Arizona and Texas Air National Guard units are scrambling. We'll have air support all the way to the LZ in Rachel, Nevada," the flight chief said.

"Rachel, Nevada? My troops need to be dropped over Kawich Peak. NORAD said we'd be landing within their ship's perimeter to set up defense positions. You realize we don't have enough transport or time to use the freeways, right?" Major Robb shouted.

"I'm sorry, sir. But even with an escort, this bird would be too easy a target to even approach the peak. Several Serkin ships are even now descending to the dig site as we speak. I'm sure the Nevada National Guard will have the latest combat vehicles in use and waiting for you. They are on the border with California—one of the last refuges of Communism on the planet; the Nevada National Guard knows how to fight," the flight chief responded.

"How about you guys fly us to the Kawich Peak's eastern edge and we get out there with the ATGMs," Major Robb began bartering.

"Okay, so long as their ships don't happen to be floating anywhere near that plateau," the flight chief said, reluctantly capitulating.

July 10, 0450 hours
Outside Rachel, Nevada

The CH85 Kodiak came in low, passing over the desert city. Roads below were packed as countless residents all fled north and east. The helicopter's occupants could see the cars' headlights illuminating the entire roadway. There were only a few flashing red and blue lights of emergency vehicles setting off the pattern. The pilots looked down as they banked the aircraft

Coming in low for a landing at the easternmost edge of the plateau, the VTOL rotated in position, hovering just above the ground. The pilots steadied the aircraft well enough for the Strike Force Marines in the back to make a running jump out the aircraft.

"That's it. Go, go, go. We aren't sticking around for long people," the pilot said over the aircraft's speaker system.

Once the last of the Marines were out of the craft, the flight engineers began handing the supplies to the Marines. The crew and Marines hurriedly offloaded while the pilot occasionally lifted upward, scattering additional dust around.

"Alright, that's enough. You're free to go," Major Robb said, releasing the pilot from their deal.

Eventually the nose of the rotors and the dust they kicked up went away. As the dust settled, the Marines ducked low to the ground—Serkin vessels could be seen in the distance despite the dark. Eric ventured forward, squatting down, but not hugging the ground like everyone else.

"What the hell are you doing, man? Last I checked, we weren't trying to see who dies first," Masa said, scolding Eric.

"Oh, please. I bet you ran all the way here. Besides, I know you'll die first. I'm the better shot. You got the long-range view finder?" Eric snapped back as he set down his equipment and rifle.

Masa took a range finder out and attached it to his helmet. "*Fakku*, how do you tolerate this crap on your helmet?" Masa asked, looking at Eric as he went prone to the ground. The attachment scanned Eric and displayed his IFF, and Masa shifted his gaze out into the desert where the Serkin ships and the Overlords were digging.

Eric flipped his sniper attachment up. "Well, it may help to keep the thing flipped up and out of the way when not in use. Now tell me what you see. My zoom tops out at one thousand meters and there seems to be a large dust cloud forming at the feet of those giant walkers."

Masa looked up at the sky, directly at the Serkin warships; the range finder told him they were two kilometers out. The Overlords seen digging when the ECS Stryker first arrived had entirely ceased their excavation operations. They had taken up a defensive perimeter, and their large legs moved like a crab's or arthropod's, marching them forward. Still, there was no way such beasts could cause dust clouds big enough to obscure the ground. Masa had to switch views on his long-range scanner. "Let's see if the passive radar shows what the hell is causing that storm."

Eric adjusted his scope, looking for the cause of the dust storm. "Careful, we don't want to draw attention. Maybe try long-range thermals?"

Masa cycled through his range finder's scanning options while the thermal imaging gathered data. He vaguely made out large clusters of heat signatures lined out in the vertical stacks that bent downwards and out. It was a perfect match for the Serkin Chiroptera dropship. "Bingo. They're packing something up to flee. It has to be big. There are at least six of their dropships loading up right now."

Major Robb sat looking out at the western sky. It was easy to see the Serkin ships looming over his head. "Mac, the clouds of dust still prevents us from seeing anything in greater detail. I do recognize the

Chiroptera dropship, however. Can you see anything more than a few transports with their engines running?"

Masa let out a sigh and tried again—this time with sonic view. He was very far away, so there was no way to collect a specific image of anything. "Sir, all I'm getting is a unique set of thumps. It's clearly different from the Overlords' signatures."

Mathew spoke up—the thumping was a haunting reminder from when Vieira was overwhelmed by the hordes of drones. He ceased digging his foxhole. "Major, that is a gaggle of Guardian drones marching. I remember it from the time those drones overwhelmed my unit on Vieira."

"Are you sure?" Major Robb asked, his reply to Masa coming through immediately. "Mac, I need you to find out if those sounds are coming or going."

Masa watched the clouds a bit longer. "I'd say leaving. The dust clouds aren't spreading outward."

Major Robb fed the data straight to command as he could easily see some of the forces approaching from the east. "Command, we have hostiles in full retreat. Requesting more information on our coming attack. I'll switch you over to the unit now."

"This is General Stone. We have orders not to engage as local high value facilities could be in the crossfire. This stand-down order comes directly from command. You are all to maintain a defensive position until further notice. These new orders are from ODIN. Hold position and only engage when engaged."

The Marines managed to dig in and were in the process of setting up the ATGM launchers. But there was much confusion among them with the rumor mill going. Several of the marines began talking to each other.

"If we don't attack, these assets will get away," Eric complained.

"What is ODIN thinking?" a marine shouted in anger. "We'll get shafted by these bastards later if we let them go. Where the hell is our fleet?"

"Hell yeah, Americans are supposed to be insane gun-ho killers!" Gabe added.

Mitch looked at the missile launcher with its Command Launch Unit. It was a 140mm diameter unit with the ability to hit a target out to the range of five kilometers, and could cut through eighty centimeters of Chobham armor. The Command Launch Unit, the tripod, and the missile were hefty and weighed in at twenty-seven kilograms. Only the power armor he wore made it less cumbersome to wield. The targeting system allowed its user to find any target via thermal imaging that could see into the UV range. Mitch could fire and then forget about the missile, or fire it and observe until it reached the target.

Mitch gave the CLU a loving pat and looked at Gabriel. "It's okay, pig, you did good. Can you believe these guys are all hopped up on Sidonian action films?"

"This pea shooter wouldn't scratch the paint on an Overlord. I don't know what's worse. Letting them go after flying more than two hours, or the fact we actually think this defensive line will work." Gabe stood up out of the small fox hole they'd dug into the sand.

Sean wanted to walk over and punch Gabe out cold. He wanted to fire every single missile he had in the Serkins' direction. But nothing was going as planned, and he slumped down into the hole. He took his helmet off and jumped up to the top plateau with his jump-jets, rules be damned.

Looking down, he could see lights illuminating several rows of M10 tanks. Their support vehicles were moving into formation in preparation for their assault on the Serkin position. Several helicopters and gunships were lined up, being prepared for anti-armor warfare. Nathan noticed Sean's broken spirit. "Don't think too much about standing down. Those assets would be too easy a target in the open desert for those Overlord walkers."

Sean spat over the edge. *I wonder how much this inaction will cost us in the end.*

Adothur, the sole Serkin commander, began issuing orders to the remaining ships. They were to regroup and retreat while his crew maneuvered their ship into Earth's orbit. "This is acting Lord Adothur to all forces. Disengage and prepare for a retreat. By order of late Prime Izha, we are retreating. Make your way toward the planet's satellite. We will exit the system with as much war material as we can. Destroy anything we can't easily take."

The Serkin ground forces followed their new commander's orders to the letter and began destroying most of their equipment; everything the humans could possibly use against them, they destroyed.

As the Serkin ships left Earth orbit and retreated, they managed to avoid the wrath of the human forces in space. The humans were too busy finishing off the ship's drone swarms.

Lord Adothur wondered what his fate would be upon returning to Serkin space, as this invasion's failure would need to be blamed on someone. Worse, he was the one who'd ordered the retreat, not Prime Izha, and he issued the order without central command approving his orders first.

His fleet lord was dead, and he had no idea how many others of his kind died attacking Earth. He watched the humans watching him prepare to flee. "Lord T'pla, our Overlords are now boarding."

Adothur stood in front of the large holographic display of the Earth. With a wave of his hand, he changed the planet display to that of Saris. "Time to go home. All ships, vector home granted, by my authority. However, before we do, these walls the humans have west of us will be destroyed by our hands. They won this day, but their greatest monuments will be ruined."

The Serkin ships evacuated the last of their equipment and troops. Spinning westward, the ships fled into the sky. But as the Serkin ships fled, each released a massive barrage of suicide drones, and Maser fire bombarded the California-American border wall.

The attack, while in the distance, could be seen on the horizon as the lights from the Serkins' warship weapons flashed. At one stage, there were so many flashes on the horizon; it looked like the sun had risen on the wrong side of the Earth. Those flashes made it clear to the troops who had stood down that their enemy had left even more ruined infrastructure while they stood down.

"On the plus side, the Californians' communists should provide us easy targets once those freaks realize they can cross the border." Gabe sighed after removing his helmet. "It'll be nice to feel unstoppable when I'm suited up. God damn these Serkins and all their drones. Even in power armor, they can make you feel helpless.

"Knowing those Californian weirdoes, they'll use those holes in the wall to rape and pillage when humans should be uniting to fight against our extinction. Instead, those selfish pricks just want us to give them a comfortable life and do as they say." Mitch's words radiated hatred, and his fists clenched. He knew the type of people who lived on the other side of that wall. Lazy, vain, and constantly looking for a new high horse to ride in upon, just like his aunt. He was grateful that the slave his aunt had purchased, who also looked after him, had fled to freedom with him at her side.

"Calm down, dude. They've done nothing and can do nothing, hell those freaks wouldn't even be good as living shields against Serkins. At best, they have a few poorly functional electric trucks that are older than the Free States of America," Sean said, noticing Mitch firing up like never before.

When Sean placed his hand on Mitch's shoulder, he reacted with anger. Nathan moved to prevent the brewing fight. "Look on the bright side. If they attack, we get to curb-stomp them if and when they try to reclaim their stolen land, or whatever BS talking point they have. We will show them the superiority that allowed us to take their land from them in the first place. They are cowardly pricks who only care about themselves. Hell, it will be nice to fight such a weak-willed and easily conquered foe."

"Hell yeah! Shoot them all in back as they flee with shit in their pants!" Mitch took a step back, knowing it was best not to humanize such a long-standing and aggressive enemy, even if they weren't very effective. He promptly put his helmet back on as he waited for orders.

July 17, 2131, ECS Moscow, Earth Orbit

The Earth's orbit, once covered by a fleet of defense and communication satellites, was now cluttered with burned hulks of both Human and Serkin ships. It was a somber view, like watching refuse and other unwanted filth wash ashore on a pristine beach. Looking it over from a viewscreen, the crew of the ECS Moscow went about their work. They were repairing the planet's communication grid, and maintaining their watch over the planet.

Some ships that were beyond repair were picked clean by civilian scavenging crews. Anything contaminated by radiation, drones would collect instead. The public scavenging process of destroyed human ships meant that the government could focus their efforts on repairing the existing military ships and satellites. Only the Serkin vessels were off limits to all. The exception was military engineers, who searched every Serkin ship still intact for new technologies and information.

The bridge crew of the ECS Moscow was tasked with keeping a watchful eye over all the workers along the patrol route it was given. The crew sat buckled into their seats as the ship drifted along their set patrol route. There was only enough gravity to keep their coffee in their thermal mugs as the steam filled the air of the bridge. It was silent except for any communications dedicated to traffic control.

"Admiral Ilic, sir. The last of the officers for the conference have reported in and are now waiting for you," the communications officer reported, taking a sip of her coffee.

"Captain Presley, ship command is yours from here on out. ODIN summoned me for a meeting. Keep watch over the aid ships and communication calls between nations." Djordje stood, looking at the flash drive in his upper left breast pocket—a top-secret direct link to an ODIN device meant to access a private communications network.

He went to the hallway and descended to the level just below the bridge via a small stairwell before coming up on a pair of Strike Force Marines. The pair was rather intimidating, even though he stood two meters tall. It was unnerving; he couldn't look either in the eye. All he saw were the blank visors of their helmets. One Marine on the right broke the silence. "You may enter Admiral. The others are waiting for you." The Marine on the left of the door remained unmoving and silent as the door opened.

"Thank you, Marine," Djordje said, entering the room. It had a large oak conference table that seemed entirely out of place to him aboard a military ship. The table was flanked by a few ODIN and Navy officers. However, the officers were not wearing their gray and gold dress uniforms. Instead, each was dressed in their on-duty uniforms that, in a bind, could be mated to a small helmet and give them some protection against the loss of air inside a ship.

"Good day officers of our victorious fleet. I welcome you to our ad hoc Strategic Defense Conference," Djordje said, chuckling slightly. He noticed the ODIN agent at the end of the table sitting slightly off to the side of a video screen at the end of the table.

The other officers, some younger and some his own age, were hardly pleased by his sardonic take on their victory. "Either way, we won. Is that what you mean, Admiral Ilic? If I may, they sent two thousand five hundred ships from their best fleets. We lost the Home Fleet, and ten of the one hundred ships we lost were Houston class battle cruisers. Those were our most heavily armed and advanced ships! Let's not even start on the loss of the Earth defense grid," Colonel Mason interrupted as Djordje began fidgeting with the door.

Djordje finished with his handy work, having removed the control panel and jamming his lucky antique quarter into the control device of the door. He succeeded in causing a temporary shutdown of the doors' electronic opening mechanism. "There, ladies and gentleman of the

Earth Colonial Space Forces, the room is now locked down. The only way in is if a person with a plasma torch or hydraulic claw comes to the door open."

"May I ask what securing the door by temporarily damaging it is good for, Admiral?" Agent Miller of ODIN questioned the admiral before he could take a seat at the table.

"I used an antique currency to break a twenty-second century lock. What I am getting at is, had our force used those antiquated nuclear bombs on the Serkin fleet sooner, things may have played out differently. I am not going to sing the praises of the propaganda, calling this an overwhelming victory. The point of our meeting is to come up with some way to turn the tide of this war by thinking outside the damn box," Djordje said, sighing as he sat down.

The ODIN operative conceded. "Well, since everyone is here, Fleet Admiral Ilic and Secretary of Treasury Ryan will represent the Earth Colonial government. Currently, the Federation's military has captured three Serkin officers. The United States Navy is under orders to raise a Serkin cruiser from the Gulf of Mexico, where it crashed. As of this time, we at ODIN are sitting on one of the biggest tactical advancements of the war. We have captured several Serkin computer terminals containing navigational data. Specifically, we know their home world's location and several of their outer colonies," Miller spoke confidently to the group.

"The Treasury department is all that remains of the civilian government, which is currently over seeing military affairs. That does, of course, still beg the question of why exactly she is here," Djordje said, interrupting and pointing to the image of the woman on the screen.

"The Senate is here because we are the ones to decide if this war's prisoners can be used to negotiate a truce. Otherwise, we must dissect them to gather information about how to more effectively kill them," Lisa Ryan answered the admiral from her bunker on Earth. "However, I won't be naïve. We've lost six worlds and ten million lives across them. As the now acting Prime Minister, above all else, I want to hit the Serkins back," Lisa Ryan continued.

"We know where to hit them and can begin a counterattack,"

Captain Kurkov interjected, already having gone over much of the data. "How many ships did they lose to us in this battle, Admiral Ilic?"

"The invasion force consisted of three thousand ships; the home fleet had one hundred capital ships, one thousand defense satellites, and five space stations. Second Fleet's losses were seventeen ships with many more limping to dry dock. They should be salvageable. May I suggest we start producing more Houston class cruisers? A victory like this is monumental, but it won't happen again. The Serkins' shields and armor are ineffective against Charge Particle Beam weaponry and Tesla cannons. If we want to go on the offensive, we need to gear up for one," Djordje stated.

"Indeed, much of the Serkin's first wave was decimated by the Houston class ships but build time for one is a year. We will need something big, certainly, but right now we have to make the enemy truly falter without grandiose displays of power. Thankfully, several key pieces of enemy technology fell into ODIN's hands in Chicago," Miller said, handing out several sheets of paper as he circled the table.

Colonel Ezra and Captain Stein each looked over the report listing things captured and a full-scale report on the Serkin military personnel. Looking over the enemy leaders named, Ezra began putting an idea together. "Excuse me, but do we have a list of the enemy commanders and access to their communication networks?"

Miller nodded as he inserted his flash drive into the computer terminal. "Yes, currently we have a small-scale algorithm keeping passive watch on them. We are copying information on any locations mentioned. It's hard right now, as full translations have been slow going. Serkin speech uses complex arrangements of consonants to make simple sounding consonants."

"Can we then track their leaders' location, or at least where their leaders will be going? If so, we have an opportunity set before us like no other that may not require large fleets." Ezra's ears and tail perked up ever so slightly when she noticed several dossiers coming up in the margins of the central screen's presentation.

"Well, yes, but right now we are simply trying to learn as much of their language as possible. Basic words and structures are down pat.

The pronunciation is the problem. Currently, we have access to their fleet doctrines and ship data," Miller continued, attempting to steer the conversation away from whatever Ezra was thinking.

Lisa Ryan looked at the display screen in the minister's bunker as an ODIN agent gave her the same presentation. "Agent Miller, Admiral Ilic has been fighting the Serkins for the past five years, only managing to contain the war to the Perseus arm. Today is all the proof the people need to realize we haven't been taking this war seriously. I'd like to hear this idea presented by the Qualurian Colonel."

"Thank you, acting prime minister. I was thinking if we know who is in command, we can deploy troops in a less direct-action way. Perhaps we can begin specifically killing enemy officers, hindering any strategic efforts they make against us from here on out." Ezra knew this idea was going to be picked apart quickly. Humans had a lukewarm relationship with the Old Clans, and she didn't blame them either.

"We need to get our most elite forces behind enemy lines and have them randomly hit enemy leaders. It's a novel idea, but Strike Force Marine Black Operation forces are incredibly expensive, and the ships required are even rarer still," Captain Stein interrupted, shocking Ezra.

"Well, we don't need to use IMSF Black Ops units per se. I don't think we're going to win this by blindly throwing our resources into building more ships," Ezra continued as she looked through the findings. "It's obvious a brute force approach won't work."

"Agreed. We should think outside the box," Lisa chimed in.

"Thank you, Minister. The report's abstract states we now know their military leaders by name and face. These are their admirals and generals. We will deploy some assets to take these targets down, but we won't use our tier one forces." Ezra began flipping through the papers. "We train several veteran troops well enough to give them a decent chance to win. But at the same time, we don't spend too many resources. If they fail, we won't lose our most valuable resources."

"The Serkin military is highly dependent on centralized command structures. Cutting the heads off their command usually nullifies their technological advantages. It's rare to see, but we've done it before,"

Colonel Mason responded as he began looking over the named Serkin commanders.

Lisa took a drink of her coffee, asking, "How big is our window to perform a head hunting operation against the Serkin leaders?"

"This kind of operation would require communication observation on a massive scale. This is far more than ODIN simply shadowing the Serkin fleet. If you would all move onto the third page, you will find what we know about the Serkin fleet," Miller commanded as a small hologram came up on the screen.

The display gave a quick flash of the Ryan Aerospace Enterprise logo of an angled fighter jet wing to the left of the words before filtering into a display of Serkin warship, all the generic Type 27 model line. The holographic display showed all twenty recorded ships with a few visually different features accompanied by different lengths.

"These are the workhorses of the Serkin fleet, all identifiable by the large Maser cannon mounted between the mandible housing on the front. The carrier variant uses long spines along the side to catch and retrieve drones as well as manned aircraft. Commonly, the length varies on all types. So far, our actions against them have killed over three thousand enemy vessels of varying sizes."

"Yes, many of us know this. We also know the ECF Space Forces only had a meager three thousand ships at the start of this war. The Serkins were able to send three thousand ships alone to attack Earth. We managed to destroy the first five hundred ships," Admiral Ilic interrupted.

"Well, the good news is the recent use of Old World nuclear weapons. It has shown their forces are prone to catastrophic malfunctions when hit with gamma radiation waves. Specifically, their systems shut down in ways that go beyond a simple EMP," Miller said, explaining a diagram.

"All well and good, but the nuclear weapons we used were built over the course of a century. Are their fleet numbers at least now even with our numbers?" Captain Kurkov asked.

"Nowhere even close. From the current dives into their system, we believe that a quarter of their fleet was deployed for this attack," Miller corrected the captain.

"Meaning our entire navy is a mere fraction of a single fleet. As of now, they have three times our ships. We seriously have to consider alternatives to throwing ships at this problem," Ezra spoke up once more.

"Well, I am the finance minister and highest ranking government official left. We worried about the consequences of a blank check mentality on military spending. Look what it got us. What would ODIN need to track enemy forces and locate their leadership?"

"We would need to have a force for this operation. It wouldn't be cheap, but it would be cheaper than a fleet of ships. The troops we pick would need the right mindset for the mission profile. It will be a team of suicide soldiers deploying to when and wherever our enemy's commanders gather. I think our best bet is to buy time," Miller said, conceding to Ezra's suggestion.

"Very well, Colonel. Ezra Adara, you are in charge of gathering the soldiers. You will be given access to the entire roster of Strike Force Marines. I will be addressing the public in seven hours. I will do what I can to sell the battle as a win without mentioning the specific gains we made in case the Serkins are watching our public communications. Shamefully, I think playing a lame duck will aid our war effort. None of you will discuss any details involving this Fire-and-Forget force," Lisa ordered before signing off.

"We should have a significant amount of time before the next meeting. Even if their ships can travel further than ours in less time, their command center is in the Perseus Arm of the galaxy. However, rest assured, ODIN will provide every algorithm and search base to form this team," Miller commented.

"So, the politician is going to sell the most surface level win to the public as we come up with a full-on Black Operations Force. I find this acceptable. I hope you like coffee and sleepless nights, Colonel Adara; we'll need that unit formed ASAP," Ilic said, moving the meeting right along.

0730 hours
Nevada Desert Staging Area

As the sun rose, the air quickly became too thin for fully loaded aircraft to keep flying, as such, they soon began making their way to nearby landing zones. The ground was active as M11 Ibexes and M9 Lees lead convoys of trucks around the ever growing Forward Operating Base. Several Hornet dropships flew overhead with fighter escorts as the hole dug by the Serkins was blocked off. Leaving for parts unknown with lord only knows what in the dropship's bellies.

All this mattered little to Eric as he threw a card from his hand on the ground. He took a long hit from Masa's vaping device and asked, "So, Mac, when do you think we'll be told who's in command of the government?"

"Not sure. But we've been here a week, watching over construction equipment for the wall and occasionally running patrol ops. We can't be without command from the civilian government. They must have issued orders for wall repair," Masa speculated, deciding what card to throw on the ground.

"I'll be glad when we can get some leave. I want to go home, but it's all made worse by our no contact orders," Masa complained.

"It'll only get worse in the coming days. We'll be lucky to get any more down time. Do you know how many missions that guy Mitch has been on with us?" Eric asked, remembering something as he threw down a card.

"Oh, fuck Mitch the Bitch as you call him, he just lasted fifteen

191

drops," Masa said, throwing down all his cards. "How much do I owe you now?"

"A hundred sovereigns now and another hundred when or if Mitch makes it to twenty drops. Although I'm not shocked you forgot the odds were totally in your favor. He's so weak, all he can do is run his mouth with complaints," Eric said, leaning down and picking up the cards as he leveled his own complaints about the younger Marine.

"Yeah, he's such a bitch, but you turn into one when he's mentioned. Let's go to one of the mess halls. Today's heat is going to be well above fifty-five degrees centigrade before noon," Masa said.

"ATTENTION ALL INTERSTELLAR MARINE STRIKE FORCE PERSONNEL AND NAVAL INFANTRY WITH RELATIVES AND IMMEDIATE FAMILIES IN THE FREE STATES OF AMERICA. PLEASE REPORT FOR A DEBREIFING AT 0800 HOURS IN THE BRIEFING CENTER. THOSE WITH FAMILY ON EARTH PLEASE REPORT AS WELL FOR DOCUMENTATION FOR LEAVE." the base intercom announced.

Mitch climbed out of his cot; he was unable to sleep. He had nothing to say to his family, but he certainly wanted to get drunk and eat food not made from meat stored in a cryogenic storage locker for years. "Hey, Nathan, wake up, man. You said you wanted to see your kid, right? You need to file paperwork," Mitch said, giving the medic a few kicks as he slept in his cot.

"Bloody hell, how many hours has it been?" Nathan sat up slowly, bringing himself to stand.

"Not sure. Mac and Eric left about an hour ago for a bit of vaping. Sean took off for god only knows," Mitch replied as he stretched in his muscle suit.

"I guess his sweetheart being out there and alive is troubling the lad," Nathan responded.

The briefing center was barely in use when the few Marines entered. The air conditioner was working, so it was at a decent temperature to be sitting around in and listen to a briefing telling everyone to keep their mouths shut. Everyone having been on Earth filed into the room and took a seat at one of the tables. Mitch, Sean, Nathan, Eric, and Masa were joined by a few other Marines they didn't recognize.

"Greeting, as you all know, you've come across some clearly questionable sights, and you may or may not be aware this base is near a questionable dig site. You're all aware that this is to be kept silent. You will not, under any circumstance, discuss this with anyone, friends and family included. If you do discuss this with others there is a colony named Waygone waiting for you and those you compromise this information. Do you have any questions?" the officer asked the quietly sitting group.

"We were told that we could file our paperwork here if we had family on Earth," Nathan said to the officer as while he looked around for any paperwork. Nathan had kept so much secret this far into his career, one more to the pile hardly mattered.

"Of course, please give us your home nation and we'll find you a transport home. For those of you who are here in the states, we have a convoy heading into Rachel, Nevada. You will have a week-long liberty pass before having to report in with your local military garrison via phone call," the officer continued. "When reporting in, you may be given an additional week's leave or receive orders at which base to report to. The convoy will leave in half an hour, so get out of you muscle suits."

The Americans all stood up and left the building, reporting to the logistical center and removing their muscles suits in exchange for utility uniforms. For many, this was the first time being entirely out of the Scorpion power suit since first putting it on at the start of the war.

To Sean, the feel of cotton-based fabric felt alien against his skin, as he no longer had a layer of second skin armor. His skin could breathe again. "Alright kid, here is your bank card. It has all the back logged pay from the last two years on it, with taxes deducted, of course," the quartermaster informed him.

Mitch slowly adjusted since he now weighed much less than before, yet without the muscle suit, his motions felt slower. He did his best to put it into the back of his mind as more important things came to mind. "Woo, beer and pizza, here I come," Mitch announced as he collected his ID and bank cards.

"Why aren't you off to see your family? Don't you have some in New York City?" Sean questioned Mitch as everyone made their way to the transport.

"Yeah, but I have no reason to go see them," Mitch said, noticing the transport. "God damn it all to hell! We have to ride in the back of a civilian truck."

"Well, at least we will be in Rachel before noon. The temperatures may have dropped globally, but thirty-five degrees centigrade is still hot." Sean climbed in right behind Mitch and the other few Marines.

A panel of wood fitted to the bed of the truck served as a bench for the group, and it was clear the vehicle was used in ranching or farming. A thick layer of hay covered the bed. The truck was a good decade old; its shape was obnoxiously boxy with weirdly shaped angles.

Mitch tapped on the glass. "Hey, driver, what's in Rachel, Nevada?"

"Oh, it's a pretty big place now since that alien memory core they found, whatever it's called. And then Nellis Air Force Base got real big when the Earth Colonial Federation needed a launch site in the west. Rachel now has a population of fifty nine thousand permanent residents. There is also a dozen post offices, and five private schools," the man in the passenger seat replied to Mitch with a thick twang accent.

"I'm old enough to remember when Rachel barely had a population of a hundred. Before, we had a couple of ugly sky scrapers to hold all those administrator offices," the driver added.

"Does that mean we'll be able to fly out? I was hoping to land in Houston, or maybe Chicago. Any place with a lot of bars and pizza shops. They had a week to clean the mess up right. It should be somewhat back to normal," Mitch said, unimpressed by the town's development into a small city.

"Why not go to New York City for all that? I mean, sure, the place is divided up with the communists, but everything east of the West 114 Street wall should be good enough for all that," Sean interrupted.

"Again, I don't want to see my uppity snob parents. Hell, they aren't really even my mother and father," Mitch snapped. "Damn, I wish my transfer to Fifth Fleet went through beaches. And cat girl babes would be better than Earth beer and pizza."

"Oh, we have some Qualurians in town running a pub," the driver added.

"Can you tell me; was the attack on Rachel as bad as elsewhere?" Sean asked, interrupting.

The question earned Sean a kick in the foot from Mitch. A silent warning not to break the rules, but Sean brushed it off. Instead, he stomped on Mitch's foot, another silent way to let the man know he had no place complaining about following rules.

"Oh, there are cows still scattered from those ships coming in, but we didn't get attacked," the truck's passenger answered.

"The military has given us access to a drone to find our cattle, but we traded it to give soldiers rides into and out of town," the driver added, slightly annoyed.

"Hydrogen prices were already high, three sovereigns at the pump and now it's almost four," the driver spat out the window.

As the truck approached the city of Rachel, Mitch looked out toward the train tracks. He noticed, among the large number of incoming trains with equipment, a single train with a passenger car now leaving the city. Shortly after standing up, Mitch sat down. "Damn it all, do you guys happen to have any knowledge of the train schedules?"

"Boy, I'm not a tour guide, and don't be moving around in my bed while I'm driving you, damn fool," the driver cursed Mitch as the truck swerved slightly.

"Sorry, look, hit a bank. I'll fill up your tank. Just get me to that pub you mentioned," Mitch shouted as he took a seat.

Nodding at each other, the men in the truck agreed to a free tank of fuel, and headed toward the center to the nearby bank. "The pub is right over there. The cats picked a decent spot to open it on the main road next to the first bank in town. We'll wait across the street."

Mitch climbed out and went to the bank to activate his card. The air conditioning was less shocking to him than the fact the bank was full of business-as-usual town folk doing their jobs. There was even a generic jingle playing on loop against the sound when he opened the door. He welcomed the normality as he stood in line behind a Qualurian with some documents and a pouch full of sovereigns.

The alien before him gave a nice view. She was slightly shorter than him but definitely well developed—a true cat woman. He noticed she had a firm, full butt just below her tail, just before the nearest teller broke his focus. "Next in line, please."

Rana noticed the man following her, but gave him no attention. "Hello Macy. I'd have had this delivered sooner, but there was an invasion and all. Did the account go into the red? I haven't been able to check the business's bank account yet." Rana handed the teller the pouch along with her ID.

The banker typed in a few commands on a keyboard. "No, your account is fine. The attack has delayed wireless purchases and transfers. We'll be seeing a lot of overtime when people start rushing in deposits soon enough."

Mitch approached the next counter as soon as it opened and laid his credentials out on the counter. "Yeah, I have a state account that I'd like to access my funds after three years of overtime. I got a lot of cash coming my way. Just need it to be verified and accessed. I'm Private First Class Mitch Davis, serial number 1309SM0027PFC."

The teller took the identification from Mitch and began working. "So, you're the adopted son of cyber security mogul Adrian Davis and his wife Alexandra. I'm sorry for your loss, sir."

Mitch had no words. He was hit hard by his wish coming true that his parents would die, but his aunt was dead, but the price was so steep. The only way to be rid of their abuse and manipulation had left cities in ruin. "Thank you for your condolences," Mitch replied as he lost focus of the Qualurian woman.

The teller returned the personal items to Mitch. "Of course, and your card is now active. Would you like any physical sovereigns?"

"Yeah, yeah. Give me enough smaller bills for a decent tip at the pub." Mitch collected his stuff, his chest feeling unnaturally heavy. He left the bank and promptly headed to the fuel station across the street where the ranchers were waiting in their truck.

"Good to see you came back. Your pals left without you though." The driver said drinking a coffee.

"Thank you, sir," Mitch said, sliding his card through the machine's payment system as a means to activate his card. After taking out the pump, watching the Qualurian leave the bank. He wanted to fill his mind with anything and everything not involving his service.

"Thanks for the fill up, kid. Want to wash my windows?" the driver asked.

"Sorry sir, I'm not full service." Mitch returned the nozzle to the pump and followed the Qualurian into the pub. He checked his watch. The lunch crowd wouldn't be around for a bit. Perhaps he could get his parents off his mind with a pint and some tail in the bathroom.

Mitch entered the pub. It was well lit by simple LED lighting with no tacky, neon stripper lights. The posters on the wall consisted of aircraft, cars, and rare, beautiful women. All were tastefully mixed and matched. Mitch sat down at the bar, the news playing out on one of the flat screens. The walls had several booths and a few tables sat between them and the bar.

"Give me the strongest beer you have, dear." Mitch slapped his cash on the bar in front of the Qualurian he'd been eye fucking for the last few moments. He slipped her his ID as soon as he noticed her pause.

Rana, satisfied with his ID, found a bottle of the strongest stuff she had. "There you are, sir—New Houston's Blackest Ale. It's a Sidonian beer. That'll be thirty-five sovereigns, that is, with the plus ten add-on. The attacks on Earth will likely cause shortages on everything not essential."

Rana paused. No sooner than she'd given the man his drink, he promptly shot-gunned it in a swift few gulps. Mitch tapped the bar for another beer.

"Keep the liquor coming and perhaps turn off the damn news," Mitch complained, seeing Chicago was the main focus of the media.

"What's wrong? Did you lose family?" Rana wondered as she went to change the channel.

"I have money, so be a cute little catgirl and pour the drinks. The last thing I need is your compassion, unless it comes with a horizontal tango." Mitch looked her up and down with a leer before finishing his third ale.

Rana poured a glass of water and threw it into Mitch's face. Before he could even think of blocking her, she smacked him across the face with her right hand. "I am not some fuck doll for out-of-town assholes!"

Rana took a sniff of her hand and almost instantly recognized the scent. "Oh shit, Mitchell Davis!"

"You're Rana, the nanny? The one who took me with her when she ran away?" Mitch rubbed his skin. Sure the upgrades made to his epidermis made being cut by a claws-out slap from a Qualurian next to impossible, but it did little to take away the stinging effect.

"How did you do it? Get a fake ID past the military?" Rana questioned him as she took the ale away and handed him the second glass of water she'd poured.

"Oh, come on!" Mitch replied, looking at his glass of water. "First up, Rana, you're a little late worrying about that. Not to mention, those asshole parents of mine won't be telling anyone otherwise about a modified date of birth in the hospital records. Now if you don't remember correctly, you and I promised each other once we escaped New York we'd find a place in the desert and live happily ever after."

Rana leaned close to him, almost kissing him, when she whispered, "This pub is very important to me. It's not mine, and your little antics could cost this place a lot. You got no reason to drink about the death of your aunt and uncle; they weren't the type of people to be missed."

"My wishing for their death got all those people killed. So don't tell me I have no reason to drink. I'll go find another bar." Mitch stood up. "My dear, if worse comes to worse; I'll just clean out a liquor store and find a hotel room."

"Damn you, you're still a little brat. Sit down and don't get drunk. You sure as hell aren't going to catch a case." Rana cursed the man for making her want to stop him. "The last thing I want is the cops wondering where you started a binge."

"Oh, thanks, you really do care." Mitch smiled, returning to the bar.

"I just don't want the ACN sniffing around this place or my past. The immigration office was only merciful once because I was forcibly brought to Earth." Rana pursed her lips, deciding to watch over Mitch. "You honestly think this invasion is your fault? You got an ego on you, boy."

"Anything it takes to see them dead. I got what I wanted now. Chicago's got two massive funeral pyres that were Arcologies where millions lived. There's also a spaceport hangar serving as a mass grave for soldiers' families, so please don't tell me I have no reason to drink."

"You gave the Serkins targeting opportunities?" Rana's lack of knowledge made Mitch smile slightly. "You lined people up and executed them. I don't like men who stink of self-pity!"

"Actually, targets of opportunity and target coordinates are two separate things. You need to give coordinates to call in fire support on targets of opportunity," Mitch replied, noticing he was getting lower quality booze.

"You noticed the cheap stuff, huh? I don't think your single wish is enough to cause the Serkins to attack. And what about the good news? The Intelligence analysts have gone on stating the tide is turning and our fleet won the second battle. They said we can turn off their drones. If you are off duty, try to be happy. Order some food and I'll change the channel." Rana handed Mitch a small menu pad. "Eat something; a stomach full of beer isn't good."

Mitch sighed. "I'll take this as a sign you want to cook for me. Oh, look, The Heart Stopper Burger: six strips of Apple Smoked Bacon on a standard pub cheese burger. Give me that suggestively named meal, please."

Rana's tail twitched with annoyance, but she still managed a genuine smile. "Right away, sir, I'll be right back with your order. Rashida, one Heart Stopper. I only tend the bar and act as the manager, Mitch. Tell me, soldier, what is it like falling from space? Do you get to where the sky ends, and the void begins? I never saw the stars on my trip."

"I wish I could tell you the drop pod is usually closed tight. There are no windows. But I admit, a Hummingbird or a Hornet is a much more pleasant trip down. I guess the good news is, ten days ago was my first combat drop from an orbiting warship. Seeing you is a nice surprise. I wasn't looking for a connection to a world I fled." Mitch rejected his beer. He didn't know why, but he suddenly didn't want his feelings numbed. "I never thought I'd see you again after the FSA split us up."

"I was told all about the stars holding romantic adventures, but it's a lifeless void. I assume you got lots of romance in the stars between planets," Rana said, waiting for the food. "What number woman will I be? Ten, eleven perhaps I'd image the Corps would allow you to sow your seed across many fields?"

"No time for any of that. Actually, it was constant interdictions, and when that was over, we plugged the gaps in the defense lines. Planet-based defense guns were our biggest edge when holding the Perseus Spur Gap." Mitch finished the low-end beer. "You would be number one."

"Christ, Mitch, I think I may have to cut you off. You just polished enough alcohol to make me tipsy," Rana commented as she looked over the ten empty bottles.

"Worried I won't be able to stand?" Mitch replied as the cook rang the bell, letting Rana know the food was finished.

"More like if you keep drinking, I won't be able to get your soldier to stand at attention. That is, only if what you want. That it's not for just for one night," Rana added, placing the food in front of Mitch. "I'm the first and only woman."

"I will promise that so long as I'm still breathing, I'll only love you," Mitch promised. "However, the first order of business is to consume some overly luxurious food."

Sean stood at the train station ticket kiosk. None of the selections for a Chicago ticket were available, so he'd settle for the next best thing: Kenosha, and travel south. "I hope the heat in Illinois is more bearable than this place. Why the Federation chose Houston for a capital is beyond me."

The train was packed at first, then large numbers of soldiers climbed off the train, heading into Kenosha, the train was all but abandoned. Sean settled into a window seat and got a scenic ride. Watching the desert turn into lush green forests comforted him. When the train came closer to civilization, he could see the much older technology used in Kenosha. Like Chicago, it used wired electricity over the more modern plasma-transmitted-electric grid of Rachel, Nevada. Once out of the station, he found the city to be a far lighter place. He could see trucks loading wrecked Guardian drones with armored vehicles driving by behind them.

Sean stuck his thumb out and waited for any vehicles heading south into Chicago. The cars largely ignored him until a private ride-share car pulled up. Sean quickly retracted his middle finger and approached the driver. "You mind taking me to 905, 14th Street?"

"That's doable, but we'll have a lot of traffic on the Sheridan, so the best bet now is Roosevelt Road. I hope you weren't looking for a scenic drive along Lake Michigan," the young man replied, clearly pleased to have a customer.

Sean climbed into the back of the car and instantly smelled it was new. The car was a Mitsubishi ZTi8 sport sedan. Inside the rear seat had a heating option and plenty of room for Sean to stretch his legs. He guessed the driver was looking for the cash to make the monthly payments. The route south was marginally clear. Though what should have been a thirty-minute drive took over an hour. The road was packed with all sorts of construction vehicles trying to head into the city. Sean, desperate for company, tried striking up conversation. "Is the reconstruction of Chicago going poorly?"

"Nope, clean-up is moving along smoothly, and most of the damage is in the downtown area. The military closed the parks to clear the mines and shit. The damage isn't wide spread, but the South Side Arcologies are being treated as graves. So far, no one has had the stomach to excavate the scene like the spaceport mass grave. It's pretty grim. I guess I'm glad I fractured my spine and never made it into the Naval Infantry. I don't think I could handle coming back and finding out my family was killed," the driver replied.

"Yeah, I'm lucky my family wasn't there that day," Sean added, watching a large convoy of military transport trucks hauling even more drones out of the city.

"That is great news, man. You know, I say taking happiness where and when you can get it is key to living a happy life," the driver replied, noticing Sean's gaze turn to the smoke coming from Chicago that could be seen as the car turned east onto Sunset Avenue.

"The Arcology fires are still burning this long after the fight?" Sean questioned the driver.

"No, the military is doing controlled demolition in the city. It's much easier to destroy things in Millennium Grant Park than ship it out live for destruction. It's going to be okay, man. We'll get through this." The driver did as much as he could to cheer up his passenger.

"Yeah, I guess we will," Sean replied, his tone signaling an end to the conversation. The ride ended at a brick three story home with an attached garage. He gave the driver a large tip before approaching the house. He could see the Civilian Ibex with its chrome trim and bright red paint that his mother Jennifer drove. The next car was his sister's Soul—at least he assumed it was Larisa's.

He headed up to the main door of the enclosed patio and rang the bell. His sister came out, clearly suppressing her emotions. He couldn't tell what she was thinking. "You're a bastard!" Larisa said, but still hugged Sean. "I hate myself for being mean to you before you left."

She had changed a lot in two years. Her training bra days had long since passed—she was now probably the girl all others envied. It was enough to make him worry about boys viewing her with the same lust he had for Sammy. He'd forgotten so much about her and now struggled to let her go. How could he leave a second time?

"I'm so sorry that I didn't bring Derek back, mom. I followed him because we were unstoppable as a pair. I was wrong, so damn wrong," Sean quietly apologized for not having come home with his brother, entering the house with his sister. "God, I failed so many people."

As the pair walked into the living room, Sean noticed new additions to the shrines on the top of the fireplace. Just off the center was his grandfather, Andrew, holding center stage, and at what was like his mother's ruling sat an image of his brother Derek and Trevor father. They each had their own white candles and a small trinkets sitting in front of their images; they'd both been lost in the war. Trevor's Chicago Police Badge leaned against his 2D picture. Sean touched the image of his father and then his brother. He let go of the images quickly grabbing hold of the mantle when he felt ill.

Seeing Sean, Jennifer dropped what she was doing in the kitchen and rushed to greet her son. She hugged him and kissed his cheeks, but barely penetrated the haze surrounding him. "Welcome home, dear. Would you like something to drink? Sammy's been here for a few days since Yuki got sent to Arizona for treatment. You've gotten so much bigger in the two years since I last saw you!"

He finally looked down at his mother, noticing her brown hair had turned dark gray. "Yeah, so where is Mother? Did she get back from Houston yet?" Sean broke away from Jennifer. "I thought she'd be home by now. It's like I stopped existing. She probably holds me accountable for so many people dying."

"No, she won't be back for some time. Please try to relax. Take a seat and relax. We have plenty of food between what I had stored up and the grocery reopening. I'll make an early dinner, something large," Jennifer replied as Sean walked away from the shrines. She knew instantly he'd had a mind wipe. "It's okay if you forgot their faces, Sean. You've been busy and it was surely stressful."

"Yes, of course, so very busy. So that's what dad and Derek looked like. I can't believe I forgot. I'm going to speak with Sammy," Sean said, sighing before heading upstairs.

Sammy sat on the roof of the back porch near Sean and Derek's old bedroom, looking toward the south toward the downtown city center that was almost an hour's drive away. Sammy heard the window open and saw Sean climbing out, and stood up to greet him.

"Welcome home, Sean. I was going to put on a cute dress, Yuki made it by hand. She modified it so you'd get me pregnant to help her cash in on the baby boom," Sammy said, blushing at the thought of sex.

"Sounds like Yuki's always looking ahead business wise and is a bit of a pervert," Sean said, watching Sammy dig into her pants pockets. It was her tale tell sign she was conflicted.

"I would hit her for being so horny all the time, but I think she would like that. I'm glad you aren't the ravenously horny monster Yuki thought you'd be." Sammy blushed, trying to broach the topic without specifically mentioning sex. She wanted more than simple pleasure. She longed to wake up each morning next to Sean, grow old with him, and be boring normal people. "Nothing turned out like I had planned.

I hoped to be in a pretty dress to go home to a barbeque, but all I got was a dead man in my shop."

"I'm sure it would've been an amazing-looking dress. Is that the medal you got for helping those children get out of the downtown area?" Sean asked, reaching out to touch Sammy's hand as she pulled something from her pocket. "You always were strong like that."

Sammy hugged Sean and began crying. "I got a medal because a man died in our store and Yuki lost an arm. My mothers are both dead and the government told me I'm some sort of community defender, an inspiration to all! I don't even know what the hell I'm going to do now. For the first time ever I feel alone and useless!"

"You don't have to be so hard on yourself. I'm glad my family had a house besides the Oak Park home. And we won't leave you alone, I promise…"

"Stop making promises. I remember all the others you made! Look at it all, we lived there!" Sammy shouted, pointing at the skyline, tears streaming down her face. "Goddess, forgive me. I'm sorry; it's not your fault. You were so right. This is a problem for humanity, and like a smug brat, I wanted you to stay with me."

He stroked her hair; not sure hushing her was the right thing to do. "Being out of town should help you with the stress. Yuki will be back soon enough." He leaned in close enough to kiss her forehead.

"If this is it, and the end is coming, I don't want to be some single amateur model and seamstress. Living with my fashion designer friend is not how I want to go," Sammy said, looking at the medal. "I want to be married to you. I know you'll go back to the war. It's what's needed, but next time you come back, you'll come back to a wife."

Sean took the medal. It was circular, with the Federation's Falcon standing guard above the flame of humanity—the civilian version of the Federal flag. He had almost forgotten what the civilian government symbols looked like- compared to the swooping falcon design the military used. "So we get married. Larisa is going to freak out over having a big sister."

"No ceremony until Yuki makes the dress, but I can file all the paperwork on the noteputer almost instantly. Give me your serial number, date of birth, and thumbprint. We'll be married in an instant," Sammy replied, looking up at Sean. "We'll probably be unable to consummate here."

"I'm game. We'll just have to go inside. There's no point in staring at the skyline midday. I am going to miss the city's night lights." Sean returned Sammy's medal. "It'll be different from our plan we made in the park, but we'll find our happiness one way or another."

Sammy let her hand rest on Sean's chest. He was taller than her and well built from constant fighting, but he seemed different, unnaturally so. "How much of you returned to me? What kind of modifications did they make? Are you a post human enhancement? You were never this big. Sure, you were tall, but this all is not you."

"Honestly, a few cybernetics in my head to control the suit, some enhanced joints and muscles. I'm still the Sean who shared a first kiss with you in Millennium Grant Park. You always said that your goddess gave me my soul. I still have my soul," Sean reassured Sammy as best as he could while her hands explored his body.

"My life as I knew it, Sean, is gone. My mothers are gone, Yuki is in the hospital, and I'm likely to be making weapons in a factory. The reality is, we can't go back to being blissfully ignorant, but I do want to be happy." Sammy lifted his shirt and noticed a large scar across his abdomen. She let out a small sigh. "When I die and I look at her feet in the great beyond, I want to tell the goddess I was a happy wife. That I grew up and worked hard to belong. If all goes well, we'll have children and grandchildren."

Sean smiled, looking at Sammy. "Well, let's go inside and get married then. If Larisa gives you shit, let me know."

"I admit, being naked most of the time is what sets her off, so if I stop that we should be alright." Sammy stepped back in through the window, Sean holding her hand. "I do have an issue with her calling me brother-stealer."

Sean sighed. "I'll take care of that. It's just that she's lost Derek and dad. Give her a bit of time; please don't be too hard on her."

Phoenix 5pm Sky Harbor International Airport

For the soldiers who didn't live in America, trying to leave the country was a haphazard event. Nathan, Masa, and Eric found this out firsthand. Any attempt at catching a flight to their respective homelands bordered on impossible. Masa suggested making a game out of the number of flights that never showed and promptly earned much contempt for cursing the lot of them.

The group waited for the better part of the day with no flights going in any direction they wished to go. The setting sun meant cooler temperatures, but Nathan was a native of Glasgow. He was truly in awe of the desert plains before him behind the windows. He bought a model UFO for his son, and a stuffed alien for his daughter, both grossly overpriced. Still, he wanted to have some gifts for his youngest children when he returned.

Eric sat reading the news on a personal reading device. Glasgow was gone and the Polish-Hungarian Empire had lost their western most city of Nice to a stray nuclear bomb. He passed the news pad to Masa. "God damn, do you want to tell him? After all this shit, Nathan lost his home, wife, and kids. They're all gone. The government he served didn't even tell him."

"They did tell him. He's just not coping so well. His oldest son is coming to get him. The one he had ages ago with his wife when they first married," Masa replied, ordering some food. "Qualurians apparently stay fertile for quite some time, but at least he has one kid left. He should be okay. His whole family isn't dead as far as I know."

"Then he hasn't lost everything." Eric took some paper sovereigns out to tip the waitress, bringing him food from the kitchen. "He should be okay. Family will help him move on."

"Look, I get it, dude. You're the hard ass, cold-blooded sniper, but the man still lost his family," Masa responded, taking a swig of his beer. "Screw this. I'm talking to someone who's less of an ass."

Masa got up to approach Nathan where he sat studying the desert. "Hey, Mac, you think my grand kid would like this stuff? Alien plushy from the old world. I think this kind of alien was dubbed *The Grays* despite being green."

"Deserts are gorgeous places. You can look at it from afar like this and it looks dead. But then you step forward, closing the distance with what looks like dead rocks and dust, then boom! You can see the hardiest life forms of land creatures with no tools, not just surviving but thriving." Masa sat down, offering Nathan a beer. "As for the aliens before we met the Yaren, Olarians, and Qualurians, a lot of hoaxes showed variations of little guys like this."

Nathan declined the beer, and ignored Masa's history lesson. "I always promised my youngest we'd build a UFO together. God only knows how many times I broke promises to my children. I got my doctor's degree ages ago, but that didn't free me up. And now I'm pushing toward my fifties. This is so weird for me. I've always had a wife and kid to go home to since I was twenty-three. Now I'm alone and my oldest is my only; he moved to the desert, hoping to search for another one of those Yaren Memory Cores in the desert caves."

The two sat together in silence for a bit. Masa knew of the data cores value he remembered as a boy imagining a grand adventure where he was the star finding the next alien database. He placed the beer he brought for Nathan between them.

"A memory core is quite the find; huge technological boons that are easily explained to those who find them. Wasn't the last guy who found one able to buy an island chain? They seeded Earth with ten of those things and we've only found two." Masa said breaking the silence.

"Apparently, the Yaren said they didn't think they would make it back to this galaxy before dying off." Nathan, despite his grief, couldn't keep the information about the Serkins they captured secret. "I just hope those assholes we captured are going to suffer for what they forced us to do."

Masa took a drink of his beer. *A bit of liquid courage and I'll talk a little longer. Fuck, I envy Eric right now.* Masa suppressed his wish of being as cold-hearted as Eric. Nathan needed a friend and Masa chose to be that friend. "Are you waiting for your son here? Convinced him to become an explorer, did you?"

"Oi, yeah, I wish he'd have given up on that, but it's why he's alive, so I can't complain," Nathan replied, finally accepting the beer Masa held out to him. "I returned to the Strike Force Marines when we lost Vieira to hold the line."

"Dad, they let me come in and pick you up," Nathan's son, Marcus, called as he approached. He was almost identical to his father: the same green eyes and scruffy hair, just with more brown than gray. The only difference from his father was the ears and tail he'd inherited from his Qualurian mother. He used his tail to take the stuffed toy alien away as he helped his father up. "Glad you got your grandkids some presents."

"Mac, this is my son, Marcus. Marcus, how goes your little treasure hunt, son?" Nathan asked, introducing the two men. "Grandkids? As in more than one?"

"Thank you for your service," Marcus said, shaking hands with Masa before he spoke to his father. "Dad, I haven't hunted for treasure in over four years. You've been disconnected for a while. You're a grandpa to a girl and a boy. Come home with me and I can introduce you."

"Well, I guess I can build this kit for the grandkids," Nathan replied, sounding somewhat more upbeat by the idea of being a grandfather twice over.

"Diana is only a few months old, but Alex would love to watch you build this kit," Marcus said, enthused as Nathan followed him out of the terminal. "Let's get going. We have over an hour's drive."

Masa smiled as he watched the two leave, feeling better now that Nathan knew he still had family. He certainly had no hope of being flown home anytime soon, but for now he felt better. "Silver linings—got to take them how you can get them, Eric. You should try it sometimes, man," Masa said, returning to their table and finishing the beers.

"I joined the military a few days after my mother died," Eric said, sharing the nachos. "You'll have to forgive me if I'm just fighting for the people next to me and don't want to be too connected."

"At least you're sharing the nachos. How many flights haven't shown up since we got here?" Masa sat down and stuffed the cheesy bite into his mouth. "I'm betting thirty-one."

"So far, it's twenty-six flights that either never took off or got redirected. We need to get on a train and head east, man. I'm thinking there may be a no-fly zone getting enforced, and no one is being told," Eric continued in a worried tone. "Personally, I'm worried about what I'm supposed to do next. I mean, without orders or an objective, I'm just a vagrant."

"No worries, man. If you want, we can hit Vegas and I'll show you how to live without the rules and regulations. You know what? Let's find a bus to Vegas. No war in history ever stopped that place from throwing a party." Masa keyed in a command at the table's shopping kiosk. "Wham bam thank you ma'am. We have bus tickets to Vegas because the busses are running!"

"Hey, look at this. It looks like the state is doing a full-on broadcast." Eric pointed to the news bulletin on the table's kiosk.

Masa clicked the alert and brought it up as a holographic image. "Shit, breaking updates on the war effort!"

"Is that the finance minister?" Eric asked as Lisa Ryan took to a podium in an unknown location. "The rumors from those 101st Airborne guys were true. Harkin and much of the ECF senate—they're all dead."

Lisa, in a fresh black pantsuit—her first change of clothes in a week—stood at a podium in front of an empty press room. "One week ago, Earth, the birthplace of humanity, was attacked by aliens. What most of us had previously consigned to dated science fiction has resoundingly come to be a reality. The Serkin invasion of Earth has forced us to accept that our previous beliefs about this conflict were wrong. It cost millions of innocent people their lives. The Harkin administration believed we were in a small-scale border skirmish, but the events of last week are proof we had buried our heads in the sand. We had hoped the conflict was isolated and diplomacy would eventually win out. We were entirely wrong."

At his family home in Chicago, Sean sat on the couch in the living room watching the news, flanked by Larisa and Sammy. Larisa perked up from her spot on the couch and added her two cents. "Harkin was always spineless. I just hope mom doesn't fuck up as bad he did. I mean, Grandpa helped Tyrone Harrison get us through the war with the Union. Mom has a lot to live up to. History class said Tyrone Harrison couldn't have been half as successful without our uncle's company."

"Be quiet, her speech isn't over," Sean hushed his sister.

Lisa continued after drinking some water. "As we speak, new combat units are being formed. Existing military personnel with experience fighting the Serkin threat will have the option of returning to front line service or withdrawing to train the next batch of soldiers. We are no longer going to debate the construction of new warships either. Research into our enemy has also begun. I will not divulge information about our military intelligence's activities. I will say, however, we are now aware of the threat and will right the wrongs of the last five years. Thank you all and please continue working with each other as you have been. Our willingness to remain individuals working toward the best outcome for all means that what we have lost will be rebuilt; we will thrive once more. The Communist Union of Colonies failed to stop us, and the Serkins will not defeat us either. Thank you."

In Rachel Nevada, Mitch and Rana took a moment to relax as they sat in her apartment, watching the news as many of the soldiers did who were released from duty. Rana folded her legs up onto the couch, cuddling up to Mitch. "You think you'll be going back to active duty?"

Mitch wrapped his arm around Rana before sighing. "I'm pretty low on the totem pole, so I can't say. I doubt I will be used to train others."

Rana kissed his chin. "You'll never be the bottom of a totem pole with me."

"I know that, Rana, I do. I am grateful for that," Mitch replied, switching the screen back to a movie.

July 22, 2131, Undisclosed location

Lisa Ryan sat watching the video footage of the two male Serkin officers and two females' interrogation. "General Stone, agent Wagner, can either of you tell me what I should be seeing on these recorded interrogations?"

Wagner stopped the video and slowly played it back. "In the first few moments of the video, all the Serkins are isolated but in the same prison block. Before the interrogation, their body language shows movements seen in conversation. I think we're looking at telepathic communications. It could explain the rapid changes in Guardian drone combat performance while our electronic warfare systems were active."

Lisa saw a few nods and took a second look at the tape, noticing the Serkins' head nods were perfectly timed. "Is there a chance they are faking this? Perhaps they have seen some old science fiction shows that were beamed into space and are playing tricks on us?"

General Stone uncrossed his arms. "They could be playing tricks on us, and in the twentieth century we broadcasted everything we knew or had imagined into the stars. However, it's impossible every Serkin would have had the time to watch over a century's worth of fictional broadcasts. It would also make little sense to train all their field officers in our fiction just to play with us if they were captured. To ensure it wasn't a trick, we moved the Serkin prisoners further apart, and it seems they can't use their telepathic communication past a few dozen meters."

"Wouldn't that make their control of the drones impossible without being in the line of danger?" Lisa was quick to ask. "And are you certain they didn't just stop using their powers to fool us?"

General Stone changed the video. "It could be that they are trying to play us, but we firmly belief their armor most likely amplifies their signals to their machines. The Strike Force Marines' helmets link to the wearer's brain for better synchronization with the suit. Serkin helmets had something similar, although slightly more advanced." The video showed the Serkin officer's helmet. "You see this pointed section on top of their helmet? It corresponds with a seventh lobe in the top of their brain."

Lisa watched the breakdown of the Serkin armor. "That is all very interesting, but why are we talking about this? We have a lot of captured Serkin armor already, none of it in this condition, certainly, but why does this all matter?"

"The technology we've captured that is in working order shows construction similar to the Yaren memory core functions," Agent Wagner replied. "We'll need to rethink letting the last Yaren queen and her people live out in the desert compound we gave them. It's clear the Serkins knew where to dig. I suggest we cease working with the Yarens in any capacity from here on out, as they may pose a security risk to our war effort."

"We can't just go down there and kill them; you know their Blade Master warriors can slice tank armor like butter and no one here regularly converses with them to begin with. We've barely begun using the memory core we have and there are millions across the stars. The Serkins could have just been using the same stuff we only recently obtained for much longer."

Lisa rubbed her temples in hopes she could dismiss his valid theory before continuing. "Now let's move on. What do we have that can help us fight the Serkins?"

Agent Wagner did as he was told, changing the view screen to display several of the blue elf aliens. "As you know, Colonel Ezra Adara has proposed Throw Away Black Operations against their leadership. We may have that opportunity and a decent enough time frame to prepare for it. Our command structure was ravaged by this attack, but their command structure has been obliterated."

The screen, at first, showed the Serkin names in their own language before the computer translated everything for Lisa. "All these Serkins are parts of what look like ten separate fleets with their accompanying troops. This is hardly a decisive victory."

General Stone uncrossed his arms. "We thought that at first, but the female Serkin, code named Eve, let slip an important detail about their operation. The Serkins built this force specifically to take out the Earth in an autonomous manner. We don't know just yet how much of their military remains, but they are going to send a new group of commanders to take over the surviving forces that hit the Earth."

Lisa took a deep breath to remain calm. "A simple shuttle trip and they will launch another attack; that doesn't sound like much of an opportunity to me, gentlemen."

Wagner selected one of the Serkin males in the command structure on the screen. "Sire Adothur T'pla is the highest ranking Serkin left from the task force meant to destroy the ECF. He can't, by their law, surrender his command until he is tried for the severity of his failure. He's likely looking at being tried and executed for a myriad of reasons. Desertion, cowardice, or their government is likely in dire need of a scapegoat. Military chatter observed has confirmed this T'pla is going to be tried as soon as possible by the replacement commanders. They are being transported by a scout flotilla of only twenty ships." Wagner then changed the screen to show a 2D version of the Milky Way Galaxy. He pointed to a location near the thirty-degree longitude.

General Stone produced a tablet with specific information before handing it to Lisa. "The Serkins have been getting numerous communications from that area. So far, they haven't detected our algorithms. It is very possible this is where their home world or main military staging area is located. We don't know the exact means they use to travel faster than light, but it seems to have the same limitations of beam space travel."

Lisa scrolled through the tablet data for a moment. "So, like our ships, they can travel any distance greater than ten thousand light years outside of a galactic arm. Signals and data sharing across stars is safe from the drift on the galactic plane, but they still have all the same safety protocols we do for ships. Those officers will need, what, six months to reach the nearest location to regroup with blue boy here?"

Wagner changed the screen to track the Serkin fleet movements. Countless star systems were displayed on the screen. Across each were various alerts, each sent from patrol craft or observation stations. "They are scuttling all ships damaged beyond repair as we speak, but we can't salvage the ships that are being sent into stars for disposal. Adothur T'pla has submitted himself to be judged where the war began. Vieira will be the world where he stands trial. Twelve of the highest known Serkin commanders will be judges. Colonel Adara may have struck pay dirt if we want to change how we fight this war. Serkins can't be tried by their equals, and it seems their brass wanted to hold the trial on a planet. In all, we could very well cripple their command structure for very little cost. A small Marine unit with just enough training could buy us the time to build up and save our more elite forces to be used in a less risky offensive strike. If they fail, we send in a small fleet to bomb the planet from orbit and forget that we ever sent in a team."

Lisa was convinced and desperate to know where on earth she was. "Name it. Whatever you need to get this team deployed ground-side to kill these bastards, it's yours. I'll call my brother, the head of Ryan Aerospace Enterprises, and tell him to work with Sidonia Dynamics to build whatever system this strike needs. If this doesn't work, we nuke the planet from orbit and hope our targets die in the blast."

Agent Wagner smiled and scrolled through some of the data before sending it to Lisa's tablet. "We are one step ahead of you; so far Sidonia Dynamics is willing to mount some of their latest stealth systems to work on some of our available ships. The stealth packages are limited by the ship sizes, but the Warrior Class Destroyers, and the Alesia and Hue class frigates, will be perfect for upgrades to insert any team behind enemy lines. The ECS Hue, which was heavily damaged, has already begun its refit to serve as a stealthy delivery ship. It may not have an operational Tesla cannon, but that could be a boon for stealth operations."

"Good, Agent Wagner. If these teams do succeed, I would like for them to be extracted if possible and used again. I've seen the cost of our current Black Operations cyborgs, and I can buy a dozen dropships for what it costs to make one of them. Using them in a suicide squad-manner would be an obscene waste of money, to say the least," Lisa added as she signed the tablet.

"The downside is that the world of Vieira is literally a ghost planet in Serkin hands." General Stone interrupted. "We may control the jump point at the Perseus Spur gap, but that's as far as it goes. Chances of retrieval of this special ops team may end in zero. Colonel Adara said it best: we will need these to be men with nothing to live for. A dedicated Strike Force Marines special ops team is beyond tier one, we can't just toss them away. We will have to find people who could be tier one but aren't. I am going to have to ask for twelve trans-human elites to do their job and die."

Lisa was in no way pleased by General Stone's hesitation, and snapped, "I'm well aware of that, and if we can't extract them, a sacrifice of twelve soldiers is fine by me. Specifically since their sacrifice will likely save trillions of lives. Make every effort to extract them.

"Though I was Naval Infantry, we had no fancy power armor or rail guns. However, we never left anyone behind, and I won't start doing that now. I won my war and I won't be the first Prime Minister of the ECF to lose a war."

"We will name new warships, colonies, and accolades for heroism after them. Look at the news, General. We cannot afford to lose this war. Green light Colonel Adara's plan immediately. Now if you do not mind, it's Sunday, meaning it's been a full week since I stayed in one place longer than eight hours." Lisa stood up and left the room.

Colonel Ezra waited in the officers' mess of the base at a table, drinking her coffee and eating her breakfast when Wagner joined her with his own meal. "How is the princess holding up after going from finance minster to prime minister?"

"She green lit the entire operation. She would like every effort to be made to extract the team we send in if they succeed. Given her history as a soldier, it was to be expected."

Ezra nearly spat out her coffee in shock. "Well, that was faster than

I expected. I thought I would need a better presentation. Did you get my request for the psychological profiles?"

Wagner began salting his soup. "My AI is on it as we speak. You wanted a diverse collection of men—self-sacrificing, morally outstanding examples of soldiers. Skilled yet troubled, and above all, preferably with no living connections. What are you thinking?"

Ezra cocked her head with a simple reply. "I'm thinking we get some of our rouges out of the way; no family means there isn't a mourning family. Those damn media critics love to exploit mourning families for their own gain. Of course, they all need to have the skills. Can you get me the soldier who shut down the drones in Chicago and saved the prime minister's kid? If we have him on our team, we could secure anything to keep our unit going."

Wagner blew on his soup to cool it before taking a sip. "Get you Sean Ryan… It's a tall order, but I can at least get him to listen to this plan. How do you intend to convince these men to join the unit? Not everyone you want will meet these requirements, nor will they all want to die in battle."

Ezra's tail stopped moving and her ears went flat as frustration took hold of her. "I think if we give them an early out with some increased benefits, they'll have a slightly higher interest in joining. Other than that, we should be alright with doing just enough to get the job done."

July 22, 2131, 0330 hours
Carl R. Darnall Medical
Center, Fort Hood Texas.

Marlow sat at the medical table waiting for the doctor when the young man entered. "Well, Staff Sergeant Presley Marlow, you are here to join the return-to-service program. You're fifty-nine years old. Perhaps you would be better off retiring. Your service in the military is over thirty years of active duty in the Interstellar Strike Force Marines. As such, I'm required to advise retirement as an option," the doctor said, donning a pair of gloves to look at how the amputation was healing. "Good news for you. I'll suggest you receive a high-end prosthetic arm with full cosmetic finish if you do retire."

The part Qualurian doctor's speech only drew Marlow's ire, who promptly decided to put the young doctor in his place. "Listen here, Doctor, I know my options, so drop that bullshit retirement spiel and I won't yank your damn tail off."

Doctor Miles Wentworth's ears flattened and his eyes widened, his smile turning devious. He knew just how deal with a grumpy geezer. "Oh, I suggest you watch what you say grandpa, given that I not only outrank you, but can make this pre-op check-up go from mildly uncomfortable to outright painful!" Miles paused, taking a deep breath to calm down. "Now then, your arm looks like it can accept a combat prosthetic replacement."

Marlow knew to get a combat prosthetic; he would need to lose the whole arm. In fact the doctor would probably enjoy taking off what remained. "How soon before I can enter surgery?"

Miles used his tail to grab his noteputer and began writing down a few notes. "Well, all the damage was to your radius and ulna bones; both are gone. Your Humerus bone is just fine, so we can graft the prosthetic directly to your elbow within the hour."

Marlow was relived he wouldn't have to wait long. "What? No medical terminology to describe more bones?"

Miles held up the noteputer and a stylus to Marlow. "If I did speak intelligently, we'd be here all day as I try to explain the terminology to your dumb ass. In all, your natural muscles have already been altered with synthetic strands to help you use Scorpion Mk3 power armor with less stress, so merging a combat-grade arm will be less invasive than back when you were young. Grafting news limbs has really advanced in the last ten years. All we need now is a signature and thumb print for consent."

Marlow signed on the line and pressed his thumb to the noteputer screen. "Last I checked, you guys would usually take the whole arm clean to the shoulder blade. That would make the connection to my body stronger, correct?"

Miles shook his head. "Only in the cases where you aren't already a cyborg would we need to do that. Your upper arm is in great shape, so we can rebuild it all from the elbow down. Your body as it is can't be made any stronger. Now, if you will excuse me, I have other patients."

In the next exam room across the hallway, Victor read through his scripture texts as he began his studies to become an orthodox priest while waiting for the doctor. When the doctor arrived, he greeted him. "Hello doctor."

Miles set his noteputer down on the counter in the waiting room. "So, you're volunteering for the IMSF. As such, I'll need blood and tissue samples; the process is largely classified, but you have a right to know what you are consenting to by law. We will be grafting several layers of titanium carbide to your bones. The blood and tissue samples are going to be used to rapid-grow new organs. A new pancreas will make your body absorb more nutrients from food and produce less waste. Your remaining organs: lungs, heart, and muscles, will have a polymer coating applied to reduce the strain from wearing the Scorpion Mk3 power armor." Miles took out a large syringe and began searching

Victor's arm for a vein. "A new liver will be transplanted allowing your body to reject toxins that would kill a normal person. Finally, your brain will be grafted with cybernetics to control your suit's flight paths. The connection port will be slightly down and behind your right ear."

"Yes, of course, take whatever samples you need, Doctor," Victor said, watching the doctor take several tools from a tray. First, he saw the device to take a tissue sample—a long, sharp hollow needle kept in a syringe. He had to look away. The tool was out of sight, but Victor felt it dig deep into his abdomen. Sure it went in and came out swiftly but he felt awful all the same. The pain caused him to hyperventilate.

As Miles finished collecting the blood and tissue samples, he spoke softly, "Calm down, take slow, deep breaths. The needles all have anesthetic coating; you should recover with no issue. They also have a coating of coagulating and antiseptic fluids that will prevent infections as the wound seals."

"I...I can't believe that was with painkillers," Victor replied. Looking down, he saw a small scar barely a centimeter long, but not a drop of blood.

Miles placed the tissue and blood sample into a sealed box, sending it on its way. He walked back to the table where he left his noteputer. "Now, there is a chance this surgery will fail, and if it does, you will likely die, but the failure rate is down to only eighteen percent. From here, you can turn back, sign a confidentiality agreement, and walk away if you like. Or you move forward and run the risk." He handed Victor the noteputer and stylus.

Victor took the noteputer and stylus. The screen displayed two files in front of him. He pressed the form to consent, then signed it. "I have witnessed miracles first-hand, and if I want to see more, I must take this risk. God will protect me in the end."

Miles a religious man himself nodded his head and collected the noteputer. "Very well. Your surgery will be this time tomorrow. Don't eat or drink anything after 2000 hours tonight."

Victor arrived early for the surgery the next day. In a surgical gown across from several men with missing limbs, he waited his turn until a nurse called him. "Victor Savinkov. We are ready to proceed with your enhancement surgery."

Victor stood up, going with the nurse. He made the sign of the cross as he swallowed his fear. "I have done many wrong deeds, so today begins the penance. But you keep your head in all situations, endure hardship, do the work of an evangelist, and discharge all the duties of your ministry."

The nurse ignored Victor as he quoted the bible, only speaking to him about important information. "This should only take about fourteen hours at most. Once you're completely upgraded, we'll transfer you to 29 Palms in West Arizona. That's where you'll recover and learn the basics of using power armor."

Victor lay down on the bed before him as the doctors approached and promptly put him to sleep. The last thing he saw was a breathing mask being placed over him as he counted backwards into unconsciousness.

Tuesday, July 26, 20:30 Hours
Las Vegas, Nevada

Las Vegas was practically unaltered as night dawned on the city. Vibrant neon lights drowned the strip in a sea of randomly colored lights that drowned out the stars above. People all poured into the casinos and clubs. Among them Masa and Eric had managed to land a ride from a rental car company and drove out to sin city.

As Masa and Eric entered a club on the strip, and Masa displayed his ID to the bouncer. As the pair entered they couldn't help but notice how the place was swarming with people, soldiers, and civilians.

"How come you are letting them in and we have to wait?" Someone in the crowd asked.

"I'm sorry sir but VIP members take priority and we are very busy tonight." The Bouncer said

As the pair walked in a bartender hand out beers to those who had just entered Eric took beer and continued into the main lounge. After a drink of his beer Eric noticed the laid back atmosphere. "Thankfully, you managed to find a club that doesn't have that obnoxious rave music playing to the point where I want to end my life."

Masa shook his head. "Oh, I get you. They call it dub step techno, aka crap. All I know is that crap went out with the manufactured conformity of punk rock. Of course, unlike power metal and hard rock, I sure as shit never want to hear that shit make a comeback. Anyway, this place is way old school. They get the best looking people possible and make them sing. They aim to take you back to when this city was first built."

Eric was pleased he could smoke. "You didn't think about taking me to Bangkok or Crete? This place doesn't strike me as a place you'd venture to for a party."

Masa laughed. "No way. You aren't the type for hookers and cocaine. I avoided a lot of things to suit you."

Eric sat back and enjoyed himself. The only noise he could hear was the on stage woman singing. He took a long inhalation of his cigarette. Seeing a waitress offering cigars to people, and with Masa paying, Eric decided to upgrade his carcinogenic indulgence. "Excuse me, miss, can I get a cigar?"

The waitress came over and smiled just as she recognized Masa. "Welcome back, Masa. Your father was in here a few months ago. We haven't seen you in almost what, nine years?"

Masa nodded. "Yeah, I joined the military almost a decade ago. This is the first time I've had a chance to come back here. Brought a friend with me this time around who needs some help to stop being a stubborn hard ass one hundred percent of the time?"

The waitress nodded and turned to Eric, giving him a paper menu. "What would you like, sir? I personally suggest the Padilla Miami cigars we have in stock. Only the gold members of our club have the option of buying the vintage cigars from Cuba. You two are just related to our Platinum tier member. Sorry about that. Policy states we give you silver tier treatment."

Eric looked at the options. Free to do as he pleased for once, he picked another brand. "How about a Drew State Natural and a proper drink to go with it? On the rocks," Eric replied, handing the woman the menu.

"I'll have the Padilla Miami and be sure to give us the finest bottle of bourbon you have for silver tier," Masa added as he turned over his own menu.

The waitress nodded before disappearing for several minutes. When she came back, she placed two glasses down and handed the men their cigars. The table displayed a quick tutorial video on how to properly smoke a cigar. "Alright sir, one Natural and our best bourbon with one glass on the rocks for you, and house choice for you Masa. If either of you need anything, just give me a ring." The waitress showed them a call button on their table; while she took out a butane lighter.

Eric took the cigar and let the waitress light it. Taking a deep breath, he savored the flavor before exhaling and turning to face Masa. "Mac, what aren't you telling me about, you Jap ass?"

Masa held up a finger and rolled his cigar, showing Eric how to smoke it correctly. "You know our suits with the back mounted jetpack? My old man is the executive responsible for oversight on Mitsubishi Heavy Industries interactions with Ryan Aerospace Enterprises," Masa said, consuming his bourbon rather quickly before continuing with a disappointed sigh. "Vegas just so happens to be home to AMNEX the Army and Marine Navy Expo. Wars are still being waged on Earth. South of the wall are the Mexican drug cartels, all well aware that the Capital of the Universe is Houston; west you have the Californians demanding the Free States return the gold mines—they exterminated the Redwoods to build; and the European Confederation is always expanding south. Earth has a lot of people who just want to cause problems. Mitsubishi Heavy Industries has wisely partnered with Ryan Aerospace Enterprises in a coalition of east-meets-west cooperation to find solutions to defend the ever-changing home front."

Eric couldn't bring himself to mock Masa. "So, are you a rich kid who spent all his time listening to daddy's sales pitches for war machines? You got sick of that and decided to make daddy notice you by being a defecator from a decadent life?"

Masa laughed, tapping the cigar on his ashtray. "No, I honestly got sick of Earth. All these throwbacks to the last century clinging to barely functional weapons, always attacking people who are trying to repair what's left of civilization. The reason for the conflict is always the same—someone refuses to admit someone else's ideas worked better than theirs. I got tired of it all, so I joined up. Find a colony and live in peace was my hope, but I didn't realize how much I missed this place."

Eric poured himself, then Masa, another round of bourbon. "You think your father will mind if we use his name to go gambling and maybe see one of those strip shows?"

Masa took his glass, nodding a thank you to Eric, before swallowing the second drink in a swift gulp. "Yeah, that's not happening, dude. My old man will already not be pleased I have yet to contact him while on Earth. Christ, I ignored checking in on my mother, too, but I saw the images all over the world. I checked my email history for the last nine years. I got an email from her weekly, but after July 9th, she went dark."

Eric had no idea how to comfort Masa. He reached out to him but decided against touching Masa. "I lost my mother ages ago, Mac. We lived in the middle of nowhere. I found a city after leaving home; I barely understood the place. The entire city and its tech was alien. I always was good at hunting, so the military seemed like a good place to go. Now all I am is the military."

Masa took a sip of his drink. "Thank you for attempting to cheer me up about this whole mess. I wanted to avoid the therapist. Can't trust nor stand the idiots with their existential bullshit claiming superiority over actual science. I'm sure a doctor can hand out a pill later at 29 Palms in West Arizona."

"West Arizona—I've never heard of that place. Mother must have given me a book that was too old," Eric replied, taking a deep hit of his cigar before exhaling.

"West Arizona was established when California defaulted on its repayment of reparations for the civil war they instigated, despite having a metric ton of gold. It happened in 2101; I saw it on the news. How did you not know? The entire operation was televised for weeks as the Free States Marines and Army invaded," Masa questioned Eric. It seemed someone his age didn't know the obvious.

Eric tapped the ashes off the end of his cigar. "I was raised disconnected from the world in the middle of Ukraine's nowhere. My real name is Erik Blake. The books I learned from were only made by the ECF before the golden age."

Masa nodded. "I see, so the world known to you had a sheltered viewpoint, how nice."

Eric exhaled, watching the waitresses in their skimpy outfits. "If you don't mind a lack of indoor plumbing and living from hunt to hunt, I suppose it's nice. Although this is nice too," Eric said, holding up his drink.

Wednesday, July 25, 2131, 1000 hours
29 Palms, West Arizona

The medical therapy building was packed with newly augmented men for the Strike Force Marines. When the nurse woke Victor woke, he saw he was in a shared room with three other men. "Welcome back, Private Victor Savinkov. Sit up slowly, please. How much pain are you in on a scale of one to ten?"

Victor took a deep breath as he sat up quickly, almost instantly, instead of slow as the nurse had asked; every muscle and joint ached. "It's mild, I would say four," Victor replied, looking at the scars across his arms and abdomen. "The pain is just everywhere at once."

The nurse stepped backwards, leading Victor. "Alright sir, step out of bed, slowly now, not as quickly as you just sat up. It will take some time getting used to your augmented body. Try to move in slow motion."

Victor grabbed the bedside, gently he thought, but bent it without meaning to. When his foot touched the cold floor, he nearly jumped up. *"Der'mo*, what the hell is wrong with me?"

The nurse gained his attention. "You're adjusting to your argumentation. Your body has to reset mental limits that we just rest. No need to worry, we have training that will help you adjust. What is Der'mo?" she enquired.

"It's thank you in Russian." Victor groaned. His whole body was sore, but he pushed on with the attempt to walk. Across his chest and arms were fresh scars. At first, he was going forward awkwardly, walking in a desultory fashion before finally gaining some semblance of normality. As he gained his balance, he looked at the nurse. "Hell, I'm going pretty good walking, aren't I?"

The nurse nodded her head as she headed out of the room ahead of Victor. She pointed her tablet at another Marine down the main hall. "Corporal Cortez, get your ass over here and help out your FNG. Then you can tell me how your leg is feeling."

Gabe closed his reader, stood up and approached Victor. He looked him up and down before focusing on the nurse's question. "It's a bit tight. The pain is down to a five when I walk, and range of motion has returned to normal."

The nurse scribbled something on her tablet. "Good to hear. It would be less painful if you stopped resting it so much. Now take the FNG through the ropes. Although he seems to be slightly ahead of the curve when it comes to dealing with his new augmentation."

Gabe knitted his brows, sighing as he would fall behind on his reading of the latest spy novel. "Fine nurse, come on Victor. I'll show you the main course for testing out your skills. The first step will be you making sure you don't crush whatever it is you pick up. If you grab a new battery or magazine for the M68 rifle, then crush it, you've reduced our force projection."

Victor followed Gabe as he led him to a different section of the hospital. "What happens next, Corporal Cortez? I promise I'll try not to be a burden to you with failure!"

"Next up, Victor, is you regain control of your body with the changes. If the nurse gave you to me, then you're probably a prodigy. No need for dedicated medical supervision. Once I saw new guy jump straight into the ceiling-all while trying get out of bed." Gabe entered the room first, opening the door for Victor.

Victor followed and went to a table similar to a firing range. There was a series of items but nothing to shoot. "I believe it must be the Lord's will for me to improve so quickly. I prayed for such strength."

Gabe ignored the religious talk and picked up the M68A2 rifle on the table. "The guns here aren't functional, so you won't hurt anyone or damage expensive weapons. This is a perfect clone of our service rifle, its magazine, and its zinc oxide battery. Fully loaded, it weighs in at twenty-five kilos, hard for any human to use, much less fire." Gabe then crushed a fake battery in his hand like piece of paper. "As you can see, we can make short work of our own weapons if we don't focus and control ourselves. I want you to try loading the battery and magazine without crushing them. When complete, unload and power the weapon down."

Victor reached for the weapon and was just about to pick it up when he remembered what Gabe had just showed him. He took hold of the fake rifle carefully and managed not to inflict any damage when he hefted it up. The weight did not register as he thought it would. "It feels like its only ten or fifteen kilograms." He then loaded the battery and rifle before removing both as he had been ordered.

Gabe collected a battery before continuing. "When you're wearing your suit, the weight will feel more manageable for combat. Now load the weapon again, but faster." Gabe held the battery up and tossed it at Victor. "Catch, but don't crush it!"

Victor snatched it out of the air instantly, then slid the battery into the butt stock successfully before sliding the magazine onto the top of the stock. "Wonderfully done, yes?"

"Don't get too cocky. The suit training will be much harder than this," Gabe replied, picking up a glass ball. "You did well here, which means you now go to school where you'll learn to use your suit in flight." Gabe threw the ball as fast as he could at Victor.

With quick precision, Victor caught the ball without breaking it and began looking it over. "I see. Will you be teaching me that as well?" Victor pressed Gabe for information about the next test.

"Damn, you didn't break that. Even I broke the ball. Fortunately for you, no. We have real pros who will train you. I'll probably be walking around the medical facilities, teaching the next group how to stand, walk, grip their guns, and, of course, clean up the mess when they crush the solid glass ball."

As Gabe began writing out a few commands on a nearby tablet, Victor nodded and offered him a hand. "Thank you for the help. When I get my priesthood confirmation, I'll keep you in my prayers."

Gabe looked at Victor's hand before shaking it. "Thanks for that.

Not sure what good it will do given every prayer I've seen uttered went unanswered."

Victor nodded, shaking Gabe's hand. "A nihilist, I see. You shouldn't look for the light. That will cause it to elude you. To see the light, you must first reject the darkness."

Gabe rolled his eyes while looking up at Victor. "Don't eat solid foods; request the mess hall staff give you a waste-free sustenance shake. Your body will need the nutrients, but you don't want the complexity and excessiveness of actual food. This will give you an edge while using your suit training, which will take place at 1530 hours at Tower B2. You'll arrive at the lower end when the rest of these fools have adjusted to their augmentations. I hope you can see that the deeds of men are more useful to you now."

Victor wanted to hit Gabe but knew better. "Perhaps we can continue this conversation another time." Victor left the building without incident, doing as he was told.

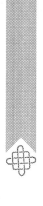

Earth Orbit, 1800 hours
ECS Hue in mobile repair
yard over Oak Valley OR

Ezra sat drinking her third cup of coffee, looking at the video screen in her office. It displayed a view of outer space. An actual window would degrade the ship's structural integrity, so the hull was covered in sensors that provided real-time images of the Earth and the repair crews. She could see the West Coast of America—how the south-west sector was a brown desert that slowly turned into a lush green north.

Ezra sighed, returning to work. *This green vegetation is so strange. I miss the bluish-purple vegetation of Vieira. To think I've called motherhood harder than the military,* Ezra thought as she began typing in commands into her computer.

Ezra scrolled through her email alerts, focusing solely on prospective Marines for her project. Seeing a promising email, she clicked it open and read:

Prospect update. Private Victor Nikolai Savinkov, age 29. Subject's recovery of motor skills after augmentation and ability to use them is above average. Subject also has no known living relatives. All past records indicate he is a hardened criminal. Current activities have confirmed an attempt to join the Russian Uniate Catholicism. We request response of acceptance to Project Nameless.

Ezra smiled as she worked, content that the algorithm was doing all the heavy mental work. She could simply approve or deny offers of membership based on skills. Replying, she approved Victor's acceptance. "Let's see how good this recruit is on the actual battlefield."

1830 hours
29 Palms

Finished training, Victor and the rest of the men now stood waiting to be removed from their suits when Mathew approached them. "Alright, maggots, I know you all did well, so now comes the real thing! I want no bellyaching. Do you get me?"

The Marines shouted in unison: "Yes, Sergeant Miller!"

Mathew looked over the group, judging them. "Our latest mission is to deploy into California, and eliminate a command post and its anti-aircraft artillery. It's more than likely this base will be used to plan future attacks on civilian protection camps in Nevada. That means we got over twelve thousand civilians in the commie's sights, and the ten of you are their shield. Load and lock, we are wheels up at 1845 hours. Everything you need is on the MULE drone outside."

The new Marines moved to the MULE supply drone and began grabbing fully charged batteries and magazines, picking it clean. Leaving behind nothing connected to live fire training, they made their way to a Hornet dropship. Mathew waited silently at the ramp with his helmet at his side. "Standing room only, ladies. This bird was set up to simulate an orbital drop. You'll have all the restraints a drop pod contains. Secure your rifle to your leg and try not to hit each other when falling."

Victor filed in and found himself a central line rack; it had several attachment points, that when he stepped in, locked his head, arms, and legs firmly in a forward position. Victor stepped into the restraints as the flight chief locked him in place. "Remember, your legs serve as better control surfaces that will help you control your drop."

Mathew, as commander, took his seat toward the rear of the dropship along its wall. As the tail ramp closed, Mathew addressed his men, "Listen up. We'll have CAS missions twenty minutes after the last Marine drops. I'm not interested in your small talk or boasting, so unless you have something useful to say, keep your traps shut."

Victor turned as best he could in his restraints. "Sergeant Miller, what is the mission objective? All we know is there's a staging area. What are we supposed to do? Just kill everyone we see?"

Matt sighed. "Yes, kill them all. It's pretty simple. Prevent anyone from leaving the staging area in any vehicle. This is a simple search and destroy mission, easy enough for FNGs like you." As soon as he finished speaking, the Hornet powered up its main engines. "Just so you know, nothing this luxury transport can do will ever equal a dead drop from orbit."

The dropship took off conventionally down the nearest runway, speeding along faster and faster until it bolted straight up. The Marines, for a time, felt utterly weightless as the dropship generated enough thrust to generate counter gravitation forces as it propelled itself slowly into low Earth orbit. Mathew scrolled through his HUD. Fortunately, no one vomited as the dropship finally leveled out.

After twenty minutes of flight, the pilot radioed in. "Thirty seconds to drop!"

The red strobe light began flashing throughout the cargo hold as the ramp opened. When the light turned green, Mathew released each row of Marines two minutes apart. One row followed the next, before his seat along the wall folded outward and sent him into free fall.

Mathew followed the rest of the Marines down. Thankfully, all the Marines followed their planned flight paths down. There was no time to show off, and he simply followed them down as an observer. He changed his drop speed to pass his recruits.

Victor noticed the observer flying slightly faster than everyone else out the corner of his eye; he wanted to look directly at his mentor but knew better than to turn. He kept following the flight path down, unlike a few others who turned to look and drifted off course.

"Stay focused, follow your flight prompts or drift off course. Worry about advanced movement later," Mathew ordered, watching over his ten Marines. "Alright, break flight paths and prepare to land." Mathew did a slow flip and fired his suit's jump-jets in preparation for landing.

The remaining Marines followed suit and came in, all landing on their feet. As they touched down, each drew their weapons. One Marine noticed they were just above their target. "Wait up. Why land here and not call in an air strike?"

Mathew nodded as he issued the order. "The mission is to test your augments in combat. The Americans have Army Rangers who have been on station keeping our LZ safe. Cover will be scarce, almost no foliage exists now. Our job is a three phased search and destroy mission. First, we take out their sentries."

Mathew sent a series of images to everyone's HUDs showing the AAA M163 Vulcans. "Second, we knock out the AAA. From what we've seen, they're antique M163 Vulcan rotary cannons mounted on a paper-thin armor chassis, but at that velocity, 20mm can kill you. Meaning you don't let the vehicle get its sights on you."

"And third, the final leg of the mission is to withdraw using jump-jets up the mountainside as the Air Force bombs the place. If you see any other vehicles, destroy them. I'll command you from here and send mortar support if you need it." Mathew dropped his hand, sending the Marines forward."

The Marines leaped down the mountainside, using their jump-jests to hop from spot to spot until finally reaching the enemy base. Victor came in using his jump-jests to grab onto the side of a watchtower; the weight of his suit rocked the tower. He shot the man inside and found himself looking at a now broken and gore covered phone. He leveled his rifle at the watchtower across from his at the other end of the base and shot the person, and then the next until all the towers' guards were dead. "This is Savinkov. Their sniper towers are gone. I'm ready to provide cover."

Mathew responded, "Negative. Those AAA guns will kill you. Move with your team. Stay in groups of five and sweep the base. Also, turn down your rifle's power. It can only function at that power for about ten shots; you have thirty-two remaining if you turn down the intensity. The drone footage shows there is a large barracks near you. Wait for your team and engage that target."

Victor dropped down and moved with the team, doing as he was ordered. The building was no barracks, and Victor kicked down the main door with ease. The room was full of armed men readying their weapons. Those who were armed opened fire; their weapons were ancient, but they still hit their targets. "Shit, the guns aren't working!" a Californian shouted as they saw their bullets bounce off the heavily armored Marines.

The Marines promptly returned fire as the small caliber rounds bounced off their armor. Mathew saw it all via their HUDs. "Damn it, you can't rely on your armor that heavily. Next time, you scan the room with your suit's sensors before you enter. Proceed with neutralizing the first AAA unit. That thing may be an antique, but it will hurt you."

"Alright, looks like whoever was manning those vehicles has been alerted. There's a crew heading to the nearest M163 Vulcan. Out the way we came and stay down," Victor ordered as he forced his team out the door.

Just as the five Marines left the building, the Vulcan vehicle opened fire on the building until it ran out of ammunition. The Marines found cover along the side of another building as the vehicle had turned on its headlights. Victor changed the battery setting on his rifle and jumped above the vehicle, opening fire on the gun area before landing and swapping out the now empty magazine. Victor contacted his unit. "Everyone else, move up and finish this thing off. The crew is dead."

Mathew looked on as the small insect-sized drone observed everything. The Marines starting to use using their mobility impressed him.

Victor's team followed him onto the roofs and began using their elevated position to kill as many of the communists who filtered out of the buildings as they could. Eventually, a M163 Vulcan drove into the courtyard of the compound and locked its sights on the Marines.

"Everybody down!" one Marine shouted.

The group dropped down behind the building and remained low to the ground as the building's second level was torn apart by the 20mm Gatling gun. "How much ammo does that thing have loaded?"

"It's an old M163, so it can't carry more than two thousand one hundred rounds. I think it fires in bursts of seven hundred rounds. So it can shoot like that three times," another Marine replied as the vehicle crew not firing made it clear it was reloaded. Several communist soldiers rounded the corner with shotguns and larger caliber rifles.

This time, no one in Victor's squad wasted any time gunning down the group before they could open fire. As they checked their kills, one Marine asked, "Wait, is this idiot of a man wearing makeup? Is it a man?"

Victor scanned the body. The bone density scan provided no clue about what he was scanning. He stopped before doing a scan of their pelvic region. "It doesn't matter; they're dead and badly malnourished from eating bug paste and other synthetic foods that aren't good for you. We should move before that vehicle reloads."

The vehicle that was chasing them exploded, shattering the nearby windows. Another Marine chimed in via the radio, "You guys cowering behind the building can come up. This villa only has three vehicles remaining, and they're parked outside the walls. How about the team with the least AAA kills buy the drinks?"

"Oh, you're going to need a new mortgage to afford buying me drinks. Now keep moving," Victor responded, ordering his men to move out to the courtyard.

Mathew watched as the three vehicles began moving into the main compound. "All jokes aside, it looks like you finished the last of the Infantry defenders. There are, however, three AAA vehicles moving in a convoy to finish you off."

"Confirmed. We'll lay down explosive charges on the ground just after the gate to cripple the vehicles as they enter." Victor ordered his team to begin laying out the explosives.

The loud metal tracks of the three vehicles got louder and louder until the main gate swung open. The first AAA vehicle rolled right over the first set of explosives. They penetrated the belly armor of the vehicle, sending fragments into its ammunition and crew. What remained of the vehicle came to a halt as its engine panel flew off, the engine and crew compartment bursting into flames. Several secondary explosions followed as the ammunition and fuel ignited.

The second and third vehicles were forced to stop with the driver of the second vehicle, who was trying his best to move the burning wreckage. The Marines opened fire on the trapped vehicles, their Gauss rifles being far too powerful for the thin aluminum armor to handle. It took no more than a few controlled bursts from each Marine for the M163 anti-aircraft vehicles to explode.

Mathew watched from the hill as the fires from the base soon illuminated the night's sky. "Alright, mission accomplished. Once everyone has withdrawn, I'll call in the airstrike. Don't let this win go to your heads. You took on dated equipment."

Victor covered the remaining Marines as they jumped up over the wall, escaping into the wilderness. Once the rest was over, he headed back to the sergeant's position. "Sergeant Miller, no casualties to report," Victor informed him.

Mathew nodded, ignoring the obvious. He contacted the bomber using the nickname he'd long since lost his identity to. "Call sign Cisco Eight. This is call sign Mute. You are cleared for bombing run. Over."

"Cisco Eight. Bombing run commencing. Thanks for clearing the path. Over," the pilot said, signing off.

As Victor slipped on the greasy polluted dirt, an Army Ranger approached him. "Can you believe this mountainside and the valley below used to be covered in trees and lush foliage? Now everything is just dunes of polluted crap. I envy your sealed suit system. The standard issue rebreathers barely work when it comes to filtering the sheer filth below."

"As a child, I saw the Californian people in the movies. The state had many hills and valleys, all green. What gives? Where did all the plants go?" Victor asked as he ran his hand through the oily dirt. "This is not what I saw in holovids."

"Combination of things over the last century changed the land. Their strip mines for gold and other resources started it all off. The other issue came when their electric cars and solar panels would no longer work. They were dumped, polluting the earth with chromium, lead, and cadmium. The fires from the waste pits make it all worse. It's why I envy you your sealed suit," the Ranger shouted as a pair of ASF-58 Rapiers swooped in over the mountain top followed by drone wingmen.

The Marines and Army Rangers all let out a roar of cheers as the aircraft moved to attack their targets. Several large explosions began going off in the city below. As the troops started celebrating the victory, it wasn't long before a UH-17 Kite arrived to pick up the two groups.

"Anyway, there's a reason why West Arizona imports all their water from Yuma Arizona," the ranger continued. "In all the ground here, water is going to be toxic for centuries to come. I swear I'm going to get cancer simply from going on recon. This toxic waste dump is a fitting punishment for the backwards Marxists. They killed billions and now have a hellish landscape to match their sick minds."

The Kite with its transverse rotors began kicking up huge piles of dust as it circled in close to the mountainside for pickup. The pilot lowered the craft to the more cliff-like section of the mountain. It was a nimble craft, and the pilot managed to turn the aircraft flawlessly on a dime so the troops could enter from the rear hatch.

"All aboard. Time to RTB," the deckhand shouted through his mask, holding out a hand to the troops.

Victor took a seat along the VTOL's wall when Mathew spoke. "Your mission was a success, but that's no excuse to avoid the simulators. You beat an easy target today, nothing more. No beers, no women, and no parties. Get some rest and prepare for tomorrow."

The flight back to base was uneventful, and looking out on the land below, Victor saw all manners of refuse. Looking south, he saw the domes that covered the last bits of civilization in the region. The domes housed the occupation forces not on duty, and their families. Victor looked at the Army Ranger next to him. "This is the fate of the godless. Hell on earth is the only place for them."

"Damn straight! These commies have sacrificed all decency," the Ranger replied.

The morning sun began creeping up slowly in the east, and another day started for Victor. He would ignore the sinners below. For now, he was content with his training in the Marines, largely unaware of things to come.

Waking up, Mitch petted Rana's large ears while she was still asleep before lovingly running his hand down to her shoulder. Rana rolled over to look at him. Yawning, she asked, "Planning on escaping?"

Mitch held Rana's face in his hand. "No, I can't sleep anymore. Perhaps I could surprise you with some breakfast?"

Sitting up, Rana crawled into Mitch's lap. "What's on your mind? Recall will be in two days, right?"

Mitch sat up and breathed in Rana's scent; maybe that's why he didn't want to love and leave her. A conscience could be the reason—they were too horny to use a condom. He cursed himself for not using one, but something in him wanted to be with her for more than a week of immature love making. Could this be the way? Without thinking much, he answered her, "You're on it, Rana?"

Rana looked down at his naked sex and smiled like the Cheshire cat. "Your penis is one hard target to miss." Rana leaned further into him.

Mitch blushed, having fumbled his words while she fluttered her eyelashes at him. "I mean, you're on my mind, and what we've been doing for the last few days isn't far behind!" Mitch tried calming down, but couldn't help but stiffen up. Her skin was the softest thing he'd felt in years, and looking into her eyes only filled him with lust.

Rana leaned into Mitch's arms, using her tail to rub his face. "You took everything from me, sir. Christ, you were rough. Tell me you were rough because your ravenous lust built up over years of loneliness. I hope you'll be nicer in the future." Rana looked him in the eyes now. "How about we have breakfast instead of another romp?"

"I got excited, and you seemed to like it rough. Anyway, a lot is on my mind. I have been lying about my age to the government for three years now." Mitch paused, watching Rana get out of bed. "I do love you, and it's not just sex."

"You lied about your age to join the military. But the medical staff should have seen through whatever nonsense your uncle taught you to bypass computer security. Perhaps things are more dire than the news said. I don't think anyone noticed, so notice me," Rana replied, stretching her legs.

Mitch sighed as Rana's leg stretching reminded him of how she moved her body beneath him and how she kept rhythm in her passion until a messy climax. He broke from those thoughts. "I'm not sure why I was so rough. You have a body any man with lustful desires could ever want. You lead the way when we escaped my degenerate excuses of parents. My aunt would still be beating me without you. I never thought I would see you again."

Rana took Mitch's hand and used it to stroke her face. "That thing was no woman, and it wasn't even human. Learn from it as what not to be. Let your misguided compassion for your family go like you should all that pain you hide." Rana looked up at Mitch as he ran his hand down to her chin. "How about breakfast in bed for my war hero?" Rana asked as they shared a languorous kiss.

Mitch broke eye contact. "Breakfast sounds great. The war hero part, not so much. I can't discuss what went down, not even with you. Thing is, we came home thinking we'd won and then boom. I'm watching the closet thing I have to a friend scrambling to find his loved ones." Mitch shook his head, trying not to remember Chicago.

Rana stepped back, sliding her panties on before taking Mitch's shirt as a trophy. "Mitch, you aren't perfect, but you did correct that failure. Now I suggest you use the time it takes to make breakfast to find work. That hideout in the desert won't buy itself and the honeymoon's wearing off." She winked, walking off.

Mitch grabbed his phone off the nightstand; he had to report in on Friday. He scrolled through his messages—most were worthless spam. The military, though, seemed to be ignoring him. Perhaps the military got tired of him, the same way his aunt grew sick of a crying, drug-addicted infant going through the pain of withdrawal. *Such is the way of any military; everyone is just meat with a shelf life.* Mitch placed the phone down and tried to relax.

Rana came in with a plate of food, placing it at the bedside. "I've been a frisky little kitty for days now, yet you're pining for the military like a love-struck puppy. What does a girl have to do to be the focus in your life?"

Mitch snapped back to reality as the scent of her cooking invaded his senses. "Sorry, I'm just not sure what the hell I can do. My uncle taught me how to be a crook. Hell, I lied to the government; they think I'm twenty-two. What the hell will I do when that hammer falls?"

"One step at a time. Perhaps they know and don't care, preferring the chance to do weird experiments on you? You know something now that I am a bit envious of. I just realized we aren't married yet. You just got an all-access pass to me with full service breakfast."

"Yeah, well, you know me so well I bet you're a dozen steps ahead of me," Mitch replied, smelling the food. "The bacon and eggs on a ship can't compare to this."

"Thank you. I didn't think you'd like my basic cooking. I've barely improved from the days before we parted ways. It's one thing I hated about the ECF. We escaped together, but they separated us the first chance they got."

"Just wait till the only thing you eat is a paste designed to minimize bodily waste and keep you going as you wear over two hundred kilos of armor. This isn't bad in any way." Mitch stopped eating. "Are you trying to convince me to quit?"

"Would it be so bad? No more crap gruel and we'll never be apart again, don't you want that? You can find a real job. You can't seriously like falling from orbit so damn much that swallowing swill would make you pass up bacon and eggs?" Rana sighed in defeat. "You actually do like falling from orbit that much?"

"It's not like that," Mitch said, finishing his food. "Did you just throw yourself at me and feed me all this to make me walk away?"

Rana rolled her eyes. "Fine, you busted me dead to rights, but why go back? Is it to prove that you're a better man than your uncle? Your uncle, a sniveling cuck who stole from idiot New Yorker trust fund trash that turned a blind eye to the fact I was bought like a slab of meat? You owe me a reason about why you're going back after all I've given you. Give me a goddamn reason why at the very least."

"I'm going back because this war isn't over. The closest thing I have to a friend turned into an emotional wreck because he couldn't find his family. We thought everything would be fine, and then we came home to a battlefield. I'm not going to walk away when this isn't over." Mitch looked over the last strip of bacon before he turned to Rana, placing a hand on her stomach. "You want to know my reason for swallowing gruel? It's because I don't want to even think of you in a protection camp. My reason is to keep you both safe."

"I was right. You are a better person than your uncle and aunt," Rana conceded, as she had to admit that Mitch was selflessly fighting for a valid cause. "I respect your choice. I don't like it, but I want a husband I can respect."

Mitch paused for a second. "Husband? So you want to marry me?"

"Yes, in all, a pregnant bar maid tends to get lower tips. Now let's ignore those scum bags and make our own future," Rana replied.

"Yeah, they were pathetic people," Mitch replied with a chuckle. "I can't believe I used to fear those fucking monsters. Is this a place with a good school zone?"

"You were a child living with abusive adults," Rana said, comforting him. "You and I did the only thing we could. We fled. As for the school zone, I'm not sure. I bought this place on the cheap."

"How about I do the dishes this time?" Mitch asked as the pair finished breakfast. About to pick up their plates, his phone vibrated ever so slightly. Setting the plates down, he looked at the phone.

PFC MITCHEL DAVIS. RETURN TO ACTIVE SERVICE MONDAY 30 JULY. REPORT TO LAUGHLIN AIRFORCE BASE BY 1100 HOURS FOR TRANSFER.

Sean woke up and looked at his phone, longing for it to ring. It was the only hope he had of ever speaking to his mother Lisa. It had been a week and no calls. *Is this punishment for my failure? Did I fail you so badly that you are rejecting me entirely? Was I that much of a disappointment?*

"Do you have to wake up so early?" Sammy questioned Sean as

she leaned up in the bed, using the sheets to cover her breasts. "I know you're a soldier, but this is time off, meaning you sleep in."

"How did you and Yuki make a business profitable enough to have a Streeterville store front by being such a slacker? It's the middle of the week and 0930 hours."

Sammy rolled her eyes. "Just say in the morning, you damn drone. As for our business, we're dedicated to our customers, whether they simply stop for off-the-rack clothing or a custom wardrobe. It helps the owner is a Nataki."

"So, D-A-D funds the entire operation," Sean said condescendingly as he slid on top of Sammy. "I guess I better find a way to put you to actual use," he said with a smile.

Sammy smiled, hiding her rage at his comment, knowing full well a marriage wouldn't always be sunshine and roses. She decided instead to kindly correct her husband. "I'll have you know her father hasn't funded that business for over a year and a half. You should be nicer given you have a nice wife who doesn't enjoy the makeup sex," Sammy said, wrapping her legs tightly around his waist and raising her pelvis to meet his.

Sean locked her hands in his. She was smiling, but one look in her eyes still showed some of the anger she'd mostly buried for his sake. "I didn't mean to hurt your feelings. My humor has gotten a bit meaner being away from civilization." Sean kissed her forehead as he pushed inside her.

"It's fine, though I wish your mother Lisa wasn't taking up so much space in your mind." Sammy winced as Sean pushed deeper and harder into her; it had been a long time since they'd been together, after all. "I'd rather not fight. We only have a little time, and it'll be over soon. I'll have to report back in a couple of days."

"I'm sorry to insult you by claiming Yuki's father funded your business. It's just hard to remember where the line in polite society is," Sean whispered as he closed the gap between their bodies. "As for my mother, the only woman on my mind now is you. Forget I mentioned her."

Sammy closed her eyes as Sean began a steady motion of thrusts;

she was his wife now, and that fact made their intimacy all the more intense. Years of emotional intimacy had finally merged their flesh into one. "Try not to change any more than you have. That's all I ask."

"What do you mean? Change how?" Sean whispered his complaint into her ear as he stopped kissing her. "I am still me, just a bit better."

"You were just fine before. Please don't lose yourself like your brother did," Sammy begged, looking at him. "Promise me that you'll come back and live."

Sean's lips crashed onto hers in a bruising kiss. "I promise when this is over, we'll do all the normal boring people stuff. When I get back, we can become mundane, routine followers."

As Sean moved to kiss Sammy again, a knock at the door interrupted the two. "Hey, breakfast is ready and waiting for you two. Also, Sammy, you have a call from your friend. Can you open up and take the phone?"

Reluctantly, Sean climbed off Sammy and she looked up at him and asked, "So it's almost ten in the morning and breakfast is only just now ready? Is that a bit lazy too? I admit, I'll have to learn some of your mom's cooking skills."

Sean dressed hurriedly. "I'm not going to touch that one. Although, you're not a bad cook as you are now."

"Tell Yuki to hold on," Sammy replied, getting dressed. She cracked open the door. "Thanks Larisa, we'll be down in a minute."

Yuki was shouting through the phone. "Hey there! How is everything going? I hope you're spending the down time making a baby! How is Sean?"

Yuki's question immediately reminded Sean of how Yuki could be far too blunt for her own good as he listened to them talking about him. "I'm well thanks, Yuki."

Yuki, despite being a disembodied voice on the phone, tried to cheer him up. "I know you, Sean. Don't beat yourself up over what happened. Now I need a favor from you, Sean, so be sure to knock Sammy up. I want to be a cool aunt."

Taking the phone off speaker, Sammy replied, "Yuki, will you stop with this nonsense? I'm glad you're doing well enough to command my husband like a prized bull, but it's still insulting."

"You got married?" Yuki's shout was loud enough Sean could hear. "No worries. When you have the ceremony, I'll design your dress."

Sammy rolled her eyes, doing her best not to sigh and let Yuki know how annoyed she was. "You know I would only come to you for a wedding dress. Now tell me why you're calling. How did you know I was here?"

Yuki sighed and got to the point. "I'm not omniscient, so don't worry that I'm watching you two rabbits. I called to let you know that after recovering our P&Ls, our business will be fine once the downtown area is opened again."

Sammy perked up. "Really? You do know our store was bombed out, and that you lost an arm."

"Don't remind me. But father has me being fitted for a customized arm. Anyways friend…" Yuki paused, her perky, upbeat tone faltering as she drew in a slow, deep breath. "Don't waste your time talking to me. Go make these last few days the best of your lives."

The call dropped off. Sammy checked the number and decided she would call back later. Yuki needed time to processes what had happened. Of course, a part of her wanted to call back immediately and scream at Yuki that she wasn't alone. Could things be fine? Sean had left for breakfast long ago, and once dressed, Sammy decided to join them.

The smell of bacon and eggs filled her nose. Would Sean expect such a luxury from her? It made her wonder how his mother pulled everything off. "Good morning, Sammy!" Jennifer said as she put out a plate for her.

Sammy picked up a fork. "Thanks, it looks as good as it smells! I rarely sit down to eat breakfast."

Sammy watched Sean pick up a fork and eat, wondering if he'd show that much enthusiasm for a meal she prepared for him. "Thanks mom." Sean's gratitude seemed so lacking to Sammy. She looked over at Larisa before eating as well.

Joining them for breakfast, Jennifer asked, "So, Sean, will you return to active duty?"

Larisa wasted no time in pressing her brother for an answer. "You'll stay here with your family and train other people to fight, right?"

Sammy sighed. She knew Larisa didn't take loss well. "Larisa, I know you want your brother back, but you need to see the bigger picture."

"Shut up. You're not the one left alone. You didn't bury your father and brother. I did, not you!" Larisa nearly spat venom at Sammy as she continued. "I'm alone with mom, waiting for the damn letter that tells me you died too. You can move on, go to your shop, and find a new man like that." Larisa snapped her fingers in Sammy's face.

Sammy punched the table. "No, you're not alone! Hate me all you want. Rant and rave, call me a slutty Wiesel if it helps you feel better. I know how much you are hurting, losing your father and brother. I lost my parents too. We're in the same boat now. So say whatever you need to say to help you accept there is no going back to the way things were. The sooner you accept it, the better I say!"

Larisa got up to leave the table, only for Sean to stop her. Before he could speak, however, Jennifer barked a command. "She's right, Larisa. Now both of you sit down and eat. I'm not going to have anyone's drama ruin my nice breakfast."

Sammy watched Sean move without question; the military taught him how to follow orders well. He would show his mother no defiance. Larisa returned to her seat as well while trying to appear defiant. "It's not fair. She just gets to tag along while we get all the next of kin notifications."

Sammy responded, "I'm your sister-in-law now. I don't just get to walk away. I wish you would at least tell me why you hate me."

"I don't exist to you. Sammy is clearly the only person who matters to you. I am nothing more than a child to talk down to, so what does it matter?" Larisa replied to Sean more than Sammy when she wasn't eating. "Just tell me what's what and leave me alone again."

"She isn't stealing me from you, Larisa. And I'm sorry I came back without Derek. Staying with you, however, is not going to help you or anyone else. How about we try to enjoy the time we have left together?" Sean interrupted, trying to calm her down.

Sammy collected the empty plates. "We can go up into Kenosha for a movie if you want in the downtown area instead of downloading something. Anything sure beats staying indoors and fighting."

"It would be nice to not listen to your arguing and other activities. Sean, take them out. I'm sure these two should be easy to handle in public. Get your sister home by 10 p.m." Jennifer gave Sammy her plate.

Larisa finished her breakfast and went to her room, but Sean followed her. "Larisa, come back, please."

As Sammy went to chase after the pair, Jennifer stopped her. "Let him deal with her for now. I'll tell you something. She probably just needs her big brother to tell her things will be okay."

"How do you do all this?" Sammy asked, motioning to the nice breakfast as well as dealing with angst ridden teenagers.

"Can I have more coffee?" Jennifer asked, handing Sammy her coffee mug. "Larisa has been alone. She is so like her father. Without him around, she thinks family is only skin deep. Being dark-skinned like Trevor and Derek, she was closer to them. That is her idea of love for the time being. Her father and big brother leaving her made her feel unwanted."

"That's so small-minded and selfish. Then again, when I was her age, I had so much more support since there wasn't a war." Sammy genuinely pitied Larisa as she gave Jennifer her coffee.

"She feels weak and alone without her doting protectors. Sean connected with her, so let him fix this, alright?" Jennifer said, drinking her coffee.

"I'm afraid of the future. I honestly doubt I can measure up to you when it comes to being a wife. Watching you make breakfast and deal with Larisa so effortlessly, it all seems so overwhelming," Sammy replied, sitting down.

"I do this because when I joined the scientific community, all my hard work got repurposed. The PTSD drug all soldiers take is my doing. My work was meant to treat long term mental health problems. Instead, the military found better uses for it and buried my hopes with the stroke of a pen. As a homemaker, I found more contentment." Jennifer paused, taking a sip, then touched Sammy's cheek. "Don't doubt yourself about this stuff. You'll be a great wife. Hell, I had all your doubts once."

"Thank you," Sammy said, putting the dishes into the washer. "Are you sure I shouldn't head up there? I can tell Larisa that I am not stealing her brother from her."

Jennifer placed her cup down. "If you really want to go up there and snoop, I would be careful not to get caught."

Sean leaned against his sister's door. "Can you tell me what's wrong? And do it to my face for once."

"Fine, come in!" Larisa swung open the door. Sammy listened in from the first floor as Sean entered his sister's room before slowly climbing the stairs. She moved silently, hoping to go unnoticed as she made her way to the second floor.

"The only letter I've ever had in the past two years is a next of kin notification," Larisa told Sean. "Look, I get it. I'm just your sister in need of protection, but you'd rather be fucking Sammy," Larisa said, walking away back to her bed.

"Oh, right, because I don't care for you. I left to protect you and every time I tried to get close to you this week, you just spit venom at me. What happened to that girl I spent weeks with? Helping dad and Derek building model planes for? The nice baby sister who happily played with them till the models broke. Never once did we get mad when you did that." Sean followed her, trying to gentle his tone. "You know, when you were four it was insanely cute- when you thought that an FA-48 Wraith at any size could break the sound barrier. Even after the F-14, F-16, and F-4 fighter planes we made you never could."

"Dad told me anything was possible if I put my mind and body into my efforts." Larisa sat up on her bed as Sean sat down at her desk. "I had no idea a 1/35 scale model lacked a functional engine."

"You were such a determined child." Sean, arms crossed, and asked, "What has you so determined to be a pain in my ass now?"

"You promised me a letter every day, but never wrote a single one; then you spend all your time with Sammy or have Sammy tag along now that you're back." Larisa went to her dresser and took out a smaller than average model plane. "Today is the first day you've given me any attention. This was one of the last planes you three built for me; I saved every piece when it broke. I think its smaller size was a sign of the end."

Larisa took another small model from the back of a dresser drawer and handed Sean the last plane. This was the last plane her men had built for her. It was the only reason Sean could imagine her keeping it. "Well, those model kits were expensive. Mother felt you'd be too much of a brat, so she put her foot down. A P-38 Lightning," Sean mused. "The only damage is to the propellers and its left wing. I can maybe put them back on in working order."

"You can?! I never was good at building things." Larisa perked up as she handed Sean the model plane's remains. "Every time I felt alone, I'd look at that and remember the days we spent together when you would let me cut the sticker sheets."

"Sure, a bit of drilling and a few metal inserts and the propeller will be as good as new," Sean replied, accepting the last bit of the model. "You know, if you feel alone, ask Sammy for a job for after school work."

"Because clothing interests me so much," Larisa complained as she lay back on her bed. "I want revenge for dad and Derek. I've been working out and Minka has helped me improve my shooting skills. I'm almost sixteen. Your mom Lisa was Field PSYOPs. I'm not as smart as her, but if I try hard, I can be Naval Infantry."

Sean wanted to smack her senseless for wanting revenge, but he knew the feeling since it also consumed him at times. "Well, I won't be able to stop you from joining. At least you aren't planning on being a lazy NEET. Be nice to Sammy, you're family now. I'll fix this for you."

"Fine, I'll be nice. Hey, Sammy. I give up, you can come in now," Larisa shouted, sitting up on her bed. "I'll share him. We can do girl stuff like braid each other's hair."

Sammy entered, arms crossed. "Are you really not angry that I was listening in? Let me guess, you were snooping on me earlier?" Sammy sat on the bed next to Larisa as she ran her hands through her hair. "Long raven locks. Keeping your hair straight goes well with your darker complexion. Braids may not be a bad idea, but I just can't braid your hair. It could come out awful, like really weird looking pigtails." Sammy grabbed Larisa's hair with a quick, hard yank.

"Hey, don't pull so hard!" Larisa let out a whine. "My hair is just fine as it is. Leave it alone."

Sammy had a slight, sadistic grin as she gave Larisa another yank. "Fair enough. I won't braid your hair, but you know you could add some brightly colored highlights. It's been so long since I've dyed only a portion of my hair beyond a solid bright purple. How about simple stripe Silver, not blonde on the left and right bang?"

"I'll stay with my natural color. The attempts to revive the punk look have never interested me. I want my hair to be all natural. Can you teach me how to ride a motorcycle?" Larisa asked. "I admit, you have a nice outfit selected for when you go riding."

"Oh, you want to know how to ride a motorcycle and look good doing it?" Sammy replied, heading to Larisa's closet. "Well, you'll need full body coverage, but that doesn't mean you need a riding suit.

As Larisa stood up to respond to the raid on her closet, Jennifer shouted from downstairs, "Sean, you have a phone call! It's your mom Lisa."

Larisa produced a key. "Hey, Sammy, you curious what they'll talk about? This key will get us into Mother Lisa's office!"

Sammy knew she should say no and stay out of Lisa's office; it wasn't right to listen in on conversations. She sighed. "Let's go. So long as you know how to bypass Lisa's security cameras, I won't mind entering her private space."

"Those only come on if the key isn't used first," Larisa replied as the two hurried to the office.

The two entered Lisa's office; it smelled like mahogany. Sammy remembered how often Lisa claimed it was her favorite wood. The library of legal books lined the left wall while a small liquor cabinet plus accessories were on the right wall. There were also a few paintings of Ryan Aerospace machines above. The room was clean, and the pair made their way to the desk mounted phone.

Larisa pressed the listen in option. "Mother never should have let me know about this option by recording a conversation I had with a boy."

"Why would she do that?" Sammy asked. "It's so rude to spy on your own family."

"Sean, how are you doing? I'm sorry for taking so long to contact you. I'm sure you understand I have responsibilities to the people?" Lisa's voice was calm but not disconnected as she spoke. "I've been very busy and security has kept me constantly moving from one location to the next until they felt I was absolutely safe. It's frustrating."

"I understand," Sean said, sounding relieved, "and I know how you feel. Larisa has been cold all week. I'm going back to active duty soon, responsibilities to other people and all."

"I'm proud of your decision. That's one thing I can say about you and all my children…" Lisa paused. "How has everyone else taken the news?"

Sean sighed. "Larisa's not taking it well, but Sammy is supportive. I have no clue how Mama Jennifer is taking it."

"Well, do what you feel is right. I'm sorry I've been so distant, Sean." Lisa yawned. "But I've been running from location to location for days. You're doing what's right, and that's what makes me proud of you."

As the conversation ended and Sean hung up, Larisa broke their silence. "That's so like her. She knows he seeks her approval and will basically keep him going in any direction she wants."

"He was already going to go back." Sammy received a nasty scowl from Larisa. "Hey, I'm not a fan of Lisa, either, but she hardly manipulates as much as you think."

Larisa rolled her eyes. "Yes, she's much worse. It's how she does so well in politics. Let's go give Sean support. It would suck to have my last memories of my brother be sour."

Sammy's eyes widened. "You promise to be more positive?"

"Do you promise to teach me how to ride a motorcycle?" Larisa asked arms crossed.

"Yes, I promise to teach the baby sister I just got how to ride a motorcycle," Sammy answered, giving Larisa a hug.

The pair walked down the stairs to meet Sean and Jennifer. "Hey girls, you two bury the hatchet?" Jennifer asked, sipping from her cup of coffee.

Sean was looking for something in the bottom cupboards. "Hey, mom, where is the model glue and the small toolkit I had in the cabinet?"

"It's out in the garage; in the small tool storage area on the second self. Your smelly glues and paints were placed out of my house. Where they belong," Jennifer stood up and headed to the backyard. "If you will excuse me, I have a book to read."

Sean went to the garage, leaving Sammy and Larisa alone. Larisa, quite proudly, announced, "I think no one is the wiser we spied on them."

"So it seems, or they don't care." Sammy crossed her arms. "Are you serious about joining the military? You're not much of a fighter. I could probably hand you your ass in a fight, Larisa. I've handled men bigger than you."

"Yeah, but you're too dainty for anything more than beating up those soft Californian rapists. Face it, Sammy, you'd need a gun to deal with real men," Larisa replied as the pair returned to Larisa's room. "When can I get my first lesson on riding a motorcycle?"

"And you would need a gun to be effective in the military. Besides needing a helmet, you'll want to have an outfit that is dense and covers your limbs entirely in the event of a crash," Sammy replied, looking into Larisa's closet.

Sean, meanwhile, was glad to be away from his sister and Sammy's bickering, even though he could still hear them. Why the hell did she always have to mimic him so damn much? Constantly trying to tag along? Larisa had never been easy to deal with and she damn well knew it. With the resin for the printer, he could fix the small plane in a few hours.

Sean opened the cabinet and began rummaging through it. Upon finding what he was looking for, he thought, *Ah, the resin I need to make a propeller. God, I'm going to have to do something extreme to keep her out of the military. The only option for the military not to take her is my death. How the fuck can I win the war and save my sister?*

Sean made his way to his room and set up the 3D printer. Sitting down at his desk, he typed in a few commands, and the machine started printing the needed replacement parts. He was thankful for the humming sound from the printer for calming his nerves.

Sammy cracked the door open. "Hey, we stopped bickering. I'm sure you'll like to hear that, right Sean?"

"Yeah, and I even got a cool outfit to go motorcycle riding!" Larisa added, walking by the door.

"Yeah, that's great, you two. I have the replacement parts coming out of the printer. I'll make a few holes in the plane and replace the propeller and wing," Sean replied as Sammy walked into the room. He looked at his clock and noticed he'd lost track of time. "Where did Larisa go? Wasn't she right behind you? Did she tire of being nice to you? I am not sure I can deal with more pouting."

Sammy sat down on the bed as Sean worked on the model airplane. "No, Larisa joined her mother on the porch. She probably went to tell her how I promised to teach her how to ride a motorcycle. Goddess made that girl high maintenance."

Sean went about cleaning the parts from his 3D printer as Sammy watched. "Yeah, she has always been hard-headed. I never could figure out the why or where she gets it from."

"She's a handful for sure. I'm not sure how you tolerate her sometimes," Sammy replied, watching Sean go to work on the model.

"Well, she is a bratty sister, but she's my spoiled bratty sister. I won't stop doing what I can to protect her and you."

Sammy raised her hands. "I understand what you're trying to do. No need to sell me on your choices."

Sean began working on the model airplane, drilling a new hole into the engine nacelle of the plane. Inserting the small peg into the hole, he attached the propeller to the peg. "Sammy, your support is probably the most important thing I have right now."

"I'll support you so long as you promise not to risk your life unnecessarily. It sounds strange to say this, but I think you'd do something needlessly extreme. I fear losing you to the extremes you already let the government modify your body and mind with. Do you have any limits now?"

"I know you distrust the system for giving me cybernetics, but I am still me. Hell, the system's why you're a successful small business owner and not taxed into poverty."

"Yeah, they're great at letting me earn a good living." Sammy paused, fighting the urge to cry. "The issue isn't the system. It's you going to the extremes for solutions that are only in your head. What will you let some government doctor cut out of you when you get it in your head that the next extreme will fix the problem? What will you cut away from your body when that plan fails?"

"That's not true Sammy! Sean made a difference by going as far as he did. Sacrificing what he did is why we are here in this house," Larisa interrupted their conversation from the door. "As for me being a difficult brat, I never thought you viewed me as your sister since we aren't siblings. I know it doesn't matter to you, but your opinion gets me."

"Well, sis, your P-38 is pretty much fixed. Look, even though I am married now, it won't stop me from caring about you," Sean said as he showed Larisa the model's spinning propellers. "Now, can you two do me a favor and not start fighting again?"

Larisa's eyes widened a bit as she looked at the model. "Nice work. This time I'll make a diorama for it, or at least give it a nice place on the shelf."

"I'm glad you kept the model all this time. It brought back some good memories. When I get back, I'll make that diorama," Sean replied, cleaning up the mess.

Sammy sat silently. Larisa's words had struck a nerve. "I'll see about finding an open craft store. That way we can have all the materials ready when you get back. Just promise me, Sean, not to do something rash for a quick solution."

Sean stood up and locked eyes with Sammy. "I promise I won't do anything for a quick solution. I am not in this for glory. I only want to do what I can to win this war."

July 30, 1045 hours
Laughlin Air Force Base

Monday had come; the border wall loomed over the base's mass driver. The gates to the base were closed off to family members who'd managed to follow their loved one this far to the call up. Countless busses lined the road into the base to deliver their occupants. Along the road side supporters and well-wishers gave the soldiers a warm send off as shuttle craft prepared to launch.

Sean sat in the back of the bus, waiting, thankful for the air condition as the window radiated with the outside heat at every touch. He sighed and watched a shuttle launch from the mass driver while playing with his wedding ring attached to his dog tags.

Mitch leaned back, not looking at Sean as he spoke. "Have you noticed this bus only has a few other members of the 3-4? I have a feeling something is up."

Sean hid his ring quickly. "I'm sure our bus wasn't meant to transport our entire unit. Seriously, calm down."

Sean did notice several new faces along with the old ones but thought little of it as the busses entered the base. Eric and Masa were all the way up front while Mute sat with Nathan. Gabe was sitting next to an unknown with several facial tattoos. It wasn't until the bus turned right while the rest of the busses went straight toward the assembly that everyone was on alert as the vehicle drove toward an empty hangar.

"Okay, now I am a bit concerned," Sean said to Mitch as the driver opened the door.

"Alright, everyone out!" the driver shouted as heat rushed into the bus when he swung the door open.

No one on the bus hesitated to grab their duffle bags and climbed off as quickly as they could. The heat hit them in earnest as the barely lit hangar did very little to reduce the sweltering humidity of Texas in July. Once everyone was off, they walked into the hangar through the opening in the main door. The hangar was empty—no aircraft, no parts, just emptiness. It was cleaner than one would expect for an abandoned section of the base. At the back wall of was a tall blonde Qualurian with a cybernetic arm in a colonel's uniform, leaning against a table.

Ezra greeted the men, arms crossed as they entered; most were slightly confused. All of them stood at attention, dropping their duffle bags when they saw her rank. She noticed several of the men began sweating. It was probably more humid than some humans could handle. She slapped her hands together. "Great, you know the basics of military respect granted to superior ranks."

Ezra walked through the center group of men, looking each over. "Some of you may know each other, but I'm sure you are all wondering why you are here. That is simple to answer. You all have proven your skills in combat and are exceptional in some way or another. Of course, you are all here for one thing above all else. All of you are connected by your willingness to do what needs to be done and won't be missed when you are dead."

Ezra's words shook many internally. Sean was confused but kept his composure. Mitch was unmoved by the Qualurian's words, watching her pass by before returning to the front of the group. "I summoned you here because I want to win the war in the shortest time possible. That means I intend to throw you at the enemy where they least expect to be attacked. If you fail, you die, and we continue the fight without you. Succeed in your mission, and I will make every effort to extract you. If you win the war, I promise increased pay, benefits, and double rank promotions. You will be a cheaper throw-away option to Special Forces, that is, if you choose to remain. If you wish to leave, go now. The bus is waiting."

Ezra pointed out to the back and several of the men left. The room went from having a full platoon of forty men to being just enough to form of full fire team. Sean remained; he'd just been given everything he wanted. This would be his chance to end the war before Larisa could join the fight. Sean knew the stakes were too high to leave. He'd failed Derek and his hometown, but now he had the chance to set things right.

Eric leaned over slightly to Masa. "Mac, you think we should have walked?"

"Shut up, man. This will be a fast track for promotion. Command can't have anything too insane for us ahead," Masa replied.

Jason stepped forward from the middle row. Jason recognized Victor looking much bigger than the last time he met him in Saint Petersburg. Two men, one Asian, and the other with a heavily scarred up face, were talking in the back; he would need to reprimand them for gossiping. However, he was thankful that he only had ten other names to remember. "My name is Major Jason West. I am both your and this unit's second in command. I will be with you all the way. From here on out, we will drill round the clock in a crash course to see what roles each person performs the best in and how to perform as a team."

Ezra placed her hand on Jason's shoulder. "Thank you, Major West. I will take over from here. The unit you all have chosen to join is unnamed and none of you are good enough to do the job needed to turn the tide as you are. The ECS Hue will be your new training ground as it transitions from Earth to the mission theater," Ezra barked at the men. Truck engines rumbled in the distance. They slowly got closer before the squealing of brakes signaled a large transport truck pulling up outside the hangar. "That's our ride, gentlemen. This truck will take you to our shuttle. Know this: when you die, no one will be around to miss you or to protest your loss."

The men collected their duffel bags and climbed into the back of the truck. Climbing in, Masa threw his hand out to help Sean up into the truck. "I'm sorry for your loss, kid. I guess your family in Chicago didn't make it."

Sean accepted the hand up into the truck. He then proceeded to lie, hoping to bury any discussion of his personal life. "Yes, and my girl left me as soon as I found my way to her. Likewise, Mac, sorry you lost your father."

"He lived honorably. I hope to do the same," Masa replied as he took a seat.

Sean pulled Mitch and Eric up into the back of the truck before taking a seat. As Mitch took his seat, he spoke up. "Let's not make this all bad news. Does anyone know why they got picked? I'm pretty sure I'm here for shutting down those drones in Chicago."

"You all got picked for several unique skills or above average performances. You need to understand one thing: having friends in this unit will only make doing your job a lot harder," James interrupted Mitch's question before he leaned in close to set the young man's ego in place. "As for you and your skills with computers, kid, if you were that important, ODIN wouldn't let you join this operation."

"Oh, I'm really liking our new major!" Eric shouted as he climbed into the truck last.

"Shut up, scar face. I know your command style well enough. You best stow your tough guy act and shoot straight. I don't have time for your shit. You will all do your best at all times and remain humble. That is an order," Jason said, watching the group of Marines look at him. Only Victor was busy reading his bible. "You become a priest after all that luck?"

Victor closed the bible and looked at the group before speaking to Jason. "Of course, and I have my first batch of souls in need of guidance."

The truck drove to the tarmac for the aircraft-like fighter jets. A smaller Hornet dropship sat alone at the taxi-way with a flight crew performing a last-minute checks. Everyone around it was clearly keeping watch as if the Hornet had been stolen. Sean wondered how much the colonel was hiding, but decided not to ask; Sammy would be pissed. She'd begged him not to do anything extreme. He'd promised her exactly that, yet here he was, joining a unit so secret it probably stole a dropship.

Fuck me, there's no other choice. I have to finish this before Larisa gets killed, Sean thought. It was obvious—to save Larisa, he had to go this far! Not that it would be something he could ever explain to Sammy. He reached for the wedding ring he kept on the chain with his dog tags. It was another problem he couldn't explain. He would be derided and ostracized in this unit if these men found out he was married, with his family being alive and well.

Ezra climbed out of the cab of the truck and began shouting as several larger dropships lifted off in the background. "Alright, there is our ride. The ECS Hue is waiting in orbit. Much of our fleet is being repaired, but the good news is the Serkins are in much the same state. Our nuclear barrage may have destroyed some of the Earth's cities, but it was a needed sacrifice. You will all get very comfortable with necessary sacrifices, or else you will fail."

The group piled out and climbed into the dropship. Mitch looked at Sean as he took a seat with his duffle bag stuck in the nearest storage locker. "You got any regrets, man?" Mitch asked as the Qualurian colonel walked past him. He did little to hide his concerns, despite knowing she could hear him.

Sean locked his duffle bag into the locker and strapped into the wall mounted seat. "Don't you dare start doubting this now. Where the hell is your arrogance?"

"Fair enough. If you have the will to go through with this, so do I," Mitch replied. He wouldn't let it slip that he'd seen Sean's wedding ring. Just because he liked running his mouth didn't mean he would spread secrets.

"Amen, let's fucking win this shit!" Masa added. Eric shook his head as he took a seat next to Mathew.

"Mute, please tell me you aren't in on this crap," Eric asked the closest man he had to a nihilist.

Mathew looked at Eric with his mechanical eyes moving slowly from left to right as the dropship's cargo ramp closed. Looking at Eric, he said, "Don't die for me."

"Death is only a guarantee for failure. This is not some death cult. We won't be performing these missions with any intent on dying," Jason interrupted. "Any of you fuck this up, I'll make you regret it for the rest of your short life."

Everyone could feel a jolt as the dropship shook when it began lifting off and angled upward. Many of the men's ears popped as the altitude changed. Finally, Earth's pull gave away as the loss of gravity; the only thing keeping the passengers in their seats now was their harnesses. Ezra sat in the gunner's seat as the pilot leveled the warship with the ECS Hue's tracking lights.

The ESC Hue extended a small rail as its airlock doors opened. The dropship drifted slowly to a stop as it attached to the arm and was slowly pulled aboard the ship. Once the dropship entered the frigate's airlock, the ship's doors closed, and the dropship was raised into the cargo hold of the ship. Gravity finally returned to the dropship as it came to a halt in the frigate's hangar.

Ezra climbed out of her seat and went to the cargo hold. "Alright guys, this ship will be our main hub of operation for the indefinite future. I cleared out an officer's barracks on deck 30, quarter number 13. It's just above your training center on decks 32 through 35. Settle in and report for your first briefing at 1100 hours."

All the men took their harnesses off and grabbed their belongings, then headed to the elevator at the back of the hangar. Stepping off the elevator before anyone else, Mitch reached the dorm first. He pressed the button to open to door. "Alright, this is our new home."

"Damn, this is nice. It's got a decent-looking table and couch in the center," Eric added, walking in as he headed to the wall where the bunks were hidden. Unpacking his belonging, he placed them in the drawer below the bed. "This definitely beats being crammed into a room with fifty people."

"They even gave us a wall with a working view screen into space." Masa activated the screen, giving everyone a live look out into space. The view of Earth was cluttered slightly as other warships began taking position alongside the Hue. He looked around and soon found a small SD card insert along the wall. "Hey, we can even use this to watch our own films if we have them on SD card!"

"Wow, look at the ships. There's our old home, the ECS Stryker's still going strong," Sean said, looking out into the void after he finished unpacking into the bunk at the second level of beds. He headed over to the washroom, finding a large mirror with eight sinks across from six urinals and six toilet stalls. One room over after that was a set of eight showers. "Damn, these quarters are enough to sell me on joining. Hell, we have our own shower stalls."

"Attention all hands. This is Captain Stein. Preparations for jump are now underway. We will be leaving the Sol system within the hour," the intercom announced.

Everyone felt the ship begin moving forward, leaving Earth's orbit as not to risk dragging any of the new satellites into beam space along with the ship.

"One hour and forty-five minutes under normal 1G thrust; we'll be at that moon and ready to jump soon enough. Our briefing will happen before jump. We should all be early," Mathew announced to the group.

"Mute is right. We have nothing better to do with our time," Eric added, standing up from the couch in the center of the room.

"I'm not very familiar with frigates; deck 40 was the main briefing room on a Destroyer class ship. So is deck 31 our briefing room or deck 35?" Mitch asked, watching the ships leave the Earth's orbit.

"We meet the colonel on deck 32, room number 9. There was a note next to the door," Mathew said, pointing to the board.

The group arrived at the briefing room just early enough to catch their colonel setting up the room in a classroom section; there was also an officer from ODIN with her. "Oh, you're early, well, good. More time for learning."

"Learning what exactly?" Mitch asked, sitting down.

"You'll learn the Serkin tongue, survival on the planet of Vieira, and navigation without GPS," the ODIN officer answered.

"Once class is complete, you will exercise and finish practicing marksmanship. There are twelve of you and this mission will take place in the central mountain range of the main Vieiran continent." Ezra clicked a remote to show the three mountains that formed a semicircle on Vieira. "These mountains will be where you will set up sniper nests. Killing the Serkins' highest known commanders as they meet to assign blame for the failed attack on Earth is your mission."

"How the hell will we be escaping after killing these guys? Vieira has been behind the lines for five damn years. If anyone got left behind, they're dead now," Eric spoke up.

"The mountains were home to the Planetary Defense Force's oldest bases with a vast tunnel network," Mathew answered. "I know this because I used to work there before we shut them down. It was deemed too costly to destroy the bases, so we just locked the doors and left. It's doubtful the Serkins would bother digging them up, so we can move around using the tunnels."

"Correct, Sergeant Miller. You can hide in the caves and use the old service tunnels to move about. So far, ODIN has confirmed that the Serkins have never entered the old bases in the mountains. The world is currently unprotected and used mostly as a base for the Serkins to rest before continuing to our space," the ODIN officer said.

"Then why are they using it for this meeting?" Mitch asked.

"Right now, the Serkins do not know we are watching their communications. Operation Tipping Point will be our opening blow and we've only got one chance at this. Most of command is not on board with my plan, and as such, you will be going behind the lines to pull this off. Once complete, our fleets should be able to launch into Serkin space and hold long enough to extract you." Ezra clicked the remote a second time, showing the faces of twelve Serkin officers. "These are the most senior staff of the Serkin military that we know of so far. Their deaths will be your only objective. We can't risk a full attack on the planet, and sending you will be a risk to the operation itself. However, it is one we must make."

"How long will we have to kill the officers in question?" Eric asked as he looked over the map he had on the desk.

"Three snipers with one backup each will have one minute and thirty seconds to take out three targets a piece. A spotter will confirm each kill." With another click, Ezra changed the screen to show a bullet. "This is a special bullet specifically meant for assassinations. Once it meets soft tissue, it fragments, releasing poison into the target's body and causes internal bleeding. In contrast to normal hollow points, this round uses a special anticoagulant designed for Serkin anatomy."

"Since you all volunteered, the question now is: does anyone of you have any objections to winning the war?" the ODIN officer asked, looking over the men.

"I have one. What are we going to call ourselves as a group?" Sean asked, raising his hand.

"Ghosts. We have nothing but our mission objective," Mathew replied.

"I like it. This unit will be called Ghosts. Any objections?" Ezra looked around at the men, but no one objected. "Very well, you are Ghosts and your objective is victory."

Printed in the United States
by Baker & Taylor Publisher Services